Heavy Metal Nightmares

A Phobica Books Anthology
Compiled by M. J. McClymont

Phobica Books
Cover design by Jorge Iracheta
Cassette tape illustration by Articult

Phobica Books
ISBN: 9798848487299

First published in 2023 by Phobica Books

Dedication

This book is dedicated to the singers, screamers, axe wielders, drum pummelers and all those talented musicians who create heavy metal thunder for our entertainment.

TRACKLIST

Phantoms

Tim Jeffreys

I first noticed her when the band started jamming during the outro to *Temple Wall*.

It had become customary for the guys to drag that song out for as long as they could. Justin would start playing a driving tom-tom rhythm on the drums which Andy's bass would lock-in with. This was Toke's cue to start throwing shapes on his guitar, getting up close to his amp and letting the feedback flow until the band got a droney trance-like sound going. While all this was going on, I'd retreat to the back of the stage and take a few minutes to recoup my energies. We always followed *Temple Wall* with the single, *Dream House by the Sea*, and I'd want to work the crowd into a frenzy for that one.

Hanging back there, behind Justin's kit, I noticed a woman pushing her way through the audience towards the front of the stage. It was no surprise to later find out her name was Summer-Rayne; she had a cute sixties flower-child look going on. Among the black t-shirt, black-eyeliner brigade that comprised most of our audience, she, with her loose blonde locks and white lace dress, looked like she'd been beamed straight down from heaven into hell. The other reason I couldn't help noticing her was because she looked directly at me. And she was smiling. It was a look I'd seen before: girls in the audience — sometimes boys too —used it to let me know that they had me in their sights.

The trance outro to *Temple Wall* started to crumble with the bass and drums falling out of synch and Toke losing control of the feedback so that it descended into one great wall of noise which he rode for a few moments before silencing. I took a gulp of water and headed back out front. Squinting against the stage lights, I looked for the woman in the crowd and was surprised to see

1

that she'd managed to elbow her way to the lip of the stage and was stood at my feet. I returned her smile, before grabbing the microphone as the bass intro to *Dream House by the Sea* began and a roar of recognition went up from the crowd. I began to leap about the stage, losing myself in the song and the wave of appreciation from the audience, but occasionally I glanced at the woman. Elbows out, determinedly holding her spot in front of the stage, she bobbed her head and mouthed the words as I sang them.

> *Dream house by the Sea*
> *Strange house among the trees*
> *Climb the stairs, she waits for me*
> *But there in the mirror her face I see.*
> *Strange house by the sea*
> *Dream house among the trees*
> *Disrobed, disrobed she waits for me*
> *Another face in the glass for eternity.*

After the gig, she appeared backstage, sliding onto the banquette seating beside me as if it was the most natural thing in the world as I chatted to a journalist from Crack Magazine. The Crack guy paused, his eyes moving from me to her, his face full of query. I decided not to question her presence and urged him on. She laid her head on my shoulder. I caught sight of Toke passing in front of the doorway, naked to the waist and with a towel across his shoulders. He saw the woman at my side, smirked, and shot me a knowing look. I couldn't help but think of our days playing the pub circuit to a handful of people. *One day we're going to have fans lined up the length of these places,* Toke would say. Back then, I'd found it hard to believe.

"Congratulations on your first sold out show," The Crack guy said.

"Thanks. It was amazing."

"Your lyrics tend to be quite dark and surreal," he went on. "Where does the inspiration come from?"

"From dreams mainly," I told him. "I have this recurring dream about a house. It's the same house but it's always in a different place. Sometimes it's on a hill overlooking the ocean, sometimes it's in the middle of the woods, sometimes it's in a field. Sometimes, in the dream, I go inside the house. Sometimes I just look in the windows."

"And what do you see?"

The woman chimed in. "Listen to the songs. It's all there."

Both myself and the Crack guy gave her a long look.

"Sorry," he said. "Who're you exactly?"

She smiled and told us. "Summer-Rayne."

"Are you with the band?"

"No." She looked at me and smiled. "Just a fan."

"You think Phantoms are going to be big?"

"I think Phantoms are going to be massive."

A few hours later, after a brief tour of Bristol's trendier bars, Summer-Rayne and I arrived at her place. It was a spacious, open-plan apartment overlooking the river. Though she smothered her accent and downplayed her public-school manners, over the course of our time together, I'd begun to suspect that she came from money. When I saw where she lived I was left in no doubt. Working behind the bar a few nights a week at Pata Negra, which was what she said she did for a living, didn't pay for a place like that. No, that was Mummy and Daddy's money. Maybe a trust fund or an inheritance. Pure privilege. Another time, this might have brought out the cynic in me, but it had been a brilliant gig that night, and I still had a good buzz going from the shots we'd done in the last bar.

"Cool pad."

She threw up her hands as if to say: *What this? This is nothing.* "Beer?"

"Sure."

As she twirled off to fetch the drinks, I noticed a cluster of framed photographs on the wall to my left and, for want of anything better to do, I examined them. There was one of a blonde-haired kid, possibly Summer-Rayne as a child, showing the camera a gap-toothed smile and hugging a Labrador. Another showed a group of older girls, among which I recognized Summer-Rayne, wearing cocktail dresses. Mixed in with the pictures of people — parents, siblings, friends? There were a few arty postcards. I recognized Klee's 'Queen of Hearts', and a Hokusai. There was a photograph of a seal poking its head out of an ice-hole. I let my gaze drift.

When my eyes lit on a black and white photograph at the centre of the cluster, I took a step back.

"Jesus."

"What is it?" Summer-Rayne said. She stood beside me holding two bottles of Stella.

"What's that?"

"That one?" she said, tilting one bottle at the picture. "Cool, isn't it?"

"Where is that place? Who took the picture?"

"I don't know actually. It's an old photograph. Not sure how old. It used to hang on the wall in a guest room at my grandparents house which I slept in sometimes as a kid. It used to freak me out a bit back then. Now I love it. After they died and we were clearing out the house, I decided to take it. It reminds me of them, of being a kid. I think it's cool." She glanced to my face. "Why? What's the matter?"

"Nothing, I…" I shook my head. "It just kind of reminds me of…"

"What?"

4

I was going to say that it reminded me of the house in my dreams, the house I sang about in 'Strange House by the Sea', the house that was always in a different place. But I knew that wasn't right. It didn't *remind* me of the dream house. It *was* the dream house. It was as if someone had entered my nightmares and taken a snapshot. Looking at the photograph gave me a cold feeling in my guts. It stopped my thoughts dead. I had an odd feeling that someone inside that house was looking back at me.

"God."

"What is it?" Summer-Rayne said, looking closely at me with an expression of real concern.

I laughed, and turned my back to the wall. "Nothing." I took one of the Stellas from her and swigged at it. "It's just creepy, like you said."

"Yeah. Who on earth would build a house right in the middle of all those trees? It doesn't make sense. It's like it's dropped out of the sky or something. Or else the woods grew up around it. And such a spooky-looking place. I used to imagine it'd be full of ghosts. Maybe if you look closely at each of the windows you'll see a face in one of them."

A cold prickle went down my spine.

"Weird," I said. I wasn't going to look closely at the picture. If there was a face at any of those windows, I didn't want to see it. I glanced at my watch instead. In a few hours I'd have to be back on the bus. Cardiff was the next stop. Not much time. I pulled Summer-Rayne to me and kissed her. Breaking away from me, she laughed.

"Don't get mad," she said, "but I kind of had an ulterior motive in bringing you back here."

"I was hoping that was the case."

"Not that." She gave a kittenish tilt of her head. "I want to play a song for you."

"A song?"

I saw it then — why hadn't I noticed it before? An acoustic guitar propped against the wall on the other side of the room. I began to get an inkling of why I was there, of where the night was going. She'd play her song then produce a CD, or a pen-drive, or perhaps just a card with a link to her Band camp or SoundCloud addresses. Then the questions would start. Did I know someone…? Could I play them the songs? Hook her up with a manager? It was all making sense. *God, not this again.* I'd thought that all she'd wanted was to screw the singer in the hot new band. But no. Like so many others she wanted to make inroads into the music industry.

"Listen, Summer…"

She raised a palm to stop my words. "Just one song, I promise."

"Well…okay. But I'm not an A & R guy, Summer, I'm a singer. I don't…"

"One song. That's it."

Taking me by the hand, she led me across the room towards the bed, grabbing her guitar on the way. Shifting some clothes from a black leather chair, she indicated for me to sit. She herself sat cross-legged on the bed. I watched, impressed, as she tuned the guitar.

"Where are you from, Summer? You're not from Bristol, are you?"

"I grew up in a village called Wringsham."

"Wringsham? Where's that?"

"About a two hour drive from here."

"I've never heard of it."

"No one ever has. Unless…"

"What?"

She shook her head. "Doesn't matter."

"Why didn't you tell me you played guitar?"

"I didn't want you to think I was out for an audition."

"Aren't you?"

She smiled. "Nope. I just want you to hear this one song. I think you *should* hear it."

"Oh yeah? What's it called?"

Glancing up, she caught my eye. "It's called The Furthest Deep."

"The Furthest Deep? Yours?"

"No, it's an old song. Very old."

"Traditional, you mean?"

"Something like that."

Her fingers began picking out a series of descending chords. I was amazed at the dexterous way she played, her long quick fingers plucking at the guitar strings, but it was her voice when she started singing that really blew me away. It was ghostly and pure, and note perfect. Like a young Marianne Faithful. For the duration of the song, she had me mesmerized. From what I could make out of the lyrics, the song was about being lost but searching. Searching for some place, and eventually finding it, some kind of paradise or heaven.

When Summer-Rayne finished playing, I stared at her in genuine astonishment.

"Wow. What was that?"

"I told you, it's called The Furthest Deep."

"It's beautiful."

"Phantoms should record that song."

"Us?" I laughed. "I'm not sure it's our style."

"You could make it your own. Imagine it with synths, maybe. Heavier guitars. You could make it sound like that Joy Division song, *Atmosphere*. Here." She reached over to her bedside table, and then there it was in her hand: the pen-drive. "There's an mp3 on here. I recorded myself singing the song."

"And I like it the way you do it, Summer. I do. Maybe…"

"Just take it. It's a very old song. There'd be no royalties to pay out." Leaning forward, she held out the pen-drive.

"We've got an album's worth of songs already recorded. Listen, I don't mean to sound…"

"Please," she said. Hers was a face you couldn't say no to. With a sigh, I took the pen-drive and shoved it into the pocket of my jeans. Summer grinned. After setting aside the guitar, she patted the space beside her on the bed.

"Now then," she said. "Come here."

When I was certain Summer-Rayne was asleep, I got up from her bed. Daylight was filtering into the apartment from behind the beige curtains, and with that I felt brave enough to take another look at that photograph of the house she had on the wall. I hadn't been able to stop thinking about it. It was all I could see in my mind's eye. I'd begun to think I must have imagined it. It couldn't be the house. It couldn't actually be the house from my dreams.

But it was. Even as I stood there half-dressed looking at it in that early morning half-light, I knew it was the house. I realized something else too. All the band's songs, all my lyrics, all those low bass notes and doom riffs… it was all somehow encapsulated by this one image. I pictured our album with this photograph on the cover, and suddenly I couldn't see it any other way. I gathered up the remainder of my clothes, checked Summer-Rayne was still asleep, and then I did something shameful. I slipped the photograph down from its nail, tucked it under my jacket, and left the apartment with it. That's right, I stole it. I stole Summer-Rayne's memories of her childhood, of her grandparents. I didn't feel good about it. I just knew that if I didn't take that picture with me, I'd regret it always.

I'd get it back to her though. Sure I would. Besides, something told me she'd understand.

The streets were full of last night's litter and weary kids on their way home from the clubs. As I was trying to work out the way back to the hotel where the rest of the band waited, my phone started buzzing. Digging into my jeans pocket, I came across the pen-drive Summer-Rayne had given me. I almost tossed it into the river, but something made me stuff it back into my pocket. I took out my phone. It was Toke.

"Where the hell are you, Danny-boy? The bus is about to leave."

"I'm on my way. Listen, Toke, I've had an idea. About the artwork for the album. I think I've found the perfect image."

"Cool. And about the album. Andy's been talking to the record company."

"Yeah? What's up?"

"They want one more song."

"One more song? What for?"

"They want a slow one. A ballad. They think the album should have a ballad on it."

I halted in my tracks. "You're fucking kidding me?"

"No" Toke said. "Why?"

"Serendipity, man. Fucking straight up serendipity."

I was in the control room reading a magazine and trying not to think about how much money the band were spending on studio time when the producer, Mick Boyle, threw down his headphones, stood up and said, "Fuck you, guys. I can't do this anymore."

The band had entered Real Take Recording Studios to record our second album at the end of August. It was now October and we still didn't have anything to show for it. Except jams. Hours and hours of worthless jams. Whenever I spoke to the executives at the record company, they told me not to worry. Phantoms were a big deal. We could afford to take our time.

As Mick headed for the door, I looked through the window into the live room and saw that Andy had nodded off while tuning his bass.

"For Christ's sake, not again."

Throwing down the magazine, I went after the producer. Mick had almost reached the exit door by the time I caught up with him.

"Mick, wait! You're not just going to walk out on us, are you?"

Mick swung around. "Too right I am! You lot are wasting my fucking time. The bass player's strung out on smack, the guitarist has a bottle of whiskey for breakfast and can't play a note by lunchtime, and worst of all there just aren't any songs!"

I noted that he hadn't mentioned Justin, who would blatantly snort lines of blow off the control room console. Perhaps because it didn't affect Justin's drumming, except that Mick often had to yell at him to give it a fucking rest.

"I've seen bands fall apart in the studio before," Mick said. "And I don't mind that, so long as we've got some music down at the end of the day. But we've been in here for months and you guys haven't produced a damn thing."

"Please, Mick," I pleaded. "Give us another chance."

Mick's expression softened as he looked into my face.

"It's not your fault, Danny. At least you've managed to stay straight, and I commend you for that. You're under a lot of pressure. But you're all fucked-up and worn out."

And with that he turned and pushed out through the double doors, letting a flood of sunlight into the corridor which blinded me. I was further dazzled as I followed Mick outside, and for a few moments I couldn't see anything except a white haze. The sunshine made my skin itch. It was as if I'd been living underground for months.

By the time I came to my senses, Mick was climbing into his car.

I put myself in front of it and threw out my arms. "Come on, Mick. We need you."

Mick leaned out of the driver's side window. "You need a break."

He pressed hard on the car's horn, forcing me to step out of its path. I watched as the car left the gravelled space behind the studio and turned onto the road.

"Great. Fucking brilliant."

Heading back inside, I realized Mick was right. The band needed some time off. As hard as we'd chased fame and recognition, none of us had been prepared for it. Not in the least. No one had expected the first album to blow up in the way it had. By the time it hit the shelves, Phantoms were on the covers of all the music magazines. We did interview after interview, photo shoot after photo shoot, with journalists questioning us as if we were the fountain of all wisdom, the people with all the answers to life, instead of four guys in their mid-twenties who happened to know their way around a chord-change and a catchy melody. We toured across the UK and then Europe for six months solid in support of the album, seeing the crowds swell at every gig we played. We started out playing the tiny basement at Bath's Moles, and finished with two sold-out nights at Brixton Academy. And as soon as those shows were over with, the record company had us back in the studio working on album number two without even a weekend off to recuperate.

It creeps in, the feeling that you're someone else's cash cow.

And Mick was also correct when he'd said that of the four band members, I was the only one who'd managed to stay straight. But that didn't mean I didn't have my own problems. My nightmares were back. That house. I saw it whenever I closed my eyes. Sometimes it was by the sea. Sometimes it was on top of a high hill. Sometimes in the middle of the woods. But always the same house. And always, whenever I looked in the windows of the house, I would see the same woman stood naked, looking back at me, and laughing.

On returning to the control room, I found Toke sitting in the chair Mick had vacated. With one hand he played with the faders on the console, while with the other he held a bottle of scotch, one-third full, to his lips. In the live room, Andy had roused himself and stood clutching his bass in two hands as if he had no idea what to do with it.

Toke swung around in the chair when I entered. He looked gaunt, his eyes shadowed. "Forget him, Danny. The man's a hack. We don't need him. We'll produce the album ourselves."

"You're kidding?" I said. "We couldn't produce a fart between the four of us." My sudden anger then surprised even me. "Look at the state of you! Look at Andy!" I grabbed the vinyl copy of Phantoms first album which we kept propped against the live room window. "See this?" I said, stabbing one finger against the cover. "This was a mistake."

Toke sat up. "A mistake? What do you mean? It's a brilliant album."

"I'm not talking about the music," I said. "I'm talking about this. This cover. People weren't meant to see this, Toke. This house belongs to some other place. I'm certain of it. Some... some place no one was meant to see. But because of me people *are* seeing it. Millions of people all over the world." I threw the album face down on the console. "I should have left that photograph where it was. In that girl's flat. And I should have left that fucking song there too."

I didn't have to say which song I was referring to. Toke dropped his eyes to the floor.

At some point during the tour, stories had started to circulate that something odd was happening. Our fans had started to go missing. The first I knew about it was when our road crew began saying they'd heard rumors about people who'd bought our album and thought there was some deep mystery to the song 'The Furthest Deep'. Then it started to get crazy. Journalists began asking us about it. They showed us photographs of teenage kids who'd disappeared. One family petitioned to have the album banned because their sixteen year-old daughter had become obsessed with 'The Furthest Deep' and then vanished off the face of the earth. Three months into the tour, we decided to stop playing that song. But after our refusal to encore with it after a show at Newcastle City Hall almost resulted in a riot, we put it back on the set list. By then, I hated singing it. Much of the blame for the disappearances was directed at me, as if was in league with the devil and had planted hidden messages in the song's lyrics. Even the other members of the band would give me odd looks whenever the subject came up. I found myself explaining over and over again that I didn't write 'The Furthest Deep'. Those weren't my words. Whatever the listener uncovered in that song, wherever it led them, it was nothing to do with me.

Except… I frequently found myself thinking about how determined Summer-Rayne had been for me to hear that song. How she'd pleaded with me to record it with Phantoms, even expounding on how we might go about it. Heavy guitars. And doomy keyboard washes like Joy Division's *Atmosphere*. I'd told the others those touches had been my idea, but they had all come from her. It was *she* who had set that song free into the world. The band and I had just been the tools she used.

By coincidence, the studio the record company chose for us to record in was out in the Somerset countryside, less than an hour's train ride from Bristol. Since the day we arrived there I'd been thinking about chasing up Summer-Rayne as asking her a few questions.

With Mick Boyle gone, it seemed the time had come. I grabbed my jacket from the couch.

"Where're you going?" Toke said. "You're not quitting too, are you?"

"No, Toke. I'm just getting out of here for a while. I need some air."

I wasn't going to spend another frustrating afternoon watching Toke fumble chords and Andy fight to keep his eyes open. Leaving the studio, I made straight for the train station. I didn't know if I could find Summer-Rayne's flat again. I didn't know the address, and I'd been half-drunk the night she took me there. But I was determined to try. I was determined to get some answers. What was that song she'd given me? Where had it come from? Why had she used Phantoms to release it onto the world? What was happening to the people who heard it? The ones who were going missing?

I arrived at Bristol Temple Meads just after five, and the city centre was busy with traffic and people leaving work. It disorientated me so much that I had to sit down on a bench and wait for a dizzy spell to pass. When the streets quietened, I tried to retrace the steps Summer-Rayne and I had taken that evening we'd spent together. I found some of the bars we'd visited. Then I thought I'd found the block where she had a flat. I waited by the entrance for someone to exit then grabbed the door. Once inside, I knew I had the right building, as I recognized a photographic print on the lobby wall of sand dunes overlooking the sea. The block only had three floors, and since I could remember climbing stairs, I went up to the second floor and, guided more by instinct, found myself standing outside what I thought was the door to Summer-Rayne's flat.

I knocked.

After some fumbling from the other side, the door opened and a man of about thirty looked out at me. He must have recognized me, as his eyes widened.

"Hi," I said. "Is Summer-Rayne here?"

His mouth worked, but he couldn't make words. Eventually, he managed to spit out, "Phantoms."

It's incredible how tiresome fame becomes, and how quickly. After years trying to get people to know who I was, to make my mark on the world, once I was famous all I wanted was to be invisible.

I nodded. "Yes. Listen…"

"You're him. The singer. Phantoms. Danny…" He fluttered one hand in the air, but couldn't get it.

"Danny Hano. Yes…"

14

"I can't believe it. Danny Hano. What… what are you doing here?"

"I'm looking for Summer-Rayne."

"Wait a minute," he said, and retreated back inside the flat. When he reappeared he was holding a vinyl copy of the Phantoms album and a marker pen.

"Do you mind?"

"Sure."

I scrawled my name across that picture of the house in the middle of the woods, thinking at the same time how strange it was that the image had found its way back to the very place I'd stolen it from.

"Thank so much," the man said when I handed back the record.

"So? Summer-Rayne. Is she at home?"

"Summer-Rayne?"

"The girl who lives here. We met about a year ago. She brought me back here. She said this was her place."

"Oh," the man said, laughing. "The blonde?"

"Yes. She in?"

"No. No. She left."

"Left? When?"

"I took over the tenancy in… February I think it was."

"Oh. She told me this was her place."

The man shook his head. "Nope. Rented."

"Any idea where she went?"

He grinned. "No idea whatsoever."

"I see. Well, I'm sorry to have bothered you."

"Hey! No problem at all, man. My pleasure. I'm a big fan. The album's awesome. Do you mind if I ask you about that one song, The Furthest Deep. Is there…?"

I cut him off. "I didn't write that."

The look in my eyes must have convinced him not to pursue the topic. He nodded. "Sure. Sure."

Before he could say anything more, I walked away.

The second album tanked, but no one cared about that because the first album was unstoppable. The record company booked us on to two world tours. I felt as if I was no longer in control. I felt like a puppet. It wasn't my music, my words, my voice; people flocked to our shows for. They came for *The Furthest Deep*, and I was the one who'd been chosen — by whom I didn't know — to deliver it to them. That had become my purpose in life. We travelled from city to city, dogged by more tales of disappeared fans and a gathering storm of enraged parents, who picketed every venue we played, demanding answers, demanding an end to it.

But we couldn't stop.

It was in Amsterdam, half-way through the second tour, that Andy OD'd. He was found dead in his bunk at the back of the tour bus with a needle stuck in his arm. Even then we didn't think of calling a halt to it, instead bringing in a session guy to finish the tour. He was a decade older than the rest of us, a family man, but even he got caught up in the dark vortex that had become the Phantoms tour machine. I knew that if it didn't end soon there'd be more casualties. Toke drank two bottles of whiskey a day, and Justin had built up a small entourage who travelled everywhere with him and with whom he partied night and day. After we encored with *The Furthest Deep* at our final show at the Olympia Theatre in Dublin, I told the crowd the song was bullshit, threw the mic down hard, and stormed off stage.

Alone in my hotel room, I told myself that was it, it was over, I was finished with Phantoms. Done. The band was history.

16

I paid three million for a sixteenth century manor house named Constantine, which overlooked the sea in Falmouth, Cornwall, and retreated there separated from everyone else in the world by four acres of land. At the time, it was what I thought I wanted. To be alone.

One day my phone rang. It was Justin.

"Have you heard?" he said.

I closed my eyes. "No. But don't tell me. Toke is dead. Right?"

"Choked on his own vomit."

"Fucking idiot."

I hung up. I didn't need to hear any more.

The days that followed were some of the blackest I'd ever spent. Toke hadn't been just the guitar player in my band. He'd been my best friend. Once.

It didn't take long for me to realize the house creeped the fuck out of me. Not only that, but I wasn't used to being alone. I'd heard it said that fame isolates you, and I didn't understand that idea until I moved into Constantine. At the beginning, I was kept busy by my phone which rang throughout the day. It began to feel as if everyone I spoke to wanted a piece of me in some way, so it stopped answering it and eventually the calls tailed off. After that the days were long and empty. I'd stand staring out of the window at the sea, or watch TV which I had set upon the box it came in. I wondered if there was someone I could call. I'd lost touch with the friends I'd had when the band started, of my bandmates only Justin remained and he and I had never been close, and when I spoke to my parents it was as if they no longer knew who I was. I made furtive, cap and sunglasses forays into Falmouth or one of the nearby villages, sometimes returning with a female in tow. They were easy to pick up. I didn't have to work at it. They would approach me. They would hang around at the house, keeping me company for a few days, until I became irritated by their cow-eyes and worshipful talk. Inevitably, they would start asking me about *The Furthest Deep*.

"I didn't write that fucking song," I told one girl. She was American and her name I think was Phoebe. Or something like that.

"Have you ever heard of Gabriel Black?" she asked me.

"Nope."

"He recorded that song in the early seventies. But his version has an extra line at the end."

This made me sit up and pay attention to her. "Does it?"

"Yes." She sang it for me. *"Don't go; don't go down to that furthest deep. Stay away, stay away and let the creatures sleep."*

I shook my head. "That's it?"

She laughed. "Don't you get it? It's like a warning. He's warning you not to go there. What freaks me out is that word 'creatures'. Let the *creatures* sleep. That's real chilling."

"It's just a song."

After Phoebe left, I typed Gabriel Black's name into Google. There wasn't much information about him online. He was a folkie who'd recorded three albums in the early seventies then killed himself. I found nothing connecting him to *The Furthest Deep*, and his version of the song wasn't available anywhere to stream.

Stay away let the creatures sleep.

I decided that Phoebe or whatever her name was had made that up to spook me after I asked her wasn't it time she fucked-off back to America.

Eventually, I stopped inviting women back to the house. Something new had appeared in their eyes which I couldn't stand to see. It was disgust. Disgust at the way I'd let myself go. I'd put on weight, sure. I'd stopped shaving, let my hair grow long, and only showered about once a week. Added to this my hair had started to recede. I no longer resembled the guy in the leather jacket and black jeans on the back cover on the first Phantoms album. That was what disgusted them the most, I think.

I stopped going into Falmouth, and had everything I needed delivered. Word had got out about where I was living, so Phantoms fans would make a pilgrimage and loiter around the town centre waiting for me to put in an appearance. The cap and sunglasses only made me more conspicuous. And what did they pester me about when they saw me? The Furthest fucking Deep. Worse than the fans were the photographers, who would gather to get a snap of me buying toilet paper then sell it to some newspaper or gossip website who'd run it with headlines like: PHANTOM SPOTTED IN BROAD DAYLIGHT or DANNY HANO HIDES OUT IN CORNWALL TO AVOID ANSWERING QUESTIONS ABOUT MISSING FANS.

One morning a Parcelforce van pulled into my driveway. When I answered the doorbell I was presented with a huge flat package which the two delivery men struggled to fit through the front door. It turned out to be a present from the record company, a massive blow-up of the cover of the first Phantoms album. It was that black-and-white photograph of the house in the middle of the woods that I stole from Summer-Rayne enlarged to six feet by six feet. I don't know why the record company thought I'd want that hanging on my wall, but I didn't. Fuck no. Though I hadn't dreamt about that house for while, the memories of those nightmares were still fresh. I left the picture where the delivery men set it down, propped against the wall in the hallway outside my lounge, with a view to getting rid of it as soon as I could, although it was too big for me to move on my own. So there it stayed. Every time I crossed from the lounge to the kitchen I had to pass it. Pass that house. Usually, I avoided looking at it. But one time I did look and, this sounds crazy, I thought I saw a movement. A figure stood at one of the first floor windows of the house. It was a woman. She was naked. And she beckoned me.

Disrobed, disrobed she waits for me.

When I saw that beckoning figure I screamed.

Then, as I stood transfixed by this vision, I began to think that there were not only trees in the picture, but trees all around me, in front, to the side of me, and behind. I was no longer standing in the hallway of my house, but in the middle of the woods. I jerked to one side and this impression vanished. I was in my hallway again.

Lying in bed that night, I still saw in my mind's eye that naked woman in the window of the house, and I became convinced that it had been Summer-Rayne. She looked exactly as she had that day we'd met, but rather than a breezy youthfulness, she exuded something darker and older. No, not older. Ancient. That's the only way I can describe it. There was something ancient about her, but it was not in her appearance. It was the look in her eyes, the expression on her face, the way she moved. It was something indefinable. Something black and ancient. Hungry.

I lay awake that night, thinking I heard someone running around downstairs. Running from room to room as if searching. It went on for hours. Back and forth. Back and forth. I didn't dare get up to look. I lay in bed rigid with fear, listening for a footstep on the staircase which never came. At one point I thought I heard a voice shouting my name, and I was convinced it had been Justin's voice. I got up and crossed to the door. Opening it a crack, I said into the darkness beyond, "Justin?"

No reply came so I closed the door and got back into bed. Somehow I managed to fall asleep.

The next morning, after I crept downstairs, I found everything as I'd left it. There was no sign of a disturbance.

Only, when I turned on the TV, I saw on the news that in the early hours of the night, Justin had driven his car at high speed into a wall, killing himself and three passengers. And I remembered how I'd thought I'd heard his voice calling out to me during the night.

I had a sense that death was circling. It had taken the other three members of the band. Soon it would be coming for me.

It began to happen more often, and not just when I stand in front of that picture. I'll be brushing my teeth in the bathroom, and in the mirror, I'll see myself surrounded by woodland. In a panic I'd run back to my bedroom and stay until I'd convinced myself I'd only imagined those trees.

I'd be watching TV and look up to realize my sofa wasn't in my living room but in the middle of the woods, and in front of me instead of the TV I saw that house, that woman at the window, naked and beckoning. It is Summer-Rayne, but her face is not as I remember. The knowledge in her face is primeval. When she looks at me, it is as if she looks into the darkest places in my mind. She looks in those places and she laughs.

Tim Jeffreys short fiction has appeared in Supernatural Tales, Not One of Us, The Alchemy Press Book of Horrors 2 & 3, Stories We Tell After Midnight 2 & 3, and Nightscript, among various other publications. His novella, *Holburn*, a ghost story set in an exclusive girl school, will be published by Manta Press in August 2022. Follow his progress at www.timjeffreys.blogspot.co.uk.

Metal Bones

Mia Dalia

The idea came to him in a dream, or rather, in that perfectly weightless moment of sleep slowly crystallizing into wakefulness. An ossuary. They would build an ossuary for a recording studio. He imagined the way the sound would bounce off the bones and it gave him the most pleasurable shudder.

The young woman tangled in the bed sheets next to him stirred, mistaking his excitement, but he wanted no more of her. It never felt right in the morning hours, as if whatever magic of the night before had worn off and all he was left with was a fairy-tale pumpkin. He looked at the dyed blonde hair, pale sleep-wrinkled skin, and tried to remember her name. Nothing came.

The room was a mess. Eddie was safe and sound in the corner in its stand. EVH striped, his pride and joy. When he finally laid hands on it, he'd forgotten all about the long humiliating hours at the local Super-Mart bagging groceries. So. Totally. Worth it. The guitar that changed the metal scene forever. Just as he believed he was destined to.

"Rex?" Her voice sounded like cigarettes and sex. In the stygian gloom of the bar last night, she was probably irresistible. She groaned. "You got any coffee?"

He waved his hand in the vague direction of the efficiency kitchenette. "Somewhere."

She slithered out of bed, wrapping the top sheet around her. It trailed her in a distinctly non-regal manner amid the debris of hard living on his floor.

Rex made his way to the bathroom and stared at his reflection in the dirty, shaving cream-speckled mirror. His long hair looked filthy, matted with gel and sweat of the night before. The darkness under his eyes echoed the storminess of his heart. But beneath it all, there was still that lean hungry daredevil look that screamed heavy metal to anyone who cared to look, cared to listen.

Almost but not quite too old to live this way, he sighed.

The laundry hamper spilled worn black denim and torn tees onto the floor like dirty secrets. Rex pissed, washed his face, and listened to his stomach growl.

He wished the blonde, whatever her name was, had left in the night, saving them both the awkwardness of the morning after.

Vanity made him avoid being seen this way. Everyone looked different on stage, however small the stage was - taller, sexier, wilder. Now with his hair flat and his eye makeup gone, wearing nothing but black boxer briefs that had seen better days, he didn't feel like a heavy metal demon, a shred master, an icon.

He felt tired and hungry and hung-over and wanted more than anything to be left alone. He plopped back on the bed, trying to remember the last time he changed the sheets. An ossuary, he thought, where did *that* come from?

The smell roused him from his reverie. His guest managed to find coffee, after all.

She handed him a mug; on it a T-Rex was shredding a wicked-looking axe. So clever, so charming. The mug never failed to make him smile but it also made him remember who gave it to him. He got rid of everything else from those years, but this one thing, his only tie to a different time, a different life.

"I didn't know how you take it," she said almost shyly, pulling the sheet closer around her.

Rex made eye contact. A nice face, a pleasant forgettable face beneath the leftover traces of too much makeup.

"Black's fine. Thanks."

They sipped in silence for a while.

"I'm Sheila," she offered. "Bet you forgot."

"I didn't," he lied. "Morning, Sheila."

"That was fun, last night…"

"Yeah." He grinned roguishly.

"I don't mean that," she nodded toward the bed. "I mean that too, but I was talking about your band. You're really good."

Rex didn't think he'd ever get tired of hearing that. "Thanks."

"Made me think of Iron Maiden. I saw them in concert last fall."

"Awesome."

Bet you didn't sleep with Adrian or Janick or Dave, he thought. Iron Maiden guitarists probably had their pick of choice every night. Rex had never been particularly selective in that department; he was a late bloomer when it came to the fairer sex and it had scarred him accordingly.

"You got a t-shirt or something you can sign for me?" she raised her eyebrow, flirting perhaps.

Rex shrugged, looked around, found a copy of a demo. "Will this do?"

She nodded enthusiastically, a groupie through and through. He'd seen them at the shows, for years now, the same radiant expressions, like sun worshippers on Solstice morning, like the music was playing for them and them alone.

"You know what an ossuary is?" he asked her on a whim.

She shook her head. "It'd be an awesome band name," she smiled.

There was something to it. Cerberus, the multi-headed hound of Hades, was a bit too abstruse for the mainstream.

He could tell she wanted more; more of him. But there was no more to give. He'd long ago shut off that part of himself or perhaps he'd given it away willingly to someone no longer close to him; either way, Sheila was getting nothing out of him besides some metal riffs and some cheap coffee.

Eventually, she got the message and left, clutching the signed demo, already rewriting this episode in her mind, romanticizing it into something infinitely more romantic and exciting.

24

Rex traced the phone cord like Perseus in the labyrinth, dug out his phone, and started calling his bandmates.

Once you let the dream drive, once you get it in your head that you're going to be a heavy metal legend that lives and dies by its killer riffs, nothing else seems too strange, too odd, too impossible.

Selling his friends on the ossuary idea didn't even take that much effort. Rex was fully preparing his best Tom Sawyer fence game, but no, they were on board, and they dug it. Then came the practical considerations.

It wasn't like they could go to the library and look up how to build one. The only reason Rex knew about it in the first place was a family trip to Paris' catacombs the summer before his parents got a divorce. It must have been their last hurrah and Rex didn't even know it. Funny that. Back then he was Richard or even the much-loathed Ricky. A nerdy skinny knees and elbows and glasses sort of kid. Before the music found and transformed him into Rex, the future king of heavy metal. It spoke to him, vibrated his bones, the thick monumental sound, the epic solos, the weighty lyrics. It sounded like destiny.

All he remembered of Paris was cobblestones glistening in the rain, the perfect baguettes, and catacombs. All those bones. It freaked him out for years back then. Now he couldn't stop thinking about it.

"So, we'll just get bones and use them as bricks essentially?" Chuck was always the reasonable one. Mild-mannered CPA by day, an animal behind a drum kit by night, the man managed his two lives with the skill of a superhero. Chuck had his own business, inherited from his father, and thus made his own hours, but the transformation was still quite striking. Had any of his clients seen him perform, they'd probably fail to recognize him. He wore a suit by day, but beneath it, his skin rippled with technicolor ink just waiting to be shown off under the stage lights. Chuck drummed shirtless, maniacal, as if chased by Cerberus himself.

"Only one place I know with bones…" Darryl drawled. A decade out of small Appalachian backwoods and all that remained was the accent. The rest was pure metal dream: the hair, the leather, the swagger.

"So we do it," shrugged Paul. Like it's that easy. He was good at making difficult seem easy, it's why his lyrics worked too. Everyone else was overworking them but Paul's songs had a clean appealing simplicity; easy to get down under your finger and easy to embellish upon.

So they did it. Night after night. One cemetery after another. They hunted down small out-of-the-way places that time appeared to forget. They were easy enough to pick out: untended graves, shaggy grass, toppling headstones.

It was still safest to go at night, away from the prying eyes of passersby.

The moral aspect of it didn't move them. The dead were dead. The bones were bones. It didn't matter. The hardest part was the digging. The shovels made their hands callus the way the guitar strings callused their fingertips.

After a while, their hands felt like giant calluses from the wrists down.

They set practice aside for their midnight excursions. Soon the dust, the smell of it permeated their dreams, their very existence.

Paul's lyrics changed, took an even darker direction. He recited them as they dug, and they layered them with power chords and solos in their minds.

There are 206 bones in an adult body. There were so many bodies. No way to know how much was enough. One night they just stopped.

They'd been saving the bones in a backyard shack, behind Darryl's trailer. The shack was on the smaller side but had a surprisingly sturdy build. Previous owners didn't feel like dealing with moving it, so Darryl inherited it in a package deal from an uncle he barely knew. The place was on the outskirts of town; a dwelling of questionable legality, but just far enough for no one to care.

Now it seemed like the best bet for a recording studio. Save some money. Their demo cost a mint and set them back significantly. Until fame came knocking, they had to be savvy.

Out of the four of them, only Paul made a decent living. The rest were scrabbling the hand-to-foot existence of the hopeful out of a succession of dead-beat, dead-end jobs, living on fumes of a dream, ramen, bummed cigarettes, and cheap beer.

They booked gigs with pleasing regularity but seldom made much at it. Got used to being paid in booze, greasy bar burgers, and promises. All it took is one right person seeing them perform.

You couldn't just superglue the bones onto the walls, that much they knew.

That was when Darryl got to utilize his years of construction gigs' experience, suggesting mortar. Easy enough to obtain and mix. Easy enough to put up.

It got tricky, though, with bones being really nothing like bricks at all.

"This is more like Tetris," Chuck complained, and not without reason.

The shapes were odd, rough, complex. Whoever had layered the catacombs in Paris must have had all the time and all the patience in the world. Perhaps, even some artistry.

The bones splintered, slicing straight through their calluses until they learned to wear work gloves all day every day. The oldest bones crumbled into dust, requiring extra care in handling. The skulls were especially delicate.

Paul's idea of a joke was arranging them faces front, rigor mortis grins and empty eye sockets mocking their efforts.

It looked clumsy, but – they had to admit – impressive. Something about each wall they finished that sent a shiver down their spine the way an epic power riff might. This *was* heavy metal. They knew it. Rex joked that he felt it in his bones. But it was true, too. Given a second chance in life, the bones around them seem to align with the bones within them, like a perfectly designed machine.

They sold and pawned everything they owned of value for recording equipment. They were never as serious about their music before, but now, after all they've done, it seemed impossible to not give it their all. Their literal sweat, blood, and tears lined the walls of their new studio.

It sounded amazing. *They* sounded amazing. Something about the vibrations made every chord sustain longer, every riff echo into eternity. The very atmosphere imbued their lyrics with a deeper meaning. They were no longer screaming their rage into the ether; this was the dawning of a new age. They were offering prophecies, requiems, and deals with the devil.

The songs came easy and sounded just as good in playback as they did in their heads.

It was time, they knew, to try it out on a crowd.

They threw one of their latest songs -live but enhanced with a prerecorded riff, all those killer bones' echoes - in the middle of a set played at The Berserker, their regular hang. In the middle of a shredding solo, the power started cutting out. They continued playing as if in trance, the sound coming out all wrong and weak.

There were sparks coming out of the plugs in the corner of the stage. Then a fire started. Followed by the screaming. Metal fans can *scream*.

The band stayed on stage as the chaos erupted all around them. Not enough people for a proper stampede even on a good night at The Berserker, but they could hear people getting trampled all the same. Darkness and alcohol didn't mix well. Maybe in theory, but not in practice.

The fire was put out easily enough. For all its edginess and slumming curb appeal, the venue was current on its fire extinguishers. The band came to no harm, their equipment was safe. Most of the audience got out safe too, but there was a body left on the floor. A brightly dressed blonde cutting a tragic figure amid the dirt and cigarette butts and spilled beer. Her limbs at cringingly unnatural angles.

Rex thought she looked familiar, but so many people did to him; when he was on stage, half-blinded by the bright lights and the sweat pouring in his eyes, everyone kind of blurred together.

He checked on her after a while. Paul knew someone who knew someone…Rex didn't feel especially guilty or responsible, but he wasn't a monster.

She made it, he found out. Would never walk again in all likelihood, but she'd live. He put it out of his mind; the music demanded his complete focus.

They continued working, completing the demo by October. They swaddled their music in hopes and dreams and bubble wrap to send out to every studio they could think of. Every name that handled all the greats. Faces on the posters that lined their walls, voices that preached through their headphones.

One day it'll be them. Cerberus on the t-shirts, sides of the tour buses, arena venues.

You had to dream big – heavy metal was an all-or-nothing proposition. You didn't just dip your toes, you dived in.

The neat stack of packages ready to be stamped and mailed lay out on the table like a pile of gifts.

It was time to celebrate, to party like they were as young and as wild as they felt on stage. All their guitars were named after the greats, and they toasted each one of them.

Chuck even splurged on some coke. Neat lines he cut using his American Express card like a Wall Street wannabe.

They lit candles – nothing else had ever really looked right in their makeshift ossuary. The lights flickered off the old bones, animated the ancient skulls into sinister glee.

They toasted them all - the sightless countenances whose rest they had so rudely disturbed for their own means – promising them their sacrifice wouldn't go in vain. Their music would give it meaning, they promised, purpose. Immortality.

They didn't know when they dozed off. The small space warmed up easily with the heat of their bodies despite the crisp autumnal night air, and the booze overrode the coke in their veins relaxing them.

Paul woke up first, the flames licking his leather jacket proved more efficient than any alarm clock. His screams woke the others.

It had to be the candles; somehow, they must have tipped over the candles. In a space that size it wouldn't take much.

Rex pushed at the door and found it locked. He twisted the keys around – they had put some good serious hardware on, to protect all that equipment, but nothing gave. The door, it seemed, wasn't so much locked as it was barred. From the outside.

He pushed. They shoved. Frantic panicked efforts exacerbated by the tightness of the quarters and the hung-over-fueled lack of coordination. Nothing gave.

They screamed for help. Screamed louder than in any of their shows. But who would hear them in this remote area?

The fire wouldn't die down. The moment they thought the flames were stomped out, more sprung up.

Rex looked around, expecting the bones to calcify and crumble, turning into ash all around them. This place, after all, had become a crematorium. He was surprised to find the bones were holding on, but then again, science was never his strong suit. Wasn't the fire hot enough? To Rex, it felt like Hell itself.

It seemed, and the terrible irony of it all wasn't lost on him, that the dead were going to outlast the living. The skulls agreed, grinned in assent, he thought.

He could hear the music, Cerberus' music. He didn't know how, but the sound traveled across the screaming, across the hissing hungry fire, across everything.

They sounded good. Strong. Heavy Metal perfect.

If that was the last thing he heard, it would be enough.

Sheila watched the flames from a safe distance. She was tired. Doing all she'd done in a wheelchair, with no assistance, took all of her strength.

Going around the shed with heavy metal chains. Securing them with a heavy metal lock. She loved the poetic justice of it all, but it wore her out. So much effort, so much planning.

Finding the address, getting here with all she had to carry. The gasoline alone. And then splashing it onto the walls and the ground until she could barely feel her arms. Starting the fire was the easiest thing. She used a long fuse, which she'd lit once she was far enough to feel safe. Then she rolled her wheelchair away like a bat out of hell.

Now, exhausted, she observed the fire with surprising indifference. She thought she could hear their screams, the terrible dissonance of it all. It should have broken her somehow, but nothing seemed to matter much anymore. Not since she woke up amid the sterile whiteness to find her life forever altered, her body mangled, her baby gone.

She came to see Rex play that night, planning on telling him afterwards. He probably wouldn't care, but a small hopeful part of her heart had 'what ifs' butterflying in her stomach. Up there on that stage, he looked like a star. She wanted to get close, to feel the reflective warmth of it. He'd noticed her once, maybe he would again. She knew every one of Cerberus' songs by heart. Wore the demo out playing it. The way Rex looked with his guitar, like a man possessed...

Sheila shook the image away; it was no use now. Dreams die. She had learned her lesson.

In the end, she was able to give him a great death. A fiery inferno of one. As epic as the best heavy metal song. Louder than sound alone. It would have to be enough.

Sheila sighed and began the long trip home, wheeling herself slowly over the uneven terrain. After a while, she reached into her bag and pulled out a pair of headphones. Fiddled with some buttons until the first power riff hit her eardrums like an angry storm. Love didn't last, but music... music was forever.

Mia Dalia is an author, a lifelong reader, and a longtime reviewer of all things fantastic, scary and strange. Her short fiction has been published by Night Terror Novels, 50 word stories, Flash Fiction Magazine, Pyre Magazine and Tales from the Moonlit Path. Her fiction will be featured in the upcoming anthologies by Sunbury Press, HellBound Press, Black Ink Fiction, Dragon Roost Press, Mystery Magazine, and Unsettling Reads. Her debut novel, Estate Sale, will be out in March 2023.

She'd like to give you nightmares...the fun kind.

Official author website https://daliaverse.wixsite.com/author

Reviews, essays, and thoughts can be found at

https://advancetheplot.weebly.com

War Born

Richard Beauchamp

Tjal could feel the vomit going up his nose and into his eyes. He spluttered but kept going, his fingers never stopping as he played through the main chorus of "Chainsaw Baptism" for the fortieth time in three days. This time he was upside down, his feet hooked into chains that kept him suspended and swinging three feet above an industrial compactor, its many metal teeth coming together in a mechanical gnashing as it eagerly yearned to render his body and his instrument to so much unidentifiable pulp. Much like the stray mutants, skinless dogs, legless hogs, and even the occasional vagrant that the other members of the band could find to toss in, causing geysers of blood and other bodily fluids to spurt up and splash Tjal as he played.

But Tjal would not let himself be distracted. He played through the two-hour set flawlessly, as he'd done many times before, in all manner of harrowing circumstance, under a litany of substances. A pound of synthetic peyote coursing through his system while he rode in the back of a war wagon while the band drove him through the Blasted Butte, scavengers and cannibals firing potshots at the vehicle while he played. Mainlining a gallon of The Berserker's homemade vat-hooch while he played on a small make shift stage in the middle of the Grim Plains, where the radiation was so concentrated that even on a mildly overcast day one's skin would boil and sizzle without protection within five minutes. Tjal had finished the set just as the last of his epidermal layer had been sluiced off, covering his bass in drooping tanned sheets of flesh that took the band's resident sawbones an hour to reattach with heaps of neurogel.

The set ended just as the chains began to lower and Tjal could feel strands of his long brown hair getting caught in the compactor, being ripped out as the punishing 350BPM outro to "King of the Whore" reached its zenith. He didn't miss a single note however, he knew it, and he knew *they* knew it as they listened, all of them biohacked into his performance as his bass was jacked into the cloud mixer.

He was set on his feet once the test was over, and as the band approached him, a half man, half machine amalgamation of suffering personified, he expected more blank stares, more demands to continue the audition, to see what he was *really* made of, his mettle forever to be tested. He steeled himself for that. He was finally starting to feel himself breakdown despite the sawbones best efforts to put him back together after each performance. But there was only so much that a stem-cauterizer and gallons of neurogel could do.

But as The Mountain approached, Tjal saw a grim admiration on the enormous man's face. The Mountain, aka The Seven Foot Death, put a grimy hand on Tjal's shoulder. Tjal forced himself to meet the vocalist's white eyes and not the pried open flesh wound of his trachea, which reminded him so much of a gaping vagina, as the big man spoke. His voice was that of ruin, of decay, a monstrous baritone augmented by the titanium mesh coating of his vocal chords. One couldn't help but watch the exposed trachea warble and pulsate as he spoke.

"You did good, Tjal of Red Water." The Mountain said, grabbing Tjal's arm and holding up the skeletal framework of his mechadigits, looking at them curiously, "Your sacrifice has paid off"

Tjal could not afford a sawbones of such quality as the one War Born had on staff, and so the suture job that married flesh to alloy was crooked and unseemly, but effective all the same. When he heard word that the heaviest band in the world was holding auditions to replace their late bassist, he knew he had to step his game up. He had to transcend his corporeal vessel and let blood in service of the riff gods. He would make himself un-whole and augmented so that he may play like them, inhumanly precise and uncomprehendingly technical. So he had his hands, his weak, human hands, chopped off, and replaced with the mechanical spiders that could easily transcend the capabilities of tarsal muscle and sinew.

The ground shook with the pneumatic swish and thud of The Berserker's iron feet, he was tiny compared to his vocalist, but the drummer was equally larger than life with the many wires and servos embedded within flesh the shade of motor oil. Long dreadlocks interweaved with bone and circuitry hung in his face as he approached and shook Tjal's hand. Sparks danced between them as metallic claw met syntha-flesh, beneath which were human tendons and bones juxtaposed with fiber optic nerve endings and mesh veins.

"Monstrous performance. Just what we like to see." The Berserker said as the sawbones hastily approached, the cauterizer already fired up and ready to rend and mend. The drummer shoved the doc away. "No, tonight this man wears his pain with pride. Tonight, Tjal of the Red Water will drink with his new clan. Today he has proven himself worthy to bleed among the War Born!" He roared. The rest of War Born roared with him, and with that confirmation, Tjal was anesthetized to the entire physical trauma they had forced him to endure over the last seventy two hours.

Tjal felt his head swim with unreality as they welcomed him aboard War Born's travelling mansion of violence and depravity: A converted troop transport and mobile command center once used by the Coalition Without Borders, a rolling behemoth of diesel and steel, the land version of the great aircraft carriers that once roamed the seas prior to their thermonuclear boiling. The red, white and blue flag of the CWB had been removed, and the band logo was vinyled in its place: Two crisscrossing laser rifles, behind which a blood red nuclear corona mushroomed upwards into jagged letters spelling out WARBORN. He had only seen the traveling war-wagon on the holo-screen, the great metal behemoth rolling up to every War Born performance, the thunderous roar of eighty cylinder diesel engines and the grate of ten foot tall tires eating up the earth hailing their fans to arms like the ancient bugling horns giving the command to charge.

"Let our newly blooded brother drink from the private reserve!" Baal said as they stood in the huge anteroom that served as a lounge and interview space for the various VR drones that came from the green zone news agencies. Once word had spread that War Born had finally found a replacement for the mighty Storm Bringer, the drones converged upon the war wagon, a million digital faces wanting their first look at the fresh blood.

Tjal stared out the window at the flooding pixelated faces of the news anchors and flipped them off with one shiny alloy finger. Then his attention turned from the window to the large crate that stood in the antechamber, a peculiar logo on it that Tjal thought he'd seen out in the great sand wastes between his hometown of Red Water and the nearest green zone: New Angeles. With a kick from his hydraulic calves, Berserker burst the crate open, and Tjal saw hundreds of rectangular bottles sporting amber fluid and black labels.

"Uncle Jack. How long has it been?" Baal said reverentially as the twin black orbs of his eyes gazed in the crate's general direction. He was blind, his eyes completely tattooed over, but some other sense keyed him into his surroundings. Tjal had yet to see the guitarist stumble or fall, and he commanded the stage better than most with full sight would. He took one bottle, twisted off the cap, and downed half of it in three huge gulps.

"Savor it, brother." The Mountain warned as he took a bottle and handed it to Tjal, who'd only ever drank the radioactive gutter hooch that was everywhere in Red Water. "This is one of a kind. Used to be everywhere before the war. Not anymore." He said, grabbing his own bottle. With a crunch of glass he bit the tip of the narrow stem off, not bothering with the plastic cap, and drank deep from the jagged opening he made. A small bit of whiskey dribbled down his neck as it wept from his tracheal opening.

36

"Where should we debut the new meat, eh?" Baal asked as they stood over the large holo screen projector in the center of the room, where generals and captains once studied maps and troop movements.

The Mountain stepped forward and pressed something on the screen. A moment later a 3d projection of the world was floating before them, the size of a wrecking ball and incredibly detailed. The whole globe was covered in various blotches of red, yellow, and green.

"Our boy is from Red Water. Closest fan base we have is New Angeles. We could play there. A kind of hometown send off, eh Tjal?" The Mountain asked, clapping him on the shoulder. Tjal shrugged.

"It matters not where we go. To be a part of War Born has been my life's goal. So long as I am laying waste side by side with my brothers, we could play the sewers of the capitol, and I would be content." Tjal said as the world slowly rotated around them. The majority of it was red, with a few pockets of yellow and a few tiny green specks showing where the last enclaves of civilization lived on as if the planet hadn't been irrevocably baptized in ionizing radiation.

"Sewers of the capital wouldn't be a bad idea actually…" Baal said as he stroked his chin, as if more than just mottled scar tissue grew there.

"You're all thinking too small. We need a *tour*. We need to show the world we're not done. We're not dead." Berserker said, and waved his hand. Around fifty arrows popped up on the map like darts, showing some of their more popular venues. Tjal looked at those arrows, each location summoning with it a memory of watching a War Born performance on the holo-vid news. Crowds tearing themselves limb by limb. Great gyrating cyclones of blood and sweat as circle pits a mile wide were started with feral mutants who'd been kept in cages until a specific point in the song. The stutter-crack of rifles going off and blending with The Berserker's own cannon blast kick drum as riots started and local governing forces (if there were any) opened fire indiscriminately.

Tjal felt adrenaline course through his patchwork body at the thought of living all those glorious moments in person, wielding that chaotic sonic power that could destroy and destabilize all in its path.

"He's right. A world tour it is. But where do we start..." The Mountain said, blood and whiskey dribbling from his lips as he tongued the jagged glass mouth from which he sucked.

The sun was high and murderous over the ruins of what was once called Stalingrad. Despite the bright day, it was negative eleven degrees Fahrenheit, only the volcanic emissions from the war wagon's idling exhaust and the row of plasma torches that lined the stage keeping the ambient temperature somewhat hospitable. The war wagon had rolled up not even an hour beforehand, and already people were lining up as The Mountain blew the great horns of the vehicle, which could be heard for miles in all directions, a distorted, warbling siren that those in even the most isolated and radiation blasted slums recognized.

Adler, their sound tech and stage manager, among other things, worked tirelessly to prepare the stage and get the massive half mile high speaker system hooked up. It was all self-contained within the war wagon and unfolded on automated plate shifters. It was the band's job to cover Adler while he set up. Indeed, being in War Born was equal parts fighting and performing, as Tjal soon found out. He manned one of the double barrel TAC cannons and set sights on the growing horde that bore down upon the war wagon, drawn by the war-horns. It was usually 50/50 whether or not the opening crowd would be hostile, depending on where they played.

Through the thermal scope he could see many limbed amalgamations running towards them, excreting a snail trail of blood and feces in their wake as they ran.

"We got gimps!" the Berserker roared as he jumped down from the war wagon, holding the home-made quadruple barrel shotgun in his arms. "Let's clear this stage for the locals, huh?" He said. While the Mountain monitored their rear, Baal began to sound check his guitar, the walls and walls of atomic powered tweeters, speaker cones and subwoofers undulated and jumped as his spidery fingers moved in a blur over the neck of the massive nine-string axe. Discordant shrieks and distorted squalls carried on two hundred decibel waves. Even the mighty TAC cannon's boom was swallowed up by Baal's pinch harmonics and gut-punching power chords as the sixty caliber depleted uranium shells slammed into the converging crowds.

Tjal switched off the thermal vision because he wanted to see the destruction he brought. Bodies exploding in great clouds of yellow and red, chunks of organ and limb flying hundreds of feet as he put an end to the hideous existence of those who'd succumbed to the harsh teeth of this world. He stopped firing once the Berserker drew close, and true to his name, the metal-legged man moved like a tornado through the sea of meat and gristle, stomping bodies flat with his pneumatic press feet and blowing apart what still stood and gnashed with four ten-gauge barrels of buckshot.

Baal's guitar abruptly stopped as Adler pulled Tjal from the cannon's seat.

"Your turn, let's see if I can get a handle on this tone of yours!" The man shouted, the cartilage cups of his ears having been replaced with strange metal apertures that resembled bullhorns. They constantly leaked blood and ear wax, the toll from being under a constant barrage of sound from the band, who were on record as being the loudest in the world.

Tjal and Baal switched spots. As Baal searched for targets with the cannon, Tjal grabbed his large 5-string bass off the stage rack sequestered behind the thick metal girders that flanked either side of the stage. A custom-made Warwick bass, an ancient model Tjal had painstakingly updated himself;

scraping what little universal credits he could get doing mine work in red water to upgrade the instrument.

The ancient magnetic based pickups were swapped out for self-contained reactor soap bar pickups he had attuned to the lowest frequency they could possibly go, so that when he struck his low B string, tuned an octave down from what the old world basses used to be kept in, the green current that surged through both pickups turned red with the plasma. The result was a snarling, sizzling tone that pushed air at around 11 Hz at the bottom and 3000 Hz at the top. Combined with his own special distortion chain and the war-wagon's sonic-weapon turned sound system, hitting the sharp staccato opening lines of "Blood Currency" it sounded more like the grunt from a world eating leviathan than a musical instrument.

Tjal watched with a big grin as the air shimmered in front of the stage as his bridge-cable bass strings were struck, stirring up dust and gore. The remaining gimps that hadn't been torn apart by the TAC cannon fell to their feet and immediately began writhing and twitching as blood spurted from even more orifices than before. A few of the boil-skinned carrion birds who'd swooped down to try and scoop up something from the pile of offal simply vaporized as they flew in front of one of the speaker towers.

"Holy shit!" Adler yelled from his armored pedestal at the back of the stage, the meters from every console and mixer he had glowing in the red after that little performance. The grizzled sound man had never seen or heard a sonic signature like that one before. He stared up at the bassist with a new level of respect.

One by one each member either sound checked of performed guard duty, and by the time they were ready to rock, the gimps had been blasted away and replaced with actual fans, non-feral mutants, war-torn refugees who were missing what their mutant counterparts had gained in terms of limbs and extra

40

appendages. Rival regional warlords and their entourages came and set aside grudges out of respect for the band. All wanted to take place in the shared catharsis of the sonic assault, all wanted to have a small taste of that pure exchange of emotion, one of the few holdovers from that world of old that they could still enjoy: Live music.

"I hope you're all ready to destroy. We've traveled a long way to be here, Stalingrad. Over the frozen hellscape of the Behring peninsula, fighting fire-serpents in the Bay of Blood, and navigating quaking fault lines just to be here, and melt your fucking faces!" The Mountain roared, his demonic voice that of a god as it came through the PA system. The crowd roared back, but their incensed ascent to destroy was lost as, without further ceremony they launched into "Demons of The Deep", the thunderous synchronized gallop of stringed instrument and kick drum pounding the air and the ground, making it feel as if though a thousand chariots from the devil himself were rolling across the blasted plains.

The blood soon flew as the music unlocked some primal rage in their brains, limbs began to flail of their own accord and firearms and other weapons were put down, not out of respect but because this type of feral bloodletting required a tactile touch. Fists, teeth, feet, legs, anything that could be swung or punched was used, filthy flesh rubbed and smacked into each other as the hyper-violence spread.

It wasn't just violence, however. Among the blood and the sweat and pus and ruptured boils, some rutted like animals, rolling around among the dead and maimed, adding their own fluids to the growing collection via bestial howls of exaltation, the rhythmic pumping of hips, and the pendulous sway of three-nippled breasts as the music brought out the primordial beast in everyone.

Tjal felt himself lost to the music and the spectacle of it. His bionic fingers moved in a blur and his greasy black hair windmilled in time with the brisk pulse of the songs, a high more pure than even the best head-shatter he'd ever slammed into his veins.

They were about halfway through the set, the crowd in a full on frenzy now, when Adler chimed in through their intra-cochlear monitors so that his voice cut cleanly through the custom-tuned mixes each one had.

"Heads up guys, we got military birds inbound. Not sure what their intentions are, they're not breaking radio silence." Adler said.

A minute later Tjal saw them; solid black and bearing the sign of the all-seeing eye, the helicopters of the Coalition Without Borders flew low and fast over the once colorful spires and gabled roofs of this Russian ruin. What remained of a world government, the CWB rarely showed itself outside of a green zone unless policing activities that could threaten the stability of a nearby green zone or well-populated yellow zone. The fact they were flying in formation in a red zone as isolated as this was… well, unheard of.

War Born ignored the squadron however, keeping up with their sonic assault until Tjal saw the glowing blue object deposited from each helicopter before they sped away. The crowd dispersed as they tried to run away from the pulsing blue orbs. Tjal had time to think they were about to get nuked when the orbs exploded, a semi-translucent shockwave traveling towards them.

"EMP!" Adler said just before the blast hit them.

Silence, so vast and consuming that Tjal at first thought he was dead. He blinked, and looked down at his hands, which hung uselessly at his sides, small sparks emitting from the finger joints. He looked over at Baal, who lay convulsing on the ground, his guitar cast aside as his scalp arced blue fire and his synthaskin boiled.

"Fucking… Bastards… Got us…" The Mountain croaked, his trachea quivering and spasming as his vocal cord augmentation short circuited. Tjal looked back at Berserker, who sat behind his drum kit, trying to get his iron piston legs moving, pulling at them with desperation. They were all crippled.

A second later he heard the *thump thump* of helicopter blades approaching. He watched as the crowd, who was mostly organic besides the few warlords who could afford chrome digs, began to point and yell at the approaching aircraft, livid that the show had been stopped. Someone picked up a rifle and started shooting at the birds.

"Oh shi—" Tjal said before his voice was lost in a roar of Gatling guns. He felt the ground shake with the barrage as red mist and bone chips flew in the air. All four of the helicopters opened up, and within a minute they had reduced the whole two thousand person crowd to hamburger. The thick stench of burnt cordite and the coppery tang of gore flowed towards the stage in waves as one chopper hovered above the stage and a rope was dropped from it. Tjal watched as three men slid down the rope and appeared before them on stage.

Crisp black uniforms that were without a single blemish. Military rankings embossed on the sleeves. One of the men was clearly a big dick of some sort; he had on a fancy hat, huge sun glasses and bore the expression of someone forever in the throes of trying to pass a kidney stone. The other two flanked him, anonymous goons in full battle rattle aiming Gauss carbines at Tjal and Berserker. The big dick idled up to The Mountain, looking up at the gigantic man as if staring at a particularly impressive piece of dog shit.

"Major Ellison. I thought you would've learned your lesson regarding these... shenanigans, last time. You know. When we killed the hairy one." The big dick said, his voice a flat monotone. Tjal blinked.

"Who the fuck you calling major? That's the mou—"

The goon was quick, using the stock of his rifle like a club and hitting a home run with Tjal's oyster's being the baseball. He dropped to his knees with a grunt. His world exploded in geysers of white stars, and from somewhere across the universe The Mountain croaked.

"Get fucked, general. Shouldn't you be coddling some fat politician in his high rise condo, pretending to be bodyguards?" He rasped, the syntha-weave of his vocal cords no longer working, making him sound like a hyena that had learned to speak.

"You mean preserving civilization and trying to keep some semblance of the world in order? Why yes, I *should* be doing that. Instead, I'm here in this prolapsed asshole, getting bathed in radiation because a certain defector won't learn when to kneel like a good dog. You've officially come under the sanction of the Coalition Without Borders, you aborted pieces of shit." The man said, taking off his glasses. Instead of human eyes, two glowing red spheres appraised the four men on stage with cold, murderous calculations, the servos whirring in his brain as his mechanical peepers took each man in. "The entity known as 'War Born'" –He said the band name as if it left a taste of mutant shit on his tongue— "Is hereby recognized as a terrorist organization in the eyes of the CWB. Magistrate Dawson, supreme commander of the Coalition, has ordered an immediate cease and desist of all operations pertaining to your...musical act."

"Under what fucking grounds?" The Mountain spat. "We don't play green zones anymore. You assholes don't even—"

"Inciting violence in war-torn regions, disrupting the peace of recently stabilized government controlled regions. Undermining continuity of government practices in places where CWB ambassador efforts have taken place. Oh, and theft of government property." He said, pointing to his feet, meaning the war-wagon. "Consider this your final warning, major. You try and setup shop anywhere in the world again, we'll know about it, your god awful caterwauling shows up on every functioning sonar rig from halfway across the world, and next time we won't fire a warning shot." The general said, and grabbed hold of the rope.

"Eat my fucking dick, General Keyes." The Mountain rasped as the three men were whisked away like spiders on their threads.

"You used to be in the CWB?" Tjal asked incredulously as they all sat in the war room, the saw bones working frantically between them all to re-solder the blown-out fuses and connections caused by the EMP. They were all thoroughly soused on Jack Daniels as The Mountain air-casted a video onto the holo-projector. The spinning globe disappeared, and Tjal was looking at War Born's last known performance with StormBringer. Tjal had watched the video a hundred times. The official word was Storm Bringer, who had a fierce addiction to head-shatter, had OD'd on stage, dropping mid song and convulsing on the ground like a man possessed.

"How do you think I got this giant turd?" The Mountain said, stomping a large booted foot on the floor, indicating the war wagon. "Yeah. I used to be military. I enlisted right when the continental army turned into the CWB, when the bombs feel. Thought we could make the world whole again. I didn't realize we'd essentially turned into a private military contractor outfit and not an actual military, meant to protect and serve its people. I quit once we started getting paid to wipe out 'problems' in the yellow zones and be lapdogs for the corpo-cocks." He said, his voice once again back to its normal booming baritone.

"And they killed Storm Bringer? He didn't overdose on shatter?" Tjal asked, his mind swimming with booze and revelations. The Mountain gestured towards the holo-vid.

"Watch closely." He said.

One minute the huge bassist with the flowing beard, mechanical torso and mechanical spider fingers was throwing down and head-banging to the brisk rhythm of "Carrion Eater". Next, he was on the ground, spasming and twitching. Tjal thought he saw the briefest flash on the camera lens. Their vocalist rewound the footage, slowed it down to half speed. That was when

Tjal saw the glimmer of a translucent projectile slam into the mighty man a split second before he went down.

"They had a sniper set up two miles away. Fired a ghost round into our boy here, a sort of compacted bullet of nano-machines that disperses on contact. Leaves no entry or exit wound. Their way of sending us a message." The Mountain said, a grimace of hatred on his face. "Fucking cowards fear us." At that, he drained the rest of his bottle in one huge gulp. "Sorry to lie to you kid. We figured if people heard the CWB wanted to ass fuck us, no one would audition." The Mountain sighed, "He was a good man, Storm Bringer." They all raised their bottles in salute to this sentiment, Tjal included.

"But… why us? Why do they care what we do? Like you said, we stay away from the green zones." Tjal asked.

"Because. They see what our music does to people. Makes them open their eyes and see that the world has given them a royal ass fucking. Enough people get riled up, and you'll have hordes of discontent half mutants descending upon the manicured lawns and shiny office buildings of the green zones. Upsetting the status quo. That's what they fear most." Berserker said. The other two members nodded in solemn agreement. "Remember last time we played in a green zone? It was fucking chaos. Those goddamn suits didn't know what the fuck hit them." The drummer said with a malicious grin. "Took them three days to quell the riots."

"We should stick it to them. One last final hoorah. One they'll never fuckin' forget." Baal said, flexing his hands with a whine of mechanical buzzing as the sawbones patched him up. "We played in a small piss hole green zone for mid level execs and all hell broke loose. Imagine if we played on the grand poobah's front doorstep." He said with a grin.

"We'd get turned into ash before we even played a single fuckin' note." The Berserker said with a sigh. "It'd be a fuckin' suicide mission."

"Shit, if I can't do this anymore, I'd rather die. It's either do this or become radiated hamburger with the rest of 'em." Baal replied.

Tjal couldn't believe he was hearing this. He'd finally achieved his life's dream, getting out of the slums of Red Water and joining his favorite band in the whole wide world, and now that all just goes up in smoke? Why? Because of some fucking rich asshole in a guarded condo high rise?

"Fuck this. Fuck all this fucking shit." Tjal said, standing and swiping a hand through the slo-mo replay of Storm Bringer falling to his knees, causing the image to vanish. "We're fucking *War Born*. They can't fuck with us! We're the heaviest goddamn band in the world!" He snarled, his blood was up.

"Yeah, and they're the CWB, the world's most powerful paramilitary organization." The Mountain said with a sigh. "You got spunk kid, but this is it. Once they put you on your shit list, you're fucked. I know from experience." He said, sounding forlorn. Seeing they were out of Uncle Jack, The Mountain hit a button on a console and an iridescent green vial of head shatter popped up from the strategy table. He popped the cork lid and laid a line out on the metal edge.

"Come on man. There's gotta be some way to sneak up on these assholes." Tjal said, eager to take a humongous shit right on the doorstep of the richest, most out of touch corpo-dick there was. The Grand Magistrate. "How much do we have in the band fund from black market sales? That's enough to buy us something, right?" Tjal said.

The Mountain was poised above the growing green line of booger-sugar and paused, as if struck by an epiphany. He then looked up at Tjal, blinked.

Suddenly he was pressing a button and Adler the soundman was on the horn.

"Hey Addy, you still got that arms dealer connect down in Sand Country?"

"I sure do boss. You trying to start a war or something?" Adler said over the intercom.

"Or somethin'…" The Mountain said, and down went the glowing green line of synthesized dope.

"Holy shit…" Tjal whispered as they came upon the huge gleaming metal gates of Eden, the biggest of the green zones and the governing seat of the CWB. He felt his asshole pucker slightly at the rows and rows of quad-barreled TAC cannons lining the ten story metal walls. The cloaking drive must've been working, or the war-wagon would've been reduced to a burnt streak on the desert floor within seconds.

"You sure you assholes wanna do this? The minute Addy fires the EMPs, there's no going back." The Mountain said, all of them were standing in the cramped confines of the folded up stage, everyone walled in by thick speaker cable bundles and speaker cabinets. They'd rehearsed it a thousand times, exactly where everyone needed to stand as the stage was unfolding so as to avoid being crushed by the stage girders and speakers as the stage configured itself. There would be no time for sound check or stage rehearsal. Adler had spent two weeks wiring the gear so that it all uncoiled neatly as the football-field sized walls unfolded and revealed the Trojan horse that had gotten past the gates of Troy.

"I was fuckin' born for this." Tjal said, the adrenaline pushing out the fear as he held his bass at port arms, standing beside Baal, who was busy cracking his neck in anticipation of what was to come.

"No place I'd rather be reduced to bone soup." The Berserker said, drumsticks yielded like nun-chucks.

The Mountain nodded.

"Show time." He said, and that was all that needed to be said.

"Woo! Ready to make history boys?!" The soundman yelled over the intercom, and a second later they heard the double percussive thud of modified cannons firing the timed EMP bombs over the gates. Detecting this faint electronic signature, the TAC cannons slowly began to swivel and converge on the war wagon.

"Come on…" Tjal said as he waited for the signal. The two EMP's were big enough to knock out power to the entire city, with the huge metal walls acting as a makeshift faraday cage to keep the pulse contained and amplified within its walls. Tjal felt his balls recede far into his body as he saw all those hundreds of barrels begin to glow red with a charging of ion energy, all directed at them, when he felt the shockwaves shake the ground of the war wagon.

"It's showtime boys! Give me a beat, B." Adler said as he drove through the sizeable gap in the wall normally protected by a ten-million-volt laser shield. They didn't even have to fire a single shot to get in.

As the war wagon proceeded forward, the Berserker began to hit out a steady single quarter note beat on his kick drum and floor tom, which was amplified through the auxiliary speakers mounted on the war wagon's front. Not nearly as loud as their actual performance but enough to shake windows and rouse the naïve bourgeois of Eden as the war wagon rolled down Paradise Square, crushing million UC hover cars and occasionally the owners of such extravagant rides as they made their way towards the center of town, where a huge skyscraper comprised of metal, marble and glass loomed over the cramped metropolis like a monolith over a place of worship.

Thump. Thump. Thump. Just like the war drums that used to play on the ancient ships of invading armies, the war wagon announced its presence with its thunderous stomping rhythm as it proceeded to the base of the magisterial palace, and the war wagon unfolded, the cloak drive powering down.

Tjal winced as the sun glinted off miles of freshly polished glass. He looked around in awe, never having been within the walls of an actual green zone before. He marveled at the lack of rust, of the shininess of everything, how the people that ran from the huge collapsing walls of the sound stage wore clean clothes and had unblemished skin, no boils or deformities or signs of living in the real world marred their bodies.

That was when the first of the foot soldiers converged on the square, filing out like drones from the ant colonies. Normally the cavalry would be called immediately, the CWB usually hid behind mechs and power armor, but they didn't have that option today. Tjal could hear the whine of small arms fire ricocheting off the speakers and girders as the sound stage rose like a phoenix from the ashes.

"Just play boys, I'll keep the cockroaches off our boots for long as I can." Adler said as he manned the single TAC cannon.

"People of Eden Square. We are War Born. We are the pain you have missed out on. We are the suffering of a world you helped create. We are the world outside these walls. And we have come to give you a fucking reality check." The Mountain boomed through the PA. People began to file out by the hundreds from balconies and porticos and shop fronts, their makeup caked on and their cosmetically enhanced faces distorted into rictuses of scared confusion. Tjal's soul burst with rage as he saw all those clean, plastic visages looming down before him.

That was when he hit the first note on his bass, the capacitors in his pickups cranked to the max, that first note so loud and thunderous that the world exploded around them in a million kaleidoscopic slivers of sun as every window within five square miles of the stage shattered. Thousands began to scream as their world rained razors upon them, the glass falling from two hundred stories and turning those who gawked on the higher levels into human Hasselback potatoes.

As blood dripped from balconies, it too painted the laser leveled streets as the TAC cannon thundered mutely in the wake of War Born's final performance. Adler, who like Major Thomas Ellison, was once a CWB recruit, his old training from the 101ˢᵗ mechanized kicking in as every carefully placed shell took out at least five CWB gunmen.

Tjal was grinning like a madman as this perfect aesthetic façade crumbled around him. He let himself be consumed by the sonic power of their own music, every member of War Born in a similar trance like state as they blasted through crowd favorites, the speakers slowly swiveling towards the magistrate's palace.

Just as the first of the helicopters squeezed through the maze of skyscrapers, having flown in from a nearby base who received the impossible SOS signal, Adler hit a Deadman switch he had rigged around his neck. This removed the compressor and quantum-limiter that kept a leash on Tjal "The Bloodletter" and his monstrous atomic powered low-end machine.

The ornate pillars of marble that made up the exterior of Magistrate Dawson's palace started to crumble, and somewhere underneath the thunderous cacophony of the band's performance there came a groan of metal coming unmoored from its foundations.

Way up high, above the clouds and the smog and ruin, a pudgy man in a silk robe screamed from his throne atop the world. Screamed as a detachment of the CWB airborne raced to climb the shuddering building, the magistrate's safety their top priority. But as huge chunks of the skyscraper fell away, crushing the ascending vehicles, Magistrate Dawson saw it would be too late.

Tjal felt himself be cut in half as the first barrage of Gatling rounds lanced across the stage. But his adrenaline kept him going long enough to watch as the sky fell upon them, the magistrate's palace imploding and falling towards them in a scream of glass and metal. Tjal smiled as the palace of god fell to crush him.

Richard Beauchamp has been writing horror and dark fiction since 2017. In that time he's had his work featured in many critically acclaimed anthologies including Dark Peninsula Press's "Negative Space: An Anthology of Survival Horror", four different volumes of Scare Street Publication's "Night Terrors" Series and most recently SNAFU: Dead or Alive by Cohesion Press. His debut fiction collection "Black Tongue & Other Anomalies" was a nominee for the 2022 Splatterpunk Awards for Best Fiction Collection.

Recce

Michael Subjack

A music video. Fuck. Adrian hadn't planned on that one. The song was about a teacher-turned-stripper. Sexy, but still insightful and even poignant. At least he thought so. When he wrote the song with Lou, the lead singer, he hadn't envisioned a music video. He imagined stoners and drunks playing air guitar to the blistering solo and giving the lyrics a perfunctory aside, citing them as "deep" and "bitchin'".

The other unexpected aspect was the location. Italy. Adrian had never been but found the prospect enticing. If nothing else, the country was known for its beautiful women. Not that it mattered if he wasn't interested. In a band of five, he was one vote and the results in this instance were a landslide. They were going to Italy to make a music video and do an interview with a guy who would spend more time on the band's salacious rumors than their artistic pursuits. Adrian didn't mind. The former was far more alluring than the latter. The problem was the timeline. The band's flight would arrive at night and they'd have to be on set the following morning. They had played enough international dates for Adrian to know that they'd be jet-lagged zombies. And while coke bumps were in the cards no matter what their schedule was, they'd likely need something much stronger to survive a twelve-hour shoot. With the contract signed, the band boarded a plane and were on their way.

They were an hour into the flight when Adrian felt a strange and unfamiliar anxiety set in. He turned to Neal, the bassist, for reassurance and saw a half-empty bottle of Jack. Not much help there. The buzzsaw-like snoring coming from the seat ahead of him meant that Lou was out of the picture, leaving Dave, the drummer, and Sid, the rhythm guitarist. As their combined

IQ was roughly equal to Neal's bottle of Jack, Adrian was better off banging his head against the window for the next fourteen hours. Instead, he focused on sleep.

And while it came, it did so with a price.

Adrian had traveled back in time. He found himself on the postage-stamp-sized stage of The Handlebar Saloon. How long had it been since they had played there? Four years? Five? If that wasn't surreal enough, he was standing a mere three feet away from Pete Sampson, the band's original rhythm guitarist. Pete had OD'd on heroin six months before they were signed. As he was a childhood friend of Adrian's, Pete's death hit him the hardest. The debut album had been dedicated to him and while his name occasionally popped up in publications like Creem and Rolling Stone, Adrian couldn't help but think that Pete was all but forgotten. Yes, he had helped write nine of the debut album's twelve songs, but save for some rough-sounding demos, Pete's contributions were ephemeral. The fan base that formed after the release of their debut album had no frame of reference and the critics simply didn't care. Plenty of musicians OD'd. To them, Pete was a dime a dozen. Although Adrian thought about him roughly thirty seconds of every day, to see him this vividly seemed cruel. He could practically smell Pete's malt liquor-infused sweat. In what had been his trademark move, Pete's leather-clad leg was perched on the amp while he pounded on his guitar like a caffeine-addled carpenter. Even compared to more famous rhythm guitarists like Malcolm Young and Rudolf Schenker, Pete was objectively one of the best. He had been taken far before his time and even if the band's platinum status continued in perpetuity, Pete's death was proof that there was no justice in the world.

When the plane landed, Adrian didn't quite feel like a zombie, but his reflection in the mirror told a different story. His face was pallid and the dark circles around his sunken eyes made him look like an aging, sickly raccoon. He didn't envy the makeup person, but long flights had never been his forte. Although the other guys wanted to party and maybe meet some hot-to-trot Italian girls, Adrian was looking forward to collapsing on the hotel bed. Call time wasn't until eleven, but even that was too soon, especially when you considered the nature of their music video. It sounded stupid to him, but Italy was one of the markets they had yet to crack. As such, they were at the mercy of the music show that had agreed to highlight them. It was to be a lengthy interview, followed by the premiere of this preposterous music video. Adrian and his band would be performing in the long-abandoned grounds of a theme park among pastel-colored inanimate dinosaurs. Adrian was already picturing the articles a decade down the road (assuming they were still together and playing):

"The band that played with prehistoric creatures are now dinosaurs themselves."

Fuck that. Adrian needed a drink.

A big one.

"This might be kind of cool," Neal said in the van the next morning. "You guys remember Land of the Lost? That was a pretty good show."

Adrian, whose one drink had turned into ten, was currently nursing a pounding headache and wasn't in the mood for Neal's vacant optimism. As he had been the last one to the van that morning, he was stuck up front. There was an advantage to that, however, as it gave him control of the radio. He turned it up, drowning out any further pearls of wisdom from Neal. The Italian DJ spoke hurriedly and the only things Adrian could glean were "Lady Diane Spencer" and "Prince Charles", likely referring to the wedding that was coming up on Wednesday.

"Man, why is she marrying him?" Sid asked. "Have you seen that dude's ears?"

"Would she be better off with you?" Lou replied, to which Sid nodded.

"Fuck yeah. I'd at least give her a fun weekend."

The band laughed but quickly fell silent again. When they were sober, there wasn't a whole hell of a lot to talk about.

"Dinosaurs," Neal finally offered in his surfer-like drawl. "Giant creatures who ruled the fuckin' Earth. We rule the fuckin' the Earth."

"Yeah, as long as the Earth doesn't include Australia and most of Europe," Lou added, earning a smirk from Adrian.

Despite his sex and booze-fueled lyrics, Lou was something of an intellectual. He spent his free time reading Proust and watching Fellini films. Adrian would occasionally join him and while he liked Lou a great deal, he just wasn't Pete. Who was? The two's closeness had spurned a number of homophobic insults in their high school days despite the fact both men were dating two of the prettiest girls in school. Admittedly, music was the only thing they were good at, but the fact it was also the ultimate aphrodisiac was a considerable bonus. More than sports, as far as Adrian was concerned. His girlfriend had been going out with the starting quarterback when she decided she was less a sports fan and more a rocker. Bad news for the jock dick head, excellent news for Adrian. Last he knew, she was married to a dentist in Sherman Oaks. Good for her. They had had their fun. And Adrian and the band were still having theirs.

At least until now.

"Shit!" Neal exclaimed, dragging the word out for several seconds.

Sid and Dave's reaction was one of baffled, barking laughter while Lou and Adrian exchanged a weary glance.

"All right, boys, let's put our game faces on," JJ the manager said in his strict but still soothing voice.

JJ didn't manage a lot of bands, but the ones he did were all platinum and managed to sell out arenas and stadiums in minutes. If JJ said you were doing something, it was in your best interest to agree. He was rumored to carry a gun, but Adrian wasn't sure how true that was. And he had no interest in finding out.

The trip had lasted over an hour and now that they were there, Adrian was tempted to jump out and run back to the hotel where he still had a partly-full bottle of Jack and a gram of top-shelf coke waiting for him. But this was it. The crew, made up of the usual gruff guys in jeans and t-shirts was setting up. One thing that softened the blow was the make-up girl. Adrian had seen enough of them to know that's exactly what she was. She wore a hip-hugging miniskirt over pink tights and the hair hanging over her forehead was dyed a deep fuchsia. She looked quite a bit like Debbie Harry, a singer Adrian greatly admired. He had met her shortly after the release of their second album and it was one of the few times he was genuinely tongue-tied. Fortunately, Ms. Harry was not put off by this and told him how much she admired not just their albums, but his guitar playing. While not in the same league as Jimmy Page or Eddie Van Halen, Adrian was no slouch, but he still accepted this compliment with a great deal of gratitude and humility. The latter was going to be the keyword for today. Six months ago, they were playing to sold-out crowds in massive arenas. Now they found themselves doing a video in front of dinosaur statues at a long-forgotten theme park. The music industry wasn't just fickle, it was downright schizophrenic.

After they parked, Sid and Dave made a beeline for the craft services table while Adrian, Lou, JJ, and Neal tracked down the director. To Adrian's knowledge, the guy mainly worked in television and had little-to-no experience doing music videos. That was another cause for concern. Music videos were still a relatively new medium, but that didn't mean you wanted to be somebody's first. And the fact this guy was wearing a fucking scarf did little to alleviate Adrian's apprehension. This mother fucker was pretentious and properly fancied himself the Bergman of Italian television if such a thing were even possible. All the ideas were to be his, regardless of shitty they were. His English was accented, but good. That didn't mean the words had any real value and he was as full of himself as Adrian suspected.

"I think I'm ready for make-up," he said when the guy finally took a breather.

The director, whose name was also Adrian, amiably nodded and waved to the make-up girl.

"Monica, Mr. Kelly is ready for you."

The make-up girl came over and smiled.

"Right this way, Mr. Kelly."

Adrian followed her into a nearby building that looked like it had been a restaurant or concession stand at one time. He honestly couldn't tell, as most of his focus was on Monica and the careful, thoughtful way she strutted her very admirable stuff.

If nothing else, at least the view was good.

She sat Adrian in a folding chair and walked over to a badly-scuffed table that contained an array of powders and creams. As she applied foundation, Adrian was struck again by her beauty and made a mental note to get his make-up redone as much as possible. Although she likely had some asshole boyfriend, Adrian had already decided that he was going to invite her to party at the hotel. He'd likely never be back here and there were still five days to go. Two for the video, one for the interview, and another two for R and R. JJ had arranged that. Usually, the record company did everything they could to make each venture as cheap as possible, but JJ had somehow convinced them that the extra time would be good for the next album. What a fucking laugh that was. They hadn't written a note.

After Monica finished applying Adrian's make-up, he made some flirty small talk before abruptly exiting. Always leave them wanting more. That had been his and Pete's philosophy and it was an effective one at that. By the end of tomorrow, Monica would be hopping in the van with them for a wild night they probably wouldn't remember. Back outside, the pretentious director appeared to be arguing with the cinematographer, which was bad, especially considering they had yet to get a shot off. The rest of the band all dutifully went to Monica for hair and make-up, but Adrian wasn't really worried about any of them. Lou was in the throes of a passionate affair with a married actress while the rest of the band focused on groupies. They liked them skanky and stupid and Monica was neither of those things. The arguing continued for almost twenty minutes. Finally, JJ stepped in and with his linebacker-like build, achieved the desired results.

The band took their place near a brontosaurus and grabbed their respective instruments. To Adrian's dismay, the guitar was a Gibson and not a Les Paul. He always played a Les Paul. His main one was painted a black so shiny it looked almost liquid. Adrian didn't believe in loving inanimate objects, but that guitar was very important to him. At present, it was nestled safely in his home studio and he was surprised at how much he missed holding it, especially given how undesirable his situation was. The Gibson was nice, but it paled in comparison to Thor (as it came to be known on their first headlining tour). Still, to make a stink now would likely result in them losing almost the entire day, as getting a new guitar would involve a two-hour round trip back to town and at this point, Adrian was willing to play a tennis racquet if it got them the fuck out of there at a reasonable time.

With their instruments in hand, the band readied themselves for the pretentious prick to call "Action". Playback was being done through a rather small and primitive tape player, a stark reminder of just how low-rent this operation was. To make matters worse, the song that played wasn't even the right one. The band let their frustration be known and their frustration was JJ's quiet rage.

"Can I speak with you?" he said to the director, who meekly nodded.

He was no longer in control of the situation. Not that he ever was, but at least now he knew it. They spoke quietly for about two minutes. When it was over, the now-ashen director waved the crew over and briefly addressed them. Within a minute of that, the right song had been cued and the shoot was underway. The most desirable effect of JJ's little pep talk was that each set-up got no more than two takes. In some instances, like a few of the close-ups and inserts, there was only one and it was captured with a speed that felt almost coke-fueled. And as far as Adrian could tell, it was. Not that was judging, of course. After three hours of nonstop shooting, they took a break. Some of them headed for craft services, but Adrian made a point to visit Monica. The only one who stayed behind was Neal, who stared intently at the large green brontosaurus that dwarfed his normally massive drum kit.

"Everything okay, Neal?" JJ called out to him.

While the concern might seem genuine and even fatherly, Adrian knew that JJ wanted to replace Neal. He wasn't exactly sure why but knew it had something to do with an altercation between the two after the last tour. While no shots were fired, it was still pretty nasty. Adrian thought the only reason JJ hadn't moved forward with the idea was that Neal was an admittedly handsome dude. Dumber than a box of rocks and probably the least talented member in the band, but as his poster adorned more walls than paint, his job was safe for the time being. Unusual for a bass player to get that kind of attention, and yes, that was something that made Adrian and the rest of the band just a little bit jealous.

"Neal?" JJ repeated, his voice taking on a slight edge.

Either Neal was willfully ignoring JJ or he was too wrapped up in staring at the fake dinosaur he had been sitting in front of for the most day.

"This thing is moving," he finally said.

Everyone that understood English stopped what they were doing. Ordinarily, Adrian would have laughed, but as he was making progress with Monica, Neal's words were an annoyance.

"The fuck are you on, man?" Sid asked, his hands full of finger sandwiches. "It ain't like those robots at Disneyland. That don't move!"

"It just fucking did!"

The rest of the band joined Sid in ribbing Neal. Before long, everyone, Monica included, was laughing.

Neal's countenance had taken on the pout that melted so many girls' hearts, only Adrian knew it was an actual pout. He was preparing his own insult when he saw something out of the corner of his eye – the brontosaur's tail.

It moved.

The rest of the band and the music video crew were still laughing as Adrian stared dumbfounded. The movement was slight at first, but what started as a twitch became more pronounced as the tail slowly moved, as if it were waking from a long slumber. In a way, that was true. Adrian just didn't know what to think. How was something like this even possible? He had seen the thing up close and it appeared to be made of some kind of plaster. Movement wasn't possible without it cracking or breaking. Just when he was about to back up Neal's seemingly crazy claim, the brontosaurus let out a deep, throaty rumble. Everyone stopped dead in their tracks. Neal turned to them, now with a look of bewilderment and triumph. A heavy silence followed and just when Neal started to speak, the brontosaurus raised one of its tree trunk-like legs. Just when Adrian realized what was about to happen, the leg came down with surprising speed, crushing Neal, who only had time to emit a short squawk.

The wet crunching of bones invaded Adrian's ears with a cruel and sickening vividness. It was a sound he'd be hearing the rest of his life, assuming they made it out of this. In the distance, the other dinosaurs, ranging from a twenty-foot-tall T Rex and a stegosaurus the size of a bus roared to life and began making their way to the terrified crowd.

After that, it was bedlam.

People were running in all directions as the prehistoric beats descended on them. The second to fall was a portly guy who had made the unfortunate error of putting himself in the path of the charging stegosaurus, who flattened the poor bastard like a pancake. It swung its spiked tail and took out several more crew members, as well as the band's equipment. A triceratops joined the fray and gored the pretentious director, as well as poor Sid. Adrian watched helplessly as his friend and band mate spewed blood while his legs dangled helplessly over the flattened grass. He felt something grab his shoulder, prompting to him let out a less-than-masculine scream. When he spun around, he saw it was Lou, his face frightened, but also determined. Standing behind him was Dave, who looked crazed as spit dribbled from his lower lip.

"We have to get to the van!" Lou shouted.

Although it looked miles away in their current situation, Adrian nodded in agreement. They started to run when they noticed Monica the make-up girl. She was on the ground, trying to crawl away from the T-Rex that had selected her as its next target. She looked at Adrian with a pleading expression, her mascara running down her face in ugly streaks. Against his better judgment, he started for her when Lou stopped him.

"Are you out of your fucking mind?"

Adrian decided that yes, he was very much out of his mind, but realized there was nothing he could do to help the poor girl. Unable to face her fear and desperation any longer, he turned away just as the T-Rex swooped down and bit into her shoulder with that now-familiar wet cracking sound. The fact it was punctuated with her agonized screams made it worse. As they got closer to the van, they saw JJ standing in front of it, a look of impossible calm on his face. In addition to the screaming, the air had grown ripe with the stench of copper.

"JJ!" Adrian yelled. "Get in the fucking van!"

JJ replied with a wan smile before bending down and lifting the flared pant leg of his tailored slacks. A pearl-handled pistol was resting comfortably in an ankle holster. So the rumors were true. With everything else that had happened, such a revelation was minor. JJ could have been wearing women's underwear as far as Adrian was concerned. JJ casually checked to make sure the pistol was loaded before turning to the three surviving band members.

"You boys be on your way," he ordered. "I'll be along shortly."

"JJ…" Lou started before whooping and pointing. "Look out!"

The Triceratops was charging at them, its horns still stained with the blood of Sid, the director, and God knows who else. JJ raised the pistol and snapped off two shots, one striking the triceratops by the mouth and the other directly through its eye. It roared with pain as a sizzling ichor shot from its wounds. Although it didn't go down, it at least changed directions.

JJ motioned for them to get into the van, using his pistol as a pointer. That was all they needed. They quickly climbed in, with Lou getting behind the wheel. Adrian sat next to him while Dave got in the back. Fortunately, the keys were still in the ignition. As Lou started it up, something slammed into the van's side, causing them to jump. Through his window, Adrian could see the panicked and bloodstained face of one of the crew members. He reached behind him and opened the door. The man managed to climb in just as Lou peeled out.

Adrian watched as JJ ambled toward the chaos, calmly squeezing off shots at the steaming, blood-soaked beasts. By the time they were a mile down the road, they couldn't hear anything. The crew member who had jumped in the van spoke in fast, gibbering Italian. Given what they had just gone through, it was a welcomed alternative. As they drove back to civilization, Adrian realized that his mind would no longer contain music and his dreams would no longer reunite him with Pete.

And if that didn't warrant a dangerous amount of booze and coke, he didn't know what did.

Michael Subjack was born in a small town in Western New York. He enjoys good cigars and going on hikes with his dog Rosie.

He lives in Los Angeles, but you can also find him on Twitter as @msubjack.

Bloodlines

Paul Sheldon

Gripping the edge of the cymbal, quieting it, laying his drum sticks gently on his snare and removing his earphones, Andy stood up.

"Thanks mate, we'll let you know."

The two Marshall guitar amps hummed in the suddenly quiet rehearsal room.

"Cheers for the opportunity guys, I really appreciate it." The audition over, the guitar wielding hopeful unslung his weapon of choice, a red Ibanez, and turned off his amp. "So, what did you think?"

Joe smiled, muting his own guitar amp. "Yeah, that was pretty good, loved the second solo."

"We'll let you know," repeated Andy, eyes on his phone.

Joe opened his mouth to say something further, and then thought better of it. The rest of the band watched quietly as the red guitar, cables, pedal board and amp were packed away, awkwardness increasing with each silent second.

"Thanks again," the no longer quite so hopeful auditionee said, as he hoisted his gear and left.

Joe turned to Andy. "I thought he was pretty good."

"He can't keep time," said Andy, still not looking up from his phone.

"His solo was-"

"He can't keep time." Now Andy looked up. "You can keep time, Joe, he can't." Andy turned back to his phone. "You're a better guitarist than he is."

Joe laughed. "Piss off; I can't play solos like that!"

"You would if you practiced more, because you can keep time. He's all flash and no basics, if you can't keep time, you can't play music."

"Then we're out of options," said Sean, removing his pale green Fender bass guitar, leaning it against his speaker cabinet and rubbing his shoulder. "Now what?"

Andy smiled and put his phone away. "Got another guy on his way, be here in about half an hour. A mate of mine told him about the audition and he sounds keen."

Sean looked at Joe and rolled his eyes. "Let's hope this one can keep time then, otherwise we're screwed."

Pete clipped his microphone back in its stand and tapped it. "Hello? Hello? Is it beer o'clock?"

Joe grinned. "Hell yeah!"

Joe took a final swig from his beer can and threw it into the bin by the mixing desk just as the next potential replacement walked in. The guy was thin, almost unhealthily so, but his long black hair, sharp features, ripped jeans and a denim jacket covered in patches from AC/DC to Whitesnake, looked every bit the part. He was obviously older than the current the band members, all in their mid-twenties, but by how much it was difficult to tell.

"Fellas," he said putting his guitar case down, "I heard you're looking for a new guitarist."

"You're John's mate, right? Mike?" said Andy.

"Yeah, we know each other. I jammed with him once, nice guy."

"He said you were really good."

"That's decent of him, but I guess you'll make up your own minds. I'll just go grab my amp, can I use that Marshall cab over there?"

"Sure, Trev hasn't come back for it yet."

"He was the last lead guitarist?" said Mike, raising his eyebrows.

"Yeah," said Andy.

"He's a fucking prick," said Pete, sneering.

Joe sighed, here we go again.

"He's a dirty dog, and he won't be back," said Andy with a tone of finality.

"Ah," said Mike, "I won't ask what happened. Be back in a second."

Joe opened another beer as he watched Mike set up. Mike pulled his guitar from its case, a flying V style, white with a black pick guard, covered in elegant black symbols and swirls, some totally abstract, others forming skulls and demonic faces, claws and fangs, the paintwork worn down to the bare wood in a couple of places. The guitar had obviously seen a lot of action over many years.

Joe whistled. "Holy shit, that's wicked." He looked at the symbol on the headstock. "What brand is it? I've never seen that before."

"I made it myself, I wanted something unique. A friend painted it for me." He looked away for a moment, as if recalling something from the past. "Anyway, it does the job."

"Dude that's metal as fuck!" said Sean, laughing.

"Ok let's get on with it, shall we?" said Andy. "Mike, what do you want to start with? Did John give you the audition list? How about Metallica's Master of Puppets or Megadeth's Hanger 18? Do you know those?"

Mike turned to Andy who was settling himself behind his drum kit once more. "I thought you guys were an original band? You've got songs on SoundCloud and an album on Spotify."

"We are, but obviously you won't know our songs yet, right?"

"I learned a couple last night," said Mike, checking the tuning of his guitar. "How about Weapon of Mass Destruction?"

"Mate, that's our toughest song," said Sean. "Trev struggled with that after six months, and he wrote the solo!" Joe saw Sean looking at Andy, who shrugged with a drumstick in each hand, emphasizing the gesture comically.

"I had a listen to it a few times last night; I think I've got it."

"Ok then," said Andy, in a matter of fact tone, and counted them in with four taps of his drumsticks.

The twin guitar harmonies of the opening bars were smooth and slick, Joe and Mike locking in together before launching into the full throttle thrash rhythm of the first verse. Joe grinned at Sean, so far so good.

After the second verse came a complicated bridge section, where the song wandered away from thrash metal for a few bars and ventured into prog metal. Mike transitioned into this flawlessly, sounding like he'd been playing the song for years. Then the bridge ended, and the guitar solo began.

By the end of the solo Joe, standing with his mouth open, missed the entry into the third verse completely, and copped some light-hearted abuse from Sean as a result. Pete was trying to sing while grinning, and even Andy was smiling behind his drum kit.

The seven minute song finally came to an end.

"So, how was that? I also learned Matter of Fact if you want to do that?" asked Mike.

Sean turned to Andy, brandishing his bass guitar. "If you say 'we'll let you know' I'm fucking hitting you with this," he said.

Joe laughed. "Shit man, you really learned that last night? Trev never played it that well!"

"Sure," said Mike. "I could hear what he was trying to do with the solo, he just didn't quite pull it off. It's actually pretty good."

"Yeah," said Andy, "it is when you play it like that."

"Who have you played with before?" asked Pete.

"A few bands here and there, mainly back east."

"You look familiar, that's all. I might have seen you play once or twice."

"Ok, let's do MoF," said Andy, going straight into the introductory drum solo before anyone could argue.

Joe stood at the bustling bar, trying to order a beer.

"A bit of liquid courage?" asked Mike.

Joe turned. Mike looked calm and relaxed.

"Yeah, I always get a bit nervous before a gig, doesn't seem to matter how many I do. How about you? It's your first gig with us, aren't you nervous?"

"Everyone gets a bit excited before a gig, but I've done a few, you get used to it." He turned and walked through the black curtains to the backstage area.

Joe eventually got his pint and followed.

Behind the curtains, Mike turned to Joe. "Just a piece of advice, mate." He gripped Joe by the shoulders. "Practice, practice, practice. The more you practice the less nervous you will feel because you'll know what you're doing. Take deep breaths and remember, everyone out there wishes they could be the one up on stage with the guitar, so don't sweat it."

Joe took a long swig of his beer. "Yeah, I hear you, it's just finding the time, you know? I wish there was some way to just, like download the genius or something. Download Van Halen, or Dimebag, or Kerry King and just get up there and rip it."

"But then everyone would be doing it, right? It wouldn't be special, would it? There would be no sense of achievement." Mike appeared lost in his own thoughts for a moment, before Andy poked his head around the curtain.

"Are you ladies ready to blow the roof off this joint?"

Joe stepped to the front, heart pounding furiously, making eye contact with the handful of head-banging diehards who'd made their way from the bar to the stage, and giving them the metal horns, he thrashed out the first riff of the night.

The gig was a blur, one frantic, thrashing song bleeding into the next, the crowd filling out as more punters left the bar and the beer garden to watch the show. This was the biggest crowd they'd ever played to, as few people usually bothered to watch the support act, and that's all they'd ever been, the support act.

Joe's playing was fast and tight, locking in with Andy's drums and Sean's machine gun bass, but his mouth stayed dry no matter how much beer he chugged between songs and his hands, while no longer shaking, were clammy with sweat.

By the fourth song though, he'd realized the crowd wasn't watching him at all. Mike's blistering solos surpassed anything his predecessor had achieved, ripping through the room like the tentacles of a Lovecraftian monster, reaching to all corners of the bar and pulling people in towards the stage. Jaws dropped and compliments were uttered, drowned out by the roar of the guitars, the thunder of the drums and bass, and Pete's screaming vocals.

Joe gritted his teeth and moved to the front of the stage, determined not to let the new guitarist have all the limelight. Banging his head furiously, long hair flying, he fed his frustration into the fast and heavy riffs. The crowd barely noticed him, they were all looking at Mike. His cheeks burned with embarrassment, and he eased his way back towards his stack at the rear of the stage. He pretended to check something on his amplifier, and then simply stayed there, in the shadows between the spotlights, watching Mike holding a legion of new fans in rapture.

Joe tried to imagine what it would feel like being a real rock star, everyone crowding in to get a closer look at their guitar hero. It seemed the bigger the crowd got, the better Mike played and the more he interacted with them, like he'd been born to it. Joe wanted that feeling more than anything, resolving to practice harder, until he was every bit as good as Dimebag Darrell or Kerry King. Every bit as good as Mike. Andy said he could be, and he was a great drummer, but he'd never played a guitar in his life, so what would he know? Joe wanted Mike to tell him how good he could be, to show him how good he could be.

70

He looked down at the set list taped to the floor beside his pedalboard and was surprised to see they only had one song left, Weapon of Mass Destruction.

He looked up and saw a sea of heads, faces all turned to the stage expectantly. The room was full to capacity, and Joe had never experienced anything like it. So why wasn't he enjoying it?

He looked across to the other side of the stage. Mike was surveying the crowd, nodding his approval, right hand raised in the metal horns salute, as if giving benediction to a faithful, worshipping congregation of metal heads. He turned to look at Joe and, moving forward, putting his heavy black boot onto the fold-back speaker at the front of the stage, as so many metal guitar legends had done before him, he raised his eyebrows and nodded. Fuck it, thought Joe, and took the same pose. Maybe he wasn't as good as Mike, but he could still share a bit of the limelight. Andy counted them in, and the twin guitars unleashed the final song's opening harmony onto the moshing crowd.

"Joe, you look like you're worn out man, you need a lie down or something?" Pete laughed as he packed away his microphone.

"Fuck you dude, you sound like a frog!"

"No shit! I've got no voice left at all, that was intense. I need a beer."

Joe turned back to the stage to fetch his amp when Pete grabbed his arm. "Seriously though, are you ok? You don't look happy, man."

Joe nodded. "I'm fine, that was an epic gig, right?" Grinning mirthlessly, he turned without waiting for a reply and jumped back on the bustling stage, into the barely organized chaos of one band removing gear while the next tried to set up theirs.

After stashing his equipment backstage, Joe went to the toilet. He barely noticed the mixed scents of piss, stale cigarette smoke and urinal freshener as he looked into the grimy mirror above the washbasin. He stared at the dark rings under his bloodshot eyes and realized Pete was right, he looked like shit. Going out drinking last night hadn't been such a great idea. He splashed some water on his face and left. "No more benders before a gig, and more practice," he muttered to himself. "Practice, practice, fucking practice."

He made his way through an above average number of punters congratulating him on a great show. "You guys were awesome, what's the band name?" One of us was awesome, he thought, but simply smiled and acknowledged every compliment. He got to the bar just as Mike was ordering a beer. "What'll you have, Joe?"

"A pint of lager, thanks."

Joe looked at Mike's face as he turned back to the bar to order the extra beer. On a bigger guy his angular features might have looked heroic, on Mike it looked hawkish. Joe still couldn't work out how old the guy was and wondered if it was a rude question to ask.

Mike handed him a pint. "Cheers, you were great up there!"

"Not really, no one was even watching me." Joe took a long drink of his beer. "You were incredible though. Fuck me, we've never had a crowd like this, no one usually bothers to watch the support act. Man, I wish I could play like you."

"You can," said Mike, simply.

Joe sighed. "Sure, I get it. Practice, practice, practice."

Mike took a long look at Joe, as if sizing him up. "Not necessarily," he said finally, getting his phone out. "Give me your number and I'll send you my address, come around tomorrow afternoon and I'll show you a few tricks."

Joe brightened immediately. "Cheers, will do." With Mike showing him some secrets, perhaps he'd be shredding in no time.

"Hey, cheers! Great gig guys," said Pete, clicking glasses with his bandmates.

"Cheers!"

"Ok I'm going to watch this next mob, I hear they're pretty good," said Mike, heading towards the stage.

Pete watched Mike walk away. "Be a bit careful with him, Joe."

"Why? He's amazing!"

"Oh, he can play, don't get me wrong, but there's something about him I don't like."

"Really? What's not to like? He's a nice guy and he plays like a demon."

"Exactly. He plays like a demon, so why has no one around here heard of him?"

"What do you mean?"

"I've been asking, no one knows him, Joe. How does a guitarist that good fly under the radar?"

"Who the hell cares? He said he played in a few bands on the east coast. Why is that a big deal? He can play, really well, you can't argue with that. And, best of all, he's playing with us."

"I'm not worried about his playing, I'm worried about who he is and why he miraculously turned up to our audition. We're not exactly famous, are we? He should be playing for the headline band, not for us."

"Fuck me, Pete! Just because he's a guitarist doesn't mean he can't be trusted. Mike wasn't the one with his hand down your girlfriend's pants, Trev was."

Pete's face darkened, but he said nothing.

"Shit man, I'm sorry, that wasn't fair. I'm just saying he's been alright so far, shit, better than alright. Look at this crowd! Imagine the gigs we'll be doing now we've got him."

"I'm not trying to be a prick Joe, I'm just looking out for us, for you. Maybe you could try not being a prick too?" He walked away without waiting for a reply.

"You look at bit better today," said Mike as he greeted Joe at the door of his apartment.

"Yeah, I crashed out after the gig last night, slept 'till lunchtime."

"You did knock back a few after our set. Anyway, let's see if we can take your playing to the next level."

Joe sat down and unpacked his guitar. "I hope so, but I should tell you I've been playing a few years now, and I've been on a bit of a plateau, you know? Be nice to make a jump and get a lot better." He pulled a couple of beers out of the cooler he'd brought with him, offering one to Mike.

"Cheers," said Mike, taking the can. "Andy reckons you're pretty good, and so do I."

"Andy likes me because I can keep time and play good rhythm, and I do what he tells me." Joe downed half the can in one go, letting out a long burp at the end. "Hair of the dog, I needed that! I think timing is Andy's only criteria for being a good guitarist."

Mike laughed. "Typical drummer! I'm surprised you're drinking though, don't you have a hangover?"

Joe sat and pulled his guitar out. "Nah, not really." He tuned the guitar, then finished the rest of his beer.

"You want another?" he asked Mike, reaching into the cooler.

"Mate I've just taken a sip out of this one. Do you always drink so much when you practice?"

"Sometimes, I guess. I like a couple, you know, makes the practice a bit more fun.

Mike looked at Joe for a moment, then reached over and took his guitar from him. "Why don't you try mine?" he said, nodding towards his guitar, leaning on a stand by the wall.

"Really?"

"Sure, you ain't gonna break it." He smiled. "Go for it!"

74

Joe reached over and picked it up, admiring the patterns on the body, both front and back. "This is seriously cool, you made this yourself?"

"Yeah, kind of. A friend helped me with the painting."

Joe pulled a guitar pick from the pocket of his jeans and sat down, resting the V of the guitar on his right leg. He strummed a few chords, getting a feel for it. "Nice action, it feels really good."

"Here, let's plug in."

Mike grabbed a couple of cables and soon they were both playing through his amp. He leaned back and closed the curtains. "Need a bit of mood, playing metal in bright sunshine doesn't seem right, does it?" He laughed. "Ok, let's start off with some basics, see where you're at."

Mike ran Joe through some basic scales and into some simple finger tapping exercises. Joe had no problem with the scales, but the finger tapping proved more difficult. "I keep hitting the other strings, it's making too much noise, I can barely hear the notes I'm playing."

"You're trying too hard, relax, this is just an exercise, we're not on stage."

"You're watching!" said Joe, smiling sheepishly, finishing off his second can of beer.

"Shit man, if you are going to get nervous in front of me, you're in trouble. Try taking a few deep breaths."

"I'll be right, the beer is kicking in already, that usually helps."

"Maybe if you eased off the booze a bit, you might get more out of your practice."

Joe ignored the comment and played through a couple more of the exercises, finding them a little easier. As he played, looking at his fingers on the fretboard, a movement caught the corner of his eye. The black patterns on the body of the guitar swirled, uncoiling and coiling back again as the notes ascended and descended the scale. He looked up and saw Mike watching him intently.

"What do you see, Joe?"

Joe looked back at the body of the guitar, the paintwork was still.

"I think that beer's going to my head, my eyes aren't focusing." He laughed.

Mike eased forward on this chair. "Try playing something else."

Joe did, finding each exercise a little easier than the last, each phrase more natural, but the patterns and symbols on the guitar remained static. Maybe the hangover was worse than he'd thought.

"Why don't you try playing something of your own, do some improvising and chuck in a bit of that finger tapping? I'll do a rhythm in the key of A, just go for it and see what happens."

Joe felt another moment of nervousness, sitting in front of the man who was becoming both his idol and his nemesis. "Ok, I'll give it a try."

Mike began, and after waiting a couple of bars to pick up the beat, Joe joined in. He started with something easy, playing around the A minor scale first position, but soon found his fingers wandering further up the fretboard. He felt the music flowing through him, his fingers picking out the notes before he'd even thought of them. The patterns swirled once more, quicker than before, catching his eye but this time without affecting his concentration. Faster phrases flowed, one after another, into a rapid-fire finger tapping run. A demon face, etched in fine black line against the beaten up white guitar, grinned up at him, cheering him on. The black filigree caught the tips of the fingers of his right hand as he picked each note. The lines crept up his fingers and across the back of his hand. He watched, fascinated, but continued nonetheless, his playing becoming tighter, faster, not frenetic but controlled, purposeful. Finally, he played a blistering sweep picked lick to perfection.

He stopped and stared at his fingers. His arm was unmarked, the black lines still, the demon's face staring away from the guitar into the distance, unmoving, just like it had when he'd first seen Mike's axe.

"Joe that was phenomenal, man!" said Mike, laughing and clapping. "You remind me of myself when I was your age," he said, wistfully, the smile fading.

"What the fuck?"

"I knew the guitar would suit you, make you play better."

"No. What the actual fuck? I don't know how to sweep pick."

"You did it naturally."

"There's no such thing as doing that naturally. It takes loads of practice. What just happened? I thought I saw, I don't know, some weird shit."

Mike got up and took the guitar from Joe, who, still staring at his fingers, didn't resist.

"The guitar likes you, my friend, you played that music together."

"I think I'm seeing things and it isn't 'coz I downed a couple of beers."

Mike laughed again and patted Joe on the shoulder. "Ok, you're coming for a little drive with me."

"Where?"

"We're going to see a man about a guitar."

They both climbed into Mike's white Toyota van, Mike quietly whistling a tune Joe couldn't make out, Joe quietly dealing with events that didn't make sense. He kept looking at his fingers, looking for the thin, black lines that had threaded their way onto his skin. He saw nothing and wondered if he'd imagined the whole thing.

Mike started the engine and turned on the CD player. The opening three notes to Black Sabbath's self-titled track came on. "Absolute classic. This is where metal came from my friend, where it all started."

Joe barely heard him as the music flowed through his ears and into his fingers. Without a conscious thought those fingers played each note, dah, dah, dahhhhhhh, over and over while Ozzy's voice rang out.

The drive took most of the album, but when Mike turned the engine off and the stereo cut out mid-song, the sudden silence broke Joe's reverie. He realized he was lost, having paid no attention to what had passed by the van's windows.

"Where the hell are we?"

"Arse end of nowhere," laughed Mike. "Let's go have a look at some guitars."

Joe's phone beeped and showed a message from Pete.

Dude, check this out, I knew I'd seen him before!

The photo above the message was of a young guitarist with a gleaming, white instrument strapped to him, a huge head of black hair and a jacket with 6 inch tassels along the arms. Below the photo was the caption 'Mickey Wraith, Speed Machine'.

Joe laughed, it did look like a younger Mike, but the picture was from the mid-80s.

He replied. *You're saying Mike was the lead guitarist for one of the biggest hair metal bands of the 80s? That would make him older than my dad, you idiot!*

Joe put his phone back in his pocket and looked around. He was standing in an industrial park, rectangular warehouses and workshops surrounding him. One looked much the same as the next apart from the odd sign here or there above the doors, all closed on the sunny Sunday afternoon. Mike walked over to a grey roller door, slid it up and led Joe into the gloomy, muggy interior.

The first thing that hit Joe was the smell of freshly sawn wood. He inhaled it deeply, the tangy scent triggering memories of his dad's garden shed and the endless little projects which Joe, or Joey as his dad called him back then, was allowed to help with. As his eyes adjusted to the dim interior, the shapes of numerous guitars appeared out of the gloom, rows of them in all styles and colors. He walked along the display looking at each one, touching them. He heard Mike talking to someone at the back of the workshop but couldn't make out what was being said. He looked at the headstocks, where the manufacturer's name or logo would normally appear and was disappointed to see, not the symbol on Mike's guitar, but the name Traveta.

"I don't think you want one of those guitars, son," said a gravelly voice behind him.

He turned.

The man standing next to Mike looked to be at least seventy, if not older, but he had a sparkle in his eye that belied the wrinkles on his face and the liver spots on his hands. His grey hair was cut short without much thought of style, the stubble on his face matching the grey on his head, his grin showing uneven, yellowing teeth.

"The good stuff is in the back here," he said, flicking his thumb casually.

"Look, I can't really afford-" Joe began, but the old man shook his head and put up a hand to halt the protest.

"I'm sure we can come to some agreement that will work for both of us, right Mike?"

Mike nodded.

Joe looked at Mike, holding his hands out in a silent protest.

Mike put a hand on Joe's shoulder as the old man turned and walked through a doorway. "Relax man, just have a look, you don't have to buy, and if you do, he's pretty cool about payment." He lowered his voice a little. "I think the guy might be secretly rich or something."

Joe followed the old man into a much smaller room that contained a heavy, beaten up timber work bench, a lathe and numerous woodworking tools. Along the rear of the room another rack contained half a dozen white guitars.

"These are the special stock, only the best tone woods, pick one you like, one that speaks to you."

Joe's eye was immediately drawn to the Flying V, just like Mike's, sans fancy paintwork. He reached out and took the guitar, turning it over in his hands. There was no doubting the craftsmanship.

The old man indicated a stool for Joe to use. "Try it on for size, see if it's the one."

"How much is it?" Joe asked, running his hand along the smooth neck, knowing just how much custom shop guitars could cost.

"More than you might think, but not as much as you would expect." The old man laughed. "What would you give to be able to play like Mike here, hmmm?"

"I'd give anything to play that well!" said Joe, playing a few tentative notes.

The old man's mouth turned up in a smile, but his eyes shone with a cold, mirthless light. "Play it."

Joe pulled out a pick and played. The neck was fast and smooth, his fingers running through scales cleanly, but when he tried what he had played earlier, at Joe's apartment, his fingers slipped off the fretboard, the strings producing an ugly, out of tune, snarl.

He sighed. "It's nice, but I think Mike's guitar is better."

"Ah," said the old man, looking at Mike for an uncomfortably long time. "You played his guitar? Well that is a special guitar, but it's not yours, you need your own guitar. Trust me, you'll be amazed what you can do with your own custom guitar."

He walked over and stood in front of Joe. "You like this one?"

Joe nodded, not taking his eyes off the beautiful instrument.

"Turn it over."

Joe did as he was instructed. The back was plain white, like the front, but with a rectangular piece cut out of the wood for the tremolo mechanism, the protective back-plate not yet fitted. He looked at the pale, unfinished wood inside the cut-out, running a finger over it, feeling its rough texture. The old man reached out and Joe felt a sting on the palm of his right hand. Turning it over he saw the first beads of blood seeping from a fresh cut, the old man holding a small knife in his hand.

"Hey, what the hell?"

The old man grabbed his hand once more and turned it, palm down, onto the gap in the back of the guitar.

"Why did you-"

"Watch the guitar, son," he interrupted.

Joe drew a sharp breath, all thought of his hand forgotten, as dark red lines traced out from under his palm, out across the pristine white body and neck, lines swirling in chaos, lines forming faces and shapes, lines appearing and disappearing, lines morphing into symbols and letters from one end of the guitar to the other.

"Now play a tritone interval," said the old man.

Joe looked at Mike and shook his head slightly. "I don't-"

Mike smiled. "Dah, dah, dahhhhhhh. The Devil's tritone dude, you know it. The unholy trinity."

The old man looked at Mike and grunted.

Joe played the three notes and the chaos of lines and swirls calmed somewhat.

"Keep playing," instructed the old man.

Joe did as he was told, ignoring the blood still dripping from his palm. Dah, dah, dahhhhhhh, over and over, accenting the final note, until the fluidity of the ethereal lines ceased, and he stared at the images formed in his own blood, now turned black. A wolf, a car with a huge supercharger poking out of the bonnet, a demon with horns, a bottle of beer and a hand with long, sharp claws gripping the top of the guitar.

The old man nodded, with a satisfied smile. "That's it, now it's your guitar, no one else's. Play it."

Joe placed his fingers on the fretboard and played, slowly at first but soon picking up pace. He played riffs he knew by heart, scraps of solos he'd learned, all of them coming easily to him. Then he began improvising, ripping through scales, the notes flowing effortlessly from his fingers, fingers that tingled with power, fingers that played as they'd never played before. The lines on the guitar, his guitar now, licked at his fingertips as they moved faster and faster, flying up and down the neck, making music like he never had in his life.

Joe stopped. He was breathless and speechless, simply staring at his instrument in awe.

The old man held out his hand. "It's yours if you want it."

Joe no longer cared about the price; he'd figure it out, somehow. Maybe his dad could help, maybe the rest of the band would chip in when they realized how good he was going to be. No more taking a back seat to Mike, everyone would be watching him too, everyone there to see him play, screaming, devoted fans who wanted to see, to hear, one thing, to hear Joe play guitar.

Joe took the old man's hand and shook it. He felt his palm tingle and looked up. The old man's smile had disappeared. Joe withdrew his hand, only then seeing a similar cut the old man had made in his own palm, a palm laced with faint scars. "That there is a bond made in blood, son. It can't be broken. I want no money for the guitar, but you are bound to me now. Every once in a while, I'll need something from you, and you'll do it, no questions."

Joe turned to Mike, to ask what he had just done, but Mike was gone.

"I'm sorry, what the hell is this? What do you mean 'do things for you'? Maybe I don't want it anymore."

The old man shook his head slowly, smiling. "You played it, you know you don't want to give it back, not for a while anyway. I saw the hunger in your eyes, boy." He laughed. "Have fun with it, make a name for yourself, get wasted, get laid! The price isn't that high."

82

Mike walked back into the workshop carrying his own guitar which he handed to the old man who took it and, without hesitation, snapped the neck across the edge of the workbench, breaking it clean off the body, the two parts hanging together only by the strings. He held it up and Joe watched as the black lines drained and blood dripped out, hitting the sawdust coated floor with soft, ugly splats.

"Mike, what are you doing? Your guitar!"

"Not any longer, it isn't," said Mike, looking at the old man.

Joe looked at Mike. His face underwent a strange transformation, at once becoming older but softer, as if a lifetime burden had been lifted but a debt of years was being paid in return.

"Oh, stop your moping kid, when you were balls deep in money, women and cocaine you weren't complaining." The old man spoke without any real malice, simply making an observation.

"When-" began Joe, remembering the picture Pete had sent.

"A lifetime ago," said Mike, still looking at the old man.

"Well, you're free now, go on, get out of here."

Mike turned his back on the pair. "Enjoy your new guitar, Joe."

Joe leapt at him, the new guitar slipping to the floor before the old man, quicker than he had any right to be, caught it.

"What the fuck have you gotten me into, you prick? What?"

Mike didn't defend himself, he just stood as Joe grabbed his shirt and shook him. "The only way out of the deal is to find a replacement. You wanted to know the secret of my playing, well this is it. You wanted to play like I played, now you will, you'll be every bit as good as me, maybe even better."

Joe pushed Mike up against the wall. "And what is it going to cost me? Huh?"

"He owns you now, and you have to do what he asks, that's all."

Joe looked at the old man. He'd laid the guitar back on the bench and was watching with arms folded, a lopsided smile on his face, as casually as one might watch a daytime soap opera.

"You tricked me. Well, I'm not doing fuck all for you with your voodoo magic shit." Joe turned back to Mike. "And as for you-" He swung his fist back, and that was as far as it got.

"ENOUGH!"

The voice sent a shock through Joe, like a bolt of electricity through his veins, muscles cramping and twitching, his ears throbbing with the power of the sound. He let Mike go and doubled over, struggling to breathe, his vision narrowing. Clutching his chest with one hand he found the edge of the workbench with the other and hauled himself up enough to look at the old man.

The workshop was gone. Joe leaned against, not the battered wooden workbench, but a block of stone that appeared to be the only object in a desolate, grey landscape of ash and smoke. He pushed himself upright, feeling his hand slip slightly on the wet stone. He stared at that hand, blood smeared across his palm. He stared at the stone, blood smeared across that too. Runes, carved into the altar, ran around the outer edge, the blood seeming to flow from one symbol to the next in an endless river of red. He coughed, the acrid vapor burning his throat.

"Would you like to hang out for a while, Joe?"

Joe's head whipped around at the sound. The old man was standing behind him, smiling, arms still folded. He didn't look so old now though, and he seemed taller, bigger, long white hair flowing down his back, an ominous presence in an ominous place. He grinned with perfect, white teeth.

Joe coughed. "Where are we?"

"Nowhere in particular, Joe. You could spend a long time being nowhere in particular, some people spend a lifetime there, or even longer. Or you could

84

be somewhere, be someone, it just costs a little more, that's all." The old man held out his hands and smiled. "So, what's it going to be?"

A rumble in the distance produced an indistinct red glow and the clouds overhead turned a shade darker.

"Are you the Devil? Is that what this is?"

The old man laughed. "If it helps you make your decision to think that I am, go right ahead. You can stay here as long as you like, Joe, I don't mind, the rent is paid." The old man chuckled at his own joke. "Or you can go back and do as you're told."

"Are you going to take my soul, is that the price I have to pay."

The old man smiled and sighed. "Oh, don't be so dramatic Joe, nothing quite that bad, this isn't eternal damnation, just relax and enjoy the benefits."

Joe looked around and saw nothing but grey ash and cloud, unable to even determine where the horizon was, where one finished and the other began. He coughed again, the smoke sitting heavy in his chest, his eyes beginning to water. His shoulders sagged and he sighed. There was no way out of this, whatever in hell, literally or figuratively, this was.

"Ok."

"Ok what?"

"Ok, I'll go back and do what you tell me."

"Attaboy Joe!"

He blinked away the tears and was again standing in the workshop. He took deep breaths of the clean, humid, timber scented air. The old man handed him the guitar without another word.

Mike was waiting for him in the van, staring straight ahead. Neither said a word on the drive back, Joe clutching the guitar as if his soul depended on it, despite the old man's assurance.

When they arrived back at the apartment, Joe turned to Mike. "What have you gotten me into?"

Mike didn't meet Joe's stare. "Some days you'll thank me, some days you'll curse me, that's just how it is."

Gripping the edge of the cymbal, quieting it, laying his drum sticks gently on his snare and removing his earphones, Andy stood up.

"Thanks mate, we'll let you know."

Joe looked around the plush recording studio where they had laid down their last four hit albums and rehearsed for three sell out world tours. "You're hired," he said, not looking at Andy.

"Thanks, that's awesome, you guys are incredible! The last album was fantastic."

Andy looked at Joe, but said nothing.

"Cheers," said Joe, "you're a great rhythm player; I think you'll fit in just perfect."

"Thanks, I can't wait. Can I ask though, why are you getting a rhythm guitarist now? You've always been a four-piece, right?"

"Not always," said Joe, turning off his Marshall amp. "We started out as a five-piece, and I feel like it's time we added a second guitar again."

"I hope you don't mind me saying, but you're like my idol man, and that guitar is insane!"

Joe popped a couple of pills, washing them down with a pull from an almost empty bottle of Jack Daniels. He stared at their new guitarist, and then he smiled.

"Would you like to play it?"

Paul Sheldon lives in Perth, Western Australia with his wife, two children and an ageing dog. He works as an IT consultant, loves to read and write horror and plays guitar in a heavy metal band. Yes, his guitar is a flying V, and no, it isn't cursed, at least not that he is aware of.

Fretboards and Fungi

Nicholas Stella

Ming rolled his wheelchair to the edge of the pit, a place of sweat and blood, broken teeth and brotherhood.

A long-haired man, easily seven foot tall, paced before the crowd, adjusting the axe in his hands. His eyes were white and blind, staring over the assembled throng.

He was ready to slay.

Ming licked his lips in preparation for the spectacle.

He had read that the lead guitarist for Angel Blood was a fourteen-fingered prodigy who had been blind since birth. Under the assumed moniker of God Corpse, he was regarded as a deity in the underground metal scene.

And at last, after the accident, Ming was well enough to attend a show.

He sat breathless in his wheelchair a few paces from the edge of where the mosh pit would erupt, his old stomping ground until the gift of mobility was taken from him. Ming was focused on the flying–V in the hands of God Corpse up on the stage, listening to the buzz of the amplifiers and the hushed conversation of the punters.

A squat little man, bald and with two full sleeves of tattoos ran from backstage and took the microphone from the cradle. His leather vest hung open, revealing a beer belly covered in faded tattoo ink. He looked out over the crowd as the rhythm guitarist and bassist strutted into position. The drummer settled in behind his kit.

The vocalist prowled the stage looking over the crowd. He stopped at the edge of the stage and his eyes widened. He grinned something not considered a smile.

A guttural roar erupted from him, driven by a prodigious set of lungs and battle-hardened vocal cords. A crunching wall of noise from the rhythm guitar whipped the crowd into an instant moshing frenzy.

Ming focused on God Corpse who stood motionless as his fellow musicians riffed, pounded and roared. The pit before him was a churning display of banging heads, flicking sweat and faded band shirts.

Ming was on the periphery waiting for the lead guitarist to lay his fingers on the strings.

The vocalist stalked the stage, snarling his rasped vocals, the drummer banged the beat on his tubs while the rhythm and bass guitars chugged and rolled.

God Corpse with his sightless, milky eyes seemed to look over the thrashing pit and directly at Ming as his fourteen digits attacked the six strings in a blistering display of musical prowess. Notes rang through the amps, born of God Corpse, immediately succeeded by others as the lead guitarist worked the strings and pounded the fretboard.

The base of Ming's spine tingled, an odd sensation, like a fizzing liquid bubbling away.

God Corpse was thrashing his head, his hair flying, dropping blistering notes into the maelstrom of music, creating beautiful carnage with his technique and timing.

Ming gritted his teeth as pain shot its way up and down his spine, back and forth, from tailbone to the base of his neck. He closed his eyes against the agony, clenching his fists as the guitar solo increased its speed and intensity, as God Corpse shredded, his guitar enslaved.

Ming cried out as the musical mayhem of Angel Blood retreated and dulled, as his sight dimmed and consciousness faded.

"Wake up, man!"

Ming's eyes flickered and opened.

Kevin was crouched in front of him, blonde hair plastered to his sweaty face, his shirt ripped at the collar.

"How can you sleep through a set of the Blood?"

"Sleep?"

"You've gone soft, man." Kevin popped a can of beer and thrust it into Ming's hand.

"I don't feel like a beer." Pins and needles sprinkled their sensation up and down the length of his spine, spreading into his legs and down to his toes.

"You dozed off like an old man and now you don't want a beer?" Kevin snatched the beer back and took a long swallow. "You want a blanket to put over your lap, old timer?"

"Piss off, Kev."

"That's the Ming I know and love," Kevin shouted and finished the beer, dropping the can on the floor.

"I wanna meet God Corpse," Ming said, looking up at the stage where the musicians were packing up their instruments.

"Yeah!" Kevin's eyes widened. "Let's meet the 'king Corpse, man!" He grabbed the handles of Ming's chair and pushed him across the floor, through puddles of beer, over empty cans, around a pond of vomit. He stopped at the base of the stage and called out to the vocalist who was packing equipment away.

"What do you want?" he shouted back, wiping at his face with the back of a hand.

"My friend, Ming, he wants to meet God Corpse."

"Does he just?" The man jumped off the stage, landing heavily, his eyes wild, his beer belly heaving. "What's wrong with me? You don't want to meet me?"

Ming was lost for words and for once, he didn't hear Kevin rattle anything off in reply.

"Just jerking your chain, lads," he said shaking their hands in turn, his grip solid and heavy.

"Blistering set, man!" Kevin blurted.

"Thanks bro," he replied, turning his attention down to Ming. "Jerry's expecting you. He's out back at the van."

"Who's Jerry?" Ming asked.

"You think his mum named him God Corpse?" the vocalist said with a laugh.

"Cool," Kevin said, pushing Ming in the direction of the open rear doors.

"Not you, blondie," the vocalist said. "You're helping me pack up."

"I'm good, Kev," Ming said, rolling himself away, knowing that his friend would be talking about the night he packed up for Angel Blood for years to come.

He shivered in the night air as he rolled outside onto the kerb, looking out over the car park.

Jerry, also known as God Corpse, sat on the tail gate of a black van, smoking a cigarette. He raised an enormous hand and beckoned for Ming to join him.

The wheelchair squeaked and creaked its way through the silence, stopping just in front of the lead guitarist.

"Do you indulge?" the big man asked, looking at Ming with clouded eyes, offering the joint.

"If you're offering." He inhaled deeply then expelled smoke up into the night. With watering eyes and a swimming head, he returned the strong leaf to the big man.

"I'll let you in on a little secret," he said, taking another pull of the joint. "Fungus is the key to a premium crop."

Ming's head lolled backwards and he looked up at the stars that jumped in and out of focus. Jerry came into view above him, his long, dark hair dangling. He ran his hands with their fourteen digits over Ming's face.

"Cut it out," Ming said, forcing the man's hands away with a clumsy push.

"It's how I see," God Corpse said, gently laying his hands on Ming again.

Ming succumbed as the massive digits covered in calluses explored his face, running over his forehead, then around his eyes, over his cheeks and down to his chin.

"You Asian?" The guitarist handed the cigarette to Ming and began to push the wheelchair away from the van.

"Half." He drew deeply. "Can you see where you're going?"

"You got a destination in mind?"

"Nah." He looked up at the firmament unblemished by any twinkling shards, now like a solid, black sheet.

"Then it doesn't matter if I can see or not."

Ming dragged on the cigarette until it burned his fingers and he flicked the ember out into the darkness. He watched it tumble and tumble, down, down, down until it was swallowed by the nothingness.

"I can help you." Jerry was towering over him, as if he were part of the dark, his eyes a dull yellow. "To get on your feet again."

"My legs haven't worked since the accident and no amount of your sweet smoke can make me think they can." Ming was unable to focus on the big man.

"We are kindred," God Corpse said to Ming. "I knew the moment you arrived at the show."

"That's not possible," Ming said, rolling away.

"There is a connection between us." He grabbed the wheelchair, stopping Ming's departure. "You've had a lung infection."

"This is getting really bloody creepy," Ming said, raising his voice

"My music got your spine firing, didn't it?"

"What's your angle?" Ming turned his chair around so he could face the big man.

"Family."

"We're not family," Ming said, wheeling away from God Corpse.

"Aspergillus."

Ming stopped. "How do you know that?"

"You've come into contact with the aspergillus spore. It entered your system and made a home in your lungs."

"And it was treated."

"It's still there." God Corpse returned to his seat on the tail gate of the van.

"How could you know that?"

"You wouldn't believe me if I told you."

"Try me."

"I think it would be better to show you."

"And I'm just going to get in a van and go off with you?" Ming asked, rolling back a little. "That's a scenario straight out of a hundred horror movies."

"I *am* legally blind."

"And *I'm* in a wheelchair."

"Look," God Corpse said. "The whole band is coming back to mine. You can either come back and smoke a little and talk a little or you can go home, have warm milk and go to bed."

"What about my mate, Kev?"

"He's welcome too."

"You'll need to help me get around."

"Anything for family," the big man said, standing and walking slowly to Ming.

Ming had no idea what God Corpse meant by that, but after months of hospital visits and sitting alone his bedroom, he was ready for something different.

"You don't walk around like someone who's blind," Ming said, as God Corpse lifted him out of the chair.

"I'm legally blind but I can still see dark and light and shapes of things in front of me." He placed Ming in the back seat and shut the door. He walked round the van, climbed into the driver's seat, the top of his head pressed against the ceiling, and started the engine.

"You've gotta be joking," Ming said, buckling his belt.

"Of course, I'm joking," he said, turning the vehicle off, laughing. "I'm fucking blind."

Once the van was loaded with the equipment and Ming's wheelchair, the heavy set vocalist jumped in the front beside Jerry. The bass player and the rhythm guitarist crammed in beside Ming, stinking of beer, smoke and perspiration.

"Aren't we missing someone?" Ming asked, looking out the window.

"Nah," the vocalist said, starting the van and pulling from the parking space. "We make Marty walk because he smells like a mountain gorilla after drumming a set."

"No, I mean Kevin," Ming said, struggling to be heard over the laughter.

"Marty's giving him a lift." The bass player gave him a wink. "He doesn't really have to walk. He has his own car."

The vocalist parked the van outside a rambling wooden house, its paint peeling and gutters sagging.

"Do you live here alone?" Ming asked.

"My mother is always around," God Corpse said, turning and regarding Ming with his clouded eyes.

"I'll need my chair."

"Too many stairs," the bass player said.

Jerry stooped and removed Ming from the van and headed for the house. It sat in the night shadow of trees with drooping branches that spilled dead leaves over the roof, and over the ground, creating a carpet that chittered in the cool breeze.

The musicians crunched through the fallen leaves, under the creaking branches and up the front steps that groaned with their weight.

"What about Kev and your drummer?"

"They'll be here soon," Jerry whispered.

The lead guitarist held Ming in a tight embrace as they ascended the stairs and entered the house. He could feel the strength in the man's arms and resigned himself to being carried, his gaze drifting to the massive hand resting on his chest with its seven outsized digits.

The house was dark but Jerry moved with confidence from room to shadowed room and down a corridor that ended in a set of stairs descending into pitch darkness.

"Can you see where you're going?"

"This is where I see at my best. I know the creak of every step, the groan of each floorboard, the rattle of each window in the wind, the gurgle of rainwater in each pipe. I came into being in this very house, born of a vast and supportive mother."

The steps groaned as the big man descended with his burden. "I can feel you trembling, but you have no cause for fear. As I have said, you and I are kindred."

"I think you should take me back outside," Ming said as he inhaled the thick smell of wet earth as they made their way further down the stairs. Jerry maintained his tight hold, a sure sign that he wasn't going to be swayed.

"I'm going to light a lantern for your benefit," he said, placing Ming on the floor.

"What are we doing down here?" Ming could feel soft earth give beneath him, felt moisture soak through his clothing, chilling his skin.

"Righting a wrong." A rising lantern glow revealed Jerry's face, his dead eyes almost golden in the light.

"I've never done anything to you." Ming squinted at the light.

"There is no bad blood between you and I," he said, hanging the lantern from a hook in the low ceiling, illuminating part of the cellar.

Patches of fungi sprouted from mounds in the soft earth, the caps pale in the light. Water dripped over brick walls tinged green with creeping mould. It fell from the damp ceiling, tapping an irregular tempo on the earth.

"I don't understand." Ming moved away from Jerry, using his hands to drag his body back to the stairs.

The big man had left the circle of light and was rummaging around in the darkness as Ming sat his backside on the bottom step, ready to move himself out of the cellar, away from the man named God Corpse.

"Down there?" A voice from the top of the stairs. "A weed cellar?"

"That's right, blondie."

It was Kevin.

"Don't come down," Ming called out. "Just leave. Get out of here."

"Hey, Ming man!" Kev bounded halfway down the stairs, followed by someone with a lantern. "You into the green already, bro?"

"There's no weed, Kev."

"Why are you down here then?" His friend looked around the small lit area of the cellar, wrinkling his nose, furrowing his brow.

"Keep going." The vocalist, carrying the lantern nudged Kev who took a few awkward steps down and half-jumped his way over Ming until he was standing on the cellar floor.

"Don't push, man. Those stairs are slippery."

"Those are the least of your problems." The vocalist turned and with the lantern in hand, disappeared up the steps, closing a door at the top.

"What an arse," Kev said.

"Grab me under the arms," Ming said. "Drag me up the bloody stairs and get us out of here."

"Hang on. Why are you down here by yourself?"

"He isn't." God Corpse emerged from the darkness with a guitar in his hand, his massive frame covering the young men in shadow.

"Why are you carrying that down here?" Kev asked.

The guitarist dropped his hand to the strings, producing a wall of noise that pounded even the seasoned ear drums of the two metal show veterans. They collapsed to the floor, fingers in their ears to stem the aural assault.

The music screamed and tore from the darkness at the corners of the room, through the small space, bounding off the walls, filling the cellar with the rise and fall of an intricate solo, where the notes weaved and segued, complemented and contradicted.

When the music stopped and the last of the notes had finished reverberating off the moldy walls, Ming removed his hands from his ringing ears and found his upper body restrained.

Kevin was curled into the fetal position a few feet away. Long pale growths had emerged from the earth and wrapped around him, ripping through his clothing, entwining themselves around his body, arms and legs.

Ming struggled with his upper body, at the tightening of cold pulsing bonds that emerged from the earth, at small feelers that ripped his clothing and sucked at his skin with tiny wet mouths.

"Kevin." The voice of God Corpse boomed in the small cellar.

"I can't get up!" Kevin opened his eyes, looking at Ming. "You've got stuff all over you, man!"

"Kevin!"

Both of the young men were able to move their heads to focus on God Corpse, his head slightly bowed, brushing the ceiling.

"What're you doing to us?" Kevin's eyes were wide, saliva spraying from his screaming mouth.

"Tell me about the swimming hole."

"What?"

"The day Ming broke his back."

"He jumped into Epworth Hole and hit a log." Kevin struggled at his bonds, grunting with the effort, giving up. "And I pulled him out."

God Corpse cut into another blistering solo, assaulting the uncovered ears of the two restrained friends.

"Okay, okay!" Kev shouted.

God Corpse removed his fingers from the strings.

"I pushed Ming in for a joke," Kev shouted, tears streaming down his cheeks. "I didn't know he would break his back!"

The music started up once more and hit Ming hard. But compared to Kev's revelation, it was nothing.

The bonds crept further around Ming, tightening their embrace, the little mouths attaching to him with stinging sensations all over his skin, awakening a burning in his spine, from neck to tailbone, enlivening dull nerves, awakening little, hot pin pricks of sensation.

He screamed and struggled against the noise and against the pulsing bonds and the sticky mouths. As the weak light waned, at the coming of the dark, he watched Kevin pulled into the earth, his friend's mouth wide in a muted scream and thought of the mushroom festooned mounds he had seen scattered through the earth in the cellar.

"The fungus has been dormant in you for years, waiting to be awakened, to help you heal."

The echoing voice of God Corpse carried to Ming from the darkness.

"I could tell you were at the show last night the minute you entered the premises. Everyone is covered in a small amount of fungus, but the organism inside you is strong."

"Fungus?" Ming was propped up against a wall in the cellar with the lantern burning dimly at his feet.

"I am caretaker for the fungal organism that lives under this house, the being that stretches under the entire suburb, even as far as Epworth Hole."

"Where's Kev?" He shifted his upper body into a more comfortable position, looking into the darkness.

"Your friend is here. He will always be here."

"Is he dead?"

The guitarist stepped from the murk. "Move your toes." He lifted the lantern from the ground, looking down at Ming with the flickering light rippling across his pale face.

"I haven't moved anything below my waist since the accident."

"A little belief goes a long way."

"You know what I believe?" Ming pulled away from the wall, dragging his legs through the earth, away from the lantern light and into the darkness. "I believe that my spinal cord was damaged when I hit that log in the water hole. I believe that it'll be years before I can walk again and even then, only in a limited capacity." He dug into the earth with his hands, looking for Kevin, his eyes closed, tears streaming down his cheeks.

"When you landed on that log, fungus was introduced into your system through the open wound. It is a part of the organism that lives under this house, stretching all the way to the water hole." Jerry was standing over Ming, the lantern providing light to the area where he was digging. "I am a sentient part of this organism, a small part of the whole, connected to the fungal matter in *your* system. I, we, can help you heal with the power of the music that enhances the connective ability of the fungal tissue. But you need to want it and to believe it."

"I want Kevin back," Ming replied, feeling a fingernail come loose as he dug through the earth.

"I am promising to heal you."

"Without Kevin I wouldn't be here in the first place."

"That is true."

Ming stopped digging. He was alive because of Kev. But he was also crippled because of him.

"Your friend can make up for what he has done. He will remain here and nourish the fungal mass that you and I are a part of."

Ming started digging again. "Even knowing what I now know, I still can't condemn him."

Ming felt vibrations through his hands as the ground shook, as the soil ruptured in the yellow light. Kevin's face appeared from under the wet earth as Ming continued to toil, digging around the body of his friend.

God Corpse pulled Kevin free, the mouths on the white tentacles releasing him, leaving welts on his pale, dirt-streaked skin.

"Is he dead?" Ming looked up at the musician.

"The fungus doesn't kill," he replied in a soft voice. "It enriches and promotes." The guitarist paused, before continuing. "And it heals."

"That trade-off is not something I could live with," Ming said, brushing loose earth from the body of his friend. "Kev saved me that day at Epworth Hole and he continues to stand by me. I owe him my life."

"Even if it is somewhat diminished?" Jerry asked, picking Kevin up and cradling him in his arms.

"I'm above ground because of Kev. I'm not going to see him go under it for me."

Jerry regarded Ming with eyes that shone golden in the lantern light. "I'll be back for you," he said, before turning away and mounting the steps.

Ming lay back on the earth, knowing he had made the right decision. Kev had acted rashly in pushing him off the ledge that day, had not thought about what he was doing or the possible consequences. But that was just the sort of person Kev was.

If Ming condemned his friend to go under the earth for him, having actually thought it through, then he'd be unable to live with himself.

He'd leave this house with Kev tonight, get his wheelchair from the van and as much as it pained him, never go to another Angel Blood show again.

Nicholas Stella can often be seen scribbling away on scraps of paper at the oddest of hours and in the most random of locations, as inspiration has no respect for time or place.

Accursed

Leon Saul

The sounds of muffled metal bled through the walls.

On his bed, Nate Dorner felt the vibrations from his sister's room bumping the back of his head, behind the drywall separating their rooms. His friends, Jeff and Shaun, stared bleary-eyed through clouds of smoke.

"Dude, why don't you use your powers to see what Erica and Layne are doing in there?"Shaun's simian face leered, buckteeth flashing between simpering lips.

"Yeah, come on, Nate. What good's ESP if you don't use it when it counts?"

Jeff's hands hovered over the glowing plasma ball on Nate's desk. His fingers traced purple tendrils of neon lightning. "Look into this magical orb and tell us what you see."

Shaun chortled and brought the glass bowl to his face. Smoke exploded from his lips. It wafted in a blue wave toward the fan near the open window. The heavy cannabis cloud jerked, ripping apart in the revolving current of air.

Lying in bed, Nate rolled his eyes, ignoring his friends' lewd remarks. He leaned his head back against the wall; despite himself, he found his ears perking upon an effort to catch any sounds beyond the muted thrash rhythms emanating from Erica's bedroom. His sister and Layne had been in there for some time. Nate knew if he focused hard enough, he might catch a sketchy glimpse of the goings-on in there. Stuff he didn't want to see.

Jeff passed the smoldering pipe toward the bed, but Nate waved it away. His mouth was cinder-dry, his tongue pasty and stale. But there was nothing to drink in the room.

Hopping on the foot of the bed, Shaun pressed his ear to the wall, eyes round with concentration. "I think I hear humping." He gawped at Nate. "Am I hot or cold?" The sole of a high-top Converse kicked him in the ribs, and the gangly teenager tumbled off the bed.

"Don't be gross, man."

"Your sister is *so* hot, "Jeff spluttered through a haze of smoke. He gagged, covering his mouth with the crook of an elbow, then laid the cashed pipe on the desk beside the plasma ball. A nest of ash gleamed in the crusted bowl. Drifting upward, smoke vanished in the fan's oscillating breeze. "I always knew she was into older guys. Never thought she'd date a metalhead, though."

"How old do you think that guy is, anyway?" Shaun asked.

Nate shrugged, bloodshot eyes gazing into the hazy foreground. Despite his repeated asking, Erica refused to tell him how old Layne, her mysterious boyfriend of six months, really was. He didn't go to their school. Thus, the minor excitement whenever he arrived at 2:30 pm to pick up Erica. In the mundane, upper-middle-class suburban high school, Layne stood out like a sore thumb: over six feet tall, gaunt and willowy. He wore black leather pants and battered combat boots, T-shirts torn to reveal aesthetic slashes of pallid flesh. Makeup powdered a sharp, angular face, giving him an almost androgynous appearance, and crow-black hair hung like curtains past the epaulettes of his studded leather jacket.

As droves of teens assembled each day in the lobby after school, they'd watch as Erica —known throughout Coffman High as being one of the hottest juniors—ran giddily into her boyfriend's arms, her slim, white legs stretching as she hugged Layne's gangling frame. He'd usually be waiting for her slouched against the trophy wall, an unlit cigarette bobbing on black-lacquered lips. Whispers would circulate amidst the gawking crowd:

"Is that Erica Dorner's boyfriend?"

"Holy shit, he looks like Iggy Pop!"

"I hear he's in a metal band."

"Yep, Wretched Angel."

"He sorta looks like a devil worshiper."

"Freaky shit!"

"I always knew cheerleaders were into bad boys."

Of course, Erica hadn't been a cheerleader since sophomore year. She'd joined as a freshman, but only because her friends had done so and it was expected of her. Since childhood, however, Erica had been a creative type, and at fifteen, she quit cheerleading to concentrate on her art.

Nate remembered how, growing up, his older sister's bedroom had been covered in watercolors and vibrant pastels. Now, the room housed different kinds of art—including her mysterious work-in-progress: the cover art for Wretched Angel's debut album, *Accursed*, which the band was getting ready to record. Much to Nate's disappointment, even he didn't have the privilege of seeing the painting, or any of the other art his sister had been working on. Her room was strictly off limits.

The few times Nate succumbed to curiosity and used the Vision, he glimpsed vague snapshots of a bedroom unknown to him. Gone were the Lisa Frank-inspired watercolors of vibrant landscapes and magical gardens, the ebullient pastels of youth.

A darker aesthetic now prevailed.

Magazine cutouts of Madonna and Whitney had been supplanted by posters for bands like Darkthrone and Cannibal Corpse. It was as if, at seventeen years old, Nate's sister had entered a dark chrysalis, metamorphosing into a black and enigmatic butterfly—albeit every bit as beautiful.

104

"I say we wait for the two lovebirds to go down to the basement and then scope it out," Shaun suggested. "I'm assuming Layne will be over tonight, since your mom's out of town."

This was probably true. Layne only came over when their mother wasn't around—probably because she had no idea Layne existed in the first place. Erica swore her brother to secrecy, and, of course, Nate would never betray her trust.

"No one's allowed in Erica's room."

"Oh *come on*," Shaun groaned. "Aren't you the least bit curious?"

"You already told us you don't trust the guy," Jeff pointed out.

"Yeah, remember, you said you think he's a major creepozoid," Shaun added. He grinned. "Then again, when has Erica ever dated a guy you liked?"

The two friends chuckled as the door opened and Erica appeared in the entrance. She wore tight Levi's frayed at the knees, maroon Red Wings, and a black T-shirt with the words *Exhorder* emblazoned in bloody letters across her breasts. She sniffed and curled her lips. "Smells like a party," she smirked.

"Care for a hit?" Shaun reached for the glass pipe beside the plasma ball.

"Um, I'm good." She looked at her brother sprawled on the bed. "We're heading to Blockbuster to pick up some tapes. Layne's staying over tonight."

"Oooh, what are we renting?" Jeff asked.

"Don't you worry about it." Erica rolled her eyes and looked at Nate. "Mom left some money for pizza. Will your . . . *friends* be staying over?"

"Absolutely," Jeff answered for Nate, drawing out the syllables and smirking. "Do we get to join you two for the movie?"

"Dream on."

Nate caught Jeff and Shaun exchange a look as the two teens ogled her peach-shaped butt exiting the doorway.

"What?" Shaun feigned innocence as soon as Erica was out of earshot. "Don't pretend you don't notice how good she looks in skinny jeans."

"Don't be a perv," Nate said. Leaning back against the wall separating the two bedrooms, he couldn't help but wonder what went on next door.

Greasy paper plates and wadded napkins littered the island counter like so much detritus. Nate tossed a wedge of crust in the pizza box and took a gulp of Coke. Belching, his eyes glanced toward the closed basement door.

He found himself straining his ears to see if he could make out any sounds, but stopped short of using the Vision. Shaun picked up the last piece of pizza from the box. As he bit into it, a membrane of cold cheese slid off the slice, dangling from his grease-stained lips; he dropped the coagulated lump on his plate and groaned. "Ugh, I'm full." He sidled over to the basement door and pressed his ear to the wood.

"Hear anything?" Jeff asked.

"Just a bunch of screaming. Not the good kind. I think it's from the movie."

Erica and Layne had been down there for about an hour. They'd picked up a couple of horror movies—*Brainscan* and *Phantasm 3*—and Erica had given explicit instructions for Nate and his friends to mind their own business and stay out of trouble.

"Nate, what's happening down there?" Shaun asked.

"How the hell should I know?"

"Use your powers!" Jeff and Shaun snickered.

"Yeah, Nate, has Layne gotten to third base yet?" Jeff said.

Almost unwittingly, Nate found himself focusing his mind's eye on the unfinished basement. He conjured an image of Erica and Layne on the scratchy sofa, a mulberry candle lit on the oak table in front of them. Erica moaned as skeletal, white hands brushed the skin of her bared legs, hot skin prickling with gooseflesh. Seconds later, Nate snapped out of it, cursing himself.

"You know, this is the perfect opportunity to check out that mystery painting of Erica's upstairs," Shaun said. "Something tells me they'll be down there for a while."

A couple minutes later, the three teenagers were skulking up the stairs. Sweat oozed from Nate's pores as they approached the forbidden room. His sister had painted her doorknob last Halloween to resemble a bloodshot eyeball, and it gaped at Nate through a network of purple veins as he reached a trembling hand to open the door. He knew Erica would never forgive him if she caught him sneaking into her room. But despite himself, he was every bit as curious to see the heavy metal painting—and whatever else his sister kept hidden inside her sanctum sanctorum.

The door groaned as it swung inward, querulous hinges squeaking like poisoned mice. Nate winced, even though Erica and Layne were two stories down and wouldn't be able to hear them.

When the door opened, a smell of jasmine entered the boys' nostrils. The room was dark, lit only by the amorphous blob of a lava lamp and a string of purple fairy lights festooning the walls. Nate crept inside, followed by Jeff and Shaun.

In awe, the three teenagers gazed around the room, which had completely transformed since the last time Nate had been allowed in. (Nate now realized that was over six months ago—before Erica started seeing Layne.) The previous robin's-egg blue of the walls had been painted a gleaming, cosmic black and was plastered with band flyers, Polaroids, and horror movie posters.

Above Erica's desk, a poster depicted two fleshless ghouls hacking into a woman's ribcage—the lower half of the woman's body a waste of viscera and bone. A bloody fetus was being extracted from the mutilated uterus, while a myriad of dead babies dangled from loops of intestine in the background. The words *Butchered at Birth* dripped in blood-red lettering under a crimson shroud.

"Fucking *gross*," Shaun said, eyes popping wide at the gruesome image. Nate shivered. It was a far cry from the posters of pop stars and Disney princesses Erica used to have adorning her room.

The boys scanned the walls, observing posters for bands called Dismember and Autopsy, Malignancy and Septic Flesh. Taped above Erica's bed was a watercolor depicting a red sea of body parts melting into one another, deformed, yowling heads emerging from the crimson waves and screaming at a stygian sky. Erica's signature was scrawled in the bottom corner.

But where was the painting?

Accursed.

The masterwork Erica had been working on for weeks, and not letting anyone—aside from *Layne*, of course—see.

"Hey, check this out." Jeff pointed to a corner of the room, where a shadowy bulk sat under a storm-gray tarp.

"Bingo," Shaun said, and started moving toward the shape.

"*Don't fucking touch anything.*" A quivering vein spasmed in Nate's throat. Jeff and Shaun paused, holding their hands up, and allowed Nate to move past them. Reaching the corner of the room, he slowly lifted the tarp.

Crinkly polyester sloughed to the floor. Underneath it was an easel, supporting a large rectangular painting.

The three teens stared, shocked eyes agape.

A crimson-black landscape glowered from the canvas. Writhing human bodies, knotted together like shoelaces, were strung over tongues of flame licking up from the cracked, barren ground. Faces of torment and agony, frozen in rictus-screams, stretched away into an abyssal void. Heads were planted on stakes leaning at angles out of the fissured ground. Clumps of viscera steamed under mutilated corpses, some nothing but fleshy skeletons. Scrawled in lurid, drippy lettering on the bottom of the canvas was the word *Accursed.*

"Dude, what the fuckkk." Shaun stared dumbly at the painting. "Your sister painted *this*?"

"This is sick!" Jeff blurted.

Both teenagers turned to look at Nate, who gawped at the image speechlessly. Looking closer, he noticed a cloaked figure in the distance, its face shadowed but for two radiant eyes like cigarette tips in a lightless room. Nate shuddered.

So *this* was the planned album art for Wretched Angel's forthcoming debut.

No wonder she didn't want anyone seeing it, Nate thought. *It's fucking terrifying.*

Shaun chuckled and shook his head. "Man. Layne is a freak. And he's clearly gotten to your sister."

"Sure ain't *Sailor Moon* she's drawing," Jeff quipped. "What's Layne's deal, anyway? Does he actually worship the devil or something?"

"Only one way to find out." Shaun picked up a black backpack, adorned with patches and pins for bands like Carcass, Slayer, and Pantera, beside the bed. "Let's see what our boy Layne packed in his overnight bag!"

"Let's . . . not," Nate stuttered, but it was too late.

The zipper slid down metal teeth, snagging once, and the bag opened like a mouth. Digging his arm in, Shaun extracted a few CDs in blank jewel cases (*Human* by Death, *Seasons of the Abyss* by Slayer; an unlabeled disc with only an *X* Sharpied on the front); a box of condoms; and, from deep within the bowels, a book, hardbound with a ridged spine. Cryptic symbols adorned its cover in bas-relief. "Aha!" Shaun hefted the tome. "Here's our demon book."

A throat cleared raspily in the room.

It came from the doorway. The boys looked at each other, then at the door. Leaning against the jamb, a lanky, emaciated figure stood with grub-white arms crossed over a sunken chest. The figure stared at the three boys rifling through its bag. Sallow skin glimmered in the faint candlelight, and long, onyx hair melted past the silhouette of its leather-clad shoulders.

Oh, fuck.

"Hey guys."

Layne's voice was stoic and monotone. He simply stood in the doorway waiting for the teens to react.

"Uh, hey!" Shaun cheeped first. "We were just, um. We wanted to see Erica's artwork, and . . ."

None of the boys knew what to say. They'd been caught red-handed.

"What do you think of the painting?" Layne took a step into the room, his steel-toed boots making the carpet creak. Shadows capered on the planes of his face. He looked like a skull wearing a Halloween wig.

"It's… nice?" Shaun glanced at the painting, then gawped at the gangling metalhead as he crept closer.

"I'm sure Erica told you," Layne looked at Nate, "this is going to be the cover of our album."

"*Accursed*, right?" Jeff squeaked, filling the silence left by Nate.

Layne turned in the direction of the timid voice, disdain curling his lips. He looked back at the painting. "Erica's such a talented artist," he said. "The moment I saw her drawings, I knew she'd be the one to create my masterpiece. In many ways, it's been a collaboration. I'm very specific about what I want."

"It's super vivid," Shaun commented. "And, uh . . . pretty gory."

"Who are they?" Jeff pointed at the chain of squirming bodies stretching away over the tenebrous landscape.

Layne's eyes glinted in the candlelight. "Those are the damned ones."

"The Accursed, yeah?" Shaun said. "That's pretty sick, dude. Got a demo?"

"As a matter of fact, I do, Shaun." Layne's lips stretched in a grin. "But you guys probably already knew that, seeing as you were going through my things."

Silence fell as the boys looked at each other. Shaun gulped. "Oh, yeah. We're really sorry about that, man. We were just curious about Erica's mystery boyfriend. We didn't mean to snoop or anything."

"Of course not."

Nate realized he hadn't uttered a word since Layne entered the room. A spike of panic had wedged in the pit of his stomach. With effort, his mouth clicked open. "Where's my sister?" he managed to croak.

Layne smiled at him. "Still downstairs, asleep. The movie bored her." Digging into the pocket of his jacket, he removed a pack of Camels, withdrew a cigarette and struck a match. In the dimness of the room, the cherry glowed like a red star through a cosmic dust of burgeoning smoke.

Layne gazed at the painting again—the vivid reds and blacks, a chain of cursed souls twisting away into a sanguine sky; corpses lying broken and twisted, some impaled, planted on stakes. His finger—long and pallid, encircled by a black stone ring—traced a line down the row of mutilated bodies. "It's almost complete," he said.

"Looks… nearly finished," Nate stammered.

Layne grinned. "Only a few more souls."

The boys looked at the painting. An eerie light was reflecting off it. Frowning, Nate squinted at the swirls of color and the crimson glow bouncing off the wretched souls, flickering over the curls of impasto that were their mangled bodies. Where was the light coming from?

Nate turned to look at Layne. His jaw dropped as two burning gleams of light stabbed outward from the metalhead's eyes. Staggering backward, Nate tripped over the edge of the rug beside his sister's bed. Jeff and Shaun also backpedaled from the painting and the gangling rock star, whose face, sans eyes, was now a red-eyed skeleton's.

The ghoulish face rotated.

Layne directed the twin beams of light at Jeff and Shaun. When the light hit them, both teenagers yelped, their skin smoking—Nate caught a whiff of burning flesh and singed hair—and then something even more inexplicable happened.

Both of Nate's friends *shrank*. A blood-red orb grew out of the air and encapsulated their diminutive bodies. With a jerk of his head, Layne propelled the crimson bubble into the surface of the painting. As the translucent sphere slammed into it and was absorbed, the canvas shook on its easel, belching out a miasma of black smoke.

Then all was still.

Nate's throat clicked. He struggled to form a sound as his understanding of reality was yanked out of whack. A new species of terror evolved in his mind.

The rays of fiery light beaming out of Layne's eyes vanished. The metalhead turned to face Nate and smiled.

Nate began to stagger toward the door—

—*I need to get to Erica*, he thought numbly, *I need to warn her*—

—but an invisible claw seized him, causing his back to arch painfully. *WHERE ARE YOU GONG, NATE?* a malignant voice seethed in his mind. *GO TO SLEEP.*

Then he lost consciousness.

Nate woke on the damp, rumpled covers of his sun-dappled bed. Birds chirruped through the open window. He still wore his clothes from the previous day, wrinkled and soaked with sour sweat.

A fucking dream, he thought as he got up, wincing as a lance of pain stabbed in his temple. Stumbling to the door, he glanced at his alarm clock and saw that it was nearly one in the afternoon.

In the bathroom, he swallowed two Aspirin, ran the faucet and splashed warm water on his face. He looked up, noting with dissatisfaction his bloodshot eyes and haggard appearance. When he turned from the mirror, he was confronted with the face of his sister. She stared at him with eyes like knifepoints, a withering sneer on her pierced lips.

"What the fuck did you assholes do last night?" she spat.

Nate's hands went up. "What are you talking about?"

"My *painting*, asshole. I told you to stay out of my room! You know how important that is to me."

Nate's brow furrowed. "Erica, we didn't do anything to your painting—"

Without a word, Erica grasped the sleeve of his T-shirt and tugged him down the hall, into her room. A few colored candles burned on the windowsill and small vanity; the air was misty, smelling of eucalyptus and jasmine. Erica dragged Nate to the easel in the corner.

Nate shivered as he looked at the sanguine landscape of the painting.

At first, he didn't notice anything different about it. Erica pointed at a corner of the canvas, where two figures were depicted—impaled on spikes that ripped through their spines and emerged out of their throats, their eyes wide and pleading.

The blood in Nate's veins congealed. He recognized the figures instantly....

"I can't believe you guys actually did it," Erica said, trembling with ire. "You actually snuck into my room last night and messed with my painting."

"Erica—"

"I can't *wait* to hear what you have to say for yourselves. Which of you did it, huh? I know *you're* certainly not talented enough to paint this...." She pointed at the two skewered bodies on the canvas.

"Erica, it wasn't us! That's... that's *impossible*. Yeah, we did come up here last night. Shaun and Jeff really wanted to see what was in here . . ."

Erica cocked a brow.

"Well—I did too. We were curious, and yes, we were snooping around. Layne came up and started talking to us. He wasn't happy we were in here either. He…"

Nate didn't know how he could possibly explain. "Erica, Layne isn't normal. He—he's a monster or something! He attacked Shaun and Jeff. His eyes went red and he . . . he sent them *there*." A shaking finger pointed at the painting.

For a moment, the tension in Erica's face slackened. She considered her brother carefully, blinking her cerulean eyes.

Then she burst out laughing.

Tears swelled in Nate's eyes, and Erica went quiet, her face serious. "Nate, are you that retarded that you think I'd believe something like that? You're telling me, what, that my boyfriend is a *demon?* And he trapped your friends in a heavy metal painting?"

Nate's hands flew up. "I can't believe it either! I thought it was a dream until just now. But *look* at it, Erica. That's Shaun and Jeff!"

Erica's eyes narrowed, and she peered closer at the painting. Although the figures were small, there was no mistaking the features of Nate's friends. "So you painted it," Erica muttered. "*Obviously.*"

"Erica, do you really think me or my friends would be able to paint… *that*, in such detail? We're not artistic like you."

"Well fuck, Nate! I don't know! What you're saying is the craziest thing I've ever heard!"

"It's the truth…"

"Why don't we give them a call? Right now."

She nodded toward the cordless phone with the Black Flag sticker on the nightstand. With a trembling breath, Nate picked up the receiver and dialed Shaun's number.

114

After a few rings, a voice squawked into the phone. "Hello?"

"Hi, Mrs. Dutton. I was wondering if I could talk to Shaun?"

"He's not with you?" Her voice was screechy and taut.

"Uh, no. I thought—"

"I haven't heard from him since he was over at your house, Nate," Mrs. Dutton crowed. "If you see him, tell him he needs to come home *straight away* and he's in trouble. He was supposed to be here at nine this morning to help prepare for his sister's birthday."

"Uh... okay, Mrs. Dutton. Will do..."

When he called Jeff's mom next, it was the same thing. He hadn't been home since yesterday.

Replacing the phone in the cradle, Nate looked at his sister with fear shimmering in his red-veined eyes.

"That doesn't mean anything," Erica stated.

"Where's Layne right now?"

Erica scrunched her nose. "Probably at Joey's. They have band rehearsal today. They're starting to record tracks for *Accursed* next weekend, so they're practicing in his garage every afternoon this week."

"Erica, *please*. You have to believe me. Layne's not normal. He's something . . . sinister."

Blue eyes rolled in thick-lashed sockets. "You never liked him."

"Let's go to Joey's. I'll prove it to you."

"You want to *spy* on them?"

"Yeah."

A sigh escaped Erica's lips as she sagged onto her bed. She looked again at the painting, at the likenesses of Nate's two best friends—his *only* friends—contorted in acute detail.

"Okay," she mumbled. "But only because my other plans fell through. *God*. Let's make this quick."

Loud music throbbed from the closed garage of the house at the end of the cul-de-sac. Drums beat a pulsing tattoo to the accompaniment of thudding bass and shrilling electric guitar. As Nate and his sister approached the garage, the sounds grew heavier, and the ground tremored beneath their feet.

A blood curdling scream escaped the confines of the garage. Nate shuddered, knowing it was Layne—the frontman of the group.

Across the garage's top, square windows were marshaled in a row. Nate and Erica crept up the pebbled driveway, then stood on the balls of their feet to get a look inside.

The garage was dim, lit only by a circle of candles arranged in a half-moon on the oil-stained floor. In the flickering glow, Wretched Angel played their music. (*Some music,* Nate thought, not particularly a fan of heavy metal . . . at least, not since Layne had entered the picture.) The bassist, a hairy, keg-shaped man with the green tattoo of a serpent rearing up on his ursine chest, banged his head, whipping straggly hair back and forth to the rhythm of the grinding, intestinal sound. Behind him, the drummer, Joey, slammed sticks like a machine, sweat leaping off the tips of his jet-black hair. Nate wasn't familiar with the guitarist. He was tall and muscular, hair worn long, like the rest. A cigarette glowed blood-red amidst the curtain of sweaty hair.

In the foreground, center stage, was Layne, a shirtless, skeletal ghoul. Ribcages sharp as branches on an autumn tree. His entire body was glossed in a liquid sheen as he clutched the microphone on the stand and screamed into it.

It almost seemed like a normal band rehearsal—until Nate caught two glowing embers amidst the snarl of hair in Layne's face as the frontman banged his head with the music. Squinting, Nate gawked at the other members of the band, all of whose eyes likewise burned an infernal red.

Nate turned to see his sister's reaction. Erica's mouth hung slack as she watched the wraith like figure of her boyfriend prance around the garage, holding the mike stand like a lover, rubbing it against his bulging crotch. The music reached a crescendo—drums sped up, bass thumped like a heartbeat, guitar shredded so loud it was a wonder the amp didn't burst into flames. All four band members banged their heads in sync with the thrashy groove of the metal. In the brief moments when their faces were visible under the sweaty mops of hair, their faces looked gaunt, ashen—even more cadaverous than usual.

The song ended, and reverb rang out in the smoky garage. Layne lifted his head. Erica let out a gasp. His eyes, still glowing crimson, sat recessed in the skull-like face. His wan visage looked like a death's head.

He peered at Nate and Erica through the window, seeing them before they could duck their heads. Black-painted lips curved in a maleficent grin. A narrow tongue slithered from the dark cavity of his mouth and licked his wormy lips.

Hello there, a voice spoke in Nate's mind as he ducked, grabbing onto his sister.

He's messing with me, Nate thought, squeezing his eyes shut and shaking his head, trying to push the demonic presence out of his mind.

You really need to stop spying on people, Nate, the voice warned. It sounded warped and heavy, like it was coming through a distortion pedal.

Grabbing his sister's sleeve, Nate spun around to flee from the house. Gears groaned as the garage door started lifting. Erica yelped and followed her brother as they fled from the house.

As Nate ran, voices taunted him. Not words like before, but bizarre and ominous sounds—

Screeching and snorting and hideous laughter—

Nate shook his head, trying to get the noises out of his skull.

Soon, vertigo overcame him. He tripped over a fallen branch. Looking up at the sky, he gaped as a fissure appeared in the sun. The wobbling sphere of light went red and tore down its middle like the image of a broken heart. Tears leaked out of Nate's eyes as he tried shaking the vision away.

After a few moments, sanity returned. He pushed himself off the grass and looked around. Erica was nowhere in sight.

"Erica?" Nate whispered. Then he screamed. "ERICA!"

But she was gone.

Hideous cackles resounded in Nate's pounding head. Cringing, he did everything he could to disregard the laughter as he staggered back toward home.

"Erica!"

Nate burst into his sister's bedroom hoping to find her there, but the room was empty. The candles on her desk and vanity had gone out, a light mist layering the air. Nate's heart thundered. Fear made a gnarled fist in his throat, obstructing his breathing. He gasped and hyperventilated.

In the corner of his mind, he felt a nudge, directing him toward the corner of the bedroom. Toward the painting.

Accursed.

Slowly, Nate crept toward the easel....

At first glance, it was the same grim landscape—red and black, a cavalcade of cursed souls stretching over a hellish landscape. But on closer view, he noticed something else.

A figure.

A woman, which, at first blush, was just another blotch of paint in the parade of lost souls. But upon closer view, was....

Erica.

It was unmistakably her. She was on a raised platform, lashed to a spike. Beneath her, mutant canines circled around cones of fire, slavering thick ropes of drool. Erica's expression, shocked and frozen, pained Nate and made him bawl. A shadowy, red-eyed figure loomed beside her.

I'm coming, Erica, Nate thought, *I'm coming for you!*

Squeezing his eyes, Nate focused all his energy on the image seared into his mind's eye. He called forth the Vision, beckoning whatever dormant powers lay within him.

Invisible screws twisted in Nate's temples and he wanted to scream. He continued focusing on the painting, willing himself to enter that evil hellscape where his sister was trapped….

For a second, the field of black behind his eyelids went red. Red as blood. The floating orbs of light behind his eyes resolved into peculiar shapes, vicious formations that made his skin crawl.

When Nate opened his eyes, he was no longer in Erica's bedroom. He was in what could only be described as hell.

The hell of Erica's painting. *Accursed.*

He trod over cracked ground that belched toxic fumaroles of smoke. In the distance, jagged cliffs clawed into the infernal heavens. A volcano disgorged not lava but green, iridescent mucus that sparkled like the ocean, swimming with ruddy chunks of human tissue and random body parts. Corpses, half-alive, crawled along the ground, grasping at his shoes. Their moans sent shivers down Nate's back. A woman with half her skull missing, a wad of brain matter gleaming from the rent in her tacky hair, looked up at him and whispered, in a hideous lisp: "*Helllppp.*"

Nate passed a phalanx of spikes stabbing upward into the sky. Bodies in various positions hung twisted on their tips. None dead, all of them moaning and horribly alive. As Nate hurried past the bodies, a withered hand clutched at him. A feeble voice spoke his name.

He looked and saw Shaun, stripped of half his flesh, lolling off a slanted spike. Half his viscera was held out like a shiny, crimson bouquet in his lap. Clutching fistfuls of guts, he held his arms out to Nate as though offering a gift.

Shuddering, Nate moved past—*I need to get to Erica*, he kept reminding himself—but was then confronted by the even more hideous image of Jeff.

His friend was now missing his body. All that remained was the face, stretched-out on the ground and flattened like a piece of stepped-on gum. It was surrounded by a lake of viscera and blood. Sickly eyes stared up at the roiling, red sky. Torn lips crawled to form words, but the only sound they could emit was a gurgling whimper. Nate made eye contact with the diseased, yellow eyes in the rolled-dough face and nearly retched.

Then another voice called his name.

Gazing ahead, Nate saw a figure lashed to a spike, thrashing in place.

Erica.

Nate bolted toward his sister. Her image wavered in the distance like a ripple of heat. Along the ground, cadaverous hands reached for him, clutching at his ankles and pleading for help. Nate ignored them.

Another figure loomed beside Erica's flailing form. Layne.

As Nate ran toward his sister, two giant, onyx-dark eyes materialized in the crimson sky. They hovered like black planets, glowering upon the scene.

When Nate finally got to his sister, Layne smirked and removed his fingerless leather gloves. Slowly, he clapped with skeletal hands that coughed up gray plumes of dust.

Now in his domain, he'd shed much of the flesh that was superfluous in this place. His face was gaunt and white, mostly bone; a few shreds of muscle and tendon clung here and there like tissue paper on a bleeding cut. His black, wavy hair glistened with bloody plasma.

The other members of Wretched Angel, also shorn of flesh—yet still wearing their torn jeans and studded leather jackets—gawked at Nate, cackling obscenely. The drummer, Joey, twirled his sticks in fleshless hands. Cocking his head, he rammed one end through his ear, till the wooden spear ejected out of the other side in a shower of blood. He grinned and snarled.

Welcome to Hell, a voice spoke in Nate's mind. Pointed teeth glimmered in the festering cavity of Layne's mouth.

Let my sister go, Nate spoke back, not understanding how he was communicating with the iniquitous, otherworldly entity. He supposed all his years of using the Vision had led up to this….

Why would I do that? Layne's eyes narrowed, leered. *I have such a fine morsel to play with.*

Slithering out of his mouth, a forked tongue elongated, flicking obscenely; it reached Erica's face and gave it a long lick.

"Stop it!" The words, shouted aloud, resounded in the hellish space. The obsidian eyes in the sky directed their gelid gaze at Nate. He could feel the energy of their stare, and every hair on his body stood erect.

DO YOU WANT YOUR SISTER? A stentorian voice spoke. It sounded like metal and thunder, like shearing, splintering glass.

"YES!" Nate bellowed. His eyes drowned in tears as he watched Erica moan and twist helplessly on the spike.

YOU KNOW WHAT YOU MUST DO, the voice rumbled.

Nate stared at the enormous eyes in the sky. Then looked back at Layne, who was moving sinuously around Erica, gliding skeletal hands over her exposed and vulnerable flesh. He winked lasciviously.

"DON'T YOU FUCKING TOUCH HER!"

With everything he had, Nate closed his eyes and gritted his teeth, focusing on the power within. Using the Vision, he saw the scene in his mind's eye—his sister lashed to the towering spike, Layne standing behind her, touching her; the vast eyes in the hellfire sky. He let the energy mount within him and concentrated all of it on Layne.

The gangling demon sneered at him.

But not for long . . .

In seconds, Layne's head exploded in a welter of gore.

Erica screamed as her face was splattered at close range. Skull chips and wads of lumpy brain matter flew into her eyes and mouth, lodged into her blood-shellacked hair. Gushing a fountain of blood from the neck, Layne's headless body remained standing for a moment—then wobbled and collapsed to the ground like a pile of sticks.

"Nate!" Erica shouted. She spat bloody mucilage out of her mouth. Nate sprinted for her, paying no attention to the all-seeing eyes in the blood-red sky.

Using his teeth, he tore at the gristly intestine lashing her to the spike, his gorge rising as his mouth filled with bile. Erica fell to the ground, shaking and delirious. Nate gathered her in his arms and held her close.

He used the remaining power in his mind to concentrate his energy on home. He did his best not to look up at those planetary eyes in the crimson sky or imagine what they might do next.

Thunder rumbled.

A wind redolent of gore and death swept over them . . .

When Nate opened his eyes, they were back in Erica's bedroom.

Silence.

Erica spun, heaving breaths. Trails of Mascara bled down her gore-caked face. When she realized they were safe, she rushed to Nate and hugged him, harder than she ever had before.

Nate held her back, his eyes squeezed shut. Sniffling and sobbing, he thought, *I'll never let you go.*

"Oh my god, Nate, I'm so sorry I didn't believe you." Erica wept into his shoulder. "You were right—right about everything."

As Nate held his sister, he opened his eyes and saw the two of them in the free standing mirror against the far wall in her room.

A portentous voice spoke in his ear.

You did well, Nathaniel. You've earned this reward. Just as you always wanted.

Nate frowned and looked at his reflection. Recessed in the sallow skin, his eyes glowed like two red-hot coals smoldering in a bed of dry ashes.

Leon Saul has published short fiction in the anthologies *Season of the Witch* (Crimson Pinnacle Press), *The Best of Bizarro Fiction, Vol. 1* (Planet Bizarro Press), and *Pernicious Invaders* (Great Old Ones Publishing), as well as magazines such as Morpheus Tales and Acidic Fiction. He lives in Southern California.

Johnny Hell

Sheldon Woodbury

When the black van crunched into the gravel lot of the Bonecrusher, he knew his metamorphosis was almost complete. It was a rainy night, the perfect setting for what lay ahead. Everything was gloomy and wet, like a splattered nightmare where something new and strange was being borne. But it wasn't a nightmare to him. It was his fevered dream to become a rock god and this was the place he'd picked for his glorious ascension.

It didn't look like much, just a crumbling slab in an abandoned part of the city. It was completely unknown except to the black clad horde of heavy metal worshippers who were already packed inside. For them it was a head banging temple where they could perform their nightly rituals away from the grinding drudgery of their daytime lives. They needed a place where darkness was sacred and howling rage was the emotion of choice. He could already hear the blistering mayhem inside that seemed to come from a much darker world.

And that was the world he wanted to rule.

It had only been a few years, but it seemed like a lifetime ago when he was a completely different person, not anything like the exquisite creation he'd now become. Back then he was just another high school dropout who spent most of his time listening to heavy metal music under the influence of whatever drug he could find. It was during the raging motherfucker of all acid trips when his destiny was revealed during a death metal dirge that ripped open a ragged hole in his scrambled brain. The acid was the magic elixir and the pounding music was the psychic road sign that told him what he had to do.

Don't just dream it... *be it*.

That's when he decided it was time to break free from his mortal bonds and become a rock god. He'd always hoped that somewhere deep inside his morbid brain there was something special that could change his life and this was it. His tiny room in the basement of his parent's house was a cluttered shrine to the hardcore bands he loved more than anything else... Cannibal Corpse, Fleshgod Apocalypse, Battleaxe, Metal Church, and Grim Reaper. They were his thundering sanctuary away from the everyday world. The crushing music was the mega-death killer of everything he hated.

And there was more than that.

In the drugged out womb of his basement room, the most depraved appetites and decadent cravings were set free. Uptight barriers were blasted away by wailing guitars and primal urges were celebrated with banshee screams. The nauseating world he felt trapped in was way too bright and rigid, a suffocating prison of stupid morality and middle-class crap. The heavy metal world was chaotic and dark, raw and powerful, a pandemonium freak show of rabid freedom and savage rage.

Don't just dream it... *be it.*

So he decided to leave the faceless mob of worshippers and become one of the metal gods he'd given his druggy allegiance to. But his dream was even grander than that. He didn't just want to join the tattooed pantheon of snarling deities, he wanted to push it to an even more mythic extreme. This part was vague, but he knew it was the breakthrough he had to pursue to the very end.

More drugs were needed, of course, and a band that shared his hardcore fierceness. It all came together in his basement room where he huddled with other misfits he found online. It was a motley group of four, including him. He was going to be the singer and write all the lyrics, the mastermind leading the way. None of them were very good, but it didn't matter. They all agreed that deafening rage was more important than anything else.

And this is when his macabre metamorphosis began.

First he came up with a new name... *Johnny Hell.*

The other members followed his lead, but that didn't matter either. They were a part of his vision, but just barely, useful pawns in his grand design. The path to his deification needed disciples, but their role was secondary. He would be the howling messiah that would scream his way to the Promised Land. He came up with the name of the band too... *The End of the World.* It captured perfectly the apocalyptic message he wanted to share.

The van grumbled to a stop in back of the cavernous building. He'd been tweaking for almost a week on crystal meth, so his frazzled brain was crackling with his dark desires. Acid had been the chemical mind-blower, but crystal meth was the slashing ax that cut away the parts of his life he didn't need anymore.

He didn't look anything like his old self. His hollow eyes were dark and quivering, like he was seeing another world trembling in a cosmic unknown. His skeletal body looked close to death, a cadaverous figure that could barely stand on shivering stick like legs.

When the money dripped in, he'd used it all on meth and tattoos. The meth sculpted his flesh and bones into the morbid messenger his vision had called for. It also dredged up the demented lyrics from the darkest places inside him. The tattoos covered his sagging skin like a gruesome stain, all in the deepest red and darkest black. They were all different monsters playing bloody guitars of human bones, except for the biggest covering his back, a giant Cthulhu creature pounding on fiery mountains Hell.

They shambled out of the black van and headed to the back door of the building. The rain soaked his skeletal body and he welcomed it as a holy anointment for the night ahead. He saw the other bands members were staring at him with a gaze that was new. His startling metamorphosis was probably too radical even for them. But there wouldn't be any non-believers after tonight.

126

They stumbled in silence down a shadowy hallway, then down creaky stairs to their dressing room. He recognized the band that was playing before them, a thrash metal group from Cleveland. He felt a surge of righteous rage rattle inside him, listening to their feeble attempts to be hardcore. The more he heard, the more it assaulted his senses. The only way he could get rid of the sickening nausea was to imagine them burning alive inside his meth soaked brain.

Don't just dream it... *be it.*

The dressing room was lit by a dirty bulb that hung from the ceiling on a twisted wire. There was more darkness than light, which was just the way he liked it. The grimy walls were covered with carved out names of all the bands that had played here before. He recognized most of them and felt the same wave of revulsion. They were all pale imitations of what hardcore metal needed to be, so the fire in his brain was now thrashing with countless more burning bodies.

They drifted off to different corners of the room and began their pre-show rituals. There was heroin, coke, pot, and pills, all of which he'd shunned as unneeded baggage as his transformation had picked up steam. Only the scorching sizzle of crystal meth gave him the transcending purity he needed. He banged a hit and pulled out his black spiral notebook with the flaming skull. He caressed it in his claw like hands, as the heart-thumping rush rocketed through his ghost-like flesh.

The dark road he'd been on the last two years had been strange and brutal, but enlightenment had finally come. His vision was driven by his desire to embody the hardcore rage of metal music and become its almighty god. But it was only after he'd purified his flesh with the sacramental meth that his way to the Promised Land was revealed. His faith had rewarded him with the power he needed.

It came from the ragged hole into the darkest depths of his morbid mind. At first there were just distant whispers, something crying out from far away, but it got louder and louder as his creepy metamorphosis evolved in even more tortured ways.

A part of him knew it was insanity, but that only excited him even more. This was the extreme he was searching for, a shattering escape from the normal world. The distant whispers turned into screams, and the screams turned into a blaring manifesto. This is where his lyrics came from, and that was the power he was given. He scribbled them down in a tweaking rush that could last for days, filling the pages of his notebook with madness and fury from the darkest of places.

He didn't tell anyone that the songs he was writing were all part of one long mystical sermon. This is where his message was hidden for the black clad horde that followed them like a midnight army. He looked down at the scribbled lyrics and whispered them hoarsely to himself. He could already feel their deviant power, because his ravaged body was suddenly flooded with even more anger and hate.

A shaggy haired figure cracked open the door and nodded his head, the signal it was time to take the stage. The music had stopped overhead, but the booming hoots and howls still echoed like a fading storm. He tottered up to his feet and felt his hanging head spin in a dizzying whir. His spectacular new metamorphosis could barely hold up his tattooed flesh, but the hard-charging meth gave him the strength he needed.

They stumbled as a silent group up the creaky stairs and down the shadowy hallway. The storm had billowed again, as the crowd began to roar their name like a gargantuan beast.

"The End of the World..."

"The End of the World..."

"The End of the World..."

When they reached the dark space next to the stage, he could hear the secret voice inside him screaming out louder than ever before. Its power made him wonder if it was the voice of a god too, and he was just an instrument of its infernal will. For a moment he felt weak and helpless, his faith suddenly shaken, but it quickly passed and his fiery vision returned.

Don't just dream it... *be it.*

He also hadn't told anyone that tonight's show would be their last, a final ceremony to celebrate the mythic extreme he'd been searching for. The extended song he'd been singing in fragments was coming to an end. It was a metal masterpiece of exalted anger and righteous rage, so the black clad horde would finally see the Promised Land.

When they took the stage, he could only see the barest glimmer of the screaming faces gathered in front of him. Matches were lit and the flickering flames gave a haunting glow to the cavernous space. It was their trademark, a heavy metal salute to... *The End of the World.*

He staggered to his place at the edge of the stage, wobbling unsteadily in front of the crowd. He pulled off his ripped black shirt and a spotlight blazed on his monstrous tattoos and shocking body. The crowd became a howling beast again as a metal blare exploded from the stage. Knowing this was going to an apocalyptic celebration of everything he'd dreamed about, he shivered with ecstasy.

They weren't very good, but that didn't matter, because their sonic rage washed over the banging heads and echoed off the crumbling walls. He was perched at the edge of the stage like a heavy metal scarecrow that couldn't stop shrieking and shaking. But it was all about the secret message that came from an insane portal in his brain.

That was the power he was given...

When they came to the final song, it was the end of the manic masterpiece he'd scribbled in his notebook with the flaming skull. He'd been a shrieking messiah on a nocturnal pilgrimage through heavy metal clubs with only one desire.

Don't dream it... *be it.*

When the song ended, he collapsed to the floor, not knowing what would happen next. Then he heard the roar of the growling beast in front of him. He looked up and saw the matches were lit again, and the shimmering faces were now different, even more monstrous than his bloody tattoos.

"The End of the World..."
"The End of the World..."
"The End of the World..."

They set fire to the building with an infernal howl, then rushed the stage with clawing hands and feral eyes. He staggered back up to his feet and raised his trembling arms, accepting the crush of worshippers with a tweaking rapture. They ripped him apart, flesh from bone, bone from flesh, his flowing blood staining the stage. At the very last moment before his death, all his morbid dreams were unleashed into the world, the first stage of his glorious ascension.

Sheldon Woodbury has an M.F.A. in Dramatic Writing from New York University where he also taught screenwriting.

He's an award winning writer (screenplays, plays, books, short stories, and poems). His book "Cool Million" is considered the essential guide to writing high concept movies. His short stories and poems have appeared in many horror anthologies and magazines. His novel "The World on Fire" was published September, 2014 by JWK Fiction. His poem, The Midnight Circus, was selected by Ellen Datlow as an honourable mention for Best Horror 2017, and his poem, The Madness of Monsters, is included in the 2021 HWA Poetry Showcase.

Black-Metal Baker

William J. Donahue

Jared Perry clapped the dusting of flour from his butter-stained apron. Flour motes hung in the air, catching the light as they descended, like snowflakes.

A tiny brass bell jangled as the front door groaned open. A man stepped across the threadbare doormat and approached the register: forty-five, fifty at most, a little doughy in the middle, gray-tinted stubble. He wore obnoxious blue pinstripes, a hot-pink tie with curls of paisley that reminded Jared of spermatozoa, and the kind of brushed-leather shoes someone in Jared's position would never buy—Oxfords, probably Italian made, three-hundred bucks easy.

The man uttered a greeting Jared did not return. He bent at the waist to peruse the baked goods behind the smudged glass. Few items remained in the display case at one-fifty in the afternoon, ten minutes before closing. The man caught Jared's eye, and Jared nodded in response.

"Chocolate croissant and a cappuccino to go," the man said.

"No hot beverages past noon. Sorry, pal."

"Just the croissant then. Two, actually."

Jared wax-papered a pair of croissants out of the case, slid them into a sleeve branded with the bakery's logo—*Butter and Mayhem*, the first word in elegant script and the third a chaotic mess resembling scratch marks, almost unreadable—and slapped the package onto the worn laminate counter. He then went to the cooler and plucked a can of nitro cold-brew coffee from the back, gave the can a halfhearted shake.

"Call it six even for the croissants, discounted 'cause they've been sitting. Cold brew's on the house."

"Mighty kind of you." The man's gaze roved the empty lobby, settling on the framed black-and-white photos tacked to the nearest wall. He picked up the croissants and the can of nitro, and headed for the exit. Jared stepped out from behind the counter, intending to lock the door as soon as the customer crossed the threshold. He undid the hair tie holding back his ponytail and unleashed his thinning brown mane.

The man stopped abruptly and turned.

"I have to hand it to you," he said. "I just love what you're doing here. Ask anyone and they'll say this city needs more places like yours—from-scratch bakeries run by ambitious entrepreneurs. Fresh coat of paint and this place could really be something to write home about."

He introduced himself as James Allan Birch, associate publisher of *Grit and Glamour*, a lifestyle magazine rooted in the arts, culture, and people of Philadelphia. Jared knew the rag, had seen its glossy cover on the few remaining newsstands nearby. Some of his friends had shared its articles and videos on Facebook, Twitter, wherever. And, if memory served, Jared had once delivered a sizeable catered order to its second-story office in Northern Liberties.

"Listen," Birch added, "we're in the process of putting out our annual 'Besties' issue—you know, best of everything in the city—and I'd love to see you in it, would love to see this place get the ink it deserves. Your croissants, best I've ever had. People need to know. I'll have one of our editors reach out and say hello. You know, help you tell your story."

"Sorry, pal. My budget doesn't have any wiggle room for advertising. Or paint, as you noted."

"No, man. I'm talking pure editorial. You won't put out a dime."

"No harm there, I guess." Jared fetched a business card; the edges of two corners dulled, and stenciled his cell number across the bottom. "Have 'em hit me up whenever."

The next morning, just before eleven, an incoming text message buzzed Jared's cell phone. She introduced herself as Mallory Quinn, a food-and-drink reporter for *Grit and Glamour*, and suggested she wanted to drop by the bakery, maybe taste some of the baked goods her colleagues kept raving about. She could stop in the following day, she wrote in follow-up, maybe just after business hours so she did not put a kink in his moneymaking.

His first reaction: a prank, someone playing a joke on him. On further reflection, Butter and Mayhem *did* crank out the best croissants in the city, not that he had ever gotten credit for the distinction. Perhaps this young woman could help spread the word, help him not have to scrimp as much, and, in turn, have Monica, his wife of three years, not have to endure so many late nights toiling in the ER.

Part of him was surprised when the reporter actually showed up the next afternoon at the agreed-upon time of two-fifteen. She was several years younger than Jared—probably twenty-six or twenty-seven to his thirty-four—and stylish, wearing a gray denim jean jacket, white linen pants, and little to no makeup. He opened the door and welcomed her in. The scents of lilac and cinnamon followed her.

She tossed her handbag onto one of the three Lancaster tables by the front window. As she circled the lobby, she studied the walls, the ceiling, the display case, taking it all in, jotting down notes. He expelled a breath as he sat in a wrought-iron chair by the display window overlooking the sidewalk, the first time he had been off his feet in the eight hours since arriving at the bakery at just before five a.m. As expected, she lingered at the three framed photos tacked to the far wall.

134

"Wow," she said. "Is that *you*?"

He rose from his seat, knees popping as he stood, to see what she was seeing. One of the photos showed Jared in his role as Grod-Korroth-Hellion, his alter ego in the black-metal band Ophiophagus: head tilted back, stage blood spilling from his open mouth and dripping from the tip of his tongue, the fronts of his teeth blacked out to resemble fangs, his face a mask of black-and-white corpse paint, while he fingered the walnut fret board of his all-black Schecter guitar. A fireball, whirling up from the barrel of an unseen FX machine on the stage, shrouded his lower half.

He loved that photo, all flame and sex and violence.

"Oh, that," he said. "Proof of my ignominious past."

In another photo, Jared and his three bandmates stood beneath a logo in unintelligible script, each of them done up in corpse paint, leather, and silver spikes: Scott Saint Germain (stage name Sathanas Faust), the lead guitarist who looked more like a demonic gorilla than a human man, an all-black hatchet clutched in his left hand; Leonard Tulio (Cyclops the Butcher), the lanky and perpetually silent bass player; and Kyle Burns (Burner-and-Basher-o-Bones), the beefy, hot-headed, and bald-as-a-Macy's-mannequin drummer.

Mallory's finger hovered above the logo. "What does this mean?"

"It's my band's name."

"That's a *word*?"

"The harder the logo is to read, the better. It's kind of 'a thing' in black metal. What can I tell you about the croissants?"

"Oh, right. Those. When and where did you learn how to bake?"

Jared described his early days working in the bakery, before he had taken over the place and renamed it Butter and Mayhem. He had started as a part-time gofer, but the bakery's French-born owner, Roger Dion, had taken Jared under his wing, figured this aimless kid from a do-nothing neighborhood in Northeast Philly could use some direction in his life. Roger mentored Jared best as he could—about baking, about business, about how to be a good human. Then, five years ago, as the neighborhood surrounding their block of Fish town began to change, Roger decided to retire and repair to the outskirts of Lake Placid, New York. He sold the bakery to Jared, his heir apparent. Roger died of a heart attack on his sun porch less than a month later.

Mallory kept eyeing the photo of Jared in action on stage—the blood, the fire, the spectacle.

"Sorry," she said. "One more question about the band."

Jared tried to hide his annoyance.

"What's the band's name?"

"Ophiophagus."

She repeated the name. "Is that Greek?"

"If you say so. Near as I can tell, it means snake eater. Do you know *Constrictor*, Alice Cooper's album from, like, Eighty-Six or Eighty-Seven?"

"I don't know who she is."

Jared winced. Someone like Mallory would not be caught dead at a metal show. Still, how the hell could she have never heard of Alice freakin' Cooper? He let the insult pass without bothering to correct her.

"The cover of the album has a photo of Alice with a snake in his mouth— hence the name," he explained. "Alice Cooper changed everything for me, opened my eyes to how awesome music could be—the makeup, the image, the attitude. I guess you could say he inspired me."

Mallory said nothing in return, and he took her silence as an invitation to continue.

"I was maybe eight years old when my older brother gave me *Alice Cooper Goes to Hell*. That was the album that did it for me. This was in the mid-Nineties, long after the album's heyday. Everyone else was listening to Nirvana and Pearl Jam, Snoop Dog, all this other lame and disaffected crap. Not me."

He returned to the counter for the spread he had arranged prior to the reporter's arrival. A dozen butter cookies, each capped with a dollop of fresh fig jam, encircled a pyramid of four croissants—chocolate, almond, apple, plain. He placed the tray on the nearest table and unfurled a hand, inviting her to dig in.

"Alice was the gateway. From there I got into other stuff—harder, faster, darker. First Dio, Ozzy, and Danzig. Maiden and Helloween. Then the likes of Possessed, Death, and Venom. Slayer, of course. Then I discovered the masters—Bathory, Darkthrone, Mayhem."

"Is that where the name of the bakery comes from—*Butter and Mayhem*? What an original name, by the way. So fun!"

He nodded, glad to have the conversation return to the bakery.

"How long did you play in the band?"

"It's been probably nine years since its earliest iteration. We've had a few lineup changes along the way, but the band refuses to die. Sort of like Jason Voorhees from the *Friday the 13th* franchise. Unkillable."

"You're *still* doing this?"

He soured at the comment. Sure, his hairline had ebbed an inch or two, and his once rail-thin frame had begun to fill out with the hint of a potbelly, but he could still pass for thirty on most days. Maybe even late twenties.

"Fewer places to gig at, 'cause most of 'em have become something else—banks and Wawas and shit," he said. "Fewer people at the shows, too. But yeah, still chugging along."

Jared could see the machinery spinning in the space behind the reporter's eyes. His fears were coming true.

"Listen," he said, "I'm not interested in you writing about some washed-up metalhead who just so happens to make baked goods in his free time. That's not my story. Now, if you want to write about the croissants, I'm all in. But I don't want to see my picture under some lame-ass headline like, 'Pastries and

Pentagrams.' The band is pretty much a side hustle at this point. Some days I'm not even sure I want to keep doing it."

"Totally understand," she said. "We'll get to the croissants in a minute. I'm just fascinated by the hustle. One or two more questions about the band, purely for my own edification, and then its right back to the baked goods. Promise."

She scrawled in her notebook. Old school, he thought. He respected old school.

"I know just enough to be dangerous here, so bear with me," she said. "Isn't black metal known for all kinds of ugliness? Racism, misogyny, anti-Christian leanings."

Jared grimaced as he considered his answer.

"Yeah, I guess some bands hit those notes—maybe a lot of them, in truth. Music scholars credit a handful of Norwegian bands forgiving birth to the genre, and a few of the pioneers have been tied to some pretty grisly stuff: murders, church arsons, other kinds of trouble that don't exactly paint the genre in the best light."

"And you wanted to continue in that noble tradition?"

"Don't do that," he said, though he did not mean to sound so confrontational. "Please don't assume. I feel about black metal the same way I feel about The Clash or David Bowie or Gwar or a dozen indie bands that woke people up and knocked 'em on their asses. Bands you've probably never heard of. The first black-metal show I ever went to, I almost couldn't handle it—all the pyrotechnics and stage blood and the wall of sound from these raw, brutal guitars. I loved the pageantry, the theatricality, the release."

"Not the devil stuff? Couldn't help but notice the tattoos."

His right hand instinctively covered his left forearm, to hide the faded blue-and-red etching of a goat skull with a pentagram between its blood-tipped horns.

"So," Mallory pressed, "you're saying it's just an act?"

"An actor on a stage, playing a part. Once you're done with the show, you take off the costume and go back to real life. Back to boredom and normalcy and utility bills."

As she crossed the lobby, her heels clicked against bare tile. She pulled one of the croissants apart—the chocolate one, his most popular item. Half of the croissant disappeared into her perfect mouth. A few flakes clung to her berry-red bottom lip.

"Wow." Her face contorted as she chewed. Her eyes beamed with delight. "This is fabulous. Like eating a buttery pillow, with a hint of ganache. From scratch, I assume?"

He poured out an espresso and set it on the table beside the croissant tray. Steam trails rose from the small white cup.

"Roger passed his genius on to me. I experimented from there. Right place, right time, I guess."

"Bravo," she said. She licked the tip of each finger. "The rest of the guys in your band, it's all make-believe for them, too?"

"Of course." He paused. The bud of an unwanted memory unfurled in his brain. "I'm pretty sure we're all in it for the same reason, but you'd have to ask them."

The vibrating cell phone shook Jared awake at a few minutes past three a.m. He picked up his phone and saw a one-word text from Scott Saint Germain, his guitar player: HELP. He scrolled to his contacts page and touched his index finger to the string of blue digits listed beneath Scott's name.

Scott picked up after the first ring. Based on the background noise, he was driving with the windows down.

"You're needed, brother," Scott said. His voice seemed to tremble.

"It's late as shit. Or early."

"Meet me at the studio."

"*Now?*"

"Come around back. I'll be there in ten."

Jared bundled up and made the eight-minute walk from his apartment to the bakery, which doubled as a rehearsal space and recording studio for Ophiophagus. A soundproofed room in the back housed the band's amplifiers, instruments, and pyrotechnic equipment.

Scott's falling-apart Cadillac Seville idled by the back door.

Jared tapped on the driver's side window, startling his friend.

"It's about friggin' time," Scott said. He looked up and down the street. His eyes scanned the second-story windows, likely scouting for nosy neighbors, but the world was still sleeping.

The smell hit Jared the second Scott popped the trunk. The metallic whiff of fresh blood. Even in darkness he could see two unmoving bodies—one male, one female. Dark blots stained their clothes. The black tomahawk Scott always seemed to have with him sat beside them, its stone blade glistening with something wet. Jared asked the obvious question.

"Are they dead?"

"Of course they're fuckin' dead."

"What the hell happened?"

"Let's talk inside. Grab his legs. We'll put 'em both in the freezer."

Scott had already pulled the first corpse halfway out of the trunk. He tried to fish his hands beneath the dead man's shoulders, but the blood-slicked body tumbled onto the ground, landing face first. Jared winced at the hollow sound of bone striking asphalt.

They moved the body through the back door, down the tight hall, into the walk-in. They did the same with the other body, the girl, much lighter than her counterpart. As Jared turned around, in a daze, he saw droplets of blood painting the floor.

140

Afterward, they stood in the kitchen, sharing cigarettes.

"Who are they?" Jared asked. "*Were* they, rather."

Deep down, Jared already knew the answer despite the bodies' butchered faces, but he needed to hear Scott say it.

"Lee Kron from Murklands. Lee and his girlfriend. Alexandra, Alexa— whatever."

Jared had recognized Lee by his strawberry-blond hair and slight build, and he identified Lee's girlfriend Analise by the bouquet-of-roses tattoo above her blood-soaked breast. He had known them both well, had liked them both. Had filled in on guitar for Murklands, Lee's doom-metal band, more than once. Had even helped Lee move into a new apartment years earlier—a two-bedroom shithole in Kensington.

"We were hanging out at Crush, the titty bar down there on Columbus," Scott said. "He kept droning on and on about shows they had lined up, about the fan base they had built, about how their Twitter following was blowing up. I just got sick of the blah, blah, blah. Like, 'I like you, Lee, but shut the fuck up already.' But he wouldn't. So, I asked them if they wanted to go somewhere and get fucked up. They're fucked up now, wouldn't you say?"

"You did this 'cause you got jealous?"

"Give me some credit, Jay. This has nothing to do with me. We have our Adam and Eve."

Nausea filled Jared as he considered the weight of Scott's words.

"Please tell me I'm dreaming," he said. "Tell me this is a sick joke."

"*They* ain't laughin'," he said, jutting a thumb toward the walk-in and the bodies inside. "This is Day One of the future we mapped out all those years ago."

Jared wagged his head. "Dude, the things we talked about back then …that was nonsense."

"No, we followed the breadcrumbs left by those who preceded us. The *Ars Goetia. The Lost Book of Solomon.* Brockum's *Guide to the Dark Dimensions.* It was all in there. We just puzzled the pieces together."

"Tell me you don't actually believe any of that crap."

"You've chosen to lose your way," Scott seethed, "but deep down I know you still believe."

"If I've lost anything, it's the taste for nihilism."

"Chaos—that's what we always wanted. Unleash the princes and presidents of Hell. Stand back and watch everything burn and crumble, and then greet the new world that grows out of the ash. We started the cycle ten years ago. I know you remember, Jay."

"There's a pretty damn big difference between vandalizing a house of worship and cold-blooded murder. Besides, I regret what we did back then."

Scott extinguished his Marlboro on a stainless-steel table near the walk-in.

"Just because you lost your religion doesn't mean the rest of us have."

Jared brought a hand to his forehead. The depths of Scott's sadism sank in. If he had killed Lee and Analise, what would stop him from taking a scalpel to Jared's throat, or the blunt edge of the black tomahawk to Jared's skull?

When Jared and Scott first met, twelve years earlier, they spent most of their free time holed up in the den of Scott's apartment. Talking about the pointlessness of life. Wishing trauma and tragedy on those who had wronged them, from former classmates to ex-girlfriends to psychologically abusive family members. Listening to the genre's standard bearers—*Under the Sign of the Black Mark, A Blaze in the Northern Sky, The Mighty Contract*—along with classics from the likes of Kiss, W.A.S.P., and, of course, Alice Cooper. Between bong hits they picked up their guitars and traded riffs that ultimately became the songs of their demo and, later, their first album. They also thumbed through the pages of ancient books about giving life to the dark forces that could bring humanity to its knees.

142

Jared had escaped the fantasy by the time he turned twenty-five. Not Scott. Clearly, not Scott.

"Oh, by the way, we're all systems go for The House of Rock Showcase on Saturday," Scott said. "We go on third, apparently."

Jared could not be bothered to think about Saturday, when they would have a three-song audition in front of a handful of agents, record-company execs, and talent professionals, in hopes of landing a recording contract. He studied a splotch of red on the kitchen tile. Someone else's blood slicked his floor, stained his clothes, tainted the flesh of his hands.

"Scott ... the bodies."

"Don't worry about 'em. We'll take 'em apart tomorrow. Yank out the teeth and cut off the fingertips, remove any tattoos—make 'em unrecognizable. Then we haul 'em out of here, one bag at a time. Maybe take a drive out to Tinicum by the airport and hurl 'em into the tidal marsh. Whatever you think is best, man."

"I shouldn't have to tell you how wrong this is." He wanted to say *all life is precious*, or something to that effect, but instead went with, "Lee was our friend."

He should have called the cops the moment Scott popped the trunk.

"Listen, what's done is done," Scott said. "All to serve the cause."

"My *cause* is to live peacefully. I'm not down with this, man. Any of it."

"Once you're in, you don't leave. You know this. What happened tonight is the first strike, opening the door inch by inch."

"Then what? Then you're going to conjure some world-ending beast from the shadow dimension and bring the hammer down on humanity's head?"

"You got a good memory, man. The unraveling of this world has already begun."

The walls throbbed, likely because the amplifiers were located on the other side of the veil of ply wood separating the stage from the so-called dressing room. The room was little more than a glorified closet with a toilet, a mirror, and three folding chairs. A sole light bulb dangled from the ceiling.

Jared applied the last white smudge of his corpse paint. He dragged a line of black makeup down from the bottom of each eye, then up toward his forehead, the way Alice Cooper had taught him, and then down either side of his mouth. Kyle and Leonard sat nearby, preparing for the task ahead.

There was no sign of Scott.

"Where is the son of a bitch?" Kyle said. He twirled his black drumsticks nervously.

Leonard, given his introversion, ran through scales on his bass without saying a word.

"He'll be here," Jared said, though he struggled to tamp down his doubtfulness.

Maybe someone had found Scott out. Maybe Scott had confessed to his crime. Maybe the cops would bust down the door at any minute and ferry Jared into a room with no windows and, later, lock him in a cage with all the other animals.

A knock rattled the dressing room door. In popped a woman of about thirty-five—Marcy, the production assistant for the showcase—rail thin with purplish-red hair and black lipstick.

"You guys all set?" she asked.

Jared was ready to bail, in part because he wanted to throw up, but also because the band could not get through a set without its lead guitarist. A shadowy figure appeared directly behind Marcy the PA.

"Ready when you fuckers are," Scott said.

"'Bout time, asshole," Kyle said to Scott, punching him on the shoulder as he passed.

Jared was the last to exit the dressing room. How could he go through with the show given the crime he had abetted?

"We need to talk," he told Scott.

"After," Scott replied.

"I haven't seen or heard from you since … the other night. We have to resolve—"

"I said after."

Marcy led them down a dark tunnel, toward the left wing of the stage. Red light illuminated the faces of the hundred or more people in the crowd—a few long-haired metalheads among them, but mostly college kids and twenty-somethings better suited for the other bands on the bill: two electronica acts, an acid-rock trio, a folk septet, an alt-country group, a pop-punk band.

"As soon as we're done here," Jared said, "you follow me back and we take care—"

Scott's hand clamped over Jared's mouth. "Shut your trap and stay focused."

Marcy the PA shot Jared a curious glance. Leonard and Kyle did the same.

A cloud of fog rolled across the stage. A funeral dirge rumbled from the house speakers—Ophiophagus's entrance music. The red light blinked out. Marcy urged them on stage, into a womb of complete darkness.

Jared took his spot at center, feeling for the microphone stand. He plucked a pick from the mike stand and turned the volume knob of his Schecter. The dirge stopped, abruptly, as it always did, and the foursome ripped into the first verse of "Sweet Nectar of the Cherub Phallus." Every note perfect, every beat landed. Guttural growls spilled from Jared's mouth.

Every bad memory, every disappointment, every kick in the teeth Jared had ever experienced—all of it melted away.

The song ended as viciously as it began. Howls of delight came from the few longhairs in the crowd. Others looked on horrified, unable to discern the chaos they had seen and heard. Jared looked toward the back of the room, where a small group congregated by a long table. The judge and jury, he figured.

145

Jared felt a presence behind him.

"Take it home, Jay," Scott said. "Brothers, you and me, from now until the end of time."

Scott's words shook Jared out of his euphoria.

Kyle counted off the second song—"Diabolos Immortalis"—and Jared missed his cue.

Then everything went off the rails.

Jared keyed his way into Butter and Mayhem, not turning on any lights until he was in the kitchen. The overheads hummed to life. He flicked on the radio and tuned to WRTI. Chuck Mangione's "Feels So Good" echoed in the open space.

Jared's mind replayed the prior night's events as he fetched yesterday's dough slabs. The showcase had been, in a word, disastrous. By the middle of the third song, Scott had unplugged his guitar and walked off stage. Scott, with guitar case in hand and corpse paint smeared from his face, told Jared as he left the stage to pitiable applause: "You'll be seeing me."

Jared tore the plastic wrap from a sheet of prepared dough and sliced the dough into rectangles, and then triangles, and folded chocolate sticks into each crescent. Row upon row of would-be pastries filled several cookie sheets ready for the oven. He went to the walk-in to gather butter for the *détrempé*—the foundation for tomorrow's croissants. His eyes automatically moved to the spot where he and Scott had placed Lee and Analise.

The bodies were gone. Not a trace.

Had he dreamed it all? He knew better. Scott must have taken them. But when? And why? A siren blared in the distance.

He followed the darkened hall toward the rehearsal room. A trickle of orange light squeezed through the space between the bottom of the door and the threshold. He yanked open the door.

"Just in time," Scott said without looking.

Scott kneeled in the center of a circle of red dust, a black square scrawled onto the floor inside the circle. A symbol—a *sigil*—was etched into each of the square's four corners. The bodies of Lee and Analise sat at the circle's edge. Cold vapors rose from their open mouths.

"This ends now," Jared said. "I'm calling the cops. Leave now and you'll have a head start."

Scott had other plans. He drizzled dark liquid—blood, it had to be—onto an object at the center of the circle: the obsidian blade and ebony handle of the tomahawk. Scott uttered gibberish, though Jared recognized the final word: *Abroghast*.

A column of smoke and flame sprouted from the tomahawk, billowing out to fill the entire room. From its center emerged a hideous beast: a sinewy, scale-covered body, the wings of a dragon, the semi-skeletonized head of a jackal. Maggot-like creatures with human faces wriggled across every inch of the beast's blistered body.

"You did it," Jared whispered, both appalled and amazed. "You fucking did it."

Scott had summoned Abroghast, a grand duke of Hell, with a legion of thirty-seven demons under his command. Spreader of disease and famine, destroyer of civilizations, slayer of hope and men. The smell of decay hung heavy in the air.

"Rise!" Scott said. "Rise and feast!"

Abroghast descended on the bodies of Lee and Analise. The beast dismantled each corpse with ferocity. Teeth snapped through frozen bone. Gore sprayed the walls. A detached finger smacked Jared in the forehead.

"Two worlds meet," Scott said, "and one consumes the other."

Jared grabbed one of his guitars by the neck and cracked Scott over the head. Scott slumped forward. Jared kicked away the edges of the circle. Abroghast roared, arms outstretched, its open maw revealing strips of his friends' shredded flesh. The cloud shimmered, spewing smoke and tongues of blue flame, and collapsed in on itself. Abroghast disappeared, but its horrid smell clung to the membrane of Jared's nostrils.

Scott rolled onto his back, groggy. Blood leaked from a gash in the back of his head.

"I can't believe you did it," Jared said. "It's madness."

He picked up the tomahawk. Somehow Scott had trapped the demon within the tomahawk. He turned the weapon over in his hands. It somehow felt alive, electrified. He smashed it against one of the Marshall amplifiers until it shattered into splinters of wood and stone.

Scott laughed quietly.

"You think that's going to make a damn bit of difference?" he said.

"Vessel's destroyed. Doorway's closed."

Scott's laughter grew in volume and intensity.

"You didn't banish them," he said. "Abroghast and his legions, they're here to stay."

Jared's hand tightened around the neck of the guitar. He lifted the instrument over his head and bludgeoned Scott, again and again, until his friend no longer moved. His chest heaving with exertion, he wiped speckles of Scott's blood from his face and scanned the room—nothing but a gore-soaked crime scene. His eyes landed on the barrel of a pyrotechnic canister staring out from the corner.

He knew what he must do.

The smell of charred wood hung in the air as Jared put in his ear buds and opened the Spotify app on his phone. He chose the *Everything's Fine* playlist. James Taylor's "Fire and Rain" led the way. How ironic.

He ducked under the police tape roping off the store front of Butter and Mayhem. Broken glass and shards of burnt timber crunched under his sneakers.

148

As he swept the detritus into small piles, the broom's bristles broke up the char and colored the pavement black.

Jared wondered if the detectives would uncover any evidence of the goings-on that led to Butter and Mayhem's destruction—the blood and body parts, the sigils used to summon Abroghast, the means Jared had used to conjure the fireball. Maybe his handiwork had burned everything to a crisp and the aftermath looked like enough of an accident for someone in charge to say, "All clear, hope your insurance check comes through."

Earlier that morning, when Monica returned home from her shift at the hospital and found him with his head in his hands at the kitchen table, she asked, "Shouldn't you be out making the doughnuts?" He then told her about the bakery's demise, choosing to leave out the incriminating bits. Toward the end, as he insisted he would find other means of employment, she cut him off, adding, "Call it a blessing, 'cause that place was a money pit anyway." She then added, "Look, I have to get some sleep. If you're around when I wake up, we can talk about the divorce then."

Not that any of it would matter in the long run.

Dark clouds rolled in from the south. A sour wind whipped down the empty street. The ominous weather seemed like a precursor to the cataclysms Hell's princes and presidents would soon visit upon the mortal world.

A thirty-something man with closely cropped hair, wearing too-snug jeans and a tight-fitting Misfits T-shirt—some poseur—approached Jared with a smart phone in hand. He stopped at the border of police tape and seemed to study Jared. His eyes moved from his phone to Jared and back again.

"Can I help you, buddy?" Jared said, though his tone suggested he was in no mood to help anyone. He removed his ear buds so he could hear the answer.

The man held out his phone to Jared and said, "This you, dude?"

Despite the phone's cracked screen, Jared could easily see the *Grit and Glamour* "Besties" logo atop an article titled, "Hail the Black-Metal Baker."

Jared's shoulders drooped.

The story featured a photo of Jared in the lobby of Butter and Mayhem. One of the magazine's graphic designers had doctored up Jared's face with sketched-on corpse makeup, and crowned his head and shoulders with cartoonish tongues of orange flame. The first paragraph introduced Jared as a locally born and bred baker who had descended into the city's "dark and seedy" black-metal scene. The next paragraph detailed Ophiophagus's basement-level spot in Philadelphia's dying rock 'n' roll scene. The description of the tattoos on his left arm as "scars of hyper masculine rage and intolerance" felt like a knife between the ribs.

So much for Mallory Quinn's promise to focus on the bakery.

Another paragraph listed two song titles from Ophiophagus's first album, *Eternal War*, both of which were off by one word. On and on the story went, suggesting that Jared, despite his "devilish leanings," seemed like a kind, quiet, and hardworking fella. A quote from Kyle, the drummer in Jared's recently deceased band, intimated the same.

The story eventually circled back to Jared's "barebones bakery" in Fishtown.

He scrolled down to the story's last paragraph: "Don't expect anything fancy. A delicate coating of flour dusts every surface. The menu board and display case could use some TLC. And the framed photos lining the scuffed tile walls display the owner's devotion to a form of artistic expression some might characterize as malevolence set to music. The chocolate croissants are pretty good, though. *Damned* good, you might say."

He handed the phone back to the poseur in the Misfits shirt and turned toward the ruined storefront. A fire-blasted hole stared back. He could not have imagined a more perfect metaphor for his life—a heap of promise reduced to a ruined shell.

As he pondered the demise of the man he had almost become, and the all-but-certain dooming of the world that reared him, courtesy of the demon he had helped unleash, he returned his ear buds to their rightful place. The chorus of Alice Cooper's "I Never Cry" filled his ears. Given the tears forming in the corner of each eye, he could not have chosen a better soundtrack.

William J. Donahue's published works of dark fiction includes the novels *Crawl on Your Belly All the Days of Your Life* and *Burn, Beautiful Soul*. When not writing stories about monsters and madmen, Donahue fosters kittens, talks to trees, and earns a living as a features writer and the editor of a lifestyle magazine and literary journal.

The Talent Scout

Rhys Hughes

The talent scout said, "I have something really special for you today. In all my years of doing the job, I never knew anything like this. They are going to be big, I tell you. I can feel it in my bones."

"You have bones?" said the music mogul with his usual mix of aggression and humor. But he was attentive enough. A slim man with a corpulent face, an elder cynic of this cutthroat world, perched on a wheeled swivel chair with such precise bearings that it could spin around in complete silence and glide over the tiled floor like an unfocussed ghost.

The talent scout reached into the pocket of his coat.

"Here!" he cried, squinting.

Jackfruit Bursts, mightiest mogul of the Almighty Racket record label now took it upon himself to lean forward until the cigar that protruded from his thick lips touched the desk and acted like a pillar to take the weight of his head while his eyes swiveled to regard the object the talent scout had set down in front of him. He gurgled as he recognized it.

"A goddamn matchbox," he spluttered.

"They are going to be massive," said the talent scout.

"Who the hell is?"

"Inside!" And the talent scout opened the matchbox, while Jackfruit leaned back and resumed his former position.

The mogul saw nothing, heard nothing, understood less.

"What are you playing at?"

"It's not me who's playing," said the talent scout triumphantly, "but them. I can't believe my luck at scoring these guys. It was purely by chance when I took a wrong turn and went to the wrong club last night. The place was empty or so I thought. But then I noticed them. Playing to themselves, to nobody, and I waited and listened and I was blown away."

Jackfruit considered the matter gravely.

"Have you been drinking?"

"Not a drop. I don't touch the stuff these days."

"Snorting drugs then?"

"Clean as a whistle, cleaner in fact, boss. Listen."

"Why should I listen to you?"

"To *them*! Not to me. Listen to them, to the band!"

Jackfruit snorted angrily.

"It's just a goddamn empty matchbox, you fool."

"No, no, you'll find out."

The talent scout looked around the room eagerly.

Jackfruit sighed in dismay.

"Do you have such a thing as a stethoscope, boss? That way, you'll be able to hear them properly. They are playing right now. They never stop playing and they only have one song but it lasts forever. It's a sort of curse, very heavy, truly monstrous. They had amplification in the club, a really elaborate set-up, and the speakers were howling like impaled werewolves, and it was horrible and it was bitter and it was magnificent. I felt the blood drain from my face and I can't say if it will ever return. I was demolished."

Jackfruit's mood abruptly changed. He found madmen to be amusing and he wanted to enjoy this encounter to the full. He planned to sack the talent scout immediately afterwards, of course.

"A stethoscope in my office? I really think that's unlikely. But there might be one you can borrow from the medical college next door. We've done favors for them in the past and I reckon they will do something for us in return. I'll be here when you get back. Waiting…"

The talent scout nodded, turned and clattered out of the office. Jackfruit smirked to himself and picked up the matchbox. He held it close to his ear and rattled it but still heard only silence.

The music business was full of lunatics and liars.

Jackfruit puffed on his cigar.

He had known the talent scout for a long time and was confident the man only spoke the truth and never lied. Therefore he must be crazy. That was logic and the mogul prided himself on his logical mind. Ruthless logic had enabled him to fulfill his ambitions, to make enormous amounts of money at this game, to be a real force in the music industry.

As for the talent scout, did he even have a name?

Jackfruit was unable to remember if he had ever known it, and he decided to dismiss the question as unimportant. A talent scout was a tool who existed to be used, and he was the ultimate user.

Fifteen minutes later, the talent scout returned, out of breath, but clutching a stethoscope in one hand, a silvery snake that would bite the eardrums of those who cared to be injected with the addictive venom of shocking music. He held it out for Jackfruit to take. An offering.

"Now we'll see what the goddamn hell you mean."

The mogul lifted the matchbox. The earpieces of the stethoscope were deep inside his ears and he pressed the other end of the instrument, the diaphragm, to the top of the little cardboard box.

His firm jaw went slack. The cigar fell out.

It landed on his leg and began to scorch a hole in his expensive trousers but he ignored the pain. He was far too engrossed in what he was hearing to care for such distractions. The infernal noise!

It was infernal but also blissful. Demonic but ecstatic.

He gibbered with delight.

The reverberation of drums, like the repeated collision of a gigantic robot's head against a hurtling asteroid in outer space. The guitars, wailing like donkeys that have fallen out of airplanes. The bass, rumbling like an earthquake below a nuclear power station. The whole thing!

Together, these miniature instruments heralded the end of the world. Sonic apocalypse. Waves of brilliant nausea.

They spelled out the word Doom in capital letters and those letters burned like phosphorus bombs in an orphanage.

It was the heaviest metal in the known universe.

Truly abysmal and atrocious and extraordinary music! Jackfruit, in a rage of revelation, yanked the earpieces out of his head, flung the stethoscope down and jumped onto his desk with surprising agility. Then he began dancing like a ripe fool, a martyred mystic or an electrocuted criminal. He yelled and drooled, a man possessed by his own incredulity.

"Genius! Genius!" he howled like a rabid mongoose.

The talent scout bowed low.

"I told you, didn't I? The best thing ever, boss!"

"The best thing ever."

Jackfruit finished his impromptu dance and a blush of shame darkened his massive cheeks as he climbed back down, with difficulty, to the ground and sat once more on his amazing swivel chair.

"I am going to sign them at once! Immediately, you hear?"

"That's for the best, boss."

"For the best and also for the worst. Yes!"

He was shouting angrily.

But there was also love in his stern voice.

Then he cooled down.

He said, "So these are little guys, huh? Microscopic life?"

"Invisible to the eye, boss."

"The *naked* eye, you mean? Not to microscopes?"

"That's quite correct."

"Tiny men. Well, now! What is the band called?"

"Chimps of Oblivion."

"OK, I get it. That's not bad, I suppose."

"But they aren't men."

"What? Are they monkeys? Tiny monkeys! Hell."

"Chimps aren't monkeys."

"Then what the hairy goddamn heck are they?"

"Apes, boss, that's what."

"So they are miniscule apes, is that right?"

The talent scout grinned.

"That's the beauty of this. The beauty and the horror. Miniature apemen. Half and half, up and down, inside and out. Men when seen from one angle but apes when seen from another."

"How do you know? Tell me quickly."

"There was a microscope at the club where they were playing. I borrowed it, with the owner's permission."

"Listen carefully. You have done good work."

"I believe so too, boss."

"Take the rest of the day off. I need to draw up a contract for this band and it's going to take me a while. You'll get a big bonus for this. I have never heard such heavy music in my life. It's so metal that it makes metal look like plastic! It's positively transuranic! A rare find."

"Chimps of Oblivion," repeated the talent scout.

"Shut the door behind you."

The talent scout went without protest. He would probably go home to bed, the mogul decided. They were essentially lazy, these people. Meanwhile, there was a lot to be done. Paperwork, reams of it, a contract with clauses of

156

various kinds, and some method needed to be found to enable the band to sign the damn thing legibly once it was prepared.

But Jackfruit Bursts was wrong about the talent scout, who slept less than normal men, not more. He was free to go about his own business and so he went to the forest on the outskirts of the city.

This was his hobby, his passion, second only to music. He slipped between the trees, pushed deeper into the woodland. As he loped, he divested himself of his clothes until he was naked. A hobby he was unable to indulge as often as he would have liked. But today he could.

He was a scout, a talent scout in his working hours but just a scout when he was alone. He reached a small clearing and dropped to his knees, digging at the soil in his secret place. His fingers soon connected with a wooden lid and with a grunt he lifted a bulky crate out of the hole. He opened it and took out what it contained. Spare clothes and a knife.

The clothes were buckskins, wide leggings and a fringed jacket, with a pair of sturdy but soft leather boots, and a coonskin cap. That was all. The knife was a Bowie, a Jim rather than a David, with a blade 9¼ inches long and 1½ inches wide and a so-called Spanish notch near the hilt. A fine weapon indeed, weighty but well-balanced and thus highly mobile.

There is a city in the United States of America called Mobile and that must be highly mobile too, thought the talent scout as he straightened up and looked around. Maybe not, he added wistfully, and then he closed his mind to mundane matters and turned his full attention to scouting. He was a scout and scouting is exactly what scouts do, come hell or high water, fire or brimstone, volcanoes or quicksands, falling trees or furious squirrels.

He chose a direction and hurried to scout in that part of the forest. Moving from the cover of tree trunk to tree trunk, stepping softly on the moss, his eyes missing no movement of leaf in the breeze, he felt the spirit of another age enter his modern body, saturating it with atavistic power. He was Davy Crockett and Genghis Khan rolled into one. A feral hero.

Feral and fatal. On most scouting trips the worst thing he did was to fling his knife at ripe apples or pears, often missing, but infrequently he would strike lucky, and today was such a happy occasion.

A solitary hiker in the woods! No, not a hiker, for he had no backpack. Just a man then, alone and unaware, a grunt, a timid, a target. Suppressing an urge to whoop, the talent scout moved forward.

The stranger seemed oblivious of everything. He was drunk or stoned, lost in the forest and not caring, a hippy making no attempt at camouflage, his long hair and beard too clean, blue tattoos signaling through the trees, stumbling and snapping twigs like the fingers of gods.

The talent scout waited for a few minutes

His approach was silent.

He came up behind the stranger and flung him roughly to the ground with a judo move. "Lookee here," he said.

The stranger blinked up at him uncomprehendingly.

"Hippy, are you, boy?"

The stranger coughed. "Man, that's wild."

"What is? Nature itself?"

"You came from nowhere. Didn't hear you. My eardrums are throbbing; I loved the gig but had to get away."

The talent scout frowned. "What gig?"

"I was at a festival, man. It's still going on. Let me get up."

"Stay where you are."

"Sure, man, take it easy, brother."

"Speak about the gig."

"On the other side of the forest. In a meadow. I'm no hippy, I'm a genuine metalhead. Listen, man. I'm half deaf now. It was phenomenal. Bands unique to our age, our place in the universe."

"Unique in what way? Describe what you saw."

"The heaviest bands, man."

The talent scout raised his knife until a rogue sunbeam, turned green by the filtering of the canopy of the lofty trees, reflected off it into the stranger's eyes, making him squint. He also wriggled on the ground and gasped, "Man," several more times. The talent scout leered.

"There are no bands heavier than the ones I know."

"That's not my fault, man."

"What were the names of these bands?"

"The heaviest of all called themselves Oxygen Deprivation. They cancelled out all the others. They are still unsigned. They are miracle workers, demoniacal and impossible. They cut me up."

"Well, it's good to know what *that* feels like."

"Maybe, man, maybe."

"Unsigned, you say? Almighty Racket Records are always on the *hunt* for new acts. Did you appreciate the way I stressed the word 'hunt'? I'm a hunter, of talent and men, of anything at all."

"Whatever, man. I'm going home to recover."

"I will check out this festival."

"Better hurry. It'll be over soon. They were halfway through their set when I left. I couldn't take any more."

"Oxygen Deprivation. Are they really so special?"

"They have a gimmick, man."

"Many of us do. But tell me about theirs."

"They play air guitars."

The talent scout recoiled in deep disgust.

"You must die," he said.

"You don't understand, man. Air guitars and all the other instruments also are air. I don't mean that they pretend to play. They really play. But guitars and bass and drums are made from air. Frozen air. You know how if you cool air it will turn to liquid? Freeze it even more and it becomes solid. Appallingly cold but solid. They have instruments like that, man. They play air guitar, air bass, air drums. They play solid frozen air!"

The talent scout was intrigued now. He decided to terminate the stranger quickly. He wasted no time flaying the fellow or even taking his scalp. He just cut his throat and finished with it.

He would return later to bury the body.

His costume would be mocked at the festival but it was too late to change back into his other clothes. He ran.

The forest was large but he was very fast.

He hurtled out of the cover of the trees and sprinted across the meadow to the collection of tents and stages where the festival was. The sound was intense and brilliantly awful, no less remarkable than the sonic assault of the Chimps of Oblivion. What a remarkable music day!

And he saw that Oxygen Deprivation were on their last song. The frontman strutted, the guitarist noodled, the drummer thrashed, the bassist gurned. And all of them had instruments of solid air.

That were translucent but not transparent.

That were frosty and evil.

And that steamed in the glare of the sun like the vapors from the clogged nostrils of sleeping snot demons. They were slowly evaporating. The musicians wore special gloves to handle them.

Now the talent scout was no longer able to repress his urge to whoop. But few heard him above the music.

"Whoooooo! Whoopeeee! Wooooooohaaaaa!"

The victory cry of a scout.

His next impulse was to wound himself in the groin, to stab his cock meat with the tip of the knife, but he successfully resisted this nudging of the imp of the perverse, the same imp that told him to jump off high buildings and plunge into dirty rivers. He ignored it.

He pushed his way through the crowd to the front of the stage. There was a mosh pit here and metalheads jumped against each other, frothing with joy and delirium, proving Newton's laws of motion with their bones and flesh, bouncing and tumbling and hopping and bruising.

"I love you!" shouted the talent scout at the band.

They played on and cascaded.

The cascade turned into a crescendo.

It was totally blistering.

The talent scout made the sign of the horns.

"Ugh! Yah! Whooooo!"

Some part of his consciousness remained cool and rational but the rest of it willingly abandoned itself to a frenzy. He seemed to be standing outside himself and watching his own antics. He saw that he was climbing on the stage, lunging for the lead guitar with outstretched hands.

The singer was bawling something at him. Telling him about gloves, about the importance of fucking right off.

The talent scout was oblivious to everything.

He just wanted to clutch the guitar tight and tell the band who he was. Tell them that he worked for Jackfruit Bursts. Win another bonus. Maybe Chimps of Oblivion and Oxygen Deprivation would end up playing on the same bill. What a delicious catastrophe that would be!

The singer tried to headbutt him. He dodged the blow.

He pounced on the guitar.

His smile froze solid and crumbled.

All the atoms in his body and soul burned coldly.

He screamed and the singer, against his will, nodded appreciatively as the talent scout reached the highest note.

In fact he was able to incorporate the scream into the lyrics of the song, the last number of the set. "I want to bum a yeti / I want to fudge his mom / I crave a clue / as to who / I can bum that yeti with…"

It worked perfectly.

But the talent scout collapsed and left his hands behind. They were stuck to the guitar. His stumps waved pathetically.

And he knew nothing more until he awoke in hospital…

He was lying on a white bed.

His stumps were bandaged and throbbed gently.

He cried softly to himself.

The door opened and a nurse came in. She was a traditional nurse, dressed in a skirt unnecessarily short with a blouse that was bursting with anticipation to reveal the generous curves of her chest. But she was brisk and professional too and her smile was full of paid concern.

"You have a visitor," she said, "waiting outside."

"A visitor?" he mumbled.

"It's a person who comes to spend an amount of time with another person. That's the dictionary definition. Look it up."

"How can I turn the pages with these?" he blurted.

He held up his stumps.

"Try an audiobook edition," she replied.

He resumed sobbing.

"Shall I show him in or not?" she asked.

He nodded and she went out into the corridor. It was Jackfruit Bursts who now came into the room, his slim body and massive head giving the impression he was a cartoon figure come to life.

"Been in the wars?" he said jovially and vehemently.

"Frozen air," came the reply.

Jackfruit nodded, sat himself down on a chair next to the bed and said with derision in his voice, "I have a gift for you."

"For me? Really?"

"Yes, a goddamn gift, Thing is, not every opportunity is worthwhile in the end. Not every avenue paved with gold leads to the hot tub of satisfaction. You understand what I'm saying, pal?"

"I comprehend you to a certain degree."

"Turns out the band was rubbish. Chimps of Oblivion! Sure, they have that one song that goes on forever and it is _heavy_, the heaviest song ever heard by a mortal man. But that's the problem. Songs need to come to an end to have a true commercial value. They need to achieve a resolution. I never heard of an eternal song that made anyone rich. I decided to drop the bastards after signing them. It means I have lost some money."

"How much?" whispered the talent scout.

"Who cares? I hate losing money, even if it's only one penny. And I doubt your hands will ever grow back, so what use are you to me? You are sacked and that's the end of our association."

"But I found another great band. Don't be hasty, boss."

"Are they microscopic too?"

"No, but they play instruments made from solid air!"

"Too bad. Goodbye, chum."

"But I have a name. You never asked me what it was. My name is Stumps. It's a horribly ironic name now!"

He waved his real stumps in the air.

"No dice," said Jackfruit.

He placed a gift-wrapped object on the bed and departed. The door closed behind him and that was all. The end.

The talent scout was hyperventilating now.

He calmed himself with effort. He gazed at the object on the bed and with jerks of his body he managed to move it closer to his head. Then he leaned over to rip at the paper with his teeth.

What was inside? What was the parting gift? He gulped as it was revealed and he struggled to put it back inside the wrapping paper, but that was futile and eventually he abandoned the attempt.

A Petri dish. Borrowed, no doubt, from the medical college adjacent to the offices of Almighty Racket Records.

The surface of the dish was black with bacteria.

No, not bacteria. Something worse.

Worse *and* better. The spores of the apocalypse.

Jackfruit Bursts had been clever and malevolent. He had transferred all the members of Chimps of Oblivion from the matchbox to the Petri dish, knowing they would rapidly multiply through division, just like amoebas. There must be billions of them on the dish, all playing.

Yes, all of them playing guitars, drums, bass, or shrieking out vocals, and there were so many of them that the noise was audible to the human ear without the aid of amplifiers or stethoscopes.

The din was incredible. It was monumental.

It was utterly deadly.

The eardrums of the talent scout began vibrating to the rhythm of the mass of music. This vibrating spread through his head and now his skull itself flexed and pulsated, the sutures grinding against each other as the separate plates were alternately pulled apart and compressed.

The force of the vibrating kept increasing. It was relentless.

He laughed and screamed.

Billions, even trillions, of atomic notes.

The nurse came to see what the trouble was, but her pace was leisurely and there was no urgency in her attitude even when she opened the door and found a mess that would take hours to clean up.

The talent scout's head had finally exploded.

His mouth had been flung across the room and the wet lips and tongue had adhered themselves to the wall with sticky drool. She turned to regard them and saw how the mouth smiled at her.

Despite her annoyance she smiled back.

Then she went to the bed and turned down the volume control on the Petri dish until there was just a faint hum.

The tiny apemen were already spilling out.

And spreading over the bed.

And the surface of the entire world.

Where would it end?

She knew the answer instinctively.

It never would.

Rhys Hughes began writing fiction at an early age and his first book, *Worming the Harpy*, was published in 1995. Since that time he has published more than fifty other books and his short stories have been translated into ten languages. He has recently completed an ambitious project that involved writing exactly one thousand linked narratives. His most recent books are the collection of flash fiction, *Comfy Rascals*, and a volume of tribute stories to authors he admires, *The Senile Pagodas*, and he is currently working on a book of weird crime stories called *The Reconstruction Club*. Fantasy, humor, science fiction, horror, satire, whimsy, adventure, irony and paradoxes are combined in his work to create a distinctive style.

A Darker Sound

M. J. McClymont

Angus stabbed the screen of the smart phone with his forefinger. The built in hands-free in the Fiesta clicked, this was followed by the distant sound of white noise and then silence.

"Great, just perfect," he said, slapping the steering wheel and pulling over on to the grass verge of the winding country road.

He snatched his phone off its cradle and looked at the screen. No bars. The 4G connection to the network had dropped, causing the SatNav app and every other app on his handset to stop working. Now he had no way of letting Sue know that he would be home later than expected.

Angus threw the driver door open with little care for passing traffic. There was no need, hell; he hadn't seen another vehicle on the road for the past eight miles or so. He cursed himself for not following the diversion signs back to the motorway when he had the opportunity. He always had to be a smart arse and trust in tech and his instincts. This had proven to be folly on more than one occasion of late. "Never mind, lesson learned, let's get back to it," he muttered, taking in his surroundings.

In the dwindling light, all Angus could make out, other than the black strip of tarmac disappearing into the distance, were trees, fields and hedges. Every variance of green and brown surrounded him. There were no notable landmarks and no signs or road markings to indicate his whereabouts. He was *out in the sticks*, as Sue had put it the last time he followed his unerring sense of direction straight to catastrophe. They had arrived late for the Iron Maiden gig Sue booked six months in advance and were initially denied admittance by a burly, power drunk security lackey with a paunch any sumo wrestler would be envious of. When they were finally given the all clear, after demanding to speak to a supervisor, they realized they had missed the opening sequence of Maiden's set. Sue had fumed about it for weeks afterwards, spurring the installation of the SatNav app on Angus's phone; a fat load of good that had done him. Now he couldn't even find his way home from work.

He entered the vehicle and pulled his seatbelt over, fastening it with a snap. *No point in burning daylight, what's left of it,* he thought as he pulled out away from the verge. The plan was to follow the road until he reached a sign for the motorway or in fact for any sign at all that would help him find his way home. It wasn't much of a plan but despite his past navigational failures, Angus felt hopeful.

From the driver's side speaker, Ronnie James Dio was telling him to, "Look out," because the world was spinning round. All Angus could see was the rolling blur of hedgerows in his periphery and the black, unmarked road in front of him which rumbled beneath the car like a treadmill.

An hour later and countless miles down the road he finally caught sight of a sign, glowing in the headlights like a beacon. He slowed the Fiesta to a crawl before he stopped and engaged the handbrake. He studied the battered metal through the open window, narrowing his eyes in an attempt to make out the words written there. After a few seconds of peering, Angus was able to decipher the faded script, BLACKCROFT FARM 2M. Next to this, an arrow pointing up indicated the direction of the farm.

Night had rolled across the landscape swiftly like an unfurled bolt of black fabric, silencing the wildlife and tiredness crept up on Angus. If he could just find his whereabouts, he would summon the energy to continue. But if he carried on down this route regardless, he may find himself nodding off at the wheel or missing an essential turn. There wasn't much of a decision to be made. With a rev of the engine and a lengthy sigh, he jerked the wheel to the left, and followed the side road to Blackcroft Farm.

The country road tested the car's suspension to the extreme but it wasn't long until Angus arrived at a set of buildings of various sizes. Two large wooden barns, steady, yet dilapidated sat at the right side of what could barely be described as a road. The wooden panels of the barn appeared jagged and crumbling where they met the damp ground like the ragged hem of a witch's dress. On the left a number of squat buildings lined the road. The buildings had once been whitewashed but time and the tempestuous British clime had worn them down to a few filthy patches here and there.

Beyond, the headlights revealed a portion of land which had clearly lain fallow for some time; a green carpet of docks had broken the surface. Angus started when, in his peripheral vision he caught the movement of something large. His heart rate slowed to a normal pace when he realized that the creature was a big brown and white mare standing forlornly. The horse flicked its tail against its barreled side intermittently and gazed towards the car. Other than the presence of the horse, the complex appeared to be deserted.

Angus exited the car leaving the keys in the ignition and the headlights on. He had taken a cautious step toward the door of the farmstead when a niggling cadence wavering on the edge of his perception caused him to pause. A high piercing whine infused with a warbling noise, shifting in pitch, redolent of the sound effects of flying saucers taking off in the old monochrome science fiction movies Angus would sneak out of bed to watch in his youth when his parents were asleep. The more he concentrated on the sound, the more it worked its way into his mind, weaving unsettling tendrils of malaise across the creases of his brain. The warbling became a thunder of down tuned guitars and the grating barrage of screaming metal vocals, but it was like no black metal he had ever heard. He mashed his ears against the sides of his head, pushing the heels of his palms hard, but this had little effect on the sound drilling into his temples.

Angus's head ached and he felt nauseous. He turned away from the homestead and crossed the rugged strip of mud and stone to the barn hoping that distance would reduce the volume of the sound and the pressure inside his skull, but it seemed to have no fixed source. It was everywhere, surrounding him in an auditory assault, penetrating his mind with dread. Then it faded. His ears could no longer detect the sound yet it still resounded inside him for a few seconds before dying.

The thunderous sound of rollers on a heavy sliding door caused Angus to turn sharply, jerking the nerves at the base of his back as he did so. He winced.

"This is private property. What are you doing here?"

An elderly man, hunched in a thin, rachitic posture and carrying a battery powered lamp stepped from the gloomy recess. Angus staggered back, silently cursing himself for his lack of nerve.

"Ah, I um, I'm afraid I've lost my way."

"What's your destination?" The stoic faced man peered over Angus's shoulder towards the Fiesta.

"The M77 actually, there were diversions, road works, you see. I was heading home from..."

The old man let out a harsh, phlegm shifting bark. "You're a long way from the M77, mate. How the fuck did you manage to get here from the motorway?"

Angus winced. "I'm a terrible navigator," he said, shrugging.

"You ought to get yourself one of them satellite navigation things."

"I have an app, and I still got lost. What can I say, I'm an idiot."

"Sounds like it."

The old man scanned Angus and when their eyes met, Angus felt discomfort rising from his core. The old man seemed to notice this and a taut smile opened across his face like a knife wound, revealing brown and yellow teeth, crooked and broken rows of ancient tombstones between hollow cheeks. He stepped close and Angus had to force himself to remain where he was, holding his breath in an attempt to avoid the weft of rot from the old man's grisly maw. His eyes were rimmed with shadow and what was left of his hair was slicked down against his pale cranium, a grinning skull balanced atop a narrow, wrinkled neck.

"Bert," he said at last, breaking the growing sense of unease Angus felt.

"Angus."

"Come away in for a cuppa." Bert motioned towards the worn structure adjacent and stepped past Angus. Despite his trepidation, Angus followed.

He entered the cottage, taking in his surroundings. The sitting room was small and cozy with candles casting a soft glow against the walls. Rows of old photographs lined an alcove above the hearth. Angus realized, with a modicum of surprise that this was the first time he had seen a functional coal fire since he had been a small child. The incandescent flames flickered and danced, rising and falling like some abstract animation, mesmerizing him. The homely surroundings were unexpected. Slowly, Angus felt his heart rate return to a normal pace.

"Have a seat. I'll stick the kettle on."

Angus thanked him, sinking into the recess of a two-seater settee and allowing his mind a reprieve from the stress that had been mounting since leaving the motorway.

Bert reached over and carefully lifted the tonearm of a retro record player and took a record from the turntable, sliding it carefully into a cardboard sleeve. Angus wondered if the record had been responsible for the bizarre sounds he had heard.

While studying English Literature in University, his then roommate had curious taste in dark and experimental music and although the noise Angus had witnessed sounded similar, the sound he heard on Blackcroft Farm didn't appear quite as innocuous as his roommate's music. Music, no matter what type should not have that affect on anyone. He pushed the thought aside when Bert left the room, appearing some minutes later with mugs of tea and a plate of digestive biscuits.

Angus's thoughts returned to Sue. She would be worried about him. He wondered how many missed calls he would have from her when he finally managed to charge his phone. He fished his mobile from his pocket and held his finger against the home button. The screen remained dark. *Damn it,* he thought.

"You don't happen to have a charger?" Angus held his phone aloft in explanation.

"Nope," said Bert, baring his rotten teeth to bite a digestive.

"Do you have a phone I could use?"

Bert shook his head. "Don't have one. No one I want to talk to these days, other than the wife."

"I don't suppose either of you have a mobile phone, do you?"

"Nope, no signal out here."

"Internet connection?"

"No need for modern technology. Can't work those computer thingies."

Angus exhaled through his smile. The way the old man had described the internet, a phenomenon commercialized in the nineteen nineties as, 'modern technology', made him wonder just how long Bert and his wife had lived on the farm, isolated from the outside world.

Bert removed a folded sheet of paper from a nearby bookcase, tossing it with little grace on to the coffee table between them. "I do have this though."

Angus picked the roadmap up and began to unfold it. "Thanks," he said.

"Keep it. I have no use for it. It may be a bit outdated but the roads are more or less the same as they have been for years around here. No one uses them, no one comes by anymore."

"I noticed. The roads are in terrible disrepair."

"Like I say, no one uses 'em. A bit off the beaten track is Blackcroft. The last time we had visitors here you were no doubt shitting nappies."

Angus scanned the room for a point of interest that would allow him to change the subject. His eyes returned to the photographs on the alcove.

"Your family," asked Angus, motioning towards the alcove. He stood and paced across the room feeling the toasty heat emanating from the fireplace on his thighs.

"My family, Moira's family, mostly photos of Moira."

Angus lifted a heavy framed picture of an older woman grinning, revealing what were undoubtedly dentures. She wore a purple top with an angular, filigree broach. He nodded his approval and returned it to the shelf. "I'm not disturbing her at all, am I? I mean, I realize it's late. She must be asleep."

Bert shook his head and barked a phlegm shifting peel of laughter at some joke Angus didn't get. "Sleeps like the dead, she does."

"I see," said Angus. He didn't. "Anyway, it's probably time I made tracks."

From outside, a bright flicker of light illuminated the dull room momentarily; this was followed by a deep rumble like the roar of some gargantuan beast looming above and a torrent or rain assaulted the window pane.

"Ah, shit," Angus said, rubbing the nape of his neck vigorously, a stress habit he had developed over time.

"Doesn't look like you're going anywhere tonight. You can stay in the guest bedroom if you like."

Angus considered this for a long moment. He did not want to stay the night, he wanted to leave and return home to his wife. After the day he had, he just needed to be in the comfort of familiar surroundings. When another peel of thunder roared and the ground beneath him quivered, he realized he had little choice in the matter. He was having difficulty locating the Fiesta through the sitting room window, visibility would be nonexistent.

"Are you sure your wife won't mind?"

"Honestly, she won't care."

"Okay, thanks again," Angus said, humbly, sitting down again. "At least your crops will appreciate the rain."

"For what little remains of them. Rain is responsible for a great deal more than the mere growth of crops," said Bert cryptically. "It can be a controller, if a somewhat capricious controller, of destiny. Even the sound of the rain can be a powerful thing indeed. Just listen." Bert cocked his head to one side, his unruly, single patch of eyebrow raised. "Many a grimoire allude to the power of the rain, of sound in general, that rapid beat and some even state that many aspects of the phenomenon can wake the dead."

"Grimoire?" Angus followed his gaze to the wide oak bookcase sitting snug against the wall. He hadn't noticed contents of the shelves before, now that he did, his eyes were drawn inexorably to their titles: *The Book of Abramelin, Magick, The Key of Solomon*. Rows and rows of what Angus identified as books on occultism.

"Ah," said Angus. "I used to dabble a bit in my youth."

"Oh, yeah?"

"Yes, the, um, The Satanic Bible and the rituals book."

Bert waved a hand dismissively. "Lesser magic for beginners. I'm talking about necromancy, conjuring, hexes."

Angus squirmed in the armchair with every example Bert gave. His reticence to stay the night grew with each passing moment. Desperate to change the subject, he poked finger in the direction of the record player and impressive collection of vinyl in the racks beneath. "A music fan, eh?"

"Hmm, metal."

"Ah, I like a bit of rock and metal, mostly stuff from the eighties, y'know? Mind if I, uh, take a look?"

"Be my guest."

Angus crouched next to the music station and began sliding records out one by one, just enough to see the covers. A plethora of black and white corpse painted faces adorned many of the covers. Others featured landscape paintings of cold, dark looking places with gothic architecture beneath illegible band names in unidentifiable font. There were no bands or titles he recognized amongst the sleeves.

"Heavy stuff, eh? I used to listen to a bit of that myself in my college days. Immortal, Bathory, Emperor, Cradle of Filth. I even saw Mayhem live once."

"What you think?"

"Huh?"

"Mayhem, what did you think of 'em when you saw 'em?"

"Oh, well, it was an experience, I suppose. I just thought it would be interesting to see what they're about with all the controversy, you know? The theatrics, their presence, the music..."

"Music, sound itself has the power to change and influence emotion. Combined with carefully selected lyrics and settings though, it can produce the most magnificent works of black magic."

Angus rubbed the nape of his neck. For the second time that evening he found himself an unwilling participant in a conversation he did not feel entirely comfortable with. It seemed like his host really wanted do discuss the dark arts with him. But perhaps Bert was harmless enough and had merely spent too long in isolation with his wife out in 'the sticks' and out of touch with society in general. Maybe that jagged mouthed smile was an attempt at humor or politeness rather than the sadistic, teasing, derisive grin Angus mistook it for.

"Black magic? I don't know much about it, to be honest. Isn't it considered a little dangerous, though?"

"Oh, it's incredibly dangerous, even to the practitioner if he doesn't know what he's doing. But it can also be used to achieve one's deepest desires. What's so wrong about that?"

174

"Depends on what one's deepest desires are."

Angus gazed steadily at Bert, who returned his gaze. Angus wanted nothing more than to leave at that very moment. He wanted to jump in the car and drive far away from Blackcroft Farm. Something just didn't feel right. All that talk of hexes and black magic had given him a creeping sensation on the nape of his neck. He cursed his poor manners but he decided that when the older man was asleep, he'd slip away during the night. A cowardly move, but self preservation was rarely dignified.

Breaking the shared silence, Bert rose from his throne. "C'mon, I'll show you to the guest bedroom. You must be shattered."

Surrounded by garish, flower patterned wallpaper, Angus lay propped up on one elbow upon the soft bedding in the guest bedroom listening intently to the sounds of Bert moving around the house. Occasionally, he parted the ancient, yellowing venetian blinds to gauge the weather, hoping that the sweeping sheets of rain would soon subside.

Hours of unproductive driving and the encounter with Bert had drained him. He tried to turn on his mobile phone once more but the battery was as drained as he now felt. Angus laid his head in the centre of the sunflower that adorned the soft pillow; it created a bright yellow halo around his dark hair. He promised himself that he would not sleep, only rest long enough to be certain that his host was unconscious and then leave Blackcroft Farm for good. Within moments, he had closed his eyes and that promise was broken.

He dreamt of an out of control train, veering round corners, its steel wheels lifting off the track. He could still hear the quick, rhythmic rattle of the train as he sped into consciousness. Then, a nauseous feeling of vertigo attacked his senses and he rolled off the bed, landing on the floor heavily. He retched and voided the previous night's tea. Groaning, he got to his feet, throwing his arms out at his sides, hoping it would be enough to keep him from falling over and then made his way to the living room. His intent was to ask Bert just what the hell he was playing at. It was the old man's house and of course he could do what he wanted but Angus was no longer in a courteous mood. He shoved the door open and stepped into the room, collecting his thoughts in preparation but the words died on his lips.

The room was empty, and the power light on the turntable was dark. The sonic dissonance was coming from somewhere outside the building. It was similar to the black metal he had listened to some years back, a subgenre he had, and occasionally still did enjoy. But there was something else, a jarring atonality that negated the usual bombast of the music, infused with multiple high pitched hums and squeals that seemed to affect his balance and made him want to puke. With the memory of the previous night fresh in his mind, Angus realized it was coming from the barn.

Outside the rain had finally ceased leaving the ground soft and resembling a mire. Angus placed a hand on the bonnet of his car and considered how easy it would be to jump in a speed off, leaving the crazy old man to whatever shenanigans he cared to pursue, but he had a niggling thought that just wouldn't go away; a thought that perhaps Bert was in trouble.

Cursing his concern for others, he entered the barn. The noise was louder in there, more insistent like knives in his skull. He felt as though his head would explode if he had to endure any more. Bert stood with a book in his hand and a pained expression. He opened his mouth and called out to Angus.

"What," Angus replied, shouting in an attempt to be heard above the cacophony and failing.

Then he saw it. Waist deep in a hole, emerging into the barn was a spectral form, wan and insubstantial, almost transparent in the candles' lambent glow. Angus didn't need to be introduced, he recognized Bert's wife from the framed photograph on the mantle.

176

Bert began to wave his hands frantically, motioning for Angus to leave the barn, dismissing him, shooing him away, but all Angus could think of as tiny needles of sound bore into skull was muting the offending noise. He took a labored step towards the turntable, clumsily barking his shin on one of the huge speakers sitting on the ground.

Up ahead, he was aware of Bert rising from his position beside the spectre of his wife, his thin arms pin wheeling. To Angus, he looked like a scarecrow at a rave, an angry scarecrow, an angry scarecrow screaming at him as Angus lowered his hand to nudge the tonearm off the spinning LP, screaming at him to...

"...uck off, noooo!"

Bert's exclamation punctuated the amplified grating of the tonearm's needle being dragged unceremoniously across the shallow contours of the record like the screech of some hungry prehistoric avian.

Seconds later, the pain receded and Angus was able to think clearly again, his throbbing mind free from the crushing bonds the music had temporarily fettered it with. Despite this renewed freedom of perception, he was still unable to make sense of the scene that confronted him.

Bert was already hobbling towards his wife, wailing. The pale light emanating from the circle began to fade as Marion sank into the ground, her hand slipping from her husband's cheek. Candles surrounding the circle began to flare violently and then the wan ethereal light was gone, supplanted with a crude circle drawn on the ground with chalk.

The lambent light from the candles cast an orange hue upon the old man's face, where deep shadows shifted, yet not deep enough to hide his grief. Bert lifted a hand and swiped away the dampness on his cheeks. He looked at Angus with pleading in his eyes. "Help her, please help her."

Angus wanted to turn in the opposite direction and flee. He didn't want any part of this madness. "Bert, she's gone."

"But she was right here. You saw her."

"That wasn't..." Angus wanted to tell Bert that the simulacrum that resembled the woman in the photographs was not his wife. He recalled the form, pale, not quite opaque, cloudy rather, like milk poured into water. He wanted to tell him to get a grip and stop messing with whatever dark magic he had gotten himself involved in. "There's no coming back, Bert. Whatever that thing was, it wasn't Marion."

"Why," he said, becoming silent for a moment as though to moderate the tone of his voice. "Why did you stop it? Have you any idea what you've done? It has taken me years to get this far. Years!"

Angus shook his head. "Bert, that sound. I thought I was going mad. I couldn't think straight."

Bert strode over to the turntable, mere inches from Angus. It wasn't difficult to tell that the old man was angry. Angus flinched at the twisted mask of rage on his face. Bert raised his finger and prodded Angus hard in the middle of the chest. "You," he said, his voice shaking. "You can fuck off. I can start again, but I want you out of here, go on, go and get lost somewhere else."

Before Angus could protest, Bert turned his back and returned to the circle. He lifted a hefty, tattered tome and began to utter sounds that Angus did not understand. Once again, the chalk circle began to glow.

"Bert," said Angus.

"I told you to go!" Spittle rained from the old man's mouth as he seethed.

At his feet, the light on the ground faded, it went dark and darker still until it resembled a slick circle of tar, fathomless and pitch dark, like nightmare's well. It began do undulate and pulse in an arrhythmic heartbeat, spilling out of its chalk boundaries. Soon, the blackness was no longer circular but an amorphous, pulsing, bleeding mass.

Angus watched in horror as a slender, undefined silhouette emerged from the blackness, writhing like a captured snake, stepping into reality with tapered,

178

mantis like legs. Unlike the spectre that resembled Bert's wife, this figure was of firmness rather than fade. Its skin glistened like distant stars in a clear night sky and its limbs appeared too long for its torso. Before Angus could alert the old man to the being, the flames on the candles snuffed out, devouring what little light remained in the barn. As the shadows closed on him, a scream tore the air, followed by a crunching sound like breaking bone and then silence.

Angus reeled. His heels collided with something he suspected was one of the oversized stereo speakers. He stumbled backwards through the darkness fearing to turn his back on the threat ahead, all the while his mind chattered like a frightened monkey. Deep in the barn the popping and crunching of bone continued. Finally, the conflict in his mind reached a resolution and he turned and fled.

Panic seized Angus as he pushed through the gap in the barn door, rolling it shut behind him with a resounding bang. He squeezed his hand in his pocket, waggling his fingers, searching for the key fob while striding at an accelerated pace towards the car. When he found it he mashed the buttons in a frenzied fashion. The Fiesta chirped, he grasped the door handle, wrenched open the driver's side door and threw his bulk unceremoniously behind the wheel. The springs in the seat beneath him twanged in protest. His finger darted forward, hitting the lock button beneath the dash once and listening carefully for the satisfying *thunk*. A ragged, labored breath sounded within the car and he let out a wail of fright before realizing that the sound had come from him.

Angus pinched the flesh of his arm hard, it smarted. It was no nightmare, the creature was real and he had a hand in summoning it. No, he would not take the blame for this; this was something Bert had done. The old man had waded in way out of his depth in dabbling with powers beyond his control. All Angus had done was turn off the record player in the barn. How on earth silencing the sickening sound had led to that thing crawling into existence, he had no clue but he was certain that the birth of such a being was something Bert should have been aware of.

With a shaking hand, after a number of failed attempts, Angus slotted the key in the ignition. He was about to start the engine when a resounding blow rocked the car.

Angus's head swiveled. A tall, elongated feminine form stood poised next to the car like a panther, ready to pounce upon its terrified prey. Angus noted the cruel black teeth in its grinning mouth. It's tongue, scarlet and forked like a snake's, flicking over cruel shards of broken coal. Angus stared in terror, a paralyzing coldness rushed through him as the creature darted forward, its head colliding with the passenger side window, leaving a small spider web fracture in the pane.

Yelling in fright, Angus turned the key and the vehicle coughed into life. He wasted no time, wrenching the gearstick before stamping on the accelerator. The car rocked back but remained stationary. The creature slapped its palms against the damaged window repeatedly, leaving a sooty residue, then, it pushed its frightening face against the window, mashing its nose and flicking its elongated tongue out, licking the black dust away.

When he realized his error, he popped the handbrake and the car shot forward onto the crude dirt track, bucking like a rodeo horse. Angus held on to the steering wheel fast while bouncing and sliding around on his seat, unwilling to stop for a second to fasten his belt. He glanced in the rear view mirror and his heart lurched when he saw the creature bolting towards the rear of the Fiesta with its legs pumping like pistons and an expression of rage. The suspension groaned in protest and seconds later the car trembled with the impact. When the trunk flipped open, Angus floored the gas. The car rocketed onto tarmac and he pushed it to its limits.

After twenty minutes of pushing eighty mph along the deserted road, Angus finally eased off and pulled over. He stepped out of the car, cautiously checking underneath before assessing the damage to the rear. The bumper was cracked and the trunk moderately dented. When Angus slammed the hatch shut it closed without any issue. The damage could be fixed or the car replaced but he didn't really care about the vehicle, he was just relieved to be free of the nightmare. That creature, whatever it was had bitten Bert, he had heard it eating the old man for Christ sakes. He felt a pang of panic rising again but staunched it by squeezing his eye shut tight as he could.

He considered calling the police, but what would he tell them, how could he begin to describe the sequence of events that culminated in the old man's death? He played the scenario over and over in his head but it always ended badly. There was nothing he could have done to save him.

After an hour of cruising back towards the motorway, he finally reached the slip road leading him back on to the M77. A trembling sigh of relief rose within him, causing a surge of emotion. He felt as though an oppressive force had left him and suddenly he realized just how tired he was. No matter, he would soon be at home with Sue. He promised himself that he would never listen to anything that extreme again for as long as he lived. It was all about the old school heavy metal from now on: Saxon, Maiden, Judas Priest, Motorhead and Sabbath.

Angus hit play on the CD player and a moment later the strident sound of rapid blast beats filled the car instead of Dio's rapturous vocals, an assault that seemed to bypass his ears and drill directly into his brain. Angus's head immediately began to swim and he pitched to one side, retching.

The Fiesta veered across a lane of traffic, eliciting in a peel of angry horn blasts. But Angus didn't hear the irate objections of his fellow road users, all he could hear was thunderous bass drum explosions and guttural roaring vocals, infused with that sound again in volumes he was unaware of the stereo being capable of. The brain stabbing whine caused him to lift both hands to his ears and he thumped his head on the driver's side window in an attempt to stop the pain.

He reached out a hand to silence the cacophony just as the car mounted the verge, throwing Angus against his seatbelt. He pitched forward violently as it began to descend a steep decline. He pumped the brakes frantically but nothing happened.

As the car tore down the embankment, Angus caught a glimpse of a dark shape rising from the back seat in the rear view mirror. The creature's obsidian eyes twinkled like glitter in the sunlight and a split tongue stabbed the air in front of its disturbing countenance as it reached for him with long, tapered fingers.

The song blasting from the stereo reached a crescendo and when the vocalist screamed, so did Angus.

M. J. McClymont is a writer of horror fiction and weird tales. He has written numerous short stories which have appeared in anthologies, magazines and websites since 2008. His work has been described as a mix of classic and contemporary, reminiscent of 70s and 80s pulp horror fiction.

Born in Scotland, he was raised in the seaside town of Ardrossan. He now lives in Kilmarnock, in the county of Ayrshire, a land steeped in history and legend by which he is constantly inspired

A Cold Slither Killing

Angelique Fawns

It was a coincidence that Michelle has just confessed to Glenna when the incident happened.

"Call me a fan of shock rock, but I absolutely love Cold Slither. The lead singer Gary Groody? He's my guilty pleasure," Michelle had said, a half-smile pulling at her glossed lips.

"Me too." Glenna gave the tanned girl's water tube a little shove. "Now I know you have the best of taste in men and music."

The 13-foot boa constrictor, Crush, was known for escaping from bathtubs when travelling with Gary Groody's entourage. The snake slid off the concrete boulder on the edge of Lake Ontario at the public beach. Glenna and Michelle were giggling at their newfound shared passion when the disturbance of the water rocked the pink tubes. Michelle screamed when the wedged head surfaced several inches from her hand. In her panicked struggle to get away from the snake, she somersaulted into the water.

Glenna laughed and rolled onto her stomach, watching her bikinied companion sputter and splash. Michelle's pure white bathing suit became see-through in the water and was obviously more for show than function.

"Would you look at that! How on earth did a Boa Constrictor end up here? You're pretty far from home buddy." Glenna trailed her hand after the ringed tail.

"Forget the snake, I can't swim." Michelle desperately tried to keep her nose above water. Her black painted nails clawed at Glenna's tube, her own having drifted several feet away.

Glenna balanced on her knees on the edge, adjusting the straps of her one-piece Speedo. "You're shitting me, right?"

Michelle couldn't answer. Her head dipped beneath the surface, black hair pooling on the oily surface of the lake. Glenna looked at the beach. There were a few people enjoying the warm fall day, but no one was looking their way. Sighing, she dove into the water but didn't immediately grab for her friend. Michelle's eyes were open under the water, the whites of her eyes unnaturally wide. Bubbles streamed out of her mouth.

Her arms slowed their thrashing.

Michelle sunk a few inches lower into the darkness.

Glenna swam behind Michelle, wrapped her arms around her torso, and hauled her to the surface. Michelle was still, limp in her arms.

Glenna kicked away from her water tube, swimming for the shore. Huffing, she strained her leg muscles. Michelle's dead weight was harder to haul through the water than she had imagined.

Michelle gave a shudder, violently coughing and spraying water out of her mouth and nose. She walloped Glenna in the head.

Glenna held her tighter. "Stay still, or you'll drown us both."

Her black nails gripped her forearms so tight there would be bruises tomorrow. Michelle still wiggled, but stopped the violent fighting. Glenna was able to swim faster. Struggling up the pebbly shoreline, she removed Michelle's death grip, and rolled her onto the sand. Her chest shuddering, Michelle rested on her hands and knees, coughing and gagging.

The few people on the public beach still paid no attention to them.

Michelle glared at her with red-rimmed eyes. "How? Why? Were you going to let me drown?"

Glenna shrugged. "I thought you were joking. Who can't swim these days?"

"Me." Michelle got slowly to her feet, marched over to where they had left their bags, and left the beach without saying another word.

"See you at work tomorrow." Glenna called after her.

Michelle ignored her.

The next day at the radio station, Michelle pointedly looked in the other direction when Glenna passed her reception desk. Glenna pursed her lips as she walked past the elegant main office into the bowels of the station. She knew she had to do something to repair the friendship. Really, the only reason she had given up her job as a morning drive anchor at CRNB 108.3 in Muskoka was to make friends with the pretty receptionist.

The public relations team had received some comped tickets to the Cold Slither Concert tonight. It took some flirting and several pointed hints, but the station manager finally came through. He gave her two tickets.

As he walked away from her desk, Glenna smothered her scream of excitement with one fist and drummed her feet on the floor. A couple of her fellow schedulers gave her dirty looks from their cubicles. There were areas of the radio station filled with music and laughter, but not in the administrative wing. Everyone here was hunched over a computer frantically assigning numbers to commercials and slotting them into appropriate on-air breaks. Filling in the daily log for Rock 999 was a deadly boring job. She often seriously questioned leaving her dream job working on-air in Ontario's cottage country. But she had an agenda. A deadly serious one. These two Cold Slither tickets, casually tossed onto her desk with a wink, were just what she needed.

These tickets were in the corporate area. Bigger seats, free drinks, and one of the best views in the house. Under the canopy. Attending concerts at Ontario Place could be dodgy. A few seats were under shelter, but many were on the grass. Toronto's notoriously rainy fall season could make sitting on a blanket, miles from the stage, miserable.

How was she supposed to concentrate now? Her heart was pounding in her temples. Her calves were throbbing. She rushed the last few inserts for tomorrow and logged out of the S4M program she was using. Making sure none of her co-workers were paying attention, she pulled up her Facebook page and scrolled through her own feed until she found a picture of her sister. They had their arms flung around each other and were drunkenly raising glasses of beer at a family reunion.

What a coincidence that "The Bloody Hunt" was playing in her headphones. She kept her eyes on the time stamp on the TV forever tuned to the 24-hour Toronto news station. As soon as it flicked to 5:00pm she felt her pulse quicken. Yanking the buds out of her ears, she ran down the twisty staircase while clutching her concert tickets in one hand. The building was state-of-the-art. Frames decorating the wall holding records for bands that had gone Gold and Platinum. Cold Slither had six platinum albums on the wall. She stopped at the receptionist's desk and waited impatiently for the Michelle to get off the phone. How did she spend all day answering calls and never smudge that black lipstick? Michelle dressed goth chic, and looked equally good in the black jeans and tank top she was wearing today as she did in that white bikini yesterday.

Glenna subconsciously smoothed her hands over her conservative skirt. Another downfall to working the corporate side. The dress code. In Muskoka, when she was the morning show talent, she could wear whatever she liked. Most of the time she wore cargos and a plaid shirt. Perfect for Northern Ontario. They all liked to joke, she had a great face for radio.

Michelle was still ignoring her, answering the phones, and doing her shtick. Her friendly grin and sexy voice charmed clients and co-workers alike. The executives loved her pretty presence at the front desk.

"Hey, I have some comped tickets for Cold Slither at the Budweiser Stage tonight. Wanna join?" Glenna asked her.

Michelle gave her a dirty look but looked interested. "Cold Slither tickets, eh?"

"Look I am so sorry about the Lake Ontario thing. I honestly didn't know you couldn't swim. Let me take you out. Make it up to you."

Sweeping her purple hair out of her eye, Michelle let a smile touch her lips. "I do love Cold Slither."

"All is forgiven?"

"You did save my life. It just took you a minute." She was fully grinning now.

"Cold Fucking Slither, right?"

Michelle jittered with excitement. "You mean Gary fucking Groody!"

"It's on baby, all is forgiven?" Glenna put her hand up for a high five.

"For Gary? All is forgiven." Michelle gave Glenna's hand a whack back. "Netflix will have to wait! I'll meet you just outside the ticket booth on the hill at Ontario Place? It's four now, I'm off in an hour."

Michelle made rock hands and stuck her tongue out.

"My logs are done, so I am going to sneak out now. Time to dust off my hair crimper!" Glenna cheeks glowed triumphantly.

Glenna found Michelle exactly where she said she would be, sitting on the hill by the lake at Ontario Place. She flopped down beside her; happy she wore jeans as she watched Michelle yanking on the short leather skirt riding up her thighs.

"Wow, you went retro." Glenna appraised the studded bracelets, Doc Martin boots, and thick chain necklace.

Michelle laughed. "Channeling my inner-goth. I haven't worn dog collar jewelry since high school."

"It suits you." Glenna pretended to strangle herself. "Wow, where did you dig up that head shop jewelry?"

"Back of the closet baby, I love your outfit too."

"Classic, right?" Glenna ran her hands over her Cold Slither T-shirt. "Shall we really do this old school and pre-drink?"

She pulled two paper bags with tallboy beers in them out of her purse.

"Absolutely." Michelle took a bag.

"Let's get away from the gate. Don't need a public drinking ticket." Glenna winked.

They ran, giggling, towards a bridge over Lake Ontario on the far side of the amphitheater. The complex sat on the edge of Lake Ontario. Green rolling hills, white building popping up like daisies in an award-winning architectural masterpiece.

Michelle hummed a few bars of "The Snake is Hungry" then swallowed a sip from her can.

Glenna admired Michelle's cool way of pouring her beer from the bag into her mouth without touching the mouth of the can. She tried to do the same, but it dribbled down her chin.

Wiping her face, Glenna leaned over the railing. "This place reminds me of my sister. We used to come here and watch Disney movies at the Cinesphere." She nodded to the big orb beside the music stage.

"You have a sister? You've never talked about her." Michelle leaned precariously over the bridge, staring down at the dark water.

"Well, she died, so I don't talk about her much."

"I am so sorry. When?"

"Last year, right before I moved back to Toronto. I had a radio show in Muskoka, but I left it to work for Rock 999. She was going to the University of Toronto for her Masters." Glenna finished her beer and gave Michelle another one.

Michelle gratefully accepted it and took a long swallow. She avoided Glenna's eyes. "Death is such a bummer."

"That's one way to put it." Glenna watched her companion fidget.

Michelle became quiet, the energy seeping out of her like an invisible succubus had latched onto her. She was looking at the dark water, lapping softly around the piers of the bridge. There was the faint smell of seaweed and long dead fish on the breeze.

Michelle leaned right over the bridge rail. "Do you ever think about throwing yourself off?"

She was hypnotized, swaying a bit. Her long purple hair hung over her cheeks and her lean torso teetered precariously on the railing.

"Like you lose your sanity for a moment and a compelling force makes you want to hurtle yourself over?" Glenna dug her nails into her palms.

From the open-air stadium the first chords of music rang over the water. Probably the opening band. Glenna wasn't a huge fan of Cold Slither's opening act, so she didn't mind if she missed them.

Michelle didn't answer Glenna but kept talking in a dreamy voice. "Sometimes when I'm driving on a cliff or bridge, I want to do it. Drive off the edge. I want to crash. I want to jump."

"Like an uncontrollable impulse?"

"No. Like a punishment." Michelle looked away from the water, met Glenna's eyes and bit her lip.

Glenna put her arms behind her back and forced a smile. "I get it! I'm afraid I will end up possessed and just for one moment some evil entity will take control of my body and hurdle it over for me!"

Michelle's eyes had tears in them, but she wiped them away. "Umm you're weird. Demonic possession, eh? That's not what I am talking about. I think I deserve it. I want to throw myself off but I don't, not brave enough."

Glenna let that hang in the air, keeping her eyes cast down on the cold lake.

"Alright, I'll bite. Why do you think you deserve to die?"

"What would you do if some bitch was making moves on your man?" Michelle tugged on a strand of purple hair.

"What would I do? Or what would Gary Groody do? Use a guillotine obviously." Glenna tried to joke.

Michelle grabbed her hand. "What would you do?"

Glenna wiggles her fingers away from Michelle. "Trust my boyfriend to choose me. And if he doesn't, then why would I want him?"

"Chuck is pretty freakin' awesome. Basically, a Gary Groody look-alike. Long blonde mullet, can rock the vinyl pants. Sometimes you got to fight for your man."

"So, what about this bitch?"

"Her name was Kim. My best friend. Drinking, smoking, hanging out. But then Chuck told me she tried to kiss him."

"Was? Her name was Kim? Why past-tense?" Glenna voice dropped an octave.

"She slipped and fell one day; we were going for a hike along the Scarborough Bluffs." Michelle threw her empty beer can into the water.

Glenna shook her head at the littering. "So, Kim slipped, did she? Was she clumsy?"

"Nope. Like a mountain goat." Michelle leaned out further over the rail and wiggled her fingers at her King Beer can floating towards the boat docks. Her heavy bracelets made a clanking sound.

Glenna looked at the back of Michelle's head, that sleek purple hair, and clenched her teeth. Michelle was teetering again, balancing her slightly inebriated self on the railing.

Glenna took a deep breath and clenched her fists, this time drawing her own blood in her palms. Should she do it? Could she do it? This was why she had given everything up. Left a dream job in Muskoka for a logging job in Toronto. This was the moment. Her "Vengeance is Sweet" (only Cold Slither's best song) moment. Plus, she said she deserved to be punished. Glenna agreed. She unclenched her hands, took a step towards Michelle, and gave her a push.

Michelle's light body flipped easily over the railing.

"Ahhh!" She shrieked, plummeting with a splash into the icy lake.

Glenna looked around quickly and was relieved to see nobody around. Unlike at the beach, the shore was truly deserted. Everyone was at the concert by now. She examined the water for any sign of a black dress or purple hair. That heavy chain jewelry. Those big Doc Martin boots.

The seconds passed impossibly... slowly... and then Michelle's head broke through the water. Black mascara streamed down her face and she screamed at Glenna.

"You pushed me! The water is freezing." Michelle's head bobbed back beneath the water.

Glenna waved at her, a smile slowly spreading across her face.

"I can't swim." Michelle sputtered, water bubbling out of her mouth.

She was desperately trying to keep her nose above water. Her black painted nails clawed at air, those thick necklaces allowing only her lips to breech the surface.

"I know, you told me at the lake, remember? I saved your life." Glenna leaned over the rail; her belly pressed into the cool metal. Relishing the cold feel of the steel. Feeling a strange peace.

"So, save me again, you can swim." Michelle's head tilted way back, water filling her mouth at the edges.

"I don't think so, I don't rescue snakes." Glenna spat into the water, the glob landing beside Michelle's purpling face.

"Help--" She submerged completely.

Her purple hair pooled on the surface, then disappeared as Michelle sunk.

"Kim was my sister." Glenna said to the ripple of water. "Chuck was her boyfriend you common cuckoo. You stole him from her."

A few bubbles formed a circle on the oily water. Glenna stepped back from the railing.

The dark water remained still.

She tilted her head, listening... No sounds from the water, but she could hear the roar of the crowd. The opening act must be done. Her heart swelled as the volume soared. Heading back down the bridge, Glenna hummed along with her second favorite Cold Slither tune. She could hear the opening chords of "Sometimes the Rat Has to Die."

She picked up the pace, she wasn't missing this concert for anything. Those corporate tickets weren't going to go to waste. She would just tell people Michelle stood her up. She was always going on dates with random guys, everyone would believe this time Michelle met her Mr. Goodbar. Not every guy was a nice guy. Like Michelle had tried to tell Kim. Chuck was no good.

After the concert she might work overseas. She knew of a radio station in Australia on the beach in Mooloolaba. Or why go that far? There were lots of media companies in San Francisco. Basically the birth place of thrash metal.

Her steps got lighter the closer she got to the Amphitheatre, dancing to the recognizable licks of a Cold Sliter tune. She especially loved his routine with the Boa Constrictor. Apparently, Gary had to get a new one for this concert. Crush had finally escaped for good. She punched a fist into the air, celebrating Crush. In Glenna's opinion, snakes belong in the water.

Angelique Fawns is a speculative fiction writer who grew up wearing Doc Martens around the Toronto Goth scene. She's the author of three guides featuring the speculative fiction market and produces a horror fiction podcast called *Read Me A Nightmare*. You can find her work in Ellery Queen Mystery

Magazine, DreamForge, Creepy, Scare Street, and a variety of other anthologies.

www.fawns.ca

KVLT

Kyle Rader

The section of the Green Mountain National Park was off-limits to the public. The numerous "No Trespassing" signs and chained-off access roads and walking trails were an attractant for Grish. The futility of man dictating his rules and whims over nature itself was laughable to him. "Let's set up over there, down in that copse of birch trees," he called over his shoulder to the rest of his band, all of whom were none too thrilled to have hiked for the past three hours in the blistering heat.

"What's so special about *those* trees anyway?" Mason said, letting the three bulky gig bags slide from his aching shoulders. In addition to being the bassist, Mason had the misfortune of serving as de facto Sherpa, simply because he was six-foot-six and more muscle than man. "They look exactly like the couple of dozen others we walked past *miles ago.*"

Grish scowled, tilting his chin down and glaring from underneath his furrowed brow, an act that he thought accentuated his perceived natural evil state but in reality, made him look as intimidating as a constipated toddler. "These trees, Mason, are the true *kvlt!* See how the light distorts through their branches? The way that one tree bows in the middle like an old man weary from a life of crushing disappointment and ready to lay down and die? These trees are the fingers of nihilism and are exactly what we need for the shoot."

Mason rolled his eyes and brushed past the lead singer-keyboardist, muttering under his breath about how stupid 'kvlt' was. Niles and Ole (lead guitarist and drummer respectively), oblivious to the uncaring nature of the trees, shimmied up them, laughing and kicking at each other as they raced to see who could climb higher. "Would you two kindly stop rubbing yourselves

194

on the fingers of nihilism? Get down here and get into character already!" Grish picked at his scalp, his coping mechanism whenever his anger took hold. His favorite spot (right side of his head near the hairline) was a trench of scar tissue; it was so thick, he'd filed his fingernails into fine points to pierce it. Grish didn't mind though. It gave him a fierce appearance, one that belied the fragility of his small frame. Mason teased him that he had to shop for clothes in the boy's section of the store. *Told him that in confidence,* Grish thought, staring at Mason as he handed *GoPro* cameras to Niles and Ole, pointing where they were to place them. *Piece of garbage had to go and tell the rest of the band.*

"Grish," Mason held a crucifix dyed red from a copious amount of blood Grish purchased from the local butcher. It was quite large, but in the bassist's hands, it may as well have been the size of a toothpick. "You absolutely sure you want to use this? The guys and I were talking and we really feel—"

"Oh, you were *talking!* Behind my back no less! How wonderful! It's so nice to know that I've been spending my free time and creative energy with a bunch of Judas goats."

"Don't be like that, Kevin," Niles leaned against one of the birch trees, smoking a cigarette. He grinned through the plume of smoke, knowing that calling Grish by his given name would set him off further, something that both he and Ole rather enjoyed as it reminded them of their little sister getting mad at them growing up. "No one is leading you wrong. We feel our style doesn't lend itself to the Satanic Panic vibe."

"We're more stoner-doom metal," Ole nodded. "Besides, aren't inverted crosses more than a little cliché?"

"About as cliché as taking promo pics in the middle of the woods, bro." Niles said, his grin widened at the sight of Grish's face, now the color of a rotting tomato.

Grish dug deeper into his scalp, his sharpened nails working the dead skin cells like a plough. *"Do NOT call me that name!* I reject it! *I* am the leader of this band, not you! Who pays for our studio time? *Me!* Who actually has a garage to store our gear? *Me!* So, if I say we're using crosses and taking pics in the woods, then guess what we're going to be *FUCKING DOING?!"*

"Whatever you say, *Kevin."* Ole sniggered at his brother, who walked away shaking his head. The sight of his turned back enraged Grish even further. Niles clearly disrespected him, had ever since Ole convinced Grish to hire him four months ago, after their original guitarist was arrested for dealing drugs outside of a *Super 8* motel. Grish felt his hand on the hunting knife he wore on his belt. (He'd never gone hunting a day in his life.) In two steps, he'd be upon Niles and the tempered steel would be deep inside of him. Grish saw himself wrench the weapon free and smiled from the way the blood came out, not as a spurt, but a gurgle. The smile peeled his lips far from his small teeth as the fantasy played out, showing the shocked pain painting a portrait across Nile's face as he turned, reaching in vain for the wound. Then, he'd stab him in the gut, just above his bullet belt, and tug across until he felt the heat from his intestines on his feet.

"Grish? *Grish!"*

"What, Mason, what?!"

"I asked if you wanted to do shots with us in makeup first or in the masks?" Mason held two of said masks before his chest; eye-level for Grish. Cheap couldn't adequately describe the level of bad they were. Stitched together from dissected trash bags and Halloween store rejects, they had the subtle visage of homeless werewolves whose appetites consisted of eating red crayons. Grish made them himself and was immensely proud of them all. (His was nothing more than a moth-eaten burlap sack; Mason's a ski mask drenched in fake blood.)

"Are you deaf as well as stupid? I mean, didn't you read *any* of the no less than fourteen emails I sent out regarding today?"

Mason's shoulders drooped. His eyes, downcast. "I just want to be certain of things, Grish. That's why I'm asking," he put a hand on Grish's shoulder and gave him a gentle shake that physically moved him back an entire step. "Look, I know you're going through a rough patch right now, you know, with the Count? Niles and Ole don't understand what he meant to you, but you know that I do."

"Your concern is as unnecessary as your questions. I'm *fine,* and I'll be even finer when you pull your head out of your ass and get things back on track. Make-up first, *then* the masks." Grish dismissed his giant bassist with a foppish wave. He waited until Mason had called the other members over into a huddle before turning on his heels and walking out of the copse. His fingers broke through the scar tissue, allowing a rivulet of blood to be born into the world.

It met up with his tears before he'd walked twenty paces.

The thing opened its eyes for the first time in two millennia.

It couldn't see naught but the same rock keeping him prisoner. Why had it awoken now? Wait. There was...*something,* distant, but approaching with great haste. It pulsated through the thing's tomb, vibrating its long dormant cells, filling them with the very need, the thirst, it had when it roamed free.

Excited, the thing pushed against the stone; futile, it well knew. The prospect of actually *seeing* anything other than rock, let alone the very means for its escape had it acting out of instinct. The vision, a sunrise in this stone Hell, moved closer and closer, the delicious pulsing taking on color. What was the color called again? It couldn't quite remember what the humans named it. It'd had forgotten much in this place, knowledge that it would swiftly seek to replenish once it was free. It had *not* forgotten what lay behind the pulsing, the power that it coveted. Blood. Yes, it must have the blood.

If its tongue weren't of stone, it'd have been salivating.

"*Bastards!*" Grish stormed through the woods, stomping anything small and green into the ground until he was good and sure it was dead. He kicked at fallen branches and churned up the topsoil. *"Goddamn bastards! Who do they think they are?!?"*

His filed nails roamed farther than his familiar scratching post. As he cursed and thrashed in his petulant tantrum, the wounds spread until half of his pale forehead was smeared red. Self-harm came second nature to him. Plus, having real blood and open wounds always played better than slapping on some white and black grease paint like a sad clown.

"True kvlt," he said, rubbing his gore in-between his fingers. "Much more than any of those lame posers think."

He walked up a slight incline where a group of glacial boulders had lived since the last Ice Age. Crusted in moss, the dampness absorbed into Grish's black jeans the second he sat down, further souring his disposition. With his blood cooling on his face, he ran through the list of grievances he had with his bandmates. "Where do they get off? *I'm* the one with the talent! *I'm* the one with the artistic drive to shape the direction of this band! There's no one blacker, grimmer, more... *kvlt*, than me!"

Grish slapped his bloodstained palm on the boulder, enjoying the brief spat of pain. His fingers found grooves in the stone and hooked them. "Who among them can say that they've not only met, but touched *the* Varg Vikernes? Niles? Please. That guy has never left Paramus. And Mason? Guy wouldn't understand what kvlt was if it smashed his seven-string over his head!"

Thinking about Mason, his closest friend and---technically---co-founder of the band questioning him had Grish's fingers clenching the grooves harder. Why did he think it was okay to bring up the Count? On today of all days? Grish had told him years ago that when they were about band business they were musicians first, business partners next, and old friends dead last. The

Count fell into that third category. "More like the *fourth*," Grish's blood found his lips, flying off in a mist as he spoke. "As in, off-limits."

He missed The Count. Every day, Grish woke up thinking that he'd still be there, waiting for him in the kitchen at breakfast and every day, Grish would stroll out there and find nothing but sorrow. Part of him appreciated the grimness. He'd tried to channel it into the music, but was only able to come up with some weak as fuck lyrics about a dying Viking child and a couple of lame chord progressions. Nothing near his usual high standards.

"Fuck the world for taking you from me," Grish relinquished the grooves of his boulder throne and slashed at his forehead, dragging his nails from temple to temple until he created crimson wetlands. "Fuck them all."

The violent outburst over, Grish tipped his head to the sky, taking in the oddly pleasant sensation of the mid-day sun on his open wounds. His hands once again found the grooves in the boulder. If he'd been paying closer attention, Grish might have noticed they weren't a byproduct of erosion, but deliberate. He might've even recognized some of them, for the very logo of his band contained similar Runic letters within it.

He might've even noticed the Runes widen as his blood sloughed off his fingers.

The thing tasted the blood and the powerful spell sealing him in weakened. Cracks appeared in the thing's vision, clearing away dirt and stone, allowing light of the day to bombard its eyes, momentarily blinding it. It attempted to sit up and break through the rest of its tomb but found that it could move no more than a few centimeters. The magick, lessened by the blood, was still powerful. The thing screamed granite, a sound that Grish's mortal ears were incapable of hearing. It knew that it'd need literal buckets of blood if it wished to be completely free. The pathetic creature, its unaware jail breaker, didn't nearly have the amount necessary.

Yet, the thing pondered, perhaps there was another avenue of escape available to it.

The thing's fingers shoved through the partially opened rune, poking through the stone, wriggling and flopping in the open air like a clew of worms after a torrential storm, until they touched Grish's skin.

"What the hell?" Grish looked down at his doom and the self-proclaimed lyricist for the ages was struck mute. The thing's entire hand was free now and seized him by his thin wrist. Equal parts rock and rot, it possessed a strength that, if Grish had the combined strength of each member of his band, he still wouldn't have been able to break free. He tried nonetheless, more of a reflexive action than a genuine attempt at fleeing. The power that lay within the thing so great that the mere movement of Grish against its talons was more than adequate to turn the bones in his wrist into powder.

Grish slid down the side of the boulder, crying out in silent agony. His hand, caught in the thing's grip, took on the appearance of a grotesque bouquet, his fingers serving as the blossoming flowers. He slapped at the hand holding him, succeeding only in breaking several fingers.

The thing was not one to play with its meal. The tips of its fingers slipped into Grish's hand, each connecting with bone. Absorbing the marrow upon first contact, the thing had no further use for them; they would not support it in the new form, humans being far too weak to contain the power it wielded. Grish howled as the bones of his hand heated and evaporated. Plumes of pink mist escaped from the entry wounds, scalding his face. Once gone, the thing planted the seeds inside the useless flaps of skin from which its new vessel would be born. Grish could only watch as the deflated sacks that used to contain his finger bones filled with the very granite of the boulder, watch and feel the jagged, uncaring edges of the stone skeleton poke out of his fingertips.

The thing worked swiftly, moving throughout Grish's body and repeating the process. The organs it found it sucked dry, leaving behind husks of petrifying meat that collected at the bottom of his pelvic cavity. The thing would excrete the useless bags later, as they'd only serve to slow it down.

It finished its ghastly task with Grish's skull and teeth. As his cranium cracked apart and evaporated, Grish's head collapsed on itself and disappeared into the hollow of his neck while bloody bone gas swirled around him. The stone skull that formed in its place was ill-fitting, snug. The self-inflicted wounds in Grish's forehead stretched to their breaking point, some splitting off into new directions under the strain. Lastly, the thing created its teeth, pushing out Grish's expensive dental work one by one in favor of stone arrowheads coated with saliva.

The thing examined its new body, clenching and unclenching its stolen hands and bending its knees. The form was unsteady and smaller than its own natural state, but it would do.

Before his host expired, the thing touched his mind. It found the ordeal detestable, but necessary if it was to negotiate this world in which it was a stranger. It knew that this man had companions close by; three of them. Their combined blood, marrow, and organ juices would be enough for the thing to complete its escape. As it set off in the direction where these sacrifices lay, something puzzled it. Throughout its host's mind, a single word kept coming up. It was a word that the thing had no prior knowledge of, and it considered itself a master of all languages known to the earth and heavens. Was it the name the poor dead host and his people had given to the thing over the ages? Was it a prayer of protection of some kind? If it was the latter, then the creatures it would soon rule over once more worshipped weak deities indeed, it thought. In the end, the thing decided that it rather liked the sound of the word and adopted it as its new moniker. After all, it had so many names already, what, really, was one more?

Through vocal chords made of gravel and over a tongue mottled with granite, the thing spoke its name; its voice raped the air around its mouth with a sound constructed of that of nightmares.

"*K…vlt. Kv…lt.*"

"*…Kvlt.*"

"He's taking a long time." Niles dabbed grease paint into his cheeks, massaging the bone white color along the contours of his face. His brother Ole, stood behind him with arms crossed and stick firmly up his ass.

"Why didn't you grab the other mirror?" Ole said. While his make-up was fully applied, his lipstick was not, and had been rather impatiently waiting another turn at the mirror.

Grinning, Niles moved to hand the tiny oval to his brother, only to pull it away at the last moment. "Because I like the way you whine, baby bro," Turning back to his makeup, and away from Ole's middle finger, Niles laughed. He loved to laugh, especially when it was inappropriate. In his eyes, nearly everything was inappropriate about this gig. If Ole hadn't shown up after work one day begging him to join up, Niles would've been sitting on his couch right this moment with a nice cup of tea and a book. Looking at his brother's pouting reflection, he sighed and thrust the mirror into his hands. "And again, our *leader* is taking an awfully long time, isn't he?"

Mason, feeling Niles eyes upon his be-leathered back, grunted. "He does this before major band events," he said, not looking up from the *GoPro* instruction manual. "He says it helps him get into character. He'll be back soon enough."

"And when will that be? Dusk? I'll tell you right here and now that there's not a hope in Hell that I'm sticking around for a night shoot. I mean, did we even *bring* flashlights?"

"Easy, bro. Grish won't do us dirty. He's eccentric and kind of a moody prick, but he's connected with the pulse of the scene."

Niles laughed. "Yeah, the scene from ten years ago, maybe. Those songs you brought home for me to learn are basically *Death Cult Armageddon* knock-offs."

"Ease off, Niles." Mason said, licking his finger to turn a page.

"Your boy is seriously deluded if he thinks that what this band is producing is anything but the same post-black metal derivative crap that's infested the scene for the past decade; *seriously* deluded. I don't know why you put up with him, I really don't. Guy's a walking, talking case of bad vibes."

"And what are you, Niles? It seems to me," Mason gently closed the instruction manual and placed it on the ground next to him. "That you're a loudmouth. A drama queen stirring the pot because you're so utterly miserable and bored in life that you can't be happy unless you're making other people miserable. *That's* what it seems like to me."

Niles stared Mason down. The bassist remained sitting on the forest floor and gave no indication that he was interested in taking the conversation to the physical level. Niles said a secret thank-you to the universe for that small favor; Mason was quite easily the largest person he'd ever seen. "Man," Niles laughed off the fairly accurate criticisms, as he did everything in his life. "You can divert the conversation onto me and my hang-ups all day long, but it doesn't change the fact that your boy---and let's face it, he's really *just* a boy---has been acting like Prince Shit of Fuck Town for *far* too long. This whole trip is just the latest in a series of temper tantrums and all-out dickheaded behavior and *you* damn well know it, Mason."

"Grish is going through a rough patch—"

"You mean *Kevin* is going through a rough patch?"

"—he just lost his best friend in the world to cancer," Mason stood, rising to his full height, looking every inch the evil, Satan-worshipping bassist he portrayed in the band. "I think that's a qualifier for giving Grish some slack, don't you?"

"Oh."

"Yeah, Niles, *oh*."

"Well, how was I supposed to know that? It's not like the little guy is forthcoming with information. I didn't even know about *this*," Niles flailed his arms at the makeshift photo shoot. "Until late last night. If he needs to take time to grieve, then he should. I mean, who died? A parent? Grandparent?"

"The Count," Mason sighed heavily, anticipating the coming onslaught of callousness from the lead guitarist. "His cat."

Sure enough, Niles didn't disappoint. The corpse paint may have given him a painted frown, but the man's smile and laughter dissipated any semblance of evil. "His fucking cat?? Aw man. That's priceless!"

"I knew you wouldn't understand" Mason shook his head and set about unpacking his bass guitar, doing his best to ignore the mocking, uncaring laughter.

"It's a *cat*! It's not like his parents died in a house-fire or something. I knew this gig was going to be shit. Ole, what the hell did you get me into here? If you weren't my brother, I'd probably kick you square in your---"

Ole was on his knees, arms limp at his sides. At first, Niles thought his brother was vomiting, as his torso retched and the all-too familiar sound of dry heaving burped through his open mouth. Two hands burst through Ole's chest, shattering the illusion along with most of his ribs. Pieces of lung and muscle clung to the fingers, dancing in the waning light of the afternoon as the murderer flexed them. The culprit moved its head into view from behind Ole's head; the drummer's eyes fluttered and his body spasmed as the thing shifted its weight.

The stretched face of Grish, now the consistency of cured leather, grinned at Niles, flashing a jaw full of bloody rocks. "Kvlt."

"OLE!!" Niles screamed, catching Mason's attention. The bassist turned in time to see Kvlt lift Ole over its purloined host's head and rip him in half. The red that lay inside of him broke apart on Kvlt's head like a water balloon. Organs and shredded tissue adhered to its rocky skin, only to become pink steam moments later. Mason and Niles watched as all of what used to be Ole was absorbed into Kvlt, paralyzed by the hissing of boiling blood and the sizzling of cooking meat.

"Kvlt."

The creature regarded the two empty halves of Ole stuck on its wrists. All flesh, all of the red, was gone, leaving behind charred bone. Kvlt shook and shook, but couldn't rid itself of the blood sacrifice. Growling, it turned to the nearest birch tree and smashed the blackened skeleton against the wood until it and clattered to the ground amidst clouds of tree bark and sawdust.

"Grish, what have you done?!" Mason said. Only when the fleeting blood coating Kvlt's eyes soaked into its skull and it regarded the large bassist for the first time, did Mason realize that he was dealing with something that his mind couldn't quite comprehend. The thing wore Grish's as if someone had shrink-wrapped a statue with freshly removed skin. It grew taught at the joints as Kvlt approached, hanging slack in discolored pockets upon resting.

Mason's eyes darted to the gig bag at his feet. Bending at the knee without taking his gaze from the monster with his friend's face, he slipped his seven-string *Ibanez* bass free. Swinging it around in his hands, it became a literal axe, surely almost as lethal as the real thing in his strong hands. Mason gripped it as if he were out in these woods to fell trees, the steel strings pressing deep grooves into the soft flesh of his palms. *"Stay the fuck back!"*

"Kvlt." The creature ran a tongue made of fossilized flesh and rock over its teeth. It pawed the air in front of Mason, testing both the range of the weapon and his resolve to use it. Mason's first swing scraped against Kvlt's talons, doing it no harm, but slicing canyons into the wide bottom of the guitar.

205

Kvlt felt the attack, but did not feel any pain along with it. It was slightly disappointed. It hadn't had the privilege of feeling anything in so long; it'd forgotten what the sensation was like. "Kvlt."

"*NILES, GET OVER HERE AND HELP ME!*" Mason risked a glance over his shoulder to where Niles was standing, hoping to see that he'd followed his example, hoping to see that stupid smirking face as he brought his own guitar on the back of Kvlt's skull.

A passing look at the back of Niles' t-shirt as it retreated into the brambles was all he saw.

"*FUCKING COWARD!!*"

"Kvlt."

"Shit!" Kvlt was right on top of him. Screaming insanity into the air, Mason lifted his bass high and brought it down on the crown of the creature's skull. A thud not heard outside of major car accidents rattled the world around them. The impact reverberated through the entire instrument, violently shaking it out of Mason's hands. The wooden body cracked, sending a tennis ball-shaped piece flying into the brush. Mason had no time to wonder if he'd hurt the creature, for Kvlt's hands were around his throat the very second the bass hit the ground.

Kvlt dug through the thick, ropey layers of skin and muscle that made-up Mason's neck and inhaled. Mason struggled for as long as he physically could, kicking and hitting Kvlt with open hand slaps, all completely pointless. His blood, marrow, and organ fluids were pulled out of him with a sickening efficiency.

"Kvlt." The word came off its stone tongue much easier than before. The scarlet gold was working quite well against the magick. Soon, it would be able to speak with the level of eloquence it'd once possessed. Perhaps it would be able to speak to the final sacrifice before it died. That would certainly pass the time, it thought.

206

It let the remains of Mason slough through its fingers, forming a hairy pile of boneless skin and desiccated organs at its feet. Kvlt regarded the broken bass guitar and, curious, picked it up. The instrument would never again play music, yet Kvlt didn't know that was its intended purpose. Its memory was not quite restored to near-omnipotence. It thought that it was a rather crude weapon, no greater than the sticks and stones some of its long-vanquished enemies used. It took a few swings with the bass and enjoyed the savagery of it. Kvlt was quite curious to see what harm it would inflict upon the fleeing meat puppet, and perhaps even more after.

"Kvlt," it pulled Grish's skin into a kind of cock-eyed grin and set off in the direction of Niles.

"OhShitOhFuckOhShitOhFuck!!"

Niles ran as fast as he dared. The uneven forest floor was covered with leaves and pine needles, all of which could've easily hidden divots or animal holes that would've love nothing more than to snap his ankles and leave him lying helpless for the monster he knew was coming for him. He'd no real clue in which direction he was fleeing. A city boy through and through, Niles could count on one hand the times he'd set foot in a forest. The terror claimed him, making the direction irrelevant as long as it was away from the creature.

Breathing came in wheezes that felt like hot knives cutting tiny cuts in his lungs. Spots waltzed in his vision and he felt dizzy. *NoNoNo,* he thought. *Don't pass out. Not now. Not now!* Staggering, Niles leaned against a crumbling boulder, propping himself up with one arm while slapping his face, hard, with the other. The boulder gave way, shifting underneath his grasp and sent him tumbling to the ground amidst a small pile of broken rocks and dirt.

"Goddamnit!" Niles looked around, trying to get his bearings. Everything looked the same to him: trees, trees, and more trees. Cursing softly, Niles brushed the dirt from his arms, discovering freshly opened cuts and scrapes,

parting gifts from his trip. He kicked the boulder and spat in the wide chasm he'd created in it. "What the hell?"

The boulder was hollow. A morbid fascination kept Niles from continuing his exodus. It was so strong that, despite the fear that had pulled his testicles taught and had his stomach twisting over itself, he could not move. He pulled down more of the rock with trembling fingers, noticing the runes carved into some of the pieces. The boulder gave way with ease, as if eager to have its millennia of existence destroyed. The opening grew to the size of a foot locker, revealing the contents to Niles in a haze of rock dust and dirt.

"It…can't be…"

The body was humanoid, but definitely *not*. It was vibrant, as if it weren't a lifeless husk, but a living, breathing thing. Seeing the thing's eyes, lifeless, yet still possessing a malevolent consciousness broke apart Niles already fragile mind. He'd no clue that he was crying, didn't even feel the warm dampness on his cheeks and, when his tears splashed against the creature's tusks, he thought it was raining.

Kvlt found him curled at the foot of the altar, rocking himself and whimpering. For a moment, the creature's violence was stayed. Niles wouldn't have been the first to think that begging for mercy would save him. Kvlt craved this kind of attention, as it was the flip-side of the coin that also contained worship, something it lusted after almost as much as violence.

Kvlt allowed Niles to continue for another ten minutes before it grew bored and drove his brains into the dirt with Mason's broken seven-string. It was highly disappointed in the mortal's efforts. All it did was mumble rapid, incoherent noise. No real pleading, no invoking of its God or Gods, and, it *soiled* itself before Kvlt ended its existence. Pathetic.

Absorbing the last drops of blood gave Kvlt the energy it needed to return to its true form. The pile of bones and skin at its feet did Kvlt a favor by removing most of the stone altar. All it had to do was reach its petrified talons

208

into the makeshift crypt and release the essence. Burning ozone and sulfur were the only evidence of the rocky creature's brief time in the world of the living.

Blinking with its own eyes, the thing called Kvlt rose from the stone, bellowing a cry of joy and triumph as the earth smooshed in-between it's scaly, clawed toes. Behind it, a pair of wings unfurled, stretching so far as to swallow the horizon. Kvlt flapped them three times, sending tornadoes of rocky dust a hundred yards away. Sunlight reflected off the gossamer of its feathers, not white, but silver, noble and beautiful. All the knowledge, the magicks, the languages it'd acquired exploded within its mind. Each step it took, it recalled a thousand things: poetry, important rulers' names, and all the things that it'd missed during its slumber, thanks to the sacrifices. By the time it'd reached the edge of the forest, night had fallen and it knew the world of man, knew that *they* did not know of it. Not anymore.

"Kvlt," it said, allowing a smirk to cross its near-angelic face.

Kvlt howled at the giant white orb in the sky like a beast might do on occasion. It was not an act born out of tribal instinct, but a direct challenge. A threat to all that worshipped under its gaze. For there was a new monster born into this world, one far greater than any of them.

And it was hungry.

Kyle Rader is the author of the novels "My BFF Satan', 'KEGGER' and 'Four Bullets'. He can be followed on Twitter @youroldpalkile or his website http://kylerader.net

One Last Duet with Davy

Ken Goldman

I'm an apprentice at death having died only once
And what bothers me most is the silence. . ."

The Dead Shed No Tears
©1995, RattSnake
The Barbosa Tapes
Available on CD and Cassette
Ramblin 'Records, Inc.

On a warm night in the early spring, David Winston Barbosa, the handsome creative genius behind the rock band RattSnake, polished off the last of his Johnnie Walker Scotch, placed the muzzle of his .45 Colt full into his mouth, and sent a bullet smashing through his frontal lobe. The slug tore a large hole through the top of the rock star's head. It carried with it a large portion of Barbosa's brain that spattered the hazelnut wallpaper inside the executive suite of Manhattan's Plaza Hotel overlooking Central Park West. Young Barbosa's gray matter freckled his bed sheets and several keyboard keys, while the blood soaked into six demo tapes that the musician had spread on the floor around him shortly before he took his Cobaine prescription.

Asked why he did it the other RattSnake members could not say. The group's bassist, Klipper O'Hara, suggested that death was an experience the young lyricist had not tried yet and thought he might like. In the narcissistic parlance of heavy metal O'Hara did not mean this as a joke.

A police officer at the scene located a large hairy flap of Barbosa's skull that had become lodged between the strings of his left-handed guitar. He passed the remark to his sergeant that here was living proof how the rock artist was a man whose mind was on his music. Out of earshot from the several reporters who were present both officers shared a hearty laugh.

Surviving Barbosa were four RattSnake members to whom he had stopped talking except in the studio, an ex-wife whose name he had not bothered to mention in his will, and an aged mother whose nursing home bills he had quit paying. Besides his music, he left behind six months 'worth of child support invoices and one extremely pissed off cocaine trafficker who had to do some heavy-duty explaining to the kingpin of an unsympathetic Colombian drug cartel.

In short, David Winston Barbosa, known simply as Davy to his fans, left his life much in the same manner he had lived it - - - in one huge fucking mess.

The media circus began immediately. One week following the shooting the National Enquirer ran an article about how the blood stains that had smeared the wall in Davy's suite formed a perfect likeness of Jesus on the cross. Some enterprising news journalist somehow obtained the police photographs to corroborate the claim. To anyone who saw them, the stains looked more like bad modern art than the Nazarene. Still, two dozen of the physically challenged from across the country camped out in the lobby of The Plaza. They begged the management to allow them to touch the wall as if it were rock's answer to the stigmata.

This was only the beginning. Eight days after Barbosa's burial four men masquerading as cleaning staff somehow gained access to the suite and stripped the wallpaper clean. Within a week the blood-soaked swatches reappeared inside commemorative glass containers sold in Cleveland's North Coast Harbor outside the main gates of The Rock and Roll Hall of Fame. Inside each container appeared the quotation "The world is but a fleeting show" from RattSnake's single, *Kill Me Before I Love Again* . The enterprising vendors scored one hundred dollars a pop.

Two weeks after Barbosa's funeral someone stole his headstone. Fearing further disturbances to the grave site the ex-Mrs. Barbosa transported the expensive silk-lined black walnut wood casket to an unmarked grave just outside the musician's home town of Little Neck, New York. The plot was within shouting distance of the garage in which Davy and his partner Klip had created the sound that was to become RattSnake's trademark. According to his ex-wife's specific instructions no member of the band was ever to know the location of the new burial plot. It didn't matter. Someone stole the new headstone too.

The candlelight vigils continued outside the Plaza for weeks. Swarming Fifth Avenue Barbosa's legions of fans droned every RattSnake lyric that had come from the musician's pen. Although no one claimed any Davy Barbosa sightings, several women insisted the rock star's resurrected spirit had appeared while they slept to impregnate them with his love child. In Seattle one young heartsick fan pointed her father's gun to her head but succeeded only in blowing out her left eye.

The whole thing played like rock and roll theater of the absurd, and it might have made bassist Klipper O'Hara laugh himself sick. But the surviving partner of the band's creative duo quickly discovered that RattSnake had lost its venom on the night Davy took the Colt's muzzle between his teeth. Anyone familiar with the band's work recognized that, of the five guys who comprised the group, only two were indispensable. Klipper O'Hara had been the other one. From the time they were kids Klip had known that his partner's words embodied the real music behind RattSnake's chart toppers.

The group's latest CD, RattSnake Bites, immediately sold out following the night Davy filled his skull with lead. But when low ticket sales resulted in the cancellation of several concert dates, no one had to ask why.

Davy had blown himself away and he had taken RattSnake with him. By midsummer the four surviving members decided to cut their losses before any of the band's royalties went into their lawyers 'pockets. The group's drummer, Dex, had already signed on with White Bronco; Rossi and Fuzz would never starve as studio musicians, although they admitted their egos might; Klipper was always bitching about wanting to fly solo anyway. There remained nothing to do but declare the band officially dead and provide the fanged serpent with a decent burial.

RattSnake's farewell concert became a surprise sellout. At midnight on August 21, six thousand two hundred and thirteen fans waved lit matches high above their heads for the final scheduled number during the otherwise disappointing 'Jesus Hates Us Tour'. Cleveland's Coliseum shone like a huge swarm of fireflies as the group performed "The Pope Ain't No Friend of Mine" with Klipper O'Hara snarling Barbosa's lyrics into the mike.

> "...I can't say I love you, Mister John Paul.
> No, I can't say you mean that much to me.
> 'Cause after I been listenin' to what you have to say,
> I know you ain't exactly Lennon/McCartney..."

The number inspired the usual fist fights among the audience of young headbangers along with several dozen death-defying leaps from the stage into the mosh pit of human arms below. For one last night it was just like old times.

"We love ya, Cleveland! We fuckin 'love ya!" O'Hara howled at RattSnake's fans. A thick-armed roadie handed the bassist his trademark bottle of vermouth. For the final time as a member of the band the rocker raised his bottle high as if he were toasting the night clouds that hovered above the Coliseum like dark ghosts.

"And here's to you, Davy Barbosa, wherever the hell you are! Satan, guard your ass!" he shouted, putting away almost half the bottle right where he stood. O'Hara's commemoration brought the house down as he headed off the stage still swigging what remained inside.

. . . and then he stopped in his tracks, stopped so suddenly that Rossi bumped right into him. In the glare of the spotlight the decision came to Klip like a revelation from God. Yet, deep within the darker caverns of his mind he had been secretly toying with the idea for weeks. Unknown to the others Klip had brought Davy's last studio tapes with him. The other self that lurked in the shadowy netherworld of his soul knew he had done this for only one reason.

"Well, why the fuck not?" he asked himself, although in the tumult no one heard him speak. The spotlight followed O'Hara like the tail of a comet as he tramped off the stage, a man with a single purpose.

He heard the echoes of his fans 'shouts for another RattSnake encore as he pushed past the huddle of backstage groupies. Surrounded by three hulking bodyguards whom his manager paid to ask no questions, he bee-lined with them down the dimly lit tunnel to his dressing room and the three gorillas waited there as he slammed the door behind him. Rifling through his carry-on bag, he pulled out a large reel-to-reel tape and shoved it into his pants.

When O'Hara returned to the stage the still-cheering RattSnake fans exploded in a pandemonium that would have muffled the exhaust fan of a turbo jet.

The roadies looked to one another, then to the band who had no choice but to follow O'Hara. Rossi and Fuzz shrugged while Dex, his face half hidden beneath a tangled mass of hair, still managed to catch their manager's eye in the wings off-stage. But he had no clue either.

Taking another long guzzle of vermouth Klip O'Hara returned to the mike at center stage. The band took their places behind him. Klipper could be one crazy motherfucker, and there was no telling what wild ride he had planned for RattSnake's send off. Although the musicians felt complete bewilderment, it would have been decidedly uncool to let it show.

But Klipper knew exactly what was going down. He knew it from the moment he had heard Davy's blood-spattered tapes. Barbosa had recorded these apart from the other guys, apart even from Klip. He had gone alone to the studio late at night in the weeks just before he had taken himself out of the game. The police presented six reels of audio tape to O'Hara in neat zip-locked plastic baggies because Davy Barbosa's suicide note had mentioned that he had wanted his long-time partner to have them. There were a good six hours of music on the tapes, admittedly unpolished stuff but definitely usable. Davy had left Klipper a gold mine. O'Hara had not played the reels for anyone else, not even for the other members of RattSnake.

. . . but that would change tonight. The boys in the band would have their shining moment courtesy of the man not present at tonight's concert but whose secret studio tapes were. Tonight Klipper O'Hara would accompany the absent David W. Barbosa, who was not live but on Memorex. Their voices would again intertwine in perfect harmony. Together their vocals would shape one upon the other in a single magic voice, a wondrous mosaic of music. This was Klipper O'Hara's gift to RattSnake's fans, one last unforgettable pairing of rock's most revered vocalists, an extemporaneous duet sung by both the living and the dead.

Of course, following a celestial moment like tonight's Klipper would have the emotional springboard necessary to launch himself into the solo career he longed for. If he required a bargaining chip to persuade any of the major labels to sign him, he also had the secret Barbosa tapes to sweeten the pot."

"Davy Barbosa couldn't be here with us tonight," O'Hara wailed into the microphone. The crowd answered with a deafening two minute frenzy at the mention of his partner's name. Klip raised his arms to quiet them. "No, Davy couldn't make it . . . *but his spirit is here and ready to kick ass on this stage with us tonight!*"

He held the single tape reel high above his head. "If you look real close you can still see Davy's blood on this reel! And if you listen real close, my friends, you can **hear** his blood on these tracks!"

An explosion of cheers filled the stadium. The members of RattSnake standing behind O'Hara looked to one another as if the floor had suddenly vanished beneath their feet leaving them hanging in midair. When O'Hara turned to them to issue a silent command they took their places like blind men, Dex to his drum set, Rossi and Fuzz to their keyboard and guitar. They looked to one another and then to O'Hara still at the mike, having no idea what he expected them to do.

O'Hara held out the tape to Bobby who worked the soundboard.

"Jesus fucking Christ, Klip! What're you doin 'to me, man? We don't know the sound levels . . . hell, we don't know jackshit about that tape to pull off this fucking three ring circ--"

"Pipe it through the system, Bobby," Klip answered without missing a beat. His eyes never left his audience. "Just do it, man."

Moments later a familiar opening guitar riff bearing the unmistakable Barbosa thumb print came through the stadium's towering speakers. Six thousand two hundred and thirteen voices fell into stunned silence as everyone waited to hear the words that no living person but the man at the mike had ever heard before.

They waited to hear Davy Barbosa sing to them from the grave . . .

"My love of life was my delusion,
so don't go savin' me against my will.
Death is sometimes the only solution,
Yeah, it's that knowledge that gives me the courage to kill . . ."

The crowd swayed with the words. Dex picked up a light drum riff to supply an improvised back beat while Fuzz and Rossi followed suit. The music had found its way into the soul of everyone present.

"Would so much rather die than to live in vain.
Would so much rather be cried for than cryin'.
So next time you see me standin' in the rain
Please understand I got my reasons for dyin' . . ."

Klip breathed heavily into the microphone as he joined Davy for the middle eight. His bass guitar had poked its way between the chords of Davy's lead, and now his voice welded itself to Davy's in an enchanted reunion of sound.

"A reason for dyin' is all I need.
A reason for dyin' is what I believe.
If you tell me different I know you'll be lyin'
Always gonna defend my reason for dyin' . . ."

The words echoed those that Barbosa had scrawled in his suicide note, secret and pained words about life that had lost its meaning. Klip had witnessed the man's pain for years, and tonight his voice wedded itself to that pain. The result was nothing short of magic. O'Hara's intuition had been correct. Tonight he had added another page to the history book of rock.

Lost in that thought Klip also lost his focus on Davy's lyrics. Calling himself back into the moment he listened to the words as he prepared to work his way back into them.

He listened to them hard.

Really hard.

Something seemed different.

Something was not right . . .

"But now in my grave I see my confusion.
Yeah, the dirt and the mud are all that is mine.
So I made myself a new resolution
Just 'cause I'm dead don't mean I must die . . ."

"They're not the right words . . ."Klip said aloud, unaware he had spoken into the mike. He turned to his band members as if they should have known this too. "Hey! They're not the words on Davy's tape!"

No one heard him. It was as if O'Hara had said nothing, nothing at all. The musicians had become lost inside Davy's lyrics, lost in the wild harmonious improvisations his genius had inspired in them.

"Goddamn it! Listen to me!" Klip shouted to anyone who might hear. *"Something is wrong! Something is fucking crazy! These words! They're not the same! They're not Davy's words! Just listen to---"*

"A reason for livin' is all that I need.
A reason for livin's what I need to believe."

218

Instead, Klip listened. He listened hard, and his mouth fell open at what he heard. Because what he heard was impossible.

"Gonna climb out of this grave and take what I can.
Gonna rejoin the livin', gonna be my own man . . ."

He heard himself singing the words along with Davy. Yet his mouth did not move, it did not move at all. Still, his voice came in sweet wails from the gargantuan speakers singing lyrics he had never heard before in his life. The voice integrating itself with Davy's belonged to him and it filled the stadium, filled it with music and words. A riot of music.

Impossible words . . .

Impossible. . . .

He covered his mouth with his palm, shoved his fist into it, and still the mammoth speakers cried Davy's lyrics in a shared duet that would not stop, that just went on and on even while he screamed.

"Shut up! Shut up! That's not Davy's words! That's not me!"

Not until he stopped screaming did O'Hara realize that someone else was sharing his mike.

"Gonna climb out of this grave and take what I can . . ."

No, not someone.

Some *thing*.

It had decayed flesh, clotted strips of it that reeked with a rotted stench. A large flap of torn skin hung from the back part of its head and a fragment of soft and spongy membrane sopping in blood peeked through the open skull. Its tattered rags dripped with pulpous slime that left dark puddles where it stood. As it sang into the microphone it held its left-handed guitar low to allow long bony fingers the freedom to work their magic.

Davy's magic . . .

The words on the tape were not the same, but they were Davy's words. O'Hara knew that now. Barbosa had tried death like he had tried everything else from drugs to women, and he had found it not to his liking.

Death had lost its romantic allure. Death had lost its kick. Now he wanted to try something else.

Something different . . .

Six thousand two hundred and thirteen RattSnake fans listened to the music. They lit their matches and swayed with the sound in the flickering light. Not one of them saw what Klipper O'Hara saw.

. . . and not one of them heard him scream as the rotted corpse of David Barbosa fell upon him center stage in the naked glare of the spotlight . . .

Inside RattSnake's limousine the group passed champagne all around. Rossi was the first to speak to O'Hara once the evening's euphoria had died down.

"Jesus, Klip. For a moment there I thought you was out of your mind playin 'Davy's tapes, man. But I guess you knew what you was about, eh? For those few minutes listenin 'to you, hearin 'you wrappin 'your voice around Davy's vocals . . ."

" . . . it was like you was both one person, man," Fuzz added. "One fuckin 'incredible person!"

The musician smiled at his fellow band members but said nothing.

"You was off in some other place, that's for damn certain," Dex said. "I mean, you ain't never been a southpaw 'long as I known you, Klip, and there you was playin 'your axe left handed just like you was Davy yourself."]

The musician's smile widened, but still he said nothing. Inside his head a single lyric played itself over and over, and he found himself humming the melody as the words rewound themselves like an audio tape that played within his brain.

"Gonna climb out of this grave and take what I can . . ."

In an unmarked cemetery plot somewhere north of Little Neck, New York, the rotted corpse of David W. Barbosa lay inside its black walnut wood silk-lined casket. Vandals and headstone thieves would be hard-pressed to find the late rocker's newest grave among the several hundred surrounding plots that looked just like it.

Klipper O'Hara prayed it would not always be so goddamned cold inside this thing...

Ken Goldman, former Philadelphia teacher of English and Film Studies, is an Active member of the Horror Writers Association. He has homes on the Main Line in Pennsylvania and at the Jersey shore. His stories have appeared in over 960 independent press publications in the U.S., Canada, the UK, and Australia with over twenty due for publication in 2021. Since 1993 Ken's tales have received seven honorable mentions in The Year's Best Fantasy & Horror. He has written six books : three anthologies of short stories, YOU HAD ME AT ARRGH!! (Sam's Dot Publishers), DONNY DOESN'T LIVE HERE ANYMORE (A/A Productions) and STAR-CROSSED (Vampires 2); and a novella, DESIREE, (Damnation Books). His first novel OF A FEATHER (Horrific Tales Publishing) was released in January 2014. SINKHOLE, his second novel, was published by Bloodshot Books August 2017.

IN EXTREMIS

Sally Neave

Pounding. That was the overwhelming sensation Julian woke up to. A terrible, all-encompassing pounding pain throbbing through every nerve and vein in his body. He tried to take a deep breath but the extra oxygen only fueled the hot agony that was the right side of his face. His first coherent thought was to check his arms. As the drummer for In Extremis, his arms were his livelihood. He could see two bloodied sleeves and nearly fainted again from the sheer relief of having an arm in each one.

He couldn't remember how he came to be in such a sorry state. He did remember that tonight was potentially the most important of his career; the band's manager told them that two premier Heavy Metal magazines had accepted invitations to send reporters to the opening night concert. In Extremis stood on the threshold of real fame and hopefully, a decent fortune. Julian didn't have unrealistic expectations of stardom or buying mansions. All he wanted was a proper income as a musician. A full-time musician.

Thoughts of the concert brought worry into his already overtaxed heart. The worry turned into panic when he realized the roaring in his ears were those of a crowd, and the throbbing behind his eyes was set to the beat of one of his latest compositions. He held a bloody sleeve up to his mouth to muffle his ragged, gurgling breaths, and he heard the steady chant of "ex-tre-mis ex-tre-mis" accompanied by a thundering of feet stomping to the heavy bass drum of their title track, Devil's Dungeon.

How was that possible? He was the drummer! Did the concert start without him? What exactly happened to knock him out and where did all the blood come from? He looked around and saw costumes hanging on clothes racks, cutout mountains and trees, and a broken trumpet. The room didn't give him the answers he wanted, but at least he knew that he was in the storage room below the stage.

Julian couldn't decide if he had to clean himself up first, or rush to the stage to see what was going on. He tried to do both, but all he managed was to add fresh, hot blood to his already soaked shirt, and shuffle slowly through a slippery red smear. The drummer tried to call out for help, but not much sound escaped his burst lips. He kept shuffling until he could see the door to the stairs that would lead him backstage. He tried to turn the doorknob but his wet red hand kept slipping.

Necessity is the mother of invention. He carefully made his way across the floor again, and grabbed a fairy costume off a hanger. With the worst of the blood wiped off his hands, he touched his face in an attempt to find the source of the blood. His face ached terribly, but so did the rest of his body. Judging from the amount of blood, he was either more injured than he thought or someone else, worse off than him, was in the storeroom. An overwhelming panic set in when he discovered he could feel his teeth and tongue where his right cheek should have been. Logic peeked through this frantic mind and he rummaged around in search of a mirror. A stage storeroom should have a mirror…he hoped. The concert above stopped being of any interest to him, he had a medical emergency that needed treatment right away. Instead of finding a reflective surface, he found chunks of flesh near the bloodstained puddle where he woke up. A shiver went through his bloodied flesh as he realized that the chunks probably came from his face. The shiver became a tremble in his hands and a deathly cold settled in his bones. He was in shock.

In desperate need of heat, Julian put on a robe that looked as if it was stored from a Christmas play. He almost laughed when blood poured from the gaping wound on his face onto the white, angelic robe. The first sort-of hit that In Extremis had, was Fallen Angel Red. The poetic justice of it turned from amusement to terror when the red bloom spread out at an alarming rate. That door needed to open before he passed out from shock and blood loss. If he didn't get help soon, he might die down here. Why didn't anyone come looking for him? Surely when he wasn't there at the start of the concert, his bandmates or manager or even security would have been concerned and started a search. He never missed a concert or even a rehearsal. Mister Reliable.

He needed to be on stage, right now, tonight! Not only were the reporters in the audience, but also a representative from the band's record company. It was expected that after being featured in two top magazines, Deathly Pale records would not only renew their soon-to-expire contract, but also sign them on for substantially more money. Terror set in at the thought of missing out on the career-maker that he had been praying for since the first day he held a pair of sticks in his hands. He hoped that the record company didn't sign the guy who was filling in for him. Spurred on by renewed desperation to get out of the storeroom, Julian made his way toward the door again. This time, with more of his blood smeared across the floor, Julian slipped. The jarring shock of the impact screamed in every exposed nerve of his ripped-open flesh. He tried to get up, only to slip again and again. The agony was too intense and he gave up the effort. From now on, he would have to crawl.

Julian inched his way on hands and knees across the red hardwood. His only goal was to escape this room that had turned into a dungeon of suffering. He made it to the door, tried to wipe his shaking hands as dry as he could, and tired the doorknob again. Relief flooded every fiber of his being when the knob turned. Relief gave way to crushing despair when the knob came off in his hands. He pounded against the door, knowing that the chance of anyone hearing knocking from below the stage during a Heavy Metal concert was zero.

With no chance of escape until the noise above stopped, Julian focused on survival. He needed to stem the flow of blood. He cried painful tears as he made his way back to the clothes rack again. On hands and knees, slowly and sobbing, he prayed. He prayed to anyone or anything that would listen. He made deals, promising anything from all the contents of his bank account to his immortal soul if he could just get out of there. Perhaps a benevolent deity would look at him and accept him as a blood sacrifice. Perhaps the deity would send an angel with bandages, or perform a miracle and manifest a pain pill out of thin air. Just in case his prayers were heard, he rummaged through the costumes in search of a pocket containing a forgotten pill. He gave up that hope when he didn't find a single pocket. Of course. The clothes were stage costumes. No one would sew a pocket onto an angel's robe or a fairy outfit.

The combination of pain and panic made the storeroom feel claustrophobic. The walls seemed to get closer, and Julian wondered about the strength of the stage. What if all the stomping and headbanging and weight of the band with the equipment caused the stage floor to collapse? The ceiling would cave in and he didn't expect he'd survive that. He wanted to live. He wanted so desperately to live.

His thoughts drifted to his life outside of his current predicament. He stopped praying and hoping, and instead tried to strike a bargain with any entity powerful enough to send someone to his cage. He didn't even care anymore that his face might be permanently disfigured. He didn't care about the reporters or the contract. He didn't care about who was playing the drums in the concert above his head. Desperately, he promised to sell his drum kit and donate the money to the local shelter. He promised to start every concert with a hymn. He promised to be the best boyfriend in the world. He vowed to visit his mother more often, to eat more healthy food, to abstain from any alcohol for the rest of his life. He would give or do anything to get out of this deathtrap. Anything.

Julian thought of all the things he had going for him. His life was worthwhile, so full of promise. At the brink of international success. Soon, he would be able to afford to buy a house of his own. He would have a steady income and a measure of fame. He was a responsible man, a man with a future. The gods must know that he deserved to live. With tears rolling down his face and stinging his raw cheek, Julian even offered his soul to the devil if only help would come quickly. The pain had reached a point where it surpassed the description of unbearable. A tortured agony as if he was atoning for a mortal sin.

He would make one last grand effort. A final attempt at escape before the pain and shock finished him off. Julian didn't have the strength left to crawl to the door. The floor was too slippery by now anyway. He slithered and slipped towards the door. With every passing moment, he had to fight more and more against the growing dizziness. It felt as if an eternity had passed when he finally reached the door. Despite his exhaustion and unsteady legs, he felt a glimmer of hope. He made it this far. If he could gather all his strength now, all his suffering would soon be just a fading memory. He imagined the siren of the ambulance that would hasten to the concert hall, the trustworthy hands of the paramedic that would let him drift off in a haze of morphine, the smiles of his family and friends when they gather around his hospital bed to joke about his sexy new scar.

At the door, Julian took a shallow, shaky breath and steeled himself for the final push to freedom. He managed to get to his feet. One last desperate prayer, this time for his shoes to keep their grip on the slick floor. He took a few careful steps back and previewed every move in his mind. With every second of his last chance carefully rehearsed, he closed his eyes and tried to steady his shaking legs. As fast as he could, Julian rushed the door. His shoulder met the door with a disappointing thud. No movement at all. No more chances. Not a scrap of energy left. Just pain and tears. He leaned against the door and stopped thinking. Thoughts hurt too much. He rested his forehead against the door and just…breathed. The concert was winding down. He recognized the ballad that the band usually played as an encore. Perhaps a security guard would pass by when the venue was quiet again, perhaps he would manage to knock his SOS on the door, perhaps he would be heard. Perhaps not. Julian didn't have the strength to care either way.

Julian's ears perked up as he heard the voice of In Extremis's lead vocalist, his best friend Steven, speak to the audience. "Today, a year ago, tragedy struck our band. As all of you know, our drummer was a broken man after Deathly Pale records chose to not renew our contract and he ended his life right below this very stage. To honor his memory, I will read out the names of the songs he composed for In Extremis: Amnesia, Bloodsleeves, Slipping in Blood, Unopened Door, Chunks of Flesh, Fallen Angel Red, In Shock, Terror, No Escape and The Haunting. Rest in peace, Julian."

The crowd roared and chanted his name. Beneath the stage, Julian fell into a bloody, crumpled heap and cried like a lost soul.

Sally Neave grew up in the era when Iron Maiden (back in the days when Bruce Dickenson was the vocalist), pre-Black Album Metallica, and AC/DC were enough to give street cred to any headbanger. The horror movies were scary but fun, and Freddy Kruger haunted teenage nightmares. Working as a ghostwriter by day and a tattoo artist by night, In Extremis is Sally's first plunge into the Horror genre.

Flee, My Pretty One

Eneasz Brodski

From up on the stage, half-blinded by the lights, all I saw of him were piercing blue eyes. The crowd churned before me, pounding music whipping them into a froth, but those eyes glittered calmly in the chaos. They shone at me, reflecting the strobe lights like jewel shards, floating over the bass pulses that rose from the floor to rattle my rib cage.

I stepped to the mic, screamed the chorus line. *"Death to all collaborators!"* His eyes never left mine.

Three beats to my guitar solo. I threw myself into it with a quickened pulse. I would never slack at a gig--this is my communion, the guitar sings my blood. And yet, there's an extra charge to it when you're showing off for someone beautiful. The blood burns a little hotter. Look at me--this is who I am inside. Eat of my body.

When the surge of emotion finally ebbed, I could breathe once more. The last notes faded, we said our thank yous, we turned away. Only his eyes remained unchanged, numinous among the vulgar. I imagined briefly that he loved to submit to vulgar, mohawked girls.

He came up to talk with us afterwards, which was too bad. Not because the rest of him sunk the fantasy. He was thin, with the delicate features that make it attractive--I like the pretty boys. No, it's because when new fans come up to see me they realize the slouch isn't a stage affectation. They see me without a guitar to hide my stance, catch me pressing my back against a wall for the relief it brings. They realize I'm twisted. Their interest fades and we both wish we'd just left the damned fantasy undisturbed.

Except he wasn't repelled by me, didn't rebound to Zoe or the guys. He smiled for me. Me alone.

"You rail against collaborators way more than the dragons themselves," he commented after introductions. "You never rage against the damn dragons. Always their human agents. You one of those non-sentience wonks?" A flutter in his voice as he said it, as if he feared challenging me, but couldn't stop himself.

From the corner of my eye I saw Liam perk up from the merch table. When his head swiveled over to us, the raised lights of the club glinted off the metal of his piercings like a flesh-and-silver disco ball. He must have been dying to jump in on this. He believed that dragons have personhood and their own motives. I wasn't so sure. There's those who theorize that the dragons are just dumb optimizers. No self-awareness, simply responding to the stimuli of human desires. We'd stayed up countless nights arguing this.

"I'm with Greenwald," I replied. "We'll probably never know, and it doesn't matter anyway. They don't have human values. The longer they stay off-leash, the worse the world gets."

My pretty fan-boy nodded. "I hear they're expecting another wave of refugees from Louisiana this month. How do you explain the repatriation collapse, if not intentional malice?" He stepped forward and motioned to the audio cables as I coiled them. "And can I help you with that?"

We continued our political bitching. Neither of us screwed up too badly in the conversation, and it'd been a while since I'd gotten any. He came home with me that night.

I woke up smiling, with that warm glow that comes from being well-laid. Restraints and toys lay scattered around the bed. I rolled over awkwardly to admire his sleeping face. I rested an arm on him, one breast pressing against his bare chest, and I realized I couldn't recall his name. I'm sure he gave it, but who knew he was going to stick around? I hadn't paid that much attention. Shit.

A fist banging against my door startled me. My band-mate Tyrell yelled through the flimsy wood.

"Jo! Wake up! You gotta see this!"

The boy beneath me stirred awake, gazed at me with bleary eyes. "Good morning," he said, and gave me a grin.

I kissed his collarbone, then his neck, and then Tyrell banged on the damn door again.

"Seriously Jo, come check this out! This is big!"

"Fine, I'm up!" I yelled back. "Give me a damn minute!"

I let my gaze wander over the boy's body and back up to his face. "Hey, look," I said, "I feel really lame about this, but I don't remember your name. I'm Josephine. And you're…?"

He laughed, and the rising sun caught his eyes, clear as the sky.

"Hi, Josephine. I'm Aiden."

I grinned. "More later," I promised. I rolled off him, and we pulled on our clothes to go eat and see Tyrell's big deal. Tyrell sat by his laptop in the kitchen, a video queued up for us.

On screen, a business-suited man left a government building. The news banner identified him as an emissary for Hirath'bur, an elder oil-and-gas extraction dragon. A gathered crowd of the unshaven and emaciated exploded in jeers as he stepped out. Hirath'bur destroyed the land where it operated-- poisoned the groundwater, blighted the soil. It had been corrupting the government for years with bribes and threats, turning our protectors into its accomplices. Whole counties had been despoiled when rich deposits were discovered. The emissary didn't spare a glance at the angry rabble. Cops corralled the protesters behind thin barriers, their hands at the pepper-spray canisters on their belts.

An unusual movement in the air drew my eye. One of those miniature quad-copters that make up any city's backdrop--routing packages or surveilling traffic or whatever they did. It had been passing overhead, and now tipped into a sharp dive, directly at the emissary. Four bursts of gray smoke erupted from its front. Simultaneously, four bursts of red liquid burst from the emissary's chest, and the man staggered. The drone shot up, high into the air, fleeing the scene. The man dropped, blood soaking his suit and spilling onto the cement. The crowd screamed, scattered, and the video cut off. I stared over at Tyrell.

"The hell just happened?" I asked.

"An assassination," Tyrell replied. "One of three, all within a few minutes, all carried out by modified delivery-drones. They targeted emissaries of major dragons."

"Holy shit. Is this what I think it is?"

"Uh huh. Looks like the resistance just got serious."

My eyes flickered to the boy I'd just met, listening to us intently.

"Um… Aiden, maybe you should go. I mean, leave me your number, last night was good, but you probably don't want to get mixed up in this."

Aiden gave me a disbelieving look.

"Are you kidding me?" He gestured to his T-shirt, which sported an image of V as Guy Fawkes, holding crossed daggers before him. Aiden grinned wildly, almost floating. "I've been waiting years for this!"

And so our relationship was born the same day as the resistance. I should have known it was a bad sign.

They hadn't always been called dragons. Centuries ago, when those incorporeal inhuman minds were first discovered, they were called some variation of "messenger" or "muse." Those less kindly inclined called them "whisperers." In an effort to remove the mysticism from the language, Adam Smith referred to them as "the Invisible Handlers."

Quickly their nature became apparent. Under their influence, country sides were stripped to their bones. Cities choked on toxic smoke. Summoners grew gross with wealth, while the commoners withered into skeletons. Karl Marx coined the term "dragons" in reference to the destructive, rapacious creatures of legend.

The first resistance started same as our current one. Small groups taking local action. Individual acts of sabotage and vandalism. Growing riots. I hadn't been in a riot yet, but that was about to change.We'd entered mid-summer. The city park bustled with activity as I helped erect the stage for a protest concert. We'd received permits and cleared everything with the authorities, because we were still playing by the rules. We hadn't yet re-learned the lessons of 1917. Not until buildings are burning do governments take you seriously. It takes a revolution to force them into restricting dragons. "From this day forward, you may not dump your poisonous waste into our water. From this day forward, you may not work our children." Not because our rulers care, but because they fear. Not discernment from above, but demands from below.

Hunched over and irritable, I struggled to lock another folding joint of the stage scaffolding. The midday sun beat down on me with spite. Every single stand and brace needed to be pummeled into submission. I was an inch from flinging the whole thing overhead and stomping off when Aiden's arms descended over me from behind.

He wrapped me in an embrace and nuzzled my hair. "Hey sexy girl."

I exhaled gratefully, relaxed back into him. He was lean, gentle affection. With maybe a hint of firmness around the crotch right now. I smiled.

"Here to help us?" I asked.

"Anything to get the show going. I still get goosebumps when you scream. But . . ." He gestured at the cops patrolling the perimeter. "It looks like we're gonna get shut down."

"Nah, don't worry about it. Everything's clear. We got a Free Speech Zone designation for the day."

It still makes me sick to think back on how compliant we were. Free speech zones? The dragons had learned to fear the power of government over the last century. Now every dragon had phalanxes of well-funded emissaries. "What is good for Genimette is good for the country," they said. They were patient. Slowly they wormed their way into the machinery of politics. Which is how you get bullshit like "Free Speech Zones." Maybe there'd been a time when cops served and protected the public. Now they're thugs who serve the dragons and protect their profits.

Our band, Against Dragons, wouldn't go onstage until 9:00 p.m., but other locals were playing nonstop from midafternoon. The music burned violent and spectacular. The cops hated it. Which meant they had to piss on anyone they could. Shouting matches erupted. Twice pepper spray hissed and they hauled off some kid in cuffs. People drifted away, not wanting to deal with the pigs. Those who stayed were on edge. Belligerent, pierced, tattooed punks, sticking it out explicitly because it did bother the police, and damn proud of it. We were in good company.

When we took the stage, the setting sun igniting the horizon, the air held a buzzing tension. Like the charge that builds inside you when a storm is rolling in, or the last pregnant note before a DJ drops the bass. I fingered my rosary as I scanned the crowd, matching my tempo to their pulse. We could use this. I pocketed the beads at *salvanos ab igneinferiori*, nodded to Liam. Zoe started us off with a bass riff.

The stage lights picked us out in a giant, harsh halo. As the sky grew darker and the heavens tightened around us, that tension worked itself into our instruments. It seeped into Liam's voice. It became a part of the music. The crowd fed it back to us, boiling, pushing us to a frantic thrashing. My hand clutched at the guitar as I choked it with my fingertips. My heart raced, and we were diving straight from one song into the next without pause. Because fuck

233

pauses, we have this burning in our throats, and we don't know any way to get it out other than to roar it at an audience and hear them scream with us.

We smashed into our breakout song and all the riotgrrrlz and punk boys below us roared in approval. We moved as one.

There's four words all piggies hate. They glare from spray-painted buildings and overpasses. They bleed from the shadows of hushed conversations. They're the chorus to this song. "Death to All Collaborators."

The chorus approached, and I stepped to the mic. Instead of looking into the crowd, I looked to the cops looming at the perimeter, and showed some teeth. I picked out one huffing like a pent-up bull. I stared him down. I screamed out my line just for him.

"Death to all collaborators!"

You could call that a mistake, maybe. But it had to start somewhere.

Halfway through my solo, a meaty hand clamped onto my shoulder and spun me around. The amps squealed as the notes died on my strings, and I stood eye-to-chest with a man in a dark blue uniform snorting fire.

"This show's over," he rumbled. "You're coming with us."

"Piss off, pig." I spat. I shrugged him off, turned back with derision. My stomach clenched in terror, but I wasn't doing this for myself anymore. This was for everyone who'd put up with their sneering abuse tonight. Put up with it for generations.

His hand shoved me from behind, hitting right at the apex of my hump. I yelped and pitched forward, but I hadn't gone one step before he wrenched my left arm behind me and screaming pain forced me to my knees.

I twisted, shrieking, as he yanked and pinned my other arm. My spine torqued, wedged vertebrae biting into calcified discs. A zip-cuff cinched one wrist, and I knew I'd be trapped like this for hours, blind with agony. Somewhere I heard Tyrell yelling, the sounds of movement, but they were dim outlines under a flood of pain.

234

Sudden sharp relief. I collapsed to the floor, gasping for breath. The stage rocked beneath me. I rolled over and saw Aiden grappling with the cop. My boy was no match for the hulking man, but as he pretzeled Aiden into submission, more angry punks leapt over me, piled on. The cop was big, but not a-dozen-angry-teens big, and he tipped over under the onslaught. His hands grasped for something at his belt and heavy boots came down to crunch his fingers before he got there.

Lights flashed, strobing blue and red. Whooping sirens drowned out the music of struggle, replaced it with the music of authority. Liam yelled into the microphone, something hot and angry, and the crowd erupted. Two nearby cops jumped onto the stage to free their trapped brother and Zoe, little Zoe, strode up behind them. She held her bass like a two-handed cudgel, back and to the side. She lunged forward, swung her guitar overhead, and brought it down on the bigger pig's head. The violent jangle of the strings breaking sounded through the park, and it was the sweetest music I'd ever heard. Bottles flew. I could barely hear the sirens over the blood-lust roar of the crowd.

Zoe picked up the mic and yelled into it. "Time to roast some pigs! Let's start some fires!"

The crowd surged like an incoming tide, bursting around the stage at the edges, breaking over the top in fury. I knew after this we were going underground. I staggered to my feet, pushed into the nearest knot of bodies, grasped for Aiden's arm. I dug him from the group stripping the pig's weapons, pulled him into the lee of one of the man-height amps. I still shook with aftershocks of pain, and I needed his attention on me. He took one look at my contorted face and wrapped his arms around me, bent his head down to mine. I clutched at him and raged against a stupid urge to cry.

"Thank you," I said. Plastic zip cuffs dangled from my left wrist. And deep inside a longing swelled, a longing I'd been beating back for weeks. It broke over my inner walls before I even knew it was happening.

"I love you," spilled out of my mouth. My heart sank. I hadn't meant to say it. Shit.

His eyes shone. "I love you too," he replied, his voice soaring.

Six months later found us hunkered down in the blacked-out basement of Liam's squat, having settled into the fugitive life. I sat on the floor, bent over my phone, resting my back against the wall. Aiden knelt beside me, kneading my shoulders and massaging along the top of my hump. He, Zoe, and Liam observed an informal remembrance of Tyrell in low tones as we waited. Tyrell had disappeared three weeks back, his door kicked in and his place ransacked. The dragons had him now.

Liam's brother Marcus arrived last, a half hour late. Over an inch shorter than Liam, with more hair and less piercings. Chemical burns ringed his eyes in flaming red. He limped in, favoring his right leg, but grinned when he saw us.

"Christ," Zoe said. "What happened to you?"

"I was at yesterday's protest at Union Station. Brought a megaphone and said some true things."

"And what'd that get you?" Liam asked, raising an eyebrow.

Marcus's grin faltered. "Someone tossed a Molly, before the pigs started cracking heads."

Liam snorted. "We should be past flinging cocktails. If this was L.A., the whole district would be in flames, and the pigs would be hiding behind barricades."

"Next time will be bigger. Next time we rush City Hall."

"It's been 'next time' for weeks. We're dying out there. For nothing."

"Hey, back off. You just call us here to bitch us out?"

"No." Liam straightened. "I have something to show you. We can still get our shit in order before they eat us alive."

236

He led us to the next room, also blacked out. He flicked on a single bare bulb hanging from the ceiling, and something glinted on the floor. A thick line of metal lay on the cement. My eyes followed it, bending smoothly, arcing around the whole room. The line of metal grazed each wall, encompassed where we were standing, and returned to touch itself. A very large circle. It looked faintly yellow. Like gold.

We were in the center of a summoning circle.

"Liam, what the fuck is this?" I asked.

Zoe gaped. "Where did you get this much gold?"

Aiden inhaled sharply and jabbed an accusing finger at Liam.

"You're going to summon a dragon? Are you insane?"

Liam looked Aiden in the eyes and spoke calmly, as if he'd rehearsed this. "Dragons are a tool. They are a goddamned amazing tool which we're leaving lying around out of ideological purity, and it's costing us lives. If you're willing to kill a man to save your species, you should be willing to use the dragons against each other."

"No." Aiden stated flatly. "Too dangerous. They get out of control. Always."

I spoke up now. "We haven't had a single politician who isn't owned by a dragon for . . . hell, longer than I've been alive. You can vote blue or you can vote red, but you can't vote against the interests of Auramagos. You want to add us to that equation too? Remove even us as an option?"

"In a gunfight, the side without a gun loses," Liam replied. "You can rage about how unfair that is, but if you don't pick up a gun, you just guarantee that the other side wins."

"Bullshit," Aiden spat.

"Cells on the west coast have already summoned some," Liam stated.

That shut us all up. He gave it a second to sink in.

"You haven't wondered how they've been doing so well?" he continued. "They've been using these things for a while. They call them Dragon-Eaters. They're advancing the struggle, and we're dragging them down. We're killing the resistance."

His words hung in the room. The circle of gold held us in its grip like a tourniquet. A bronze bowl rested against one wall, the athame inside it lay in wait. Overshadowing them, a tall wooden crucifix held a beautifully carved corpus of Christ, twisted in agony up toward the heavens. His eyes gazed at me from under the barbed crown, asking me how much I was willing to give to make the future better. How much of myself would I sacrifice for the good of others?

Liam's brother spoke up first. "I'm willing to die for the resistance. I don't want that to be for nothing. If this is what it takes . . . I'll do it."

Zoe nodded. "If this is a mistake, it's not permanent. We're the summoners, we can always banish it."

Aiden looked back and forth among us in dawning disbelief. "Oh no . . . you guys aren't buying this. You can't be buying this."

I opened my mouth to agree with him. A mental image of Tyrell being tortured stopped me. "We can't let them keep getting away with it," I said instead. "If we're defeated, it could be generations before people rise up again. Maybe never. I can't live in that world."

Aiden stared at us, a fire in his eyes. His breathing came heavier. His hands clenched into fists.

"You unbelievable idiots. You're damned if you go down this path. You're all damned, and you're doing it to yourselves."

"Aiden, we're losing. We have to try." I extended a hand, not used to his opposition. He jerked away from me.

"No. Fuck this. I'm outta here. Damn yourself by yourself."

238

He turned and stormed out. The door creaked slowly in his wake, as if buffeted by the fury of his passing.

"He'll come around," I told the group, ignoring the pinch of doubt in my guts. "I'll bring him over."

Zoe and Marcus murmured agreement.

Liam began the summoning. He knew exactly what he was doing; he'd been preparing for weeks. Within minutes the athame sliced over my palm. The blade split the skin neatly, drawing a perfect red line that wept into the bowl. It mingled with Liam's, Zoe's, and Marcus's. I stared at it as Liam worked, a buzzing in my head. Or was it in the room? It shifted, doubled, spawned low hums.

The gold ring thinned, evaporating, and the air grew heavy with an alien presence. Not just the air. Everything grew heavy--my clothes, my body. Breath came hard. The light from the bulb distorted and played over the walls as if filtered through choppy waters. A foreign mental process shoved against my mind, pushing my thoughts in unwelcome directions.

I glanced at Zoe. Under the distorted light her spiked hair looked like tarantula tufts. Strange shadows shifted behind her, giving her the appearance of having extra limbs. I saw a spider whose life consisted of the constant knitting of webs of emotional dependence, until her entire identity was a tangled social net and the upkeep it required. She crept into the lives of others, insinuating herself under the guise of extroverted friendship. Only by manipulating people did she accomplish anything.

This was the first gift of the dragons--the dragon sight. It strips away the facades we monkeys erect to make ourselves feel noble and pure. It reveals that we are simply biological constructs, responding to incentives, executing crude survival strategies. I looked to Marcus. I saw him wither into little more than a fluttering shadow. Unable to make his own way in a confusing world, he leached vitality from his brother's desperation. Dark tendrils slipped from his lethifold form, grasped after Liam, hanging onto another's life since he couldn't direct his own.

Liam had become a shimmering mirage in the wavering light, almost not there at all. His defiance paled into the flailings of a man who couldn't compete with his peers. He was plain, so he mutilated his face with pounds of metal. His voice couldn't soar, so he screamed and growled instead. Everywhere that he couldn't excel, he carved out his own pool of excess. He couldn't even fight the revolution with his natural talents, so he'd do it as a dragon-summoner.

I'd lived in a dream world where people ran on ideals. The dragon sight stripped that away, showed us our true motivations. I refused to look at myself.

As we gazed at each other, the light stabilized, and the droning hums and buzzes shifted. Wove together. They coalesced into a scratchy whisper--the dragon's murmurings, the second gift. The invisible presence hooked its claws into my psyche. From now on, a part of it would be with me, always. My chest swelled with power as the creature spoke. It began--

If you wish to prevail against dragons, this is what you must do . . .

We kept our dragon sight suppressed most of the time. Permanently living in a world stripped of its masks would have driven anyone crazy. I did use the dragon sight on Aiden later that week, though, after five days of him refusing to take my calls or respond to my texts. I'd have done it sooner, but I had trouble tracking him down. I saw an insubstantial, hollow-boned thing that lived vicariously through the emotions of others. He rejoiced when I took my pleasure from him. He exulted in my passion when I raged against the dragons. But above all, he was addicted to the concentrated distillation of emotion that made up primal music. Soaring high in that jet stream was the only time he felt alive.

Immediately I found a new drummer for Against Dragons. As we released new music, Aiden spiraled in closer around me, pulled by a gale of desire, until all I had to do was reach out and pluck him back in. I got what I wanted, but it left a sour taste in my mouth. I'd seen him as a biological construct responding to incentives, rather than a person. I didn't use the dragon sight on him again.

Months later, I sat on the remains of a couch in the remains of an apartment, my guitar in my lap. I fingered the strings absently. Sunlight streamed in from glass sliding doors, still intact, that led out to a balcony twelve stories above an alley strewn with trash. From the kitchen came the smells of Aiden frying us eggs. I pondered, examining the dragon problem, again. For their entire existence, dragons lived only as long as they produced wealth for their summoners. Failure to do so meant "banishment." Death. A single unprofitable year could kill a dragon, regardless of how great the rewards for sacrifice would be five years down the line. With incentives like that, no wonder they scorched the earth to achieve the results we demanded. They were only responding to the survival pressures humanity had placed on them.

A pang of regret cut me, knowing that I couldn't discuss this sort of thing with Aiden anymore. He wouldn't even talk about our Dragon-Eater. He couldn't rejoin our cell, not being a summoner. Fortunately he was extremely valuable as the leader of my sub-cell, as our part of the resistance had flourished in the months following the summoning. Recruiting had skyrocketed. It became so much easier when we saw what motivated people, what kept them loyal, what they could be pushed to do. The dragon sight let us estimate what each member could contribute, how much they were worth. It brought us successes--devastating guerrilla strikes with very acceptable losses on our side. Success was the biggest draw of all; I couldn't believe how quickly our ranks swelled.

Even the smattering of recent failures were easily turned into rousing stories of sacrifice. Nothing fired up our people like a strong martyr.

Aiden emerged from the kitchen carrying two plates loaded with greasy eggs and sausage. A niggling irritation scampered in my mind, scratching away at the corners of my brain like a rat. It nipped at my thoughts, but every time I looked for it, there were only tattered worries and rodent droppings.

Aiden's eyes caught the sunlight, sparkling cerulean blue. I smiled. They brought me back into the living, breathing world. He didn't smile back, but I didn't mind.

"Hey sexy boy," I greeted, and set my guitar aside. He sat down by me mutely and handed me a plate. I finally noticed his distant expression, his troubled brow. A weight of guilt smothered my hunger. How long had he been like this? I'd been ignoring him again, fretting over last week's barely-salvaged disaster.

"Did I keep you up too late last night?" I asked.

"It's not that. I woke up dreaming of Zoe again."

"Oh." I crossed myself. "Shit, sorry."

"I keep trying to picture her last moments." His voice came timid, as if scared to confide in me. That hurt. I pushed down the urge to use my dragon sight. "I wonder if she was terrified when she ran for the explosives. Was she already shot and bleeding out? Or did she detonate them defiantly, triumphantly? I think I like that better. I can see her with a detonator in hand, yelling at the top of her lungs that they'll never take her alive." A slight smile twisted his face. "Took a hell of a lot of pigs with her."

I nodded and ignored the piece of me searching for an answer that would make it better. Instead I forced up the core of dread that had been smoldering inside me for weeks, hot coals of regret. They burned me when I spoke. "It wasn't a fair trade."

A strong knock startled us. The front door swung open and Liam stepped inside, eyes hard. His brother Marcus followed, as well as a man I didn't recognize. The dragon whispered inside me--*he's brought along extra muscle. Something is going down.*

"Liam?" I asked as he closed the door behind them. "Who's this?"

Liam pursed his lips. His eyes moved to Aiden, his face darkened. That pestering rat at the back of my mind started scurrying again.

"Jo, why haven't you been freaking out about our failures over the last month?"

I hesitated, felt the dragon's cunning prodding my thoughts. "Our estimates are off. We're absorbing the data and adjusting our probabilities. It happens. We'll just have to be more conservative for a while."

Scratch, scratch, scratch. Gnaw, gnaw, gnaw.

"They're off in a consistent way," Liam said. "It looks like chaos at first, until you change a simple basic assumption. Then it becomes a predictable flaw."

Aiden's hand came to rest on my hip. "What are you trying to say?" he asked.

Claw, claw, claw. Bite, bite, bite.

Liam pierced me with a stare. "You should be able to see it."

The rat in my mind leapt at his words, and rapidly everything tumbled into place.

Don't look at the data in one pool--split it into two populations. The operations I'm not involved in, failing and succeeding roughly at the rate expected.

The operations I do have a hand in still succeeding often enough, but at a lower rate. Those that do succeed get us less supplies, less info, or cost more lives than expected. Enough success to keep us in the game, but costly enough to slowly bleed us dry.

He was right, I should have been the first to see it. The data is explained if I'm a mole, working with the old dragons to rot us away from inside.

But if they were convinced that I'm a mole, I'd be dead right now, came the whisper. The fact that they were here, appealing to me, was evidence they'd reached a different conclusion.

A chill spread from where Aiden's hand rested on my hip. Ice crept up my spine and sunk claws into my chest. Suddenly I couldn't breathe. I turned around to look at Aiden.

"What's up?" he asked, confusion in his eyes.

I looked through the dragon sight. Before me sat a man who only ever saw my hunched back as part of what made me who I am. I wasn't ugly to him. That was rare enough, but out of all the men who weren't turned off by me, how many would I be compatible with? How many took sex the way I loved to give it? How many would be caring and sweet, and love my bitchiness and aggression? How many could know all of me, and love me anyway?

No one else. I couldn't lose him.

So when I'd realized what was happening, I'd suppressed that knowledge. I knew, somewhere, what he'd done. The knowledge skittered in my mind like a rat in the walls. Hiding from sight but sometimes heard fleetingly, hatefully.

I didn't see Aiden below me. I saw my own lies. I'd endangered the resistance with my selfishness. Destroyed resources. Lost advantages. Killed Zoe.

"Oh, God no." The words escaped like smoke rising from my lungs, trickling from my mouth. I stepped back, back, until I stood pressed against the wall.

"Jo, are you ok?" my lies asked me, concern in his voice. He sounded ignorant, innocent. *He lies well.*

I closed my eyes and banished the dragon sight. Around me the sounds of three men stepping forward, laying hands on Aiden. A brief struggle I couldn't watch. My eyes burned.

"Jo, help me! What the hell? Get off me!"

244

I opened my eyes and gazed at Aiden, bent over, arms wrenched behind him. Confused, pained.

"Why?" I asked. But I already knew. Biological constructs running off simple incentives. Aiden secretly working with the dragons for months? That kind of bitter dedication only came from someone deeply wronged.

He drew a shallow breath. "Like you care," he said quietly. "You declared humans don't matter. Dragons are the true players in the world, humans are just the pieces they play with. Even you admitted it. Even you. I hope you burn."

We studied each other. He looked so fragile, bound up by angry friends. It hurt to see him like that. To see that in the end, he had been driven to the dragons, too. Aiden had realized that you could only seek vengeance upon a summoner by turning to a dragon of your own. When it came to something he truly, desperately wanted, even Aiden had succumbed. And I had set that precedent.

"Get him out of here."

The other three wrestled him out the sliding door, onto the patio. It overlooked a dozen floors of empty space, terminating in concrete far below.

Aiden struggled, thrashing. "No! Jo! Stop them! Please, Jo!"

Slowly I shuffled up to him on the balcony. My hands trembled. The words scraped my throat on their way out:

"Death to all collaborators."

They heaved him over the edge, and for one infinite split-second he hung in the air, surprise still on his face. Then gravity took him.

He fell, screaming, shattering the serenity of the sky. As he plummeted something bulged under his shirt, something large and swelling. The shirt shredded at the shoulders and downy growths burst from his back.

Long graceful wings, thick with snow-white feathers, erupted from the flesh. They snapped open, spanning yards across, and caught the air in a full embrace.

I should have been terrified. I should have recoiled in horror at this invasion into our material realm. The dragons had found a way to affect physical reality. The war was escalating, and there was no knowing where it would go now.

Instead I sank to my knees in gratitude, choking on sobs of relief. Tears spilled down my cheeks. I watched Aiden through a liquid blur as he swooped up, up into the endless blue sky, free of me finally and forever.

I haven't seen him since. I am grateful. The war grows bloodier, and our world grows bizarre. Yet I still craft the most volcanic music I can at night. I scream it into the sky, my personal siren songs. Sometimes I think I can see Aiden's figure far above, suspended from outstretched wings. I imagine he can hear my violent hymns, and I wonder how he would answer my rage. My accusations, my inquisitions.

When the dragons are finally ground to dust, I fear I may snare him and find out.

Eneasz Brodski lives in south Denver, and has a number of meaningful relationships of many varieties. He was born in Poland, and raised in an apocalyptic Christian sect. While he's left that behind, it still colors much of his writing.

Eneasz's short works have been published in Analog magazine and Asimov's Science Fiction. He was a winner of the 2018 Writers of the Future award.

246

In his ever-dwindling free time, Eneasz produces an audio fiction podcast at www.hpmorpodcast.com. He blogs at www.DeathIsBadBlog.com. He's always willing to strike up a conversation with anyone in dark clothes and eyeliner.

It Grows on You

Pedro Iniguez

It was five in the evening when the knock came at the door. Startled, Becky Castro nearly flung her book into the whirling blades of the ceiling fan.

Becky sucked in a deep breath and let her heart settle back into place. After adjusting her glasses, she tiptoed toward the window, knocking over a small stack of pogs along the way. She gently parted the curtains and saw Suzy DeMarco waiting below with crossed arms. In the distance, the sun crawled behind the hills of Los Angeles, causing the trees to spit forth long, gnarled shadows over the street. She frowned and made her way downstairs.

When Becky opened the door, Suzy was already scowling, her brows furrowed. Worst yet, her crimson lips curled upward like a snarling dog. Suzy had looked almost unrecognizable; she'd let her hair down and she was rocking a slick leather jacket and tight blue jeans.

"I've been calling and calling," Suzy said jabbing a finger into Becky's chest, "and all I get is a dead ringtone. If you thought I'd forget about picking you up, you are sincerely mistaken."

"Aw, come on, Suze," Becky said fidgeting with her glasses, her face starting to flush. All week she had wondered how long she could delay the inevitable. "You already know I don't like going out. Besides, it's getting dark and my mom doesn't like me being out this late."

"Come on! It's the fucking weekend," her friend said placing her hands on her hips. Her shoulders tensed and a faint trail of veins appeared on her head. "Besides, it's not every day I get to borrow my dad's car." Behind her, the cherry-red Cadillac sat parked in the driveway, its engine ticking as it cooled.

She wasn't conscious of it at first but she found herself closing the door a smidge. "I-I don't know..."

Suzy huffed and eyed the book in Becky's hands. Her shoulders eased a bit as she tilted her head to the side. "Watcha reading about this time, dork?" she said with cruel snark. "Killer cyborgs? Hungry mutants?"

"No," Becky shook her head, now opening the door and holding up the page where she'd left off. "It's this story about aliens and how they plan to conquer Earth by turning humans into mindless, droning herds."

"I'd say they've already succeeded." A smirk split across Suzy's face. "You know its aliens who dispersed that AIDS stuff into the world, right?"

"R-really?" Becky's lips quivered.

"Yup. They're everywhere. A whole cabal of 'em walking among us, wearing our flesh, waiting to colonize us all."

"Oh, my God," Becky said clutching the book to her body. She felt her heart race again. "How do you know all this?"

"I'm just kidding, dork. See? That's your problem, you're so cooped up at home reading this junk, that you're oblivious to the world. Sacred of it, even. It's the nineties; you gotta get out of the house. Get hip, you know? You have to learn to acclimate to the world and stop being a loser."

Becky sighed and dipped her head. Suzy had been right, of course. All her life she had been a homebody and making friends was almost impossible. She was shy, socially awkward; a downer at parties and school group projects just the same. Truth was, Becky did like having people to talk to, she just wasn't any good at it.

Besides, the fear of being judged had always scared her away from even trying.

If it wasn't so sad, it'd be funny: she wasn't cool enough for the popular kids and she was too quiet for the nerdy kids.

Suzy, on the other hand, was born to be social; an attention-seeker from birth. Sometimes it had even landed her in detention. Why she'd stuck around since kindergarten was beyond her. But Suzy understood her better than anyone else; all she wanted was for Becky to break away from her sheltered bubble and enjoy what life had to offer outside of it.

"You're not totally hopeless," Suzy said playfully thrusting an elbow into Becky's side.

"Really?" asked Becky, smiling.

"Yeah. You're a smart, sweet girl and there's no better way to integrate you into human society than a Nekrotik Korpse show." She pulled out two tickets from her purse and fanned them in Becky's face. "It'll be fun."

"I'm not sure, Suze. You know I don't like those crazy European black metal bands, much less their music."

Suzy snatched Becky's wrist and flashed a mischievous smile. "Come on, it grows on you."

By the time they arrived, darkness had settled into all the dingy nooks and alleys of the city. Packs of drunkards huddled around buzzing lampposts and the flickering window lights from the all-night diners, like children at bedtime finding sanctuary from the creeping dark.

It was late October in Los Angeles, when the days were warm and the nights were frigid. Becky shivered beside Suzy underneath the marquee, both of them awash in red neon light as they waited for the doors to open.

The line had steadily grown for the better part of an hour but it hadn't surprised her. The Roxy had been the trendiest joint on Sunset Boulevard, even Becky knew that. All the seniors at school talked about how they'd sneak off on weekends to catch their favorite up-and-coming bands just to say they saw them before they made it big. Lots of big acts had made a name for themselves there: *Gun N' Roses. Poison. Ratt.* Though, she'd known next to nothing about

250

today's music. She hadn't been too keen on MTV, or whatever passed for popular these days. She preferred the quiet comfort of reading beside a desk lamp in the safe confines of home.

Years of prodding from Suzy had convinced her that she needed to belong to something, anything other than being a prisoner in her own room.

Becky told herself tonight was healthy. It would be good to get out of the house and mingle, soak up some life for once instead of having her nose shoved in a book. She wasn't sure she was convincing herself.

Her mother's voice echoed in her mind, like teeth gnawing on the back of her brain stem. Something she'd said through the years. *There are bad people out there, Becky. They'll get you, sooner or later.*

Who were *they*? Perverts? Killers? Aliens? No one ever seemed to have a specific answer. Not her family, not her books. Like a phantom, the uncertainty had stalked her all her life.

She sighed and leaned against the wall, trying to make sense of her thoughts. She turned to Suzy, who swung and swayed and shook her hips, losing herself to the music throbbing from her Walkman headphones. It was hard not to be jealous of her friend. How nice it must have been to live so carefree, so open to the world.

A gust of wind blew in, nipping at her legs like tiny blades. Becky frowned. She already hated tonight before it even began. She eyed a payphone across the street and thought about phoning home. She could ask her dad to pick her up and pay Suzy back for the extra ticket. He'd probably be more than happy to do it. She shoved a hand in her pocket and rubbed two quarters between her thumb and index finger. Yes, that's what she would do.

Before she could break it to Suzy, heavy footsteps scraped against the pavement. Becky turned. A pair of men stumbled past, eyeing her up and down like hungry jackals. They smelled of beer and sweat and they cackled manically before they hobbled away into the night. Their predatory stares caused Becky to shrink within herself. She pulled her jacket in tight.

They'll get you, sooner or later.

Suzy must have seen her discomfort as she cradled her headphones around her neck and turned to her. She popped a pink bubble and slurped the deflated chewing gum back in her mouth. "I can tell you're tense. Just relax, it's only a show. We're all safe here."

"I'm just a little nervous is all," Becky said gazing at the people beside her. "Besides, I hear girls are getting murdered left and right these days."

"Oh, for God's sake, Becky. These people aren't here to hurt anybody. They're like you or me."

Becky observed the crowd waiting in line, which had now wrapped around the block. Glassy-eyed men with long bleached hair wore sleeveless vests, revealing muscular, tattooed arms. Many even wore black t-shirts bearing skulls and the logos of their favorite bands in metallic fonts.

They looked like trouble. Like the kind of guys who'd get rowdy at bars and start fights.

Damnit, Becky, stop being so judgmental. She looked them over again.

A few guys passed a joint around as they bunched up together to stave off the cold. Others drank beer covertly from paper bags. They all seemed to be enjoying themselves. And they weren't hurting anyone.

Becky had seldom seen people dressed like that in the daytime. They were Los Angeles' own anti-social freaks, she supposed, scurrying about town after nightfall, avoiding the judging glances of *proper* society, whatever that meant. She knew what that was like. Maybe, she thought, she had more in common with them then she'd want to admit.

"That paranoia? That's your mother talking," Suzy said draping an arm around Becky's shoulder. "You've got to learn that not everybody is out to get you. Besides," she said shaking her head, "You keep thinking like that and you'll never fit in anywhere. You'll be a single, crazy cat lady the rest of your life. Gag."

Becky forced a smile. "We can't have that, I suppose."

Suzy hugged her. "I won't allow it. Not on your life, kiddo."

The theater doors creaked open, producing a tall man wearing tight black jeans and a long, raggedy coat. The man limped outside; his strides awkward like a person nursing an old injury. Becky felt a shiver tingle up the back of her neck. The man's gait was frightening, unnatural, like those classic Hollywood monsters she'd seen on TV with her dad.

The man stepped under the marquee's red glow. He was bald and his face was pale, like a body drained of all its blood. His skin sunk around his cheekbones, revealing pockets of drooping pink flesh underneath his eyeballs. Becky thought the red lighting made him appear demonic.

"I think that's Heinrich Von Goethe, the owner of the joint," Suzy whispered in Becky's ear. "He's booked all the talent in this town for ages."

"What a sickly-looking man," Becky said under her breath. "He gives me the creeps."

Von Goethe's eyes glazed over the crowd with what appeared to be contempt. He bowed and swept a dramatic hand across the threshold. "Please," he said in a soft Germanic voice, "come in."

The crowd stampeded inside, jockeying for prime position on the floor. Suzy clutched Becky's hand and pulled her into the theater.

Becky didn't know why, but she turned and offered the payphone one last glimpse. Before the doors locked shut behind her and the darkness of the theater swallowed her whole, Von Goethe locked eyes with her and smiled.

They shoved through hordes of eager fans, wading past flying elbows, stumbling over steel-toed boots and discarded plastic cups. There were a few near-slips in the dark as they treaded over mysterious puddles.

Becky clenched her teeth as she felt the caress of stray hands stroking her arms. Even worse, were the pelvic thrusts, the not-so-subtle grinding against her backside while she shimmied past. She wanted to disappear, to turn invisible in the worst way.

She thought about breaking free from Suzy's grasp and running home to cry. Instead, she bit her lip and allowed Suzy to drag her toward the stage.

After a few grueling minutes of revolting human contact, they managed to nudge themselves just in front of center stage. The stage was just out of hand's reach, where a pair of amplifiers leveled evenly with their heads. The illegible scrawl of graffiti was etched into the front of the stage, where generations of youth had made their mark for all time.

"Here we can see everything," Suzy said clasping her hands together like a person in prayer. "Aren't you excited?"

Becky feigned a smile and nodded. Billows of smoke began to wisp around the air as people sparked up. Suzy's face suddenly became fuzzy, distorted, her shape a mangled silhouette of muted colors. The combination of heat and smoke had caused Becky's glasses to fog. She wiped them with the tail of her shirt and looked around the theater.

The Roxy was windowless and dark like some gothic sepulcher. If it wasn't for the dim purple spotlights in the rafters, Becky wasn't sure she'd be able to see much of anything other than the feint, indiscernible features of the people around her.

Just left of the stage she could make out a few columns of underlit picture frames. Pictures of famous musicians and singers through the years, smiling, many alongside Von Goethe himself. He looked as irritable and sickly as he had outside, except he'd appeared only scarcely older now. Some of the pictures must have been at least thirty years old. How was that possible? The thought unsettled her, made her want to retch, for some reason.

Suzy gawked around in awe. Becky understood; it was hard not to be impressed. Tonight, the venue had corralled a few hundred rabid fans. Chants of "Nekrotik Korpse," broke out, at first sporadically, until eventually, like a wildfire, it caught everywhere. The ground rattled as every boot in the theater stamped the floor. Behind them, an ocean of faceless outlines waved their arms in the air.

The energy in the theater was electric. It took Becky a moment before she realized she had been smiling.

Suddenly, there came a lull in the din as if the oxygen had been sucked from the theater. Every spotlight in the building began to strobe until five men in leather costumes sprinted onstage. Their faces were covered in black-and-white corpse paint, reminding Becky of demonic mimes. The crowd erupted into a chorus of cheers and whistles.

The band lifted their instruments in the air like offerings to the gods and stuck their tongues out. The singer, a long-haired blonde, closed his eyes and threw up devil horns.

The drummer twirled a pair of drum sticks before smashing them down on the snare and crash. The music blasted forth; a wave of pulsing sound that reverberated up and down Becky's spine. The drum beats rattled the foundation of the stage and the bass notes vibrated deep inside her chest. The guitars screeched like alien death rays and the singer growled like a woodland beast.

Becky covered her ears. The noise pounded inside her head, disorienting her. Is this what a concert was like?

Suzy threw her hands up and screamed, though Becky couldn't hear anything other than the sonic onslaught blasting from the amps. This went on for what felt like an eternity.

After the song ended, Suzy leaned in and tapped Becky's shoulder. "Hey," she shouted, "I gotta go whiz. I'll be right back."

Becky nodded, and her friend shoved through the mass of thrashing youth.

A pair of men scrambled over each other, filling in the gap where Suzy had stood. One of them, a stocky, bearded man, blew her a kiss. Becky folded her arms across her chest and looked away. She inhaled a breath of stale air and hoped Suzy would return soon.

Nekrotik Korpse played on. In spite of being nauseatingly loud, some of the tunes were catchy, though the lyrics, hard to understand, almost dealt exclusively with nihilistic tales and morbid delinquencies. She wasn't sure the genre was something she could get behind. When tonight was over, she would have so many questions for Suzy.

A few songs into the set and Suzy still hadn't returned. Becky looked at her watch. It had been too dark to make out the time, but it had surely been longer than twenty minutes. She turned around but couldn't spot Suzy among the crowd. For a brief moment she thought she saw Von Goethe's lofty outline lurking in the back row near the bar.

She faced the band again. The lines for the bathroom must have been incredibly long. She told herself everything was ok, to just relax and enjoy the show. But her mother's words found her again, nibbling on her brain stem like they always had.

They'll get you, sooner or later.

A trickle of sweat dripped down Becky's head. Her glasses fogged over again. The place had grown hotter since Suzy had left. What was the point? She tucked the glasses inside her jacket pocket. Five blurry shapes now marched about stage in a haze of purple light and smoke like a jarring nightmare.

The same was true for the audience around her; they had lost all their discerning features, becoming instead a mass of dark, writhing limbs.

Where was Suzy?

She turned again and witnessed blurry black forms melding into an ocean of black. Behind a curtain of smoke, a tall silhouette hobbled its way forward.

Von Goethe?

A strange sensation suddenly washed over her. It was a feeling that countless eyes had settled upon her. She scanned the people in her vicinity, but their faces were obscured.

They'll get you. Sooner. Or. later.

Tiny glints of light flashed like fish scales on the stage directly in front of her. She leaned forward and squinted her eyes. Fragments of what appeared to be fingernails had been lodged deep into the wood. The illegible graffiti scribbled onto the stage now looked a lot like scratch marks.

She spun around. The tall shape glided closer. Her heart beat against her chest. Had Suzy been right? Were aliens among us? Wearing our flesh? She ran a hand through her hair. *No. You're being irrational.*

It had been all those books, or her mother perhaps, sowing fear since she was a child. And now the dread had manifested itself into the paranoid delusions of a teenage girl's tormented psyche. All she had found repulsive in life had now taken shape and sprouted legs out in the darkness of the theater. Movie monsters, strange men, the dark, faceless terrors; all of them out to get her. That's all it was and nothing more, she told herself.

As if to invoke some sort of prayer, she shut her eyes and allowed the music to envelop her. She nodded her head to the beat, letting it carry her away from all she feared.

Behind her, she felt cold fingers part away the hair on her neck. The hairs on her arms went prickly. She shut her eyes tighter until they began to hurt.

"Welcome, child," the Germanic voice whispered, "to a new life."

She suddenly heard a familiar voice. "No," Suzy said. "She's my friend. Let me do it."

Then came the quick, piercing sting on her throat and the warm, wet drip down her neck. She kept her eyes closed as a wave of lethargy swept over her. She slumped into the embrace of a strong pair of arms.

"You're one of the family now," Suzy's voice said softly against her ear. "There aren't many of us yet, but soon, there'll be enough of us to convert the whole city, then no one will ever judge you again."

When Becky opened her eyes, her friend—looking like a cold, lifeless corpse— stared back through a warm, loving gaze. She smiled, bearing a set of bloodied fangs.

Becky's eyes adjusted to the dark.

All around, a slew of dark shapes thrust upon the throats of screaming concert-goers. The screams gave way to gurgled whimpers, and then, silence as they collapsed lifelessly on the floor.

Blood flowed freely from punctured throats, pooling underneath their bodies, soaking into their clothes.

Becky tried to gasp but no sound came. Her throat was dry, itchy.

One by one, the dead rose, pushing themselves slowly off the slick, dark floor. Fangs now sprouted from their blue lips like daggers.

Everywhere, the smiles of pale strangers greeted her. A slew of frigid hands rocked her shoulders gently, welcoming her, pulling her in to their masses. She felt a rush, then. Something akin to pride and love.

The band played on as they gazed upon her with loving, bloodshot eyes.

Already Becky felt her body changing in inexplicable ways, but that didn't matter. Now she felt strong, confident. She'd found her people. Her family. She would finally belong to something, to outcasts like herself and it was enough to fill her heart with joy, up until its final throbs.

And as for the music: it was finally starting to grow on her.

Pedro Iniguez is a speculative fiction writer and painter from Los Angeles. His work has appeared in Nightmare Magazine, Helios Quarterly, Star*Line, Space and Time Magazine, and Tiny Nightmares, among others.

He can be found online at Pedroiniguezauthor.com

Horns of Abaddon

Jason R Frei

"He was so young," said Lip, looking down at his friend nestled in a solid black casket. In fact, Robert "Blaze" Trudow, lead vocalist for the death metal band Goat Scrote, had turned thirty-two less than a month ago.

Blaze was adorned in his normal band attire—leather pants, Doc Marten's, Judas Priest t-shirt, leather biker jacket and a jeans jacket with cut-off sleeves. His auburn hair, neatly curled, cascaded down to his chest. The mortuary cosmetologist did a great job of making him look like he was asleep, including covering up the ligature marks on his neck from the rope he hung himself with.

Dante and Greg shuffled forward and stood next to Lip, paying their respects. Goon stepped up and tucked a bottle of Jack Daniels in the crook of Blaze's arm. Noodles patted Goon on the back, his gaze flitting everywhere but on the corpse.

Emma, Blaze's widow, approached the men.

"Brandon Lipinski," she said.

Lip turned and bowed his head.

"Good to see you Emma, even under the circumstances."

The two embraced.

"Thank you for coming. Blaze loved you all very much. He considered you brothers."

Dante hugged Emma and said, "It's because of him that Horns of Abaddon got so big. I just wish we were still touring together."

Greg chuckled. "I remember our first night on tour. Blaze introduced us to the crowd like we were the headliner and they were the opener."

"I think I singed my eyebrows with all the pyrotechnics they had," said Noodles, a small smile playing on his thin face.

"I'm surprised Blaze's hair didn't go up in flames with all the Aqua Net and whiskey in it," said Goon. He gave Emma a tender embrace, belying his strapping exterior.

Lip pulled Emma to the side. "Emma, Blaze and I went way back. He really was like my big brother. I just don't understand why he would have done this to himself."

Emma shook her head. "I don't understand it either. The last few weeks, he just wasn't himself. He locked himself in the studio for hours. I'd hear him talking, as if he was having a conversation with someone, but no one else went in or out."

She pulled a large yellow envelope from her purse. "One of the last things he told me was to give this to you in case anything happened to him."

"What is it?"

"I don't know. He said to give it directly to you and only you."

Lip took the envelope and gave Emma another hug. "I'll be around if you need anything. We're going into the studio, but we'll be available."

"Thank you Lip." Emma gave him a quick peck on the cheek.

My Brother of Metal,

If you are reading this, then shit went south. Way south. I know I fucked up a lot, but I always tried to do right by my family, both with Emma and with the metal community. Especially with you.

I fucked up big this time though. During our last European tour, I drunkenly stumbled into an antique bookstore somewhere near Budapest. I don't know exactly why I was there, but I was looking for something to leave as a legacy—something to give my family that would last forever.

That's where I found an old, thin book that led me down this road. The jacket was mottled tan and had a distinctive odor. Stale, but sweet, like smoked beef jerky in an old library. It felt like velvet, smooth and supple. Liber Musicorum Daemoniorum was stamped into it in scarlet lettering.

Although the book was written in Latin, I could somehow understand the words on its vellum pages. The small text was a manual for writing music, music that could change a person's destiny. I devoured the words, looking to create a song that would leave its mark on the world.

When we got back from the tour, I locked myself away to create my masterpiece. I leave my legacy in your hands. Please don't fail me.

A warning though, if you will. The music written must be performed together, never separately. That is the mistake I made and why this music is now in your hands. Live long, my brother.

Metal forever,

Blaze

Lip read the letter twice before folding it up and setting it down. He shook the envelope and out slid a paper-clipped pack of notation sheets. Scrawled atop the first page in Blaze's spiky lettering were the words "Canticum Damnatorum".

With a beer in hand, Lip took the sheet music to his desk and spread the pages out. All of the parts were layered over each other—bass, guitars, drums and lyrics. He hummed the intro. Almost instantly, his head spun and the notes echoed back like he was underground in a large cavern. Nausea bubbled up inside of him. A trickle of blood dripped from his nostril and spattered on the desk, barely missing page three.

He stood up quickly and the room tilted, throwing him to the floor. He crawled to the waste basket and emptied his stomach into it. Lights strobed through Lip's head as he passed into unconsciousness.

He awoke bathed in silver. A gibbous moon hung in the night sky, shining down through the bay window in his studio. His head ached.

Groaning, he rolled over and stood up, keeping a hand on the desk to maintain his balance. The shimmering light of the moon danced over the music sheets. The notes seemed to float slightly above the paper like a 3D image. They emitted an eldritch green light that hurt Lip's eyes. Whispers swam through his throbbing head.

His cellphone lit up on the desk. Lip picked it up and found fifteen missed messages—his bandmates wondering where he was. They were supposed to be getting together at the studio to start working on their next album. He checked the time and found that six hours had passed.

"Shit." The word came out hoarse and slurred.

He grabbed his gig bag and threw the music in. Slinging his guitar over his shoulder, he rushed to the studio.

"Where you been, man?" asked Dante. His voice was nasally when he spoke, making him sound more like whining than the growling he did as the lead singer.

"Yeah," said Dante's younger brother Greg. "You were supposed to be here hours ago." His voice was naturally gravely and if he wasn't such a good rhythm guitarist, he would have been the first pick for vocalist.

"Sorry, guys," said Lip. "Something weird happened and you aren't going to believe it."

He pulled the sheet music out of his bag and set it on the mixing board table.

"What's this?" asked Noodles, picking up the first sheet. "Something new?"

The bassist rested his thumb on the E string and Lip yanked the sheet out of his hands before he could pluck a single note.

Noodles scowled.

"Sorry, man, but just hold up a second."

Lip unfolded Blaze's note and handed it over. "Read this first."

The rest of the band huddled over Noodles and read the letter.

"What's he mean, never separately?" asked Goon, twirling a drumstick in his left hand.

Lip took a deep breath and let it out slowly. "Look, guys. Like I said, I know this is going to be weird, but hear me out."

He told them what happened when he read the music and then hummed the intro. The uneasiness still washed over him in waves. He couldn't shake the feeling that something bad was released into the world.

Noodles shook his head. "That's bullshit, man."

He looked at the music again and slapped out the first four or five notes. A twang cut through the bass and the G string snapped like a gunshot in a closet. Noodles whipped back his head and let out a shriek. An ugly red line creased his face from his forehead diagonal down to the corner of his lip, missing his eye by less than half the width of the string. For a brief moment the red line stood out in sharp contrast to his pale face, then blood flowed out, covering the bottom half of his face in a crimson sheet.

Greg tore off his Slayer t-shirt and wrapped it around Noodles' face, partially to staunch the flow, but also to muffle the scream coming out of the bassist's mouth. Dante and Lip held him down while Goon called for emergency services. After Noodles was carted off in the ambulance, the rest of the band processed what happened.

"I think Blaze's letter is pretty clear. We can't play this music individually. It has to be the whole band."

Dante grabbed the sheet music and took out his lighter. "Fuck that. I say we burn it back to Hell where it belongs."

"Hold up," said Goon. "That's a bit extreme. I mean, if this music can truly help us hit the big time..."

"We don't know that for sure," said Dante, his lighter poised below a corner of the pages.

Greg put his hand on his brother's arm. "You're right, we don't know for sure. But we do know that both Lip and Noodles experienced some freaky shit by going solo. If that can happen, why couldn't it do what Blaze says?"

"Then we put it to a band vote," said Lip. "All those in favor..."

Goon shook his head and waved his hand. "The whole band ain't here right now. I say we put this away somewhere and wait until we see Noodles."

"Agreed," said Greg and Dante together.

Lip nodded his head. "Alright. Since I know what this thing can do, I volunteer to keep a hold of it until we're back together."

The others agreed. Lip folded the sheets, put them back in the envelope and then jammed the whole thing inside his gig bag. Together, they went to the hospital.

Noodles was in good spirits when the rest of the band got to the hospital. The cut across his face was nothing more than a scratch requiring no stitches.

"Not even a cool scar?" he asked the attending doctor.

"I'm afraid not, young man."

"Why did it bleed so much?"

The doctor took off his glasses, huffed on them and wiped them on the sleeve of his white coat. "Capillaries are small blood vessels that exchange carbon dioxide for oxygen and other nutrients. They are like very thin veins networked close to the skin, especially in the face. When the string sliced through your skin, several capillaries were severed, releasing their blood."

Dante grunted. "So, it just looked a lot worse than it was?"

"Correct." The doctor put his glasses back on and squinted at the group. He looked at Noodles and nodded his head at the band. "Friends of yours?"

"More like family," said Noodles.

Goon laughed. "Any chance you can fix his face, doc?"

"The scratch will heal in a few weeks. As for the rest of his face, I'm afraid he's stuck with what he was born with."

The group laughed as the doctor made his leave.

Lip sat on the bed next to Noodles. "So, do you believe me now?"

A solemn looked crossed Noodles' face and he nodded his head. "I do, but there's more. When I played those few notes, I felt... sick, or just wrong somehow, like the world was spinning and I was standing still. When the string cut me though, I saw something else.

"I saw us up on the stage absolutely shredding the hell out of that song. The crowd fucking loved it! I saw major record contracts and platinum records and big, fancy cars and even bigger, fancier houses. This song is a gold mine."

Lip pulled the sheet music from his bag and spread it out, face down, on the bed. Noodles moved back, but didn't shy completely away from it.

"Before we came here, we were going to have a vote."

"What kind of vote?" asked Noodles.

Dante flipped open his Zippo. "Whether we should burn it or learn it."

Lip nodded and looked at each other member of the band. "So, what do you all say? Those in favor of learning it..."

Lip, Noodles and Goon put up their hands immediately. Greg looked at Dante for a moment and then added his hand to the rest.

Dante crossed his arms. "Well, I guess that's a majority, but we need to lay some ground rules."

The other bandmates agreed.

"First, no one practices alone. We do this all together or not at all."

"Agreed," said Noodles.

Greg piped up. "I think we should only practice this in the studio. It'll give us a way to control some things just in case."

Dante clapped his brother on the back. "Excellent suggestion, bro."

"What should we do with the sheets?" asked Lip.

"I think we keep those locked up in the studio, too," said Greg. "We should get a small safe and stash them there. I'd hate for anyone else to look at them and end up like Lip and Noodles."

Goon smiled. "You heard the doc. Noodles was just born with that fucked up of a face."

Horns of Abaddon spent the next three months in the studio writing and recording their new album. In between takes, they practiced the *Canticum Damnatorum*, always together. There were a few minor mishaps with the piece.

Once, halfway through the song, a strong storm momentarily knocked out the power to the studio. The instrumentalists stopped when the electric went out, but Dante, his eyes always closed when he was lost to the music, continued with the lyrics. The power came back on as he was still singing. The electricity surged through the microphone and coursed into the singer's face. The resultant shock cracked a tooth and left a scorch mark on his cheek.

Even that event did not deter the band from continuing with the song. They could feel its power. Small bits and pieces of the unholy canticle found its way into their new music. Two days after their new album dropped, it went straight to number one on the Billboard charts with five of the twelve songs reaching the top ten on several music charts in multiple countries. Within the month, the album hit Double-Platinum and would be certified Diamond by the end of the year.

Their recording company lost no time in organizing a World Tour, set to start in Tampa, Florida, the death metal capital of the world. Horns of Abaddon practiced their new songs and continued working on the *Canticum*. They couldn't help but feel that it was the source of their newfound glory.

The first night in Tampa was sweltering. Fifteen minutes before show time and it was still 100 degrees.

"This heat is fucking up my hair," said Dante while applying another coat of Aqua Net.

"Seriously," said Goon. "I'm afraid to tighten my drum heads anymore or they'll snap."

Originally, the band was to be decked out in all their leather glory, but quickly opted for tank tops and ripped jeans when Lip almost passed out from heat exhaustion.

Noodles cornered the main stagehand. "We need all the fucking fans you can get, man. I'm not going limp out there."

Lip sat on the floor, chugging water from a gallon milk jug. "What a way to start the tour. It's like we're truly in hell right now."

"You going to be able to play?" asked Dante.

Lip grinned up at the vocalist. "Not even Satan himself could stop me."

Greg looked out from the side of the stage. "Holy shit, guys. It is fucking *packed* out there. The floor is just a sea of people."

The other members peeked out, huge grins spreading over their faces.

"We finally made it," said Dante in an awed whisper.

The main stagehand ran up to them. "You're on in five minutes. The fans on stage are loud, so we cranked up the monitors, but you should be nice and cool."

The Horns gathered in a huddle.

Dante looked around the group. "This is our time, guys—time for the Horns of Abaddon to finally make a huge name for itself. We've been working toward this moment for years now, and it's finally here. Let's go out and kick some ass!"

Greg laughed. "Your pep talks are getting better. Still a good thing you don't write the lyrics yourself though."

Dante laughed and punched Greg in the shoulder. They stood shoulder-to-shoulder for a moment more, basking in the glory.

"Go time!" yelled the stagehand.

Horns of Abaddon took the stage.

The crowd was deafening. Even with the monitors turned all the way up, Dante had a hard time hearing himself. In between songs, he screamed out to the crowd, goading them on to get even louder. A mosh pit opened up on the floor in front of the stage. Metalheads, punks and skins windmilled, spin-kicked and 'bow-threw their fists and boots and other body parts with abandon.

Horns of Abaddon finished their second set to thunderous applause. Screams for an encore echoed through the stadium. The band gathered offstage.

"This is fucking nuts," said Dante.

Goon wore a grin from ear to ear. "I can barely hear my drums over the crowd."

"What song should we encore with?" asked Greg, going over a mental list of choices.

Lip laughed and slung his arm around Greg's shoulder. "What fucking song? We do the *Canticum*, of course."

Noodles wiped the sweat from his face and ran a finger over his non-existent scar. "Fuck yeah we do!"

Dante grabbed a bottle of bourbon, took a deep slug and passed it around. Excitement played at the corners of his mouth. "Let's do this!"

The crowd exploded into a cacophony of raw noise as the band hit the stage. Dante tapped the mic and the clamor died almost instantly. His voice boomed out through the stadium.

"We'd like to thank all of our fans here in Tampa tonight! You've made our dreams come true by filling this fucking place. In gratitude, we're gonna play you a brand new song. Now, make some fucking noise!"

The audience roared, shaking the walls of the stadium. Goon tapped out a three count with his sticks and the *Canticum Damnatorum* started.

The intro rolled along as a slow dirge-like hymnal. The guitars resonated in distorted rhythm playing through a discordant scale of flats designed to incite fear and awe. The bass thrummed like the tolling of a bell. Goon's drums played a beat that did not match the rhythm of the guitars or the bass, but instead, wove their own intricate pattern of kick, snare and high-hat. Dante's voice entered the fray with a low, almost throat-singing chanting in Latin. One minute into the song and Goon struck a hard swing on the china, jarring the music into something different.

The guitars broke rank. Greg continued playing the same discordant scale, but sped it up to thrash speed. Lip shredded a solo filled with sixteenth notes and long, distorted slides. Noodles slapped up and down the neck of his bass seemingly at random, his hands crossing over each other as they held or slapped the notes. Dante's voice vacillated between the guttural growl of a demon and the high-pitched keening of an angel.

The crowd picked up on the change and pitched into a frenzy. The mosh pit became a blur of leather, spikes and chains. Blood slicked the floor. The music swelled and swayed like a fearsome thunderstorm. The floor and walls reverberated with the chaotic melody. Cracks snaked through the facade and made their way across the ground. Doorways shattered cutting off all exits. The band played on as if possessed.

A skinhead in the middle of the mosh pit staggered as the floor buckled. He threw his hands out for support and screamed as a literal pit opened up beneath him. Smoke and heat belched out of the red-glowing abyss. A horde of locusts sprang forth. They bit and stung anyone they encountered. Cries of pain and agony echoed through the venue.

The music reached its crescendo and then abruptly stopped with a jarring wail from Dante. The panic of the crowd died with the music. They gathered around the infernal pit in the middle of the venue.

A hand reached out of the abyss and grabbed onto the splintered floorboards. Scabrous sores blistered and oozed across the back of it. Long, ragged nails sunk into the boards. From out of the hole crawled a man. His skin glistened with decay and putrescence. Long auburn hair dripped from its peeling head, bits of skull showing through. The revenant turned toward the band, a rotten and toothy smile on his face. Lip instantly recognized the worm-eaten Judas Priest shirt and gore-slicked leather jacket.

He gasped. "Blaze?"

Their undead brother walked toward the stage, parting the crowd before him like Moses at the Red Sea. Behind him, more corpses clambered forth from the hole.

"So, my brother, the song worked. This"—Blaze spread his arms, as if crucified—"is my legacy."

A low howling issued from the pit and sparks shot up into the rafters. Shadows flitted across the smoke.

Blaze turned back to the pit and went down on one knee, his head bowed.

A crimson hand the size of a bass drum cleaved the smoke and slammed down on the ground. Black talons tipped the massive fingers. The muscles bunched up in the hand as the rest of the creature pulled itself from the pit. The thing's head resembled a mix of a human and a horse, with a twisted, black crown resting on top. Long, black hair flowed down its sinewy back. Two dark-

271

feathered wings sprouted from the shoulder blades. A pitted, tarnished breastplate adorned its bulky chest. Its legs were covered in scales all the way down to its hooves.

Blaze kept his head lowered. "Master."

The demon strode toward the stage.

"Ahh, my namesake children. As you can see, I traded in my horns for a crown." His voice buzzed like electricity in water. "Thank you for summoning me and providing me with all of these"—He swept his arm to the side, indicating the crowd—"souls. What is it that you desire?"

"Desire?" asked Dante. "Souls? What the fuck is this?"

Abaddon snorted, black smoke billowing from his nostrils. "The song you played was a summoning spell—*my* summoning spell. You provide me with sacrifices, and I provide you with gifts. Now, what do you desire?"

Dante opened his mouth, ready to let loose a tirade on the infernal being. Greg put his hand on his brother's arm and pulled him back. Dante turned on him.

"What?"

"This could be our big chance. We can ask for anything, man."

"But at what cost?" asked Goon. "Look out there, Greg. Tell me what you see?"

Greg's eyes took on a weird shine. "I see a fucking goldmine."

Dante slapped his brother across the face. When Greg turned back, his eyes were normal again.

"I...I'm sorry. I don't know what came over me."

"Greed," said Abaddon, his voice coiling around them like a snake. "I can make you rich beyond your wildest dreams. Money, fast cars, women. Anything you desire."

Lip stepped up to the edge of the stage. "Thanks, but no thanks, asshole. We'll get there on our own."

272

The rest of the band stepped up with him, forming a line of solidarity against the Prince of Hell.

The demon hissed. "Fools! Tell me your desire or join these heathens in eternal damnation."

Lip looked directly at Blaze. "You wrote this song, man, and what did it do for you?"

Blaze stared back, anguish and grief in his eyes. "A one way ticket to Hell, my brother. I'd hoped it would do better for you."

"Well, you can see how that worked out. What can we do?"

Abaddon stomped his cloven foot. "Nothing, mortal!"

He closed his fist around Blaze's body and raised him into the air. The cracking of joints and bones resounded through the hall. Blaze tried to scream, but his lungs were crushed under the pressure. His arms flailed as he tore his shirt off his body and threw it to the stage. Abaddon brought his other meaty hand up and crushed the undead man's head like squeezing a swollen tick.

Lip cried out and dropped to his knees. He picked up Blaze's shirt and held it reverently before him. Tears streamed down his face, but a wild, maniacal grin spread across his face. He jumped up and grabbed Dante.

"Get the crowd to rush Abaddon and keep him busy." He shoved the t-shirt into Dante's hands and slung his guitar on.

Dante looked at the shirt, grinned, grabbed the microphone off the stand and shouted to the crowd, pleading with them to hold Abaddon back.

"What's the game plan?" asked Goon.

"We need to pull a 'Better By You Better Than Me'."

Noodles's face lit up. "You mean play the song backwards?"

"Right. It should reverse the summoning and send that fucker back to Hell."

The other bandmates grabbed their instruments as Lip pulled out the song sheets. He placed them near Goon and they all gathered around the drum kit.

Goon once again tapped out a three count and the music started with an inhuman pig squeal from Dante.

The guttural screech died in Dante's throat and another malevolent shrieking took its place, resounding through the stadium. Abaddon staggered under the weight of twenty metalheads. They pounded on the demon with chains and spiked fists. The undead shuffled around, ineffective.

The song's feverish pitch and thrashing guitar solos fell back into the opening crescendo, but instead of being discordant and uneasy, the music became somber and forbidding. The walls of the venue shook as Abaddon flailed and buffeted the fans assaulting him. The riotous throng drove the living dead back into the hellish pit.

The *Canticum* was nearly finished and took on a choral tone. Abaddon reeled across the floor drunkenly. He spun around once and fell backward into the pit from whence he came, two punks clinging to his wings. The song ended as the floor reknit itself with a crunching, grinding noise, leaving not a trace that it had ever been there. The dead lay strewn across the floor, but many more survivors checked on each other and helped those who could not help themselves.

Blood frothed on Dante's lips. He made to speak, but could utter nothing, his vocal cords damaged from the chthonian singing. Scorch marks marred the surface of Lip's guitar and blood flowed freely from his fret hand. Noodles and Greg lay unconscious on the floor, twined together. Blood flowed from Goon's ears that would no longer hear.

Newspapers called the event a catastrophic failure brought on by faulty equipment. The record company disavowed any wrongdoing and fired the band. The Horns of Abaddon were no more.

Months after the doomed concert, Lip sat alone in a rundown studio apartment. He could no longer play guitar. The damage done to his hand left it numb and lifeless.

On the table in front of him were the singed and blurred pages of the *Canticum Damnatorum*. Most of the lyrics and notes were illegible. An open and blank music notation book sat in front of him. He held a small coffee-colored leather bound book in his good hand. Scarlet ink covered the onion skin pages in small cramped Latin. Lip placed the book down and stamped into the spine were the words Liber Musicorum Daemoniorum. He took a deep breath, picked up a pencil and began transcribing the music surging through his head.

Jason R Frei lives in Eastern Pennsylvania where he works as a therapist with children and adolescents. He writes speculative fiction culled from the experiences of his life and those he works with. He blends science fiction, fantasy and horror into new creations. Visit him online: https://facebook.com/odinstones

Sonitus Satanae

Heinrich von Wolfcastle

They handed me the cassette in a clear, non-descript case. The black marker scrawled across the side of it teased, *For a Good Time.*

"It won't be anything like you're expecting," they warned. "There are no guitars, and no one even utters, 'Satan.'"

"Well, that seems like a missed opportunity," I suggested.

No one laughed.

It began with a drum. The beat was slow.Steady. I counted the seconds between thumps just to be sure that there was, indeed, a structure to what I was hearing.

The static hissed and panned its way back and forth between my ears before finding residence at the center of my skull. And then the thumping began. Between beats, there wasn't silence exactly. I'm not quite sure what it was—a dry resonance. I imagined someone with sharp fingernails dragging their hand across a sheet of leather. And that's when I realized it was working, because I saw it.

I was in a damp basement with concrete walls painted in firm shadows. There was a girl bound to a wooden chair under the glow of a hanging light bulb. Her face was hidden from me—her head slumped forward, tucked awkwardly onto her chest.

I was overcome by a burst of excitement as I approached my gift from behind, admiring the grooves carved into her back like trails of cherry-colored rivers. I went to caress their depths, but was taken aback by the appearance of my fingers.

Heavy Metal Nightmares

My hands, my arms, my entire body was translucent, like I had been remade out of jellyfish flesh. I waved my hand over her, mesmerized by the glow of my non-skin, and then gently lowered a fingertip to her wounds. I could almost sense the curvature of her lacerations—the raised tissue bulging to create defined valleys—even though I couldn't actually touch her.

I pressed into those gashes, feeling her molecules scatter as they made way for my own, and if I had a voice, it might've uttered a sound of pleasure.

What should have been disbelief of the entire experience was replaced by exhilaration as I examined my surroundings—gleeful to find myself in another time, another place. It had been such a long pursuit to find this rumored world between worlds that I had almost doubted it existed.

A long staircase led from the basement to the rest of the house, and I wanted to explore further to find where—and when—I might be. But it was too hard to leave the girl.

I made my way around the chair, wondering what her face might look like. I hoped she had dimples.

Her chin sat in a pool of vivid, red blood that had collected across her ample chest. I imagined that she was exhausted; tired from thrashing about during whatever torture she endured. I lowered myself to look into her eyes, and to my delight, I found that they had been removed.

I drifted closer with a curiosity for what might happen if more of our parts overlapped. But my attention was snagged by a long, dull, dragging sound. It pulled across the floor above me in shuddered movements.

It seemed impossible. The only thing that could *move* in a place like this would have to be someone—or something—like me. A momentary hint of intrigue formed at the thought of finding camaraderie after such a lonely, misunderstood life. But the feeling quickly deflated as I considered the likelihood that I would again be shamed and judged for my earnest wants. Needs.

With agitation tearing at my elated mood, I made my way to the base of the staircase. I paused to listen for the sound again, but it had become so faint that I wasn't quite sure I was even hearing it.

A strange effect from the tape, I considered. I longed to return to the girl so beautifully fixed in her agony. But it didn't matter. I wouldn't be able to fully invest my attention back to her without first surveying the rest of the house.

I moved easily over the steps, recognizing for the first time how much my physical body regularly labored in its movements. Without it, I simply glided with no wasted effort.

My ascent led me to a dark kitchen where a set of broken blinds traced slices of moonlight across a linoleum floor. The kitchen table was covered in the shredded remains of a newspaper. An article about withdrawing troops from Vietnam had been soiled by what I presumed were bodily fluids and other organic materials.

The whole room seemed to be furnished in nauseating gold and orange patterns. A clock hanging from the wall stared back at me, its hands pinned in place.

A long hallway extended beyond the kitchen like a portal into darkness. I listened intently, examining its shadows from where I stood. There was no sign of any life at all.

I surprised myself with my own hesitation to venture into that dark tunnel. I mean, what was there to fear, anyway? Yet, between the shadows, I could've sworn I saw something move.

A terrible screeching sound ripped at my eardrums, and I awoke back in my bedroom, gasping for air as I tore the headphones from my head. They were drenched in sweat.

My pulse thudded so loudly in my ear that it was difficult to think straight. I dabbed my forehead as I rewound the tape, readying myself for a second journey.

Part of me wanted to go search for a news story about kidnapped or tortured women in the 1960's, but I would need more information to find anything worthwhile. I needed something tangible, *like an address*, I thought. But, let's be honest, I just wanted to see *her* again.

That steady, dry drumbeat panned slowly, then rapidly, between my ears. Then came the static hiss over the sound of someone raking their fingernails through flesh. With the exhale of a deep breath, I found myself in the basement again.

The girl was bound to the wooden chair just as before. But I could swear there was another wound on her back—something long and jagged that ran from her shoulder down and around her torso. I hadn't seen that one before. *Had I? But it must have already been there*, I told myself, because it certainly wasn't something *I* was able to create.

Habitually, I raised a hand to touch her, forgetting that it would be impossible. Nonetheless, I moved my fingers into that delicate space between her ribs just beside her silent heart. Her molecules scattered the same way they did before. I lingered, hoping to eventually find a sense of their friction. What good was her body to me if I couldn't *affect* it?

I could feel the seams of my composure starting to fray as flashes of rage built in my mind, and then the dragging started again in long, slow movements. There was no time to waste with the girl anymore. I made my way for the kitchen.

I rooted myself at the table and peered into the great darkness of the long hallway. I could make the outline of something scaly—humanoid in form. It crouched over what I presumed was the body of a dog.

279

I shrank back as the sudden heft of the situation collapsed upon me. I truly knew nothing of the beings that lurked here—their wants. Their needs.

I pressed backwards until, to my surprise, I found myself outside.

"Mind your cord," came a soft voice.

I turned and saw a slim, feminine silhouette lurking in the shadows of a bush from a neighbor's yard. She seemed to read my confusion.

"Your cord," she urged again.

I looked down and saw a thin silver thread protruding from my stomach. It ran back through the wall of the house. But she was right; it was snagged on the physical structure of the wall.

"If that breaks," she started.

I struggled to find any kind of voice to communicate with her. Before I could even utter a sound, she retreated into the shadows of the bushes and seemed to disappear altogether.

I tugged on the cord, but as it stretched, it looked as if it might tear. I loosened my grip and returned to the wall hoping to make slack. It drooped to the ground like an effervescent fishing line.

As I stood at the wall of the house, I recognized for the first time that something seemed off about the world I was in—as if the measurements weren't quite right. I turned my attention to the individual bricks of the wall and placed my hand upon them. I couldn't feel their texture, but I could feel *them*. It was as if I developed a new sense of touch that could detect something, even if I didn't quite have the vocabulary to describe it. The house—the whole world I was in—felt ill.

I placed my ear closer to the wall, wondering if I might detect something else. It had no sensation at all until it began to quiver. Then it started to tremble.

I pulled back and saw the hideous, scaled face of a man-shaped worm pushing its way through the wall. It lunged at me, its mouth open, suckling, and squelching the air. I flew backwards until the tension of the silver cord briefly caught me and then snapped with a *pop*.

My eyes shot open and I was back in my bedroom. I settled my gaze on the rotating fan above my bed as I caught my breath. The tape droned on with its distorted drumbeat. I removed my headphones before it could reach its screeching end.

I wondered if I managed to wake up before the cord had severed. And maybe *waking up* was the right way to think about it altogether. *What if it all was just a dream?*

I rose from the bed, contented by my usual reflection as I caught a glimpse of myself in the mirror. I needed to process what I experienced. I needed answers, and I thought to return to the group who sold me the tape.

The door of my bedroom opened to the hallway, and I walked in a daze out to my car with images of the girl racing through my mind. Just as I made it way outside, I realized I had forgotten my car keys. I turned around but was halted by the brick wall of *the house*.

It was night again, and everything looked the same as if I hadn't woken up at all. But my hands, my body, everything about me was physical.

"What the fuck is going on?" I muttered. Hearing my own voice brought me relief that I could speak again.

I placed my hand against the wall and was comforted to feel its real texture this time, but I pulled back as I remembered the face of the scaled creature.

"Hey!" I called out, turning to the shadows of the bushes. "Help!"

I was met by silence.

I moved closer, searching the shadows for outlines of somebody hiding there. A strange mound of something hid in the twigs and branches of the foliage. I grasped for it and managed to pull it out with a tug. It was unmistakably a flayed hand. It looked like the skin had been sucked right off of it. The muscle tissue glistened with gore as I rolled it over in my grasp.

"Who the—"

Behind me, a terrible slurping sound belched out from the wall of the house. The creature stepped through it as if it were merely a hologram.

I ran to the street—anywhere to get away from the nightmare thing dragging its long, wet tail across the ground after me.

The street was empty except for long shadows cast by the moon's glow. If the measurements of this place were off before, they were entirely fucked by the time I made it to the road. Houses bent on strange angles, and the sidewalks seemed to swirl into an infinite distance. I felt like I was inside a shrinking soap bubble.

"It's something like that," I heard a voice suggest. It was the same smooth whisper I had heard before, but I couldn't find where she was coming from.

"What?" I asked. "What the fuck is going on? Help me!"

But I was met by silence.

"Help me!" I called again.

The worm creature continued after me. It was slow but it didn't seem to tire.

I ran up a driveway to a door and felt a burst of hope as I turned the doorknob and found it unlocked.

I darted inside to look for anything that might help me—a way out, a weapon, anything! But when I came to the kitchen, I froze with a horrible realization: I had entered the very same house I was running from.

I backed slowly away from the long black hallway, away from the kitchen, until I was at the staircase, unsure of how I ended up back where I started from. With resignation, I returned to the darkness of the basement, illuminated by glow of one hanging light.

It swung, throwing shadows across the damp concrete walls. The girl, unconscious in her chair, sat poised over the pool of blood at her feet. I crept towards her, examining the stilted movement of her chest.

"Who are you?" I asked in a whisper. "What is this place?"

She lifted her head slowly as she came to consciousness, peering at me through her absent, black socket eyes.

Her jaw fell open, unsheathing a deafening, shrieking scream.

I moved my hands to my ears, but they could do nothing to abate the sound of her shrill, squealing voice.

"Stop!" I shouted. "What do you want from me? Just stop screaming!"

And she did stop. In a whispering voice with the same dry resonance of the recording she told me, "You sought truth, and you have found it."

"What does that mean?" I asked. I peered past her and found shadow, something that looked like the start of a dark passageway. "What do you want?"

"It is what *you* want—knowledge, power, otherworldly delights."

I nodded, dumbly, while wondering if I could make it past her to the tunnel.

"We have given you this knowledge."

"This isn't knowledge. This is a wormhole," I spat. I felt my body tense as I shifted my weight and prepared to run.

"The tape you listened to did not bring you anywhere but within. You are experiencing your true nature." She staggered forward in stuttered movements as she spoke. The tops of her feet dragged across the floor, as if she were suspended by an invisible noose.

"But, my cord." I gestured to my stomach with panic.

"You are within your own mind, inhabiting a world of your own creation." She paused, waiting for her words to register. "This is the greatest secret of all truths; it is all you—in here just as it is in your physical world out there." She gestured to the shadowed hallway behind her.

"What the fuck?" I protested. "Who are you?" I asked.

Her open mouth stretched to form a pained smile. "I am you, born to suffer for your pleasure."

I grimaced as she approached.

"We are all you—*you* reincarnated into all existences simultaneously with a mere illusion of separation."She raised her hand up to reach for me, but I sidestepped her and dashed for the blackness of the shadowed doorway.

"Just as we suffer, so too shall you!" she called after me.

The tunnel was cold and dark with trails of bones littering the ground. It was long, but it looked like there was an end to it. A window of light rippled in the distance like a mirage. It grew in size as I approached it, but it also seemed infinitely far, as if I might never reach it.

It was like peering into another world. There was a collage of ceiling tiles and a track-lighting system. I was looking up at a man in a white doctor's coat. He was gesturing towards the window but speaking to other people I couldn't see.

"Unfortunately, there is nothing else we can do for him but wait. His brain activity is excellent. This is truly unlike anything I have ever seen before."

"But when I talk to him, it looks like he understands me," a voice sobbed. I recognized it instantly. It was my mother.

"Like I said, his brain activity is excellent. We just can't find a source for the paralysis. But that's all this is: paralysis. He's not in a coma."

My mom continued to sob.

"Listen, this is going to be a long journey, and I don't just mean for your son." The doctor paused, shifting his approach. "Go home. Have a good dinner. Get some rest. This isn't the kind of thing you wait out and overcome, but rather something you have to learn how to live with."

My mom continued to cry quietly.

"I can't tell you if he will wake up from this in a week or a year or decades from now. I think you and your husband need to have a conversation about what it will be like to live with your son in this kind of condition indefinitely."

"I understand," my mom relented between choked sobs.

"I want to give you the name of someone to talk to." He scribbled something on a piece of paper as he went on. "I think it could be good to process this with a therapist who specializes in helping families make adjustments—to figure out what this 'new normal' is going to look like. But for right now, it's one day at a time."

I watched on, looking blankly at the ceiling tiles as the doctor moved about the room.

"Take care of today, and tomorrow will take care of tomorrow," he encouraged. Several keyboard clicks punctuated the silence as the door to the room opened and closed. The doctor stood in the frame of the window again, looking right at me.

"Can you see me?" I asked.

He sighed.

"Look at me!" I shouted, jumping up and waving my hands. "I'm right here! You can hear me!"

The doctor brought two fingers to the window, paused, and gestured it closed—encasing me in darkness.

My stomach dropped and I fell to my knees with a burst of loneliness. And that's when I realized I wasn't alone at all. Somewhere in the dark behind me, a squelching grumble reverberated through the blackness followed by a shuddering, wet dragging sound.

Heinrich von Wolfcastle is an affiliate member of the Horror Writers Association and a member of the Great Lakes Association of Horror Writers. His work has appeared in multiple anthologies and magazines. Most recently, you can hear his story "Things in the Attic" presented on the Scare You to Sleep podcast and read his story "The Ones in Between" in <u>Blackberry Blood</u>. Though he lives the life of a recluse, he has been known to emerge from the shadows for Trick-or-Treaters on Halloween night.

Father of Lies

Gary Power

When [the devil] speaks a lie, he speaks from his own resources, for he is a liar and the father of it. —*John 8:44*

The dream was always the same: corpulent, albino creatures with pin-prick eyes and slashed, gaping mouths, chasing him through dark labyrinthine corridors. The passages would get narrower, his shoulders grating against coarse brick, tighter and tighter; but there was no turning back. Finally he'd find himself trapped and at the mercy of the slavering beasts. And as they smothered him with sweaty folds of white bloated flesh, he'd wrench himself from sleep. Emerging from the nightmare was like dragging his body from quicksand. Finally, breathless and drenched in sweat-sodden sheets, he'd cry out.

"Holleee…"

The sheer desperation of his waking cry stayed with him long after the images had dispelled; getting back to sleep was no longer going to be an option.

And so, it was in the early hours of a muggy Sunday morning, after a generous measure of Chateau de Beaulon Cognac, Frank Travis left his luxury apartment on the Albert embankment and took a stroll along the South bank of London's river Thames.

In his lifetime he'd been a chain-smoking, drug taking, womanizing alcoholic, but that was a long time ago. His intense and uncompromising work ethic earned him a reputation for being one of the most divisive figures in the music industry. With those hedonistic times just a distant memory, it seemed that he had fared remarkably well. Some would say uncannily well.

He was somewhere between Lambeth Palace and Westminster bridge when he found himself experiencing intense feelings of déjà vu. Twenty-seven years ago he'd walked the same walk, except then he'd been on the verge of bankruptcy. A couple of disastrous business ventures had left him penniless, homeless and on one occasion suicidal. Fate dictated that he share a squat with four dilettante musicians. Recognizing their talents, he took over their management. Over the next couple of years he got them gigs, publicity and, by sheer bloody-minded determination, a lucrative recording contract.

The 80's had become stagnant pool of sterile pop music, and with punk music on the decline Frank provided the perfect antidote in the form of four hell-raising anti-heroes known as the 'The Stoned Angels'. Their decadent behavior became as legendary as their short-lived career and spectacular demise. Miraculously, Frank survived with his reputation intact and moved on to become one of the UK's most successful music promoters, confounding critics with his remarkable success.

One name still haunted him though, and that name was Holly Parker - an innocent caught up in a world of drugs and debauchery, whose fate was dictated by her own naiveté and a chance meeting with the Stoned Angels over two decades ago.

Taking a contemplative swig from his cherished silver hip flask, he rested his eyes on the stippled reflections of London's city lights and sighed deeply - and it was at that moment the gently hummed chorus of a familiar song drifted into his ears.

He recognized it as 'Father of Lies'. Usually performed as a rousing anthem, it had been a trademark song for the Stoned Angels. Three young women, slightly the worse for wear but elegantly dressed, strolled by. Normally Frank would have ignored them, but the flame-haired beauty straggling behind - the one humming the Angel's song - caught his attention. A sheer silk dress clinging to her body like a fine coat of mercurial paint did little to protect her from the night air. One of the straps had slipped from her shoulder and she'd drawn a hand across to stop it falling off completely.

"Heaven must be missing some angels," he remarked just loud enough to be heard, and with a friendly smile added. "… all for one and one for all?"

The leading two giggled and continued on, but the trailing temptress slowed to a halt.

Momentarily distracted by a stale and unpleasant smell that he dismissed as river effluence, Frank placed his flask on the embankment wall and sat down next to it.

The young woman teased him with a provocative smile and precocious stance. In the sulphurous promenade light, he caught the glint of a filigree pendant about her slender neck depicting what appeared to be the initials 'HP'.

"So which one of the musketeers are you?" she asked.

"Aramis, with a smidge of Porthos." he replied after pausing for thought.

"Interesting. So you see yourself as a sort of… ambitious… philanderer."

He chuckled at that. She was educated as well.

"So, what's your name?"

"Melody." she replied coyly.

There was an alluring innocence about her that intrigued him. But there was something else. Beneath that childish façade he sensed a devilish streak, and that intrigued him even more. Her pale complexion was flawless, her demeanour captivating and her feisty gaze, strangely sensual. Had he looked more closely he'd have glimpsed fine cracks on the surface of that alabaster skin and a spidery web of blood vessels within the yellow orbs of her eyes. But it was night and Frank was not at his best.

"Nice name. Unusual." he mused.

"Take me home and play some music." she slurred with a lick of her lips that promised ineffable pleasure, and then she slipped a hand beneath the sheer material of her dress and held it to her breast. A few decades back and the only thing on his mind would have been to notch up another conquest.

"Tell me your name." she asked drunkenly.

"Frank." he replied apathetically, and then, beginning to feel uncomfortable with the situation, added, "… and it's time I made a move."

"No. I won't let you.' she said, grabbing his arm, 'I like you Mr Frank, and I want to come back with you to listen to some decent fucking music, 'cos that's what you do, don't you? You make decent fucking music."

"Look Melody, I think it would be better if you caught up with your friends." he told her firmly.

In an instance her smile evaporated and her mood changed.

"Oh, I don't think so, Frank. There are things we need to talk about. Tell me, does your conscience ever prick you? Do you ever worry that your past might catch up with you?"

Seeing the look of confusion on his face, she burst out laughing and became frivolous again. But Frank was already walking away.

"Well I don't know about you, mister music man, but I'm going for a swim," she shouted after him. Glancing over his shoulder, he saw her balancing precariously on the riverside wall. "Is this what you want, Frank?"

She walked towards him as though in a lurid Soho strip joint. Letting the straps of her dress slip from her shoulders, she teased him with provocative glimpses of flesh.

"Oh dear, Frank. Look. You've left your silver drinkie thing on the wall." she said, and with a deft kick sent it flying into the river.

Frank watched in disbelief, furious at seeing his precious flask disappear into the blackness of the Thames.

"That's going to be you, if you don't stop pissing around.' he yelled at her, "This river doesn't take prisoners… and don't think I'm jumping in after you."

"Ahhh, Frank's frightened for me. Maybe I'll get down if he invites me home." and then, staring him in the eye, she warned, "Maybe if he doesn't, I'll fucking jump."

"You're crazy!" he snapped.

"Like a fox!" she countered with a defiant grin.

"Okay. You can come back to mine and listen to some decent fucking music if that's what you really want."

"Sure?" she replied as she teetered on one leg.

"Yes, Melody. I'm sure. Now please get down."

Instead she went into some kind of psychotic state, glaring into space and muttering gibberish.

That was the final straw. She was either mentally unbalanced or on drugs, and he had no time for either.

"Jump then, you stupid girl; make yourself yesterday's news because in a few days that's all you'll be. Just another forgotten headline," and then he shouted at her, "JUMP!"

And, obediently, she did as he said.

In disbelief, he stared at the space where she'd been. He could just make out her fiery hair in the darkness but already the current was drawing her away. His options were simple; save her or leave her. Without further thought he pushed his jacket behind a bush, mounted the wall and jumped in.

Frantically treading water, he looked for Melody in the darkness, repeatedly calling her name. His clothes were weighing him down and a strong undercurrent was dragging him into the body of the river. With a touch of cruel irony, he looked up and caught glimpse of his apartment building. He could even make out the light flickering from his own TV.

"Fuck!" he shouted, cursing the moment he set eyes on the lunatic flame-haired tramp. He should be back in his penthouse flat chilling out, Louis X111Cognac in hand, Debussy serenading his ears.

Melody was out of sight, so reluctantly, Frank's focus shifted to preserving his own life. Exhaustion kicked in as he swam against the river's unrelenting flow. The main thing was, he'd tried to save her. And he was nearly there, just a few feet away from reaching the bank when a piercing cry stopped him mid stroke.

"Frank! Help me! I can't swim!"

Her shrill cry ran through him like a sword; desperation, panic and sheer terror – it was all there. Treading water, he turned and saw Melody thrashing around and bobbing below the surface. Just a few moments ago he'd have happily pushed her head under, but now she was within reach, and they were close to the bank.

He'd almost reached her when she slipped beneath the surface, this time not coming back. At the same time the water began to surge about him, gently at first but then spiraling into a vortex that sucked him down. His body tumbled helplessly with the descending current and he found himself lost in a topsy-turvy world of darkness. River effluence surged into his mouth as he lifted his head fleetingly above the surface and gasped for air. With his lungs feeling like they were about to burst and consciousness fading, he sank towards the silt bed of the Thames.

Frank woke to find himself lying on a warm stone floor with Melody sitting cross-legged in front of him. They were both unclothed.

"You okay old man?" she mused.

He groaned a reply.

A dull thud pounded behind his eyes as he struggled to remember what had happened. He'd jumped into the Thames to save Melody, and by some miracle they'd both survived. Now they were in what looked like a cellar. He tentatively prodded his scalp and felt scabs of blood in his matted hair.

Melody looked back with a childish grin on her face. He scratched at the scabs again. They felt dry.

"What happened?" he grunted.

"No idea. I woke up here just like you."

"How long ago was that?"

She shrugged, "A couple of hours I guess."

Frank shuffled uneasily and moved his hands to cover his modesty. "What happened to my clothes?"

"We were drenched. You'd have caught your death so I undressed you. It's pretty warm in here - they'll soon dry. And anyway, it's liberating like this, don't you think?"

"Not really. It certainly is warm in here though; it's like a sauna. Have you any idea where we are?"

Melody shrugged again.

"Some kind of cellar, I think. There's a bricked-up door over there." she said, pointing vaguely towards a shadowy recess, "… and there's some kind of shaft leading into a pit in the corner behind you; that's where the weird light's coming from."

The light was a curious mix of lurid green and shimmering red and took the appearance of a luminous mist.

Frank got up to take a look but slipped on the floor as he got closer. Melody laughed. "Oh, there's gooey stuff on the ground–I meant to warn you about that."

Looking closer he found patches of foul-smelling slime prints spread across the floor, like huge footprints. "What the hell made those?"

From way Melody grinned back, it obviously didn't bother her.

He looked around at the drab, bare bricked surroundings. Shadows and darkness concealed just how spacious the room was. There were nooks and crannies that might lead somewhere; if only he could somehow clear his hazy head. The balmy air was tainted by a musty aroma that while pungent was not particularly unpleasant. Most disconcerting though was the droning hum that filled the air, like a soft chorus of baritone voices.

Frank was still angry though. Not just with Melody, but with himself for being stupid enough to get mixed up with such an obviously disturbed young woman who seemed incredibly at ease with her own nakedness.

"Don't you feel vulnerable sitting there like that?"

"No.' she said, "…do you?"

Letting his silence be his reply, he retrieved and slipped on his boxer shorts.

"Any ideas how we're going to get out of this hell hole?"

She produced a mobile phone from behind her.

"It was in your pocket."

"… and it still worked with half the Thames in it?"

"Long enough for me to phone some friends."

"Soon be out then." He replied sarcastically." "Give me."

"Okay, but it's broken."

"Broken? How did that happen?"

"I threw it at the wall. I get angry. You might have noticed."

Frank examined it; the screen was cracked and it wouldn't turn on. When he looked at her she just grinned pathetically and uttered, "… oops."

"How did you get past my pin?"

"I asked you and you blurted it out. Anyway, I found something else when I was looking around - something that might turn that frown upside down."

Disappearing behind a wooden partition she reappeared with a dusty bottle of red wine. Begrudgingly, he took it, examined the label…and a smile broke through his sullen expression.

"Bloody hell Melody… Chateau Mouton Rothchild 1952."

"Is that good?"

He laughed.

"Yeah, several hundred pounds good. Getting older isn't all bad, Melody. Not when you learn to appreciate stuff like this."

"So you'll want these then." She held up two glasses and an antiquated corkscrew.

"I found them with the wine. There's a whole rack of bottles back there, and other stuff too."

Frank was soon working at the cork. If ever he needed a drink it was now.

"Well, we're certainly not going to die of thirst." he said.

He savored the aroma and after a contented sigh poured a glass and swilled his first mouthful.

With the bottle soon empty, and feeling a little more acquiescent, he asked, "How long did you say we've been here?"

"I told you already, fuzz-brain. Hours. And let's just say… things got interesting."

Frank looked surprised. "I was conscious?"

"More like delirious. Your dad called you Frank after Frank Sinatra."

"I told you that?"

Melody laughed. "Oh, there's more."

She started giggling, so much so that for a few moments she struggled to talk.

With the wine taking effect, Frank found himself chuckling with her.

"Come on girl… spit it out."

Her laughter stopped in an instance and she fixed him with an unnerving stare. "We fucked." she said, and her face darkened.

Frank laughed nervously.

Shaking his head, he replied, "I don't think so."

But as he looked into her eyes, images slipped into his head: of naked flesh bathed in shadows and light; of writhing bodies glistening with sweat; of

295

Melody on top of him, arching her back; of her taut abs and small breasts thrusting over him; of crimson light playing on her goose-fleshed skin as she brings their union to an exquisite crescendo.

"Don't let the Devil in." she whispered in his ear. "Mean anything to you?"

Frank looked truly shocked. The pounding behind his brow started again with a vengeance and his concentration faltered. The wine, it seemed, had gone straight to his head.

"It… it was one of the Angel's more controversial numbers." he slurred.

"Tell me about 'the crazy days." she demanded impatiently.

He tried to think; that was what he and his cronies used to call the hedonistic early years. He studied the bewildering young woman with trepidation, wondering what else he'd said, or done.

"They were crazy, and that's all I'm saying."

"Okay. Tell me the secret of your success then?"

"Umm…I play by my own rules and…and I don't compromise," he told her. "…and…what's with all…the questions…anyway?"

He sounded drunk, and for some reason that amused Melody.

"I'm nearly finished. Humor me."

With a shrug of resignation, he told her, "One more."

"Who have you worked with?"

"Stones, Sabbath - rock royalty; the best. They want fame and money and I just want money."

"…and sex." she added.

He chuckled at that, lingering his gaze as he studied the creature so enigmatically poised before him. The shadowy gloom seemed to enhance her beauty; if that was possible. For a moment, as he looked at her, his concentration faltered and his mind slipped into a wistful state.

"How did you keep them happy?" she said,

"Who?" replied Frank as he emerged from reverie.

"The Stoned Angels, stupid."

He shook his head indifferently. For some reason he felt strangely euphoric.

"Drugs?" she prompted.

"Drugs, yes drugs, of course."

"Women?"

Frank smirked at that.

"It's rock n' roll, baby."

Melody swayed gently from side to side and began to hum a song. Resigned to the fact that rescue was not going to be imminent and feeling particularly chilled, he laid back and listened. Her voice was angelic and perfectly pitched.

"Hmmm…Angie. Rolling Stones." he said, closing his eyes.

"It's your funeral song," she remarked, 'well, either that or "In a gard… in… a"'

That made Frank laugh.

"In-A-Gadda-Da-Vida; seventeen minutes of classic rock. That one's for all the bastards I don't like that come to gloat. Make 'em listen to some decent music while they're a captive audience. So what else did I divulge about my riotous past?"

"Rick Silver." she said.

An uncomfortable silence followed as Frank considered her words. He got up, stepped cautiously over to the shaft and peered down, into the pit. Murky light shimmered far below – the effulgent glow flickered and shadows danced in a way that suggested movement.

Warm air was rising and carrying with it a muted resonant beat, like tribal drums.

Turning his head, Frank listened a little more intently. He could hear screaming, or laughter, or even cries of ecstasy - it was difficult to tell.

"So tell me about Rick Silver."

Frank drew his breath deeply at that.

"'Slick' Rick Silver, lead singer of Stoned Angels… now why on earth did you bring that lemming into the conversation?"

"My mother worshipped him. I suppose I'm intrigued by someone who had such a profound effect on her life."

Frank nodded knowingly; his femme-fatale was becoming a little less mysterious. Melody's mother knew the lead singer of the band that he managed so successfully; suddenly it seemed that their accidental liaison might not be such a coincidence.

"Rick Silver was the thorn in my side, and at the same time one of the most charismatic performers I've ever met. The Angels would have been nothing without him. I loved him…and at times I truly hated him. He developed an obsession with the black arts. He saw music as a recruiting ground, preying on fans' naivety and cherry picking those most vulnerable."

Melody stood up and, despite her nakedness, performed a pirouette while humming contentedly. Frank couldn't help but be enthralled by her erratic behavior.

"Not exactly shy, are you?" he said.

"My mother was a brazen cow– I got it from her. Anyway, she's dead now."

The light in the cellar dimmed a little and the air briefly chilled. Melody stopped dancing and sat despondently on the floor.

"You got women for rock stars didn't you?" she mumbled sulkily.

"In a way, yes."

She gazed into his eyes; her stare reached deeply.

"Be honest with me Frank. You arranged for young women to have sex with the band didn't you?"

"I'd facilitate mutually acceptable meetings, what happened after that was up to them. Melody, what's this all about? Did your mother have something going with Rick?"

"Well mister smarty pants. You should know; you were the one that introduced them."

"You make me sound like a pimp. I was young and ambitious. I wasn't responsible for what others did with their lives. Now I don't mean to change the subject, but are those friends of yours ever going to get us out of here?"

Ignoring his question, Melody rose and stood over him.

"Rick took advantage of her. He betrayed her trust and defiled her. Do you have a daughter Frank?" she asked pointedly.

"I don't have children."

"All that drinking, all those drugs - maybe you do Frank."

She held the palm of her hand to her iron-board belly.

"Maybe you do now. We weren't exactly careful."

In Frank's world that wasn't a problem.

If she was, he'd pay for an abortion. Anything to get the crazy young woman out of his life.

Running a clammy palm across his forehead, he wondered again how they'd ended up in such a dank and gloomy cellar. The air was stifling and uncomfortably warm and yet his breath was condensing as though on freezing air.

'Look, Melody, I work with people who have an almost inhuman drive to be someone.' he explained, 'Famous people lead bizarre and unsettled lives. They have to be inspired if they're going to make it and that's where I come in. I maintain their creative ability without tipping them over the top…or letting them kill themselves which in my business is always a distinct possibility. Part of that lifestyle involves sex, especially on tour.'

Melody paced over and clasped his hand in hers.

"Tell me more about the crazy times. Tell me about these 'women' who followed the band."

With a heavy sigh, Frank told her.

"Your mother was one of those women; they were known as groupies. We all do wild things when we're young don't we, Melody? And these were times when inappropriate behavior was the norm." he said accusingly. "I certainly wasn't a saint, but I learned from my mistakes. I moved on."

"But you were responsible Frank, and some of those women were barely more than kids."

Resentment was creeping into her tone, that and anger. 'They trusted you, they looked up to you. You could've stopped things before they went too far.'

Frank shook his head. "I'm sensing real hostility here, Melody."

Melody glared back, holding her pendant so that he was forced to look at it.

"HP, Frank. Holly Parker. She was my mother."

Now there was condemnation in her tone.

Frank fell silent.

"You remember her, don't you?"

"It was a long time ago."

"So you did know her?"

"I know the name. She was just an acquaintance though. One of many."

"Okay, let me remind you then. You introduced her to Rick and his band. They fucked with her body then they fucked with her mind and when they'd taken all that they wanted they just let her die."

Frank shook his head.

"The Holly Parker that I knew, and we're talking over twenty-five years ago, was a young woman looking for excitement at a time when rock idol hysteria was at its peak."

"That's not true Frank. You sampled the merchandise first and passed her on to the others. They were animals, she was meat. They fed her drugs like they were sweets and whiskey like it was lemonade and then they used her to satisfy their own depravity. And then the next morning, to their stupid astonishment that body was a corpse. Not quite so fuckable then was she?"

Frank looked away in disgust.

As far as he was aware Holly Parker disappeared. Life went on, times got crazier, fame and fortune followed. Drugs and denial clouded the past. Controversy could have ruined them so Frank's 'people' sorted it out; no questions asked.

"Where's all this going Melody. What do you want from me?"

"I want to hear you confess–it's good for the soul, apparently. And it might help your case."

Frank scoffed at that, and then he became momentarily distracted by the increasing intensity of the monastic chanting rising from the shaft.

"Look, you need to understand a few things. Lives and careers depended on the Angel's success. Nobody knows what happened to Holly. What you're telling me is pure speculation."

That seemed to amuse her. She wandered about chuckling and muttering to herself. When she came across Frank's shirt, she draped it loosely around her shoulders.

"Do you know who I am?" she asked him bluntly. "I mean, who I really am."

Frank remained silent.

"I'm the ghost of your conscience."

He snorted at that. A sound of scuffling from a shadowy corner briefly took his attention.

"My conscience is clear." he told her as he studied the darkness.

"Oh, I don't think it is. I'd say it's more like a festering cesspit."

The way she glared at him sent a shudder through his body. The hate in her eyes was palpable.

"Maybe I'm the ghost of Holly Parker come back to haunt you."

Something strange was happening with her voice. It had become deeper and resonant and more bizarrely, it had slowed down.

Frank's heart began to pound. He heard scuttling somewhere in the room again, this time louder. Too big for a rat. There was another noise as well, like the fractious cooing of a baby. Things were turning distinctly weird, but Melody just stood there watching him.

"You're obsessed with the past, girl. I don't know what you want and frankly, I don't care."

Melody let out an infuriated scream.

"I'll tell you exactly what I want, Frank. I want to drink Louis Roederer champagne. I want to eat Filet mignon. I want to swim with dolphins and I want to feel cock inside me, preferably from a man who actually fucking cares."

Frank had heard enough. Her friends were obviously not coming and he doubted they even existed. He'd have to find his own way out. Climbing down the shaft was a possibility. The sides were steep and craggy but if he could just get a foothold, he could probably do it.

Melody had other ideas though. She leapt at him like a feral cat, screaming wildly and scratching at his face, but Frank saw it coming and, wrapping his arms about her waist, lifted her onto his shoulder.

She screamed again and in that same moment the cellar was plunged into darkness —and her body disintegrated in his hands.

"Melody?" he called.

A shrill cry, like that of a baby, cut through the air and his blood ran cold. The scratching got louder. Some kind of living thing was scrabbling towards him. Something with claws. Something big. He lashed out.

"Melody. Answer me, for God's sake."

But there was no answer. Darkness pressed against his chest, closing in like a smothering shroud and sucking the breath from his lungs. His heart pounded and his head felt light.

The movement was just a few feet away now, and the air had become tainted by the suffocating stench of decomposing flesh. Frank held a hand to his mouth and gagged. A radiant mist was flowing from the shaft like a shimmering cloud and he saw, to his mounting horror, beneath that soft blanket of light…the naked, emaciated corpse of what appeared to be an old woman.

"What the fuck?" he gasped.

Edging closer, he observed the wretched figure to be little more than skin and bone. As the mist dissipated so the woman began to twitch spasmodically, and then, to his horror, she glared at him through black marble eyes and then scuttled away like a spider on disjointed limbs.

Frank could only wonder if he'd actually tipped the scales of madness.

Staring into the blackness before his eyes, he noticed two small crescents of light - and Melody called his name.

Her voice moved eerily about him, taunting and teasing him in the way of a spirited child.

"Frank…I'm here…over here…Frank…no here…over here," again and again until he was quite disorientated.

The glimmering from the shaft grew brighter and revealed, stood against a far wall, the cadaverous woman.

Around her scrawny neck, Melody's pendant glinted briefly as though just for him.

Frank backed away, his mouth dry as parchment and his heart pounding against his ribs. The ever changing madness was unrelenting and it seemed there was no escape.

"Mister music maaaaan," rasped the woman.

He closed his eyes and tried to dispel what surely was nothing more than a grotesque hallucination.

When he opened them again the woman was gone, but in her place stood Melody, radiant in her silk evening gown and close enough for him to smell the sweet scent of her skin.

"Frank,' she said. She moved closer and caressed his face with her fingertips. "You look like you've seen a ghost."

He laughed nervously and stared blankly into her eyes.

'Where did you go?" he mumbled.

"I've been here all the time, trying to find a way out. You're behaving very strangely. You haven't been taking drugs have you? Or have you got something on your mind?"

He reached out and touched her. She was warm. She was flesh and blood.

He laughed in a slightly unhinged way and combed his fingers through her hair.

'What are you?" he said.

Seeing him so confused amused her.

"I'm the woman that never was," she replied.

With the balance of his sanity teetering on a knife edge he took a deep breath and calmly told her, "I'm going to climb down the shaft. I'm going to save us."

She didn't respond. Instead she leaned forward and whispered in his ear.

"I'm Holly Parker."

She was holding something by her side but he couldn't quite see what it was.

"No, you're Melody," he told her.

She scoffed at that.

"No, that was just now. At the moment I'm Holly Parker, just before she fucking died." She struck him on the side of his head with a 1937 Chateau Latour premier grand cru - and the world went black.

When he came to, Frank found himself face up on the floor with a gloating female succubus in Melody's evening dress standing over him.

"Time's not been kind to me has it?' rasped the dead thing, 'Imprisoned here for 25 years; no food or light and nothing to drink-not good for a girl's complexion - great for the figure though." She pinched the flesh of her thigh and cackled as blood-stained pus oozed from the putrid tissue and dripped onto his face. When she smiled patches of necrotic skin split open revealing livid strands of muscle and stark white bone beneath.

With his mind struggling to make sense of the insane situation, he whimpered, "I didn't leave you here."

"You were the one person who could've saved me, Holly Parker – but you didn't. Let me take you back to that place: Holly, just a teenager, is at a concert and having more fun than she ever thought possible. Frank Travis, like a predatory beast, spots the sexy young thing and plucks her from the audience. He gives her the opportunity to meet the band and the entrance fee is that she pops a few pills, and then he shags her in a squalid dressing room, granted he was probably too stoned to remember. She's taken to a hotel room, to entertain four drunken, drugged up musicians. Who gave them the alcohol Frank? Who supplied the amphetamines and cocaine? She was abandoned and left at the mercy of four bigoted degenerates. She was made to do things that she'd never done, and would never have done."

"I wasn't responsible for what happened," he protested, "Holly wanted to be with them."

"Do you know what happened to me, Frank? They found me the next morning, my body broken by their vile abuse. I'd suffocated on my own vomit. Was that the way that an innocent young woman should end up?"

Frank stared into space, his eyes darting about as he tried to remember. "Holly Parker disappeared. She was never found."

"Money and power overcome all, Frank. Your lies are vacuous drivel. Disposing of a few pounds of flesh and bones wasn't difficult for your people…which leads us conveniently to this place. Do you know where we are?"

He stared blankly at her.

"We're in an embankment cellar that you used to use for all the 'crazy day' parties. I thought you might recognize it. The cellar was sealed up after I was dumped here. I wasn't dead though. I was dying…not that anybody cared. I woke in darkness, too weak to move. I cried for help and scraped my fingers to the bone trying to get out." Holly held her hands before him showing him the bloody stumps of her fingers.

"I lasted a long time."

"I didn't know they put you down here. I paid people to sort things out. I didn't ask questions. I thought they gave you money…and sent you on your way."

"Liar!' she screamed. 'You made a pact with the devil, Frank, and I was part of that bargain. I've suffered more than you could ever fucking imagine, and now it's payback time."

Frank scrabbled to his feet and lunged at her with one thing on his mind - to tear her scrawny body apart and rid himself of the cursed monstrosity forever. In the real world, she no longer existed so she wouldn't be missed.

With a single swipe that defied her feeble appearance, she struck him to the ground. "Here's one more revelation for you, Frank. I was pregnant and

I'd say there was a pretty good chance that you or one of your degenerate friends was the father."

Frank could take no more. He grabbed her about the waist and slammed her frail body into the wall. The violence of his assault shattered her bones and made rags of her cellophane skin, but still the cadaverous creature mocked and taunted him.

"You're going nowhere." She growled. He stared into her maggot infested eyes and wretched. A throbbing soreness pressed behind his eyes and he fell to the floor crippled by pain. Fractious baby noises filled the cellar and from the shadows he saw a hideously deformed foetus crawling towards him.

With a piercing cry, Holly retreated into the shadows. The baby thing smiled and cooed as it got nearer, and Frank recoiled in horror.

"I must be off, Frank," he heard a voice say. Melody's voice echoed eerily from the shadows. "I've got an appointment with your jacket. I do hope your keys and credit cards are safe. After all, you don't want them falling into the wrong hands now do you? Maybe I'll do a bit of flat sitting for a while. How much is in that safe of yours? Quite a lot of rainy day money I imagine. Oh, and that thing you believe about not being able to change history? You're in for one big, fucking surprise."

Holly stepped forwards as Melody, her face radiant and dressed just as he'd seen her on the embankment.

"Time to pay the ferryman," he heard her say as she moved closer to the edge of the shaft and peered down. "My redemption was part of the bargain. Your bargain. You of all people should read the fine print."

"What are you talking about?" he said.

"Oh, everything costs. You should know that - in this world," she told him as she climbed into the shaft, "and in the next."

Psycho baby was mauling Frank's leg, dribbling strings of acrid phlegm onto his skin and gnawing his flesh with pin sharp teeth.

And just as Frank thought things couldn't get any worse, the oppressive drone of ominous secular incantation rising from the shaft became even louder.

"Daaaddddeeee," whimpered baby thing in guttural tones that were far from cute.

Frank screamed out, 'I'm not your fucking daddy." He kicked wildly at it, laughing insanely as its twisted body flew through the air and dropped neatly into the pit like a well-placed rugby ball.

"Yesssss." he cried, pulling a punch from the air, and then he began to gibber in a way that suggested he had finally entered the kingdom of madness. He found himself contemplating the last words of Melody or Holly or whatever the fuck it was had said.

"There'll be a price to pay."

"There'll be a price to pay alright!" he bawled into the gaping hole like a lunatic.

The air rising from the pit was warm and pungent and had about it an unworldly scent, like eastern incense. The peculiar aroma made him light-headed and induced a feeling of distance from the world. His limbs became heavy and slowly, drained of energy, he sank to the ground unable to even crawl away.

With mounting horror he watched as fat, white limbs began to reach out from the pit.

"Oh fuck, no," he groaned, "not the nightmare. Anything but the nightmare."

For this was his dream made flesh and unfolding before his eyes. This time though, the dream was real.

Watching incredulously as several albino creatures emerged into the cellar, he whimpered and cried. Apparently blind, they sniffed at the air and then, having picked up his scent, crawled in his direction leaving viscous trails of slime in their wake. They were obese, repulsive beings enveloped in folds of flesh that glistened like cold, wet tripe; with rasping tongues that lashed from gashed mouths and pin prick eyes that stared blindly from grotesquely swollen faces. Organs throbbed beneath translucent patches of skin, so thin that it looked as though the skin might rupture and spill out the visceral contents of their obese bodies onto the warm stone floor. With Frank helpless to resist, they lifted him from the ground and carried him into the pit.

Having rested him on a stone plinth at the centre of a commodious chamber, they humbly retreated to the out walls of the spacious cavern. Small fires scattered all around gave life to shadows that danced wildly across the walls and floor. High on a granite pedestal stood an imperious figure, neither man nor beast, its eyes burning like hot coals, its naked flesh bristling with flaxen hair.

'Frank Travis,' boomed the unholy beast. "Twenty-five years ago you were solely responsible for the death of Holly Parker."

"I didn't kill her," he stuttered. His mouth was dry, like parchment and his head filled with such panic that he feared he might have a stroke. With trepidation, Frank looked around. The cave had about it the appearance of a dingy courtroom. A veritable army of obese, albino creatures, recumbent upon rocks, surrounded him. The air was thick with their flatulent stench and the floor covered with excrement. They stared at Frank with hungry impatience as though waiting for something to happen; for what though, he dared not contemplate.

"Your assertion of innocence is of no importance.' boomed the voice, 'You begged for redemption from your crime and you were heard."

"I...I was high on drugs." he stuttered, "I was drunk. I didn't...didn't really believe all that satanic crap."

A sheet of paper fell from the air and landed at his feet. Frank studied the parchment - a contract signed by him in blood.

"Rubbish." he uttered as he tore it to shreds. But in its place fell another. He tore that up too only to have another float gently down before his eyes. The scrawl was indeed his, and the memory burned into his head. At the time Rick Silver had become obsessed with Faustian rituals and convinced him that a ceremony would solve their dilemma. Like so many other bands Satanism had become an immoral obsession. And then Holly Parker had fallen victim to their depraved ways. In a fit of drug induced madness and with Rick's questionable guidance, Frank pledged his soul in return for resolution. He drew a blade across the soft pad of his thumb and in his own blood, committed himself to a diabolical pact. In his head, it was a desperate act of drunken madness. But in his heart, it was a solemn pledge. The next morning, when sensibility had returned, dismissing it as an act of idiocy, he burned the contract and scattered the ashes into the Thames.

"You, Francis Travis, procured an arrangement in which, as an ambitious and unscrupulous person, you surrendered your moral integrity in exchange for money and redemption. Now the time has come to pay the price and join my wretched legion."

Frank turned his attention to the gathering of vile monstrosities that surrounded him and he wept as a man who was fated to an eternity of misery.

As he protested so his body began to swell and he became gripped by agonizing pain. Colour drained from his skin bringing to it a deathly pallor. He cried out in horror as his hair fell out in bloody clumps and weeping sores appeared on the surface of his fat, white skin.

A droning chorus of approval filled the chamber as the creatures rejoiced in Frank's grotesque metamorphosis and his affiliation to their legion. He tried to speak, to continue to protest his innocence and beg for mercy, but his tongue, like a plump slug in his mouth, was too swollen for him to form a coherent sentence. His teeth had become like chalk and all but crumbled away leaving bloodied stumps, stark against the his new, white flesh.

310

And he realized in that fateful moment he that the vile stench of his own putrid flesh would remain with him for eternity.

The Present

Dave had worked with River Security Surveillance CCTV for more years than he cared to remember but in all that time he'd never seen anything as bizarre as this.

"What do y'reckon, Syd?"

His colleague is mulling over the previous night's footage of a man leaping into the Thames.

"He's been on the lash. Schizo as well, by the look," he replies in a broad Manc accent.

Dave nods his head. He thought he'd seen it all.

"Play it again; I think I saw something else." Leaning in closer, he points to the screen.

"The guy chats up the two women but they move on, probably thinking he's a nutter. Then he starts talking as though there's someone else there. Funny thing is, if you look closer, there is something there, like a shadow."

"Yeah, I see that."

"He gets really animated and shouting like someone else is there."

"He's one pissed off geezer." agrees Syd.

"Now pause it and zoom onto the wall."

"Okay."

"See the flask."

"Yeah, I see it."

"Now play itslo-mo."

"Jesus...fuck..." utters Syd.

"That's what I thought."

The flask is suddenly projected from the wall and into the river. They play it again and again. No matter how many times they watch the clip, it still defies rational explanation.

"…and see the guy now. He really flips this time."

Syd whistles. "Like someone's peckin' his head big time."

"Okay, now for the really weird bit. Play it slow again and watch above where the flask was."

A few feet above the wall is a smudge of darkness that has the appearance of a hazy figure. The image is fleeting but for a split second there's a glimpse of a woman's ghostly face with mad staring eyes - eyes that briefly but intently look directly into the camera.

Syd rewinds, freeze frames and zooms in.

The woman's eyes glare back as though she can see them.

What the two men haven't noticed is the sudden drop in temperature, and that their breath is condensing on the air.

Syd shudders.

"That's some scary shit."

"Sure gives me the creeps. Like Blair Witch, eh?"

The rest of the recording shows the man hastily thrusting his jacket behind a bush and then jumping into the river.

"You reported it?"

Dave nods his head.

"It happens a lot apparently; nutters, drug addicts. They just wait until a body gets washed up or someone's reported missing."

"So was there anything else?"

"Ooh, yesss"

Dave skips forwards a few hours. It's twilight, there's a storm brewing and the south bank of the Thames is deserted. A howling wind and sweeping rain make it difficult to see properly, but a slim woman wearing a sheer evening dress and oblivious to the weather wanders into the scene. She retrieves the man's jacket from behind the bush, examines it and then walks away.

"Wow, how did she know that was there?"

"Beats me."

Suddenly the screen flickers, goes blank and then springs back to life and the two men find themselves looking at the same rain soaked promenade. The woman in the evening dress is back. She's looking up towards the camera and smiling in a way that scares the crap out of them –because it's as though she can see them.

"What time was this?"

"It isn't." says Dave.

"eh?"

"It's live. It's now."

They look at each other.

The woman grins smugly as she moves slowly towards the camera, which is strange because the camera's mounted on a pole, twenty feet in the air.

The screen flickers again and the bizarre image breaks up. For a few seconds there's just fuzzy interference and white noise, and then the picture returns, but now her face fills the screen. And her appearance has changed. Her wrinkled flesh is ghostly white and covered with weeping sores. Cataracts cover her eyes and her teeth are yellowed crumbling stubs. As they both recoil in horror, the lights go out and the room is plunged into total darkness.

A woman laughs and the two men suddenly fear for their lives.

Because the laughter is in the room.

Gary Power is a UK based author of weird, wonderful and occasionally shocking short stories. His work has appeared in popular anthologies such as When Graveyards Yawn (Crowswing Books), several volumes of 'The Black Book of Horror' (Mortbury Press), Jeani Rector's, The Horror Zine for which he was featured author of the month and 'Years Best Body Horror 2017' by Gehenna and Hinnom publishing.

Most recently his novella, 'The Art of Anatomy' was published by Mannison Press (US) to excellent review.

He has been a keen member of the British Fantasy Society since 2006 and attended several conventions where he has participated in signings.

He has been shortlisted for the Ian St James short story award and is a registered Amazon author. He is also a member of Allen Ashley's 'Clockhouse London Writers' group.

You'll find more information and a lively gallery at - www.garygpower.com

Thanks

We received an overwhelming volume of great story submissions for this publication, making selection a difficult process. We want to thank all the authors and artists who created the fantastic images and stories included in *Heavy Metal Nightmares*. We also want to thank those who wrote the stories we did not have space for. We enjoyed reading each and every tale.

Thank you to Lee Millar and Anthony Long for their time reading through a couple of story submissions. A special thanks to James Thomson, who read pages and pages of story submissions and gave his invaluable opinions, it is appreciated.

This publication has been a real labor of love. It has also been an education, and I suspect there are more lessons to come.

Most of all, if you're holding a physical copy of *Heavy Metal Nightmares* or reading it on your Kindle or eReader then thank you for your purchase. We hope you enjoyed these stories and we'd encourage you to follow the authors on social media and check out their websites and Amazon author pages.

For more great horror fiction titles, visit us at . . .

www.PHOBICABOOKS.CO.UK